Foreign
Fictions

Foreign Fictions

*25 Contemporary Stories from
Canada, Europe, Latin America*

Edited by JOHN BIGUENET

VINTAGE BOOKS
A Division of Random House
New York

A Vintage Original, March 1978

FIRST EDITION

Library of Congress Cataloging in Publication Data
Main entry under title:

Foreign fictions.

Bibliography: p.
1. Short stories. I. Biguenet, John.
PZ1.F738 [PN6014] 808.83'1 77-92630
ISBN 0-394-72493-3

Manufactured in the United States of America

*Grateful acknowledgment is made to the following for permission to reprint previously
published material:*

George Braziller, Inc.: "Tropism: V" from *Tropisms* by Nathalie Sarraute, translated by Maria Jolas. Copyright © 1963 by John Calder, Ltd., Librairie Gallimard 1956.

Campbell, Thomson, McLaughlin, Ltd., A. M. Heath & Company, Ltd., Italo
Calvino: "The Argentine Ant" by Italo Calvino, translated by Archibald Col-
quhoun. Originally published as "La Formica Argentina" from *I Racconti* © 1958
Giulio Einaudi editore S.P.A., Torino.

Joan Daves: "Undine Goes" from *The Thirtieth Year* by Ingeborg Bachmann,
translated by Michael Bullock. Copyright © 1964 by Michael Bullock. *The Thirtieth Year* was originally published in German as *Das Dreissigste Jahr* © R. Piper
& Co. Verlag, München, 1961.

Joan Daves and Farrar, Straus & Giroux, Inc.: "The Bound Man" from *The
Bound Man and Other Stories* by Ilse Aichinger, translated by Eric Mosbacher.
Copyright 1956 by Ilse Aichinger.

Editions Gallimard: "The Great Theater" from *Astyanax* (1964) by André Pieyre
de Mandiargues, translated by John Biguenet; "I Am Writing to You from a Distant Country" from *L'espace du dedans*, pages choisies (1966) by Henri Michaux.

For my mother and my father

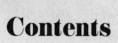

Contents

Introduction

"It has always spoken, it will always speak, of things that don't exist, or only exist elsewhere . . ."

—Samuel Beckett

Realism has declined as a force in fiction. At the least, our conception of what realism encompasses is far broader than it was just a few years ago. The limitations of probability and possibility no longer bind the imagination as strictly as when they entered into every calculation made by a writer. Today, many authors around the world portray a random, indifferent and absurd universe through images that are foreign to everyday consciousness. They have chosen to transfigure common experience into a startling, original vision, and thus are very consciously constructing *fictions*, fully aware of the possibilities of creation limited only by their ability to express it. Having abandoned the strictures of realism in favor of more inventive narrative techniques, these writers test the full capabilities of language.

The tradition of the fantastic in literature is ancient and

the injunctions of realism were imposed only fairly recently. Probability was not a consideration in *Gilgamesh, The Odyssey* or *Sir Gawain and the Green Knight.* Realism is an invention of the industrialized world. Its concern with the visible and the palpable places it outside the dominant traditions of Western literature. John Barth has said, ". . . unlike those critics who regard realism as what literature has been aiming at all along, I tend to regard it as a kind of aberration in the history of literature." Even the masters of realistic writing did not hesitate to imagine other worlds. Flaubert's initial work on *The Temptation of Saint Anthony* immediately preceded the composition of his realistic masterpiece, *Madame Bovary.* However, although we find numerous examples in every period of literary history, the fantastic elicits a unique response from the modern mind.

When Milton re-created the warfare of angels in *Paradise Lost,* his readers accepted the actuality of the struggle. Their imaginations, anchored in faith, could unblinkingly include the supernatural with the mundane. But the modern reader must find substance in Milton's fantasy without the aid and comfort of religious belief. What religion describes as mysterious is simply incomprehensible to the secular mind. The stories in this anthology depend upon the failure of religion to explicate the predicament of modern man, whose confusion is thus denied the dignity of mystery. Just as the indignity of death became the source of much medieval humor, the discomfort of the bourgeois citizen confounded by an incomprehensible reality amuses the modern reader.

Certainly the most common source of the fantastic throughout history has been mythology. Each culture produced its heroes and deities who were unfettered by human limitations. Most importantly, mythology helped to establish a system of metaphors with which the present could be coherently understood. In most of the stories in this anthology, a kind of diminutive myth-making is taking place. Their authors offer metaphors that seek to illuminate life in the twentieth century.

If these stories have a particular literary antecedent, then perhaps they derive from the introduction into France and subsequently into England early in the eighteenth century of *The Thousand and One Nights,* a secular masterpiece. A growing taste for the exotic in Europe fostered its popularity. Its stories, unlike those of *The Decameron,* another popular collection, freely mix the vividly realistic with the supernatural. The influence of this and other works dealing with the fantastic later combined with a nostalgia for the Middle Ages that gripped England and the continent to produce an enduring genre, the Gothic tale. In it, the ordinary good sense of the heroine (and the reader) constantly falls victim to deep psychological fears as she wanders through unfamiliar regions of the subconscious. Much of the great writing that was to follow depended upon this correspondence between internal reality and external circumstances.

The publication of Goethe's *Faust* carried the tradition of the fantastic into the nineteenth century. Meanwhile, Jacob and Wilhelm Grimm had begun their compilation of folk tales, many of which placed considerable emphasis on magic. In the United States, Hawthorne experimented with folk-based tales of the supernatural, but the brooding, psychological stories of Edgar Allan Poe proved far more influential.

When Poe declared that certainty could only be found in dreams, he was planting a seed that would blossom in the next century as a tenet of the surrealist movement. However, his manipulation of the short story as a form was quite conscious, and the effects he achieved demonstrated a disciplined talent. His importance to succeeding writers included the technical lessons his work offered, as well as something more significant: Baudelaire described Poe as a man out of tune with himself. Poe's morality is traditional—evil deeds invoke the supernatural. But the sensibility of the narrator is far from traditional; it is, in fact, distinctly modern in its paranoia and alienation. For Poe, a state of mind is often more convincing and detailed than exterior circumstances, which grow vague or are supplanted entirely by the particulars of a world created by the imagination. The fantastic is a product of this tension between the mind and the world. Borges has said of Poe that in him "the dream was exalted to a nightmare."

Franz Kafka, who is certainly the most obvious influence on the writers in this anthology, also concerned himself with consciousness and reality. As in Poe's stories, point of view is at the heart of his work. But Kafka's subject is not a deranged mind. Rather, he describes an inexplicable world. If one is arrested and brought to trial for no discoverable reason, or if one is turned into an insect, there is really not much to be done about it. Determination in the face of the truly hopeless is as ridiculous as it is heroic. Thus, Kafka's characters are often quick to submit to the unexpected and sometimes even force the logic of a situation to an inexorable conclusion despite circumstances that are unhurried and more or less indifferent to their fates. It is the victim who presses for his own victimization. In *The Trial*, for example, K. returns to the court for interrogation although no one has summoned him. Dignity and freedom are never in dispute since they are never available to Kafka's characters, who react as best they can in an incomprehensible world. Nietzsche's madman in *The Gay Science* attempted to explain the predicament of such characters when he proclaimed that God was dead. Although the foundation of all values was shattered by the revelation, the world continued to follow its daily course. Many of the stories in this anthology, such as "The Southern Thruway," "Rhinoceros" and "A Very Old Man with Enormous Wings," are simply elaborations on the theme that the mundane is never seriously interrupted by the extraordinary. Kafka shows that to struggle against the absurd is useless; one must learn to live within its confines.

It remained for a small group of artists and writers under the leadership of André Breton to establish the most thorough defense of the fantastic in history, surrealism. The methods employed by surrealists to pursue the subconscious were varied, but foremost among them was the practice of placing an everyday object adjacent to the unexpected in order to jolt the viewer or reader out of his habitually blasé attitude. A fur-lined cup and saucer, for instance, were exhibited as an example of surrealist art. Dreams were preferred to waking consciousness; the fantasies of a vagrant mind were esteemed above the intellections of a diligent brain. As in so much other art of the fantastic, the dialectic of surrealism juxtaposed the mundane to the extraordinary. Many of the writers included here continue that tradition. Calvino's inescapable ants, Cortázar's endless highway and Lispector's tiny woman are all surrealist objects.

Other writers are related to a later development in art. Abstract expressionism demonstrated that a common experience does not exist; only the multitude of perceptions of a particular moment constitute that moment. Exterior reality disappears in the variety of sensations it evokes within the observer. Only point of view exists. This is not to say that there are, in fact, abstract expressionist *writers*, but that the fiction of such authors as Samuel Beckett, Severo Sarduy and Margarita Karapanou uses language in much the same way that Jackson Pollock used paint. Their stories progress word by word rather than sentence by sentence. Their narratives are intriguingly concealed within poetic monologues. Fiction is reduced to point of view and becomes, therefore, total invention.

The philosophy of existentialism comes closest to summarizing the major characteristics of fantastic literature during the last hundred years, particularly in its elaboration of the alienation of man from his world. As Beckett suggests, words are all we have and they are not enough. Sartre's *No Exit* and Camus' *The Plague* are exemplary both of existential literature and of the mood of stories in this collection.

Out of this long tradition, of which only the briefest outline is sketched here, come the writers of *Foreign Fictions.* Descendants of Poe or Kafka, Breton or Camus, they seek both to escape and to depict the human condition. Common human experience is no longer accepted as the necessary subject of their prose. The enormous universe of the imagination alone offers them sufficient room to stage their dramas and comedies. Within the last twenty years, examples of their fictions have become available in English translations and have begun to influence our own writers. The originals appeared throughout South America, Canada and Europe.

Some of the writers, such as Sarraute, Robbe-Grillet and Borges are studiously pursuing the notion of *fiction*. Robbe-Grillet, like Sarraute, carefully constructs a reality so precisely like the one in which we exist, so burdened by the details of our world, that it remains foreign to us, a fiction. Borges, as skeptical as Descartes, wonders if he is, in fact, the author of his own stories or, perhaps, a character in someone else's.

Others invoke the absurd. Calvino, Ionesco, Bioy Casares, Lind, Böll and Cortázar introduce characters who, confronted by the inexplicable, patiently knit it into the fabric of their mundane lives. Kundera, the citizen of a bureaucratic state, recounts equally absurd tales, though we have no trouble believing the likelihood of his fictions. Kociancich uncovers the fantastic in the relationship of a husband and his wife. Is the story metaphorical, or does the wife actually lose her hands, her eyes and finally disappear altogether? How, in fiction, can one distinguish between metaphor and a created reality?

Extended metaphors are common in these stories. Guimarães Rosa, Aichinger, Yates, Mandiargues and Mrozek conceive parables that astonish us even though they refuse to establish any moral. Yates has described an image as "one of an infinite number of entrances to an arena where something ineffable has always been going on." His comment is particularly applicable to the images in these stories. Lispector, Michaux and Bachmann also create stories around fantastic conceits. García Márquez's angel and McEwan's geometrical magic, too, must be included among these carefully constructed fantasies.

A broader perception of life is taking form in these fictions. This new perception reassesses the power of man, his free will, his achievements and his notions about the nature of reality in a random universe. The new man is often a victim. He is distressed but seems to be the only one who notices that anything is wrong, does not precipitate his crisis through evil deeds and understands language to be both the key and the maze. Through these foreign fictions we will come to know the bewildered person who inhabits the world we live in.

Julio Cortázar has explained that "if the totality of any narrative work can be classified as 'fiction,' it is clear that fantastic literature is the most fictional of all literatures, given that by its own definition it consists of turning one's back on a reality universally accepted as normal, that is, as not fantastic, in order to explore other corridors of that immense house in which man lives." *Foreign Fictions* offers a reader the opportunity to walk down some of those corridors.

—JOHN BIGUENET

Foreign
Fictions

The Argentine Ant

ITALO CALVINO

Translated by Archibald Colquhoun

When we came to settle here we did not know about the ants. We'd be all right here, it seemed that day; the sky and green looked bright, too bright, perhaps, for the worries we had, my wife and I—how could we have guessed about the ants? Thinking it over, though, Uncle Augusto may have hinted at this once: "You should see the ants over there . . . they're not like the ones here, those ants . . . ," but that was just said while talking of something else, a remark of no importance, thrown in perhaps because as we talked we happened to notice some ants. Ants, did I say? No, just one single lost ant, one of those fat ants we have at home (they seem fat to me, now, the ants from my part of the country). Anyway, Uncle Augusto's hint did not seem to detract from the description he gave us of a region where, for some reason which he was unable to explain, life was easier and jobs were not too difficult to find, judging by all those who had set themselves up there—though not, apparently, Uncle Augusto himself.

On our first evening here, noticing the twilight still in the air after supper, realizing how pleasant it was to stroll along those lanes toward the country and sit on the low walls of a bridge, we began to understand why Uncle Augusto liked it. We understood it even more when we found a little inn which he used to frequent, with a garden behind, and squat, elderly characters like himself, though rather more blustering and noisy, who said they had been his friends; they too were men without a trade, I think, workers by the hour, though one said he was a clockmaker, but that may have been bragging; and we found they remembered Uncle Augusto by a nickname, which they all repeated among general guffaws; we noticed, too, rather stifled laughter from a woman in a knitted white sweater who was fat and no longer young, standing behind the bar.

And my wife and I understood what all this must have meant to Uncle Augusto; to have a nickname and spend light evenings joking on the bridges and watch for that knitted sweater to come from the kitchen and go out into the orchard, then spend an hour or two next day unloading sacks for the spaghetti factory; yes, we realized why he always regretted this place when he was back home.

I would have been able to appreciate all this too, if I'd been a youth and had no worries, or been well settled with the family. But as we were, with the baby only just recovered from his illness, and work still to find, we could do no more than notice the things that had made Uncle Augusto call himself happy; and just noticing them was perhaps rather sad, for it made us feel the difference between our own wretched state and the contented world around. Little things, often of no importance, worried us lest they should suddenly make matters worse (before we knew anything about the ants); the endless

instructions given us by the owner, Signora Mauro, while showing us over the rooms, increased this feeling we had of entering
troubled waters. I remember a long talk she gave us about the
gas meter, and how carefully we listened to what she said.

"Yes, Signora Mauro. . . . We'll be very careful, Signora
Mauro. . . . Let's hope not, Signora Mauro. . . ."

So that we did not take any notice when (though we
remember it clearly now) she gave a quick glance all over the
wall as if reading something there, then passed the tip of her
finger over it, and brushed it afterward as if she had touched
something wet, sandy, or dusty. She did not mention the word
"ants," though, I'm certain of that; perhaps she considered it
natural for ants to be there in the walls and roof; but my wife
and I think now that she was trying to hide them from us as
long as possible and that all her chatter and instructions were
just a smoke screen to make other things seem important, and
so direct our attention away from the ants.

When Signora Mauro had gone, I carried the mattresses
inside. My wife wasn't able to move the cupboard by herself
and called me to help. Then she wanted to begin cleaning out
the little kitchen at once and got down on her knees to start,
but I said: "What's the point, at this hour? We'll see to that
tomorrow; let's just arrange things as best we can for tonight."
The baby was whimpering and very sleepy, and the first thing
to do was get his basket ready and put him to bed. At home
we use a long basket for babies, and had brought one with us
here; we emptied out the linen with which we'd filled it, and
found a good place on the window ledge, where it wasn't damp
or too far off the ground should it fall.

Our son soon went to sleep, and my wife and I began
looking over our new home (one room divided in two by a
partition—four walls and a roof), which was already showing
signs of our occupation. "Yes, yes, whitewash it, of course we

must whitewash it," I replied to my wife, glancing at the
ceiling and at the same time taking her outside by an elbow.
She wanted to have another good look at the toilet, which was
in a little shack to the left, but I wanted to take a turn over
the surrounding plot; for our house stood on a piece of land
consisting of two large flower, or rather rough seed beds, with
a path down the middle covered with an iron trellis, now bare
and made perhaps for some dried-up climbing plant of gourds
or vines. Signora Mauro had said she would let me have this
plot to cultivate as a kitchen garden, without asking any rent,
as it had been abandoned for so long; she had not mentioned
this to us today, however, and we had not said anything as there
were already too many other irons in the fire.

My intention now, by this first evening's walk of ours
around the plot, was to acquire a sense of familiarity with the
place, even of ownership in a way; for the first time in our lives
the idea of continuity seemed possible, of walking evening after
evening among beds of seeds as our circumstances gradually
improved. Of course I didn't speak of those things to my wife;
but I was anxious to see whether she felt them too; and that
stroll of ours did, in fact, seem to have the effect on her which
I had hoped. We began talking quietly, between long pauses,
and we linked arms—a gesture symbolic of happier times.

Strolling along like this we came to the end of the plot,
and over the hedge saw our neighbor, Signor Reginaudo, busy
spraying around the outside of his house with a pair of bellows.
I had met Signor Reginaudo a few months earlier when I had
come to discuss my tenancy with Signora Mauro. I went up to
greet him and introduce him to my wife. "Good evening,
Signor Reginaudo," I said. "D'you remember me?"

"Of course I do," he said. "Good evening! So you are our
new neighbor now?" He was a short man with spectacles, in
pajamas and a straw hat.

"Yes, neighbors, and among neighbors . . . ." My wife began producing a few vague pleasant phrases, to be polite: it was a long time since I'd heard her talk like that; I didn't particularly like it, but it was better than hearing her complain.

"Claudia," called our neighbor, "come here. Here are the new tenants of the Casa Laureri!" I had never heard our new home called that (Laureri, I learned later, was a previous owner), and the name made it sound strange. Signora Reginaudo, a big woman, now came out, drying her hands on her apron; they were an easygoing couple and very friendly.

"And what are you doing there with those bellows, Signor Reginaudo?" I asked him.

"Oh . . . the ants . . . these ants . . ." he said, and laughed as if not wanting to make it sound important.

"Ants?" repeated my wife in the polite detached tone she used with strangers to give the impression she was paying attention to what they were saying; a tone she never used with me, not even, as far as I can remember, when we first met.

We then took a ceremonious leave of our neighbors. But we did not seem to be enjoying really fully the fact of having neighbors, and such affable and friendly ones with whom we could chat so pleasantly.

On getting home we decided to go to bed at once. "D'you hear?" said my wife. I listened and could still hear the squeak of Signor Reginaudo's bellows. My wife went to the washbasin for a glass of water. "Bring me one too," I called, and took off my shirt.

"Oh!" she screamed. "Come here!" She had seen ants on the faucet and a stream of them coming up the wall.

We put on the light, a single bulb for the two rooms. The stream of ants on the wall was very thick; they were coming from the top of the door, and might originate anywhere. Our hands were now covered with them, and we held them out open in front of our eyes, trying to see exactly what they were like, these ants, moving our wrists all the time to prevent them from crawling up our arms. They were tiny wisps of ants, in ceaseless movement, as if urged along by the same little itch they gave us. It was only then that a name came to my mind: "Argentine ants," or rather, "the Argentine ant," that's what they called them; and now I came to think of it I must have heard someone saying that this was the country of "the Argentine ant." It was only now that I connected the name with a sensation, this irritating tickle spreading in every direction, which one couldn't get rid of by clenching one's fists or rubbing one's hands together as there always seemed to be some stray ant running up one's arm, or on one's clothes. When the ants were crushed, they became little black dots that fell like sand, leaving a strong acid smell on one's fingers.

"It's the Argentine ant, you know . . ." I said to my wife. "It comes from South America. . . ." Unconsciously my voice had taken on the inflection I used when wanting to teach her something; as soon as I'd realized this I was sorry, for I knew that she could not bear that tone in my voice and always reacted sharply, perhaps sensing that I was never very sure of myself when using it.

But instead she scarcely seemed to have heard me; she was frenziedly trying to destroy or disperse that stream of ants on the wall, but all she managed to do was get numbers of them on herself and scatter others around. Then she put her hand under the faucet and tried to squirt water at them, but the ants went on walking over the wet surface; she couldn't even get them off by washing her hands.

"There, we've got ants in the house!" she repeated. "They were here before, too, and we didn't see them!"—as if things would have been very different if we had seen them before.

I said to her: "Oh, come, just a few ants! Let's go to bed

now and think about it tomorrow!" And it occurred to me also to add: "There, just a few Argentine ants!" because by calling them by the exact name I wanted to suggest that their presence was already expected, and in a certain sense normal.

But the expansive feeling by which my wife had let herself be carried away during that stroll around the garden had now completely vanished; she had become distrustful of everything again and made her usual face. Nor was going to bed in our new home what I had hoped; we hadn't the pleasure now of feeling we were starting a new life, only a sense of dragging on into a future full of new troubles.

"All for a couple of ants," was what I was thinking—what I thought I was thinking, rather, for everything seemed different now for me too.

Exhaustion finally overcame our agitation, and we dozed off. But in the middle of the night the baby cried; at first we lay there in bed, always hoping it might stop and go to sleep again; this, however, never happened and we began asking ourselves: "What can be the matter? What's wrong with him?" Since he was better he had stopped crying at night.

"He's covered with ants!" cried my wife, who had gone and taken him in her arms. I got out of bed too. We turned the whole basket upside down and undressed the baby completely. To get enough light for picking the ants off, half blind as we were from sleep, we had to stand under the bulb in the draft coming from the door. My wife was saying: "Now he'll catch cold." It was pitiable looking for ants on that skin which reddened as soon as it was rubbed. There was a stream of ants going along the windowsill. We searched all the sheets until we could not find another ant and then said: "Where shall we put him to sleep now?" In our bed we were so squeezed up against each other we would have crushed him. I inspected the chest of drawers and, as the ants had not got into that, pulled it away

from the wall, opened a drawer, and prepared a bed for the
baby there. When we put him in he had already gone to sleep.
If we had only thrown ourselves on the bed we would have soon
dozed off again, but my wife wanted to look at our provisions.

"Come here, come here! God! Full of 'em! Everything's
black! Help!" What was to be done? I took her by the shoulders. "Come along, we'll think about that tomorrow, we can't
even see now, tomorrow we'll arrange everything, we'll put it
all in a safe place, now come back to bed!"

"But the food. It'll be ruined!"

"It can go to the devil! What can we do now? Tomorrow
we'll destroy the ants' nest. Don't worry."

But we could no longer find peace in bed, with the
thought of those insects everywhere, in the food, in all our
things; perhaps by now they had crawled up the legs of the
chest of drawers and reached the baby. . . . We got off to sleep
as the cocks were crowing, but before long we had again started
moving about and scratching ourselves and feeling we had ants
in the bed; perhaps they had climbed up there, or stayed on
us after all our handling of them. And so even the early morning hours were no refreshment, and we were very soon up,
nagged by the thought of the things we had to do, and of the
nuisance, too, of having to start an immediate battle against
the persistent imperceptible enemy which had taken over our
home.

The first thing my wife did was see to the baby: examine
him for any bites (luckily, there did not seem to be any), dress
and feed him—all this while moving around in the ant-infested
house. I knew the effort of self-control she was making not to
let out a scream every time she saw, for example, ants going
around the rims of the cups left in the sink, and the baby's bib,
and the fruit. She did scream, though, when she uncovered the
milk: "It's black!" On top there was a veil of drowned or

swimming ants. "It's all on the surface," I said. "One can skim them off with a spoon." But even so we did not enjoy the milk; it seemed to taste of ants.

I followed the stream of ants on the walls to see where they came from. My wife was combing and dressing herself, with occasional little cries of hastily suppressed anger. "We can't arrange the furniture till we've got rid of the ants," she said.

"Keep calm. I'll see that everything is all right. I'm just going to Signor Reginaudo, who has that powder, and ask him for a little of it. We'll put the powder at the mouth of the ants' nest. I've already seen where it is, and we'll soon be rid of them. But let's wait till a little later as we may be disturbing the Reginaudos at this hour."

My wife calmed down a little, but I didn't. I had said I'd seen the entrance to the ants' nest to console her, but the more I looked, the more new ways I discovered by which the ants came and went. Our new home, although it looked so smooth and solid on the surface, was in fact porous and honeycombed with cracks and holes.

I consoled myself by standing on the threshold and gazing at the plants with the sun pouring down on them; even the brushwood covering the ground cheered me, as it made me long to get to work on it: to clean everything up thoroughly, then hoe and sow and transplant. "Come," I said to my son. "You're getting moldy here." I took him in my arms and went out into the "garden." Just for the pleasure of starting the habit of calling it that, I said to my wife: "I'm taking the baby into the garden for a moment," then corrected myself: "Into our garden," as that seemed even more possessive and familiar.

The baby was happy in the sunshine and I told him: "This is a carob tree, this is a persimmon," and lifted him up onto the branches. "Now Papa will teach you to climb." He burst

out crying. "What's the matter? Are you frightened?" But I
saw the ants; the sticky tree was covered with them. I pulled
the baby down at once. "Oh, lots of dear little ants . . ." I said
to him, but meanwhile, deep in thought, I was following the
line of ants down the trunk, and saw that the silent and almost
invisible swarm continued along the ground in every direction
between the weeds. How, I was beginning to wonder, shall we
ever be able to get the ants out of the house when over this
piece of ground, which had seemed so small yesterday but now
appeared enormous in relation to the ants, the insects formed
an uninterrupted veil, issuing from what must be thousands of
underground nests and feeding on the thick sticky soil and the
low vegetation? Wherever I looked I'd see nothing at first
glance and would be giving a sigh of relief when I'd look closer
and discover an ant approaching and find it formed part of a
long procession, and was meeting others, often carrying crumbs
and tiny bits of material much larger than themselves. In
certain places, where they had perhaps collected some plant
juice or animal remains, there was a guarding crust of ants stuck
together like the black scab of a wound.

I returned to my wife with the baby at my neck, almost
at a run, feeling the ants climbing up from my feet. And she
said: "Look, you've made the baby cry. What's the matter?"

"Nothing, nothing," I said hurriedly. "He saw a couple of
ants on a tree and is still affected by last night, and thinks he's
itching."

"Oh, to have this to put up with too!" my wife cried. She
was following a line of ants on the wall and trying to kill them
by pressing the ends of her fingers on each one. I could still see
the millions of ants surrounding us on that plot of ground,
which now seemed immeasurable to me, and found myself
shouting at her angrily: "What're you doing? Are you mad?
You won't get anywhere that way."

She burst out in a flash of rage too. "But Uncle Augusto! Uncle Augusto never said a word to us! What a couple of fools we were! To pay any attention to that old liar!" In fact, what could Uncle Augusto have told us? The word "ants" for us then could never have even suggested the horror of our present situation. If he had mentioned ants, as perhaps he had—I won't exclude the possibility—we would have imagined ourselves up against a concrete enemy that could be numbered, weighed, crushed. Actually, now I think about the ants in our own parts, I remember them as reasonable little creatures, which could be touched and moved like cats or rabbits. Here we were face to face with an enemy like fog or sand, against which force was useless.

Our neighbor, Signor Reginaudo, was in his kitchen pouring liquid through a funnel. I called him from outside, and reached the kitchen window panting hard.

"Ah, our neighbor!" exclaimed Reginaudo. "Come in, come in. Forgive this mess! Claudia, a chair for our neighbor."

I said to him quickly: "I've come . . . please forgive the intrusion, but you know, I saw that you had some of that powder . . . all last night, the ants . . ."

"Oh, oh . . . the ants!" Signora Reginaudo burst out laughing as she came in, and her husband echoed her with a slight delay, it seemed to me, though his guffaws were noisier when they came. "Ha, ha, ha! . . . You have ants, too! Ha, ha, ha!"

Without wanting to, I found myself giving a modest smile, as if realizing how ridiculous my situation was, but now I could do nothing about it; this was in point of fact true, as I'd had to come and ask for help.

"Ants! You don't say so, my dear neighbor!" exclaimed Signor Reginaudo, raising his hands.

"You don't say so, dear neighbor, you don't say so!" exclaimed his wife, pressing her hands to her breast but still laughing with her husband.

"But you have a remedy, haven't you?" I asked, and the quiver in my voice could, perhaps, have been taken for a longing to laugh, and not for the despair I could feel coming over me.

"A remedy, ha, ha, ha!" The Reginaudos laughed louder than ever. "Have we a remedy? We've twenty remedies! A hundred . . . each, ha, ha, ha, each better than the other!"

They led me into another room lined with dozens of cartons and tins with brilliant-colored labels.

"D'you want some Profosfan? Or Mirminec? Or perhaps Tiobroflit? Or Arsopan in powder or liquid form?" And still roaring with laughter he passed his hand over sprinklers with pistons, brushes, sprays, raising clouds of yellow dust, tiny beads of moisture, and a smell that was a mixture of a pharmacy and an agricultural depot.

"Have you really something that does the job?" I asked.

They stopped laughing. "No, nothing," he replied.

Signor Reginaudo patted me on the shoulder, the Signora opened the blinds to let the sun in. Then they took me around the house.

He was wearing pink-striped pajama trousers tied over his fat little stomach, and a straw hat on his bald head. She wore a faded dressing gown, which opened every now and then to reveal the shoulder straps of her undershirt; the hair around her big red face was fair, dry, curly, and disheveled. They both talked loudly and expansively; every corner of their house had a story which they recounted, repeating and interrupting each other with gestures and exclamations as if each episode had been a huge joke. In one place they had put down Arfanax diluted two to a thousand and the ants had vanished for two days but returned on the third day; then he had used a concentrate of ten to a thousand, but the ants had simply avoided that part and circled around by the doorframe; they had isolated another corner with Crisotan powder, but the wind blew it away and they used three kilos a day; on the stairs they had tried Petrocid, which seemed at first to kill them at one blow, but instead it had only sent them to sleep; in another corner they put down Formikill and the ants went on passing over it, then one morning they found a mouse poisoned there; in one spot they had put down liquid Zimofosf, which had acted as a definite blockade, but his wife had put Italmac powder on top which had acted as an antidote and completely nullified the effect.

Our neighbors used their house and garden as a battlefield, and their passion was to trace lines beyond which the ants could not pass, to discover the new detours they made, and to try out new mixtures and powders, each of which was linked to the memory of some strange episode or comic occurrence, so that one of them only had to pronounce a name "Arsepit! Mirxidol!" for them both to burst out laughing with winks and comments. As for the actual killing of the ants, that, if they had ever attempted it, they seemed to have given up, seeing that their efforts were useless; all they tried to do was bar them from certain passages and turn them aside, frighten them or keep them at bay. They always had a new labyrinth traced out with different substances which they prepared from day to day, and for this game ants were a necessary element.

"There's nothing else to be done with the creatures, nothing," they said, "unless one deals with them like the captain . . ."

"Ah, yes, we certainly spend a lot of money on these insecticides," they said. "The captain's system is much more economical, you know."

"Of course, we can't say we've defeated the Argentine ant

yet," they added, "but d'you really think that the captain is on the right road? I doubt it."

"Excuse me," I asked. "But who is the captain?"

"Captain Brauni; don't you know him? Oh, of course, you only arrived yesterday! He's our neighbor there on the right, in that little white villa . . . an inventor. . . ." They laughed. "He's invented a system to exterminate the Argentine ant . . . lots of systems, in fact. And he's still perfecting them. Go and see him."

The Reginaudos stood there, plump and sly among their few square yards of garden which was daubed all over with streaks and splashes of dark liquids, sprinkled with greenish powder, encumbered with watering cans, fumigators, masonry basins filled with some indigo-colored preparation; in the disordered flower beds were a few little rosebushes covered with insecticide from the tips of the leaves to the roots. The Reginaudos raised contented and amused eyes to the limpid sky. Talking to them, I found myself slightly heartened; although the ants were not just something to laugh at, as they seemed to think, neither were they so terribly serious, anything to lose heart about. "Oh, the ants!" I now thought. "Just ants after all! What harm can a few ants do?" Now I'd go back to my wife and tease her a bit: "What on earth d'you think you've seen, with those ants . . . ?"

I was mentally preparing a talk in this tone while returning across our piece of ground with my arms full of cartons and tins lent by our neighbors for us to choose the ones that wouldn't harm the baby, who put everything in his mouth. But when I saw my wife outside the house holding the baby, her eyes glassy and her cheeks hollow, and realized the battle she must have fought, I lost all desire to smile and joke.

"At last you've come back," she said, and her quiet tone impressed me more painfully than the angry accent I had expected. "I didn't know what to do here any more . . . if you saw . . . I really didn't know . . ."

"Look, now we can try this," I said to her, "and this and this and this . . ." and I put down my cans on the step in front of the house, and at once began hurriedly explaining how they were to be used, almost afraid of seeing too much hope rising in her eyes, not wanting either to deceive or undeceive her. Now I had another idea: I wanted to go at once and see that Captain Brauni.

"Do it the way I've explained; I'll be back in a minute."

"You're going away again? Where are you off to?"

"To another neighbor's. He has a system. You'll see soon."

And I ran off toward a metal fence covered with ramblers bounding our land to the right. The sun was behind a cloud. I looked through the fence and saw a little white villa surrounded by a tiny neat garden, with gravel paths encircling flower beds, bordered by wrought iron painted green as in public gardens, and in the middle of every flower bed a little black orange or lemon tree.

Everything was quiet, shady, and still. I was standing there, uncertain whether to go away, when, bending over a well-clipped hedge, I saw a head covered with a shapeless white linen beach hat, pulled forward to a wavy brim above a pair of steel-framed glasses on a spongy nose, and then a sharp flashing smile of false teeth, also made of steel. He was a thin, shriveled man in a pullover, with trousers clamped at the ankles by bicycle clips, and sandals on his feet. He went up to examine the trunk of one of the orange trees, looking silent and circumspect, still with his tight-lipped smile. I looked out from behind the rambler and called: "Good day, Captain." The man raised his head with a start, no longer smiling, and gave me a cold stare.

"Excuse me, are you Captain Brauni?" I asked him. The man nodded. "I'm the new neighbor, you know, who's rented the Casa Laureri. . . . May I trouble you for a moment, since I've heard that your system . . ."

The captain raised a finger and beckoned me to come nearer; I jumped through a gap in the iron fence. The captain was still holding up his finger, while pointing with the other hand to the spot he was observing. I saw that hanging from the tree, perpendicular to the trunk, was a short iron wire. At the end of the wire hung a piece—it seemed to me—of fish remains, and in the middle was a bulge at an acute angle pointing downward. A stream of ants was going to and fro on the trunk and the wire. Underneath the end of the wire was hanging a sort of meat can.

"The ants," explained the captain, "attracted by the smell of fish, run across the piece of wire; as you see, they can go to and fro on it without bumping into each other. But it's that V turn that is dangerous; when an ant going up meets one coming down on the turn of the V, they both stop, and the smell of the gasoline in this can stuns them; they try to go on their way but bump into each other, fall, and are drowned in the gasoline. Tic, tic." (This "tic, tic" accompanied the fall of two ants.) "Tic, tic, tic . . ." continued the captain with his steely, stiff smile; and every "tic" accompanied the fall of an ant into the can where, on the surface of an inch of gasoline, lay a black crust of shapeless insect bodies.

"An average of forty ants are killed per minute," said Captain Brauni, "twenty-four hundred per hour. Naturally, the gasoline must be kept clean, otherwise the dead ants cover it and the ones that fall in afterward can save themselves."

I could not take my eyes off that thin but regular trickle of ants dropping off; many of them got over the dangerous point and returned dragging bits of fish back with them by the teeth, but there was always one which stopped at that point, waved its antennae, and then plunged into the depths. Captain Brauni, with a fixed stare behind his lenses, did not miss the slightest movement of the insects; at every fall he gave a tiny uncontrollable start and the tightly stretched corners of his almost lipless mouth twitched. Often he could not resist putting out his hands, either to correct the angle of the wire or to stir the gasoline around the crust of dead ants on the sides, or even to give his instruments a little shake to accelerate the victims' fall. But this last gesture must have seemed to him almost like breaking the rules, for he quickly drew back his hand and looked at me as if to justify his action.

"This is an improved model," he said, leading me to another tree from which hung a wire with a horsehair tied to the top of the *V*: the ants thought they could save themselves on the horsehair, but the smell of the gasoline and the unexpectedly tenuous support confused them to the point of making the fatal drop. This expedient of the horsehair or bristle was applied to many other traps that the captain showed me: a third piece of wire would suddenly end in a piece of thin horsehair, and the ants would be confused by the change and lose their balance; he had even constructed a trap by which the corner was reached over a bridge made of a half-broken bristle, which opened under the weight of the ant and let it fall in the gasoline.

Applied with mathematical precision to every tree, every piece of tubing, every balustrade and column in this silent and neat garden, were wire contraptions with cans of gasoline underneath, and the standard-trained rosebushes and lattice work of ramblers seemed only a careful camouflage for this parade of executions.

"Aglaura!" cried the captain, going up to the kitchen door, and to me: "Now I'll show you our catch for the last few days."

Out of the door came a tall, thin, pale woman with fright-

ened, malevolent eyes, and a handkerchief knotted down over
her forehead.

"Show our neighbor the sack," said Brauni, and I realized
she was not a servant but the captain's wife, and greeted her
with a nod and a murmur, but she did not reply. She went into
the house and came out again dragging a heavy sack along the
ground, her muscular arms showing a greater strength than I
had attributed to her at first glance. Through the half-closed
door I could see a pile of sacks like this one stacked about; the
woman had disappeared, still without saying a word.

The captain opened the mouth of the sack; it looked as
if it contained garden loam or chemical manure, but he put his
arm in and brought out a handful of what seemed to be coffee
grounds and let this trickle into his other hand; they were dead
ants, a soft red-black sand of dead ants all rolled up in tight
little balls, reduced to spots in which one could no longer
distinguish the head from the legs. They gave out a pungent
acid smell. In the house there were hundredweights, pyramids
of sacks like this one, all full.

"It's incredible," I said. "You've exterminated all of these,
so . . ."

"No," said the captain calmly. "It's no use killing the
worker ants. There are ants' nests everywhere with queen ants
that breed millions of others."

"What then?"

I squatted down beside the sack; he was seated on a step
below me and to speak to me had to raise his head; the shapeless brim of his white hat covered the whole of his forehead and
part of his round spectacles.

"The queens must be starved. If you reduce to a minimum the number of workers taking food to the ants' nests,
the queens will be left without enough to eat. And I tell you
that one day we'll see the queens come out of their ants'

nests in high summer and crawl around searching for food with their own claws. . . . That'll be the end of them all, and then . . ."

He shut the mouth of the sack with an excited gesture and got up. I got up too. "But some people think they can solve it by letting the ants escape." He threw a glance toward the Reginaudos' little house, and showed his steel teeth in a contemptuous laugh. "And there are even those who prefer fattening them up. . . . That's one way of dealing with them, isn't it?"

I did not understand his second allusion.

"Who?" I asked. "Why should anyone want to fatten them up?"

"Hasn't the ant man been to you?"

What man did he mean? "I don't know," I said. "I don't think so. . . ."

"Don't worry, he'll come to you too. He usually comes on Thursdays, so if he wasn't here this morning he will be in the afternoon. To give the ants a tonic, ha, ha!"

I smiled to please him, but did not follow. Then as I had come to him with a purpose I said: "I'm sure yours is the best possible system. D'you think I could try it at my place too?"

"Just tell me which model you prefer," said Brauni, and led me back into the garden. There were numbers of his inventions that I had not yet seen. Swinging wire which when loaded with ants made contact with a battery that electrocuted the lot; anvils and hammers covered with honey which clashed together at the release of a spring and squashed all the ants left in between; wheels with teeth which the ants themselves put in motion, tearing their brethren to pieces until they in their turn were churned up by the pressure of those coming after. I couldn't get used to the idea of so much art and perseverance being needed to carry out such a simple operation as catching ants; but I realized that the important thing was to carry on continually and methodically. Then I felt discouraged as no one, it seemed to me, could ever equal this neighbor of ours in terrible determination.

"Perhaps one of the simpler models would be best for us," I said, and Brauni snorted, I didn't know whether from approval or sympathy with the modesty of my ambition.

"I must think a bit about it," he said. "I'll make some sketches."

There was nothing else left for me to do but thank him and take my leave. I jumped back over the hedge; my house, infested as it was, I felt for the first time to be really my home, a place where one returned saying: "Here I am at last."

But at home the baby had eaten the insecticide and my wife was in despair.

"Don't worry, it's not poisonous!" I quickly said.

No, it wasn't poisonous, but it wasn't good to eat either; our son was screaming with pain. He had to be made to vomit; he vomited in the kitchen, which at once filled with ants again, and my wife had just cleaned it up. We washed the floor, calmed the baby, and put him to sleep in the basket, isolated him all around with insect powder, and covered him with a mosquito net tied tight, so that if he awoke he couldn't get up and eat any more of the stuff.

My wife had done the shopping but had not been able to save the basket from the ants, so everything had to be washed first, even the sardines in oil and the cheese, and each ant sticking to them picked off one by one. I helped her, chopped the wood, tidied the kitchen, and fixed the stove while she cleaned the vegetables. But it was impossible to stand still in one place; every minute either she or I jumped and said: "Ouch! They're biting," and we had to scratch ourselves and rub off the ants or put our arms and legs under the faucet. We did not know where to set the table; inside it would attract more ants, outside we'd be covered with ants in no time. We ate standing up, moving about, and everything tasted of ants, partly from the ones still left in the food and partly because our hands were impregnated with their smell.

After eating I made a tour of the piece of land, smoking a cigarette. From the Reginaudos' came a tinkling of knives and forks; I went over and saw them sitting at table under an umbrella, looking shiny and calm, with checked napkins tied around their necks, eating a custard and drinking glasses of clear wine. I wished them a good appetite and they invited me to join them. But around the table I saw sacks and cans of insecticide, and everything covered with nets sprinkled with yellowish or whitish powder, and that smell of chemicals rose to my nostrils. I thanked them and said I no longer had any appetite, which was true. The Reginaudos' radio was playing softly and they were chattering in high voices, pretending to celebrate.

From the steps which I'd gone up to greet them I could also see a piece of the Braunis' garden; the captain must already have finished eating; he was coming out of his house with his cup of coffee, sipping and glancing around, obviously to see if all his instruments of torture were in action and if the ants' death agonies were continuing with their usual regularity. Suspended between two trees I saw a white hammock and realized that the bony, disagreeable-looking Signora Aglaura must be lying in it, though I could see only a wrist and a hand waving a ribbed fan. The hammock ropes were suspended in a system of strange rings, which must certainly have been some sort of defense against the ants; or perhaps the hammock itself was a trap for the ants, with the captain's wife put there as bait.

I did not want to discuss my visit to the Braunis with the Reginaudos, as I knew they would only have made the ironic comments that seemed usual in the relations between our neighbors. I looked up at Signora Mauro's garden above us on the crest of the hills, and at her villa surmounted by a revolving weathercock. "I wonder if Signora Mauro has ants up there too," I said.

The Reginaudos' gaiety seemed rather more subdued during their meal; they only gave a little quiet laugh or two and said no more than: "Ha, ha, she must have them too. Ha, ha, yes, she must have them, lots of them. . . ."

My wife called me back to the house, as she wanted to put a mattress on the table and try to get a little sleep. With the mattresses on the floor it was impossible to prevent the ants from crawling up, but with the table we just had to isolate the four legs to keep them off, for a bit at least. She lay down to rest and I went out, with the thought of looking for some people who might know of some job for me, but in fact because I longed to move about and get out of the rut of my thoughts.

But as I went along the road, things all around seemed different from yesterday; in every kitchen garden, in every house I sensed streams of ants climbing the walls, covering the fruit trees, wriggling their antennae toward everything sweet or greasy; and my newly trained eyes now noticed at once mattresses put outside houses to beat because the ants had got into them, a spray of insecticide in an old woman's hand, a saucerful of poison, and then, straining my eyes, the rows of ants marching imperturbably around the door frames.

Yet this had been Uncle Augusto's ideal countryside. Unloading sacks, an hour for one employer and an hour for another, eating on the benches at the inn, going around in the evening in search of gaiety and a mouth organ, sleeping wherever he happened to be, wherever it was cool and soft, what bother could the ants have been to him?

As I walked along I tried to imagine myself as Uncle

Augusto and to move along the road as he would have done on an afternoon like this. Of course, being like Uncle Augusto meant first being like him physically: squat and sturdy, that is, with rather monkeylike arms that opened and remained suspended in mid-air in an extravagant gesture, and short legs that stumbled when he turned to look at a girl, and a voice which when he got excited repeated the local slang all out of tune with his own accent. In him body and soul were all one; how nice it would have been, gloomy and worried as I was, to have been able to move and joke like Uncle Augusto. I could always pretend to be him mentally, though, and say to myself: "What a sleep I'll have in that hayloft! What a bellyful of sausage and wine I'll have at the inn!" I imagined myself pretending to stroke the cats I saw, then shouting "Booo!" to frighten them unexpectedly; and calling out to the servant girls: "Hey, would you like me to come and give you a hand, Signorina?" But the game wasn't much fun; the more I tried to imagine how simple life was for Uncle Augusto here, the more I realized he was a different type, a man who never had my worries: a home to set up, a permanent job to find, an ailing baby, a long-faced wife, and a bed and kitchen full of ants.

I entered the inn where we had already been, and asked the girl in the white sweater if the men I'd talked to the day before had come yet. It was shady and cool in there; perhaps it wasn't a place for ants. I sat down to wait for those men, as she suggested, and asked, looking as casual as I could: "So you haven't any ants here, then?"

She was passing a duster over the counter. "Oh, people come and go here, no one's ever paid any attention."

"But what about you who live here all the time?"

The girl shrugged her shoulders. "I'm grown up, why should I be frightened of ants?"

Her air of dismissing the ants, as if they were something

to be ashamed of, irritated me more and more, and I insisted: "But don't you put any poison down?"

"The best poison against ants," said a man sitting at another table, who, I noted now, was one of those friends of Uncle Augusto's to whom I'd spoken the evening before, "is this," and he raised his glass and drank it in one gulp.

Others came in and wanted to stand me a drink as they hadn't been able to put me on to any jobs. We talked about Uncle Augusto and one of them asked: "And what's that old *lingera* up to?" "*Lingera*" is a local word meaning vagabond and scamp, and they all seemed to approve of this definition of him and to hold my uncle in great esteem as a *lingera*. I was a little confused at this reputation being attributed to a man whom I knew to be in fact considerate and modest, in spite of his disorganized way of life. But perhaps this was part of the boasting, exaggerated attitude common to all these people, and it occurred to me in a confused sort of way that this was somehow linked with the ants, that pretending they lived in a world of great movement and adventure was a way of insulating themselves from petty annoyances.

What prevented me from entering their state of mind, I was thinking on my way home, was my wife, who had always been opposed to any fantasy. And I thought what an influence she had had on my life, and how nowadays I could never get drunk on words and ideas any more.

She met me on the doorstep looking rather alarmed, and said: "Listen, there's a surveyor here." I, who still had in my ears the sound of superiority of those blusterers at the inn, said almost without listening: "What now, a surveyor . . . Well, I'll just . . ."

She went on: "A surveyor's come to take measurements." I did not understand and went in. "Ah, now I see. It's the captain!"

It was Captain Brauni who was taking measurements with a yellow tape measure, to set up one of his traps in our house. I introduced him to my wife and thanked him for his kindness.

"I wanted to have a look at the possibilities here," he said. "Everything must be done in a strictly mathematical way." He even measured the basket where the baby was sleeping, and woke it up. The child was frightened at seeing the yellow yardstick leveled over his head and began to cry. My wife tried to put him to sleep again. The baby's crying made the captain nervous, though I tried to distract him. Luckily, he heard his wife calling him and went out. Signora Aglaura was leaning over the hedge and shouting: "Come here! Come here! There's a visitor! Yes, the ant man!"

Brauni gave me a glance and a meaningful smile from his thin lips, and excused himself for having to return to his house so soon. "Now, he'll come to you too," he said, pointing toward the place where this mysterious ant man was to be found. "You'll soon see," and he went away.

I did not want to find myself face to face with this ant man without knowing exactly who he was and what he had come to do. I went to the steps that led to Reginaudo's land; our neighbor was just at that moment returning home; he was wearing a white coat and a straw hat, and was loaded with sacks and cartons. I said to him: "Tell me, has the ant man been to you yet?"

"I don't know," said Reginaudo, "I've just got back, but I think he must have, because I see molasses everywhere. Claudia!"

His wife leaned out and said: "Yes, yes, he'll come to the Casa Laureri too, but don't expect him to do very much!"

As if I was expecting anything at all! I asked: "But who sent this man?"

"Who sent him?" repeated Reginaudo. "He's the man

from the Argentine Ant Control Corporation, their representative who comes and puts molasses all over the gardens and houses. Those little plates over there, do you see them?"

My wife said: "Poisoned molasses . . ." and gave a little laugh as if she expected trouble.

"Does it kill them?" These questions of mine were just a deprecating joke. I knew it all already. Every now and then everything would seem on the point of clearing up, then complications would begin all over again.

Signor Reginaudo shook his head as if I'd said something improper. "Oh no . . . just minute doses of poison, you understand . . . ants love sugary molasses. The worker ants take it back to the nest and feed the queens with these little doses of poison, so that sooner or later they're supposed to die from poisoning."

I did not want to ask if, sooner or later, they really did die. I realized that Signor Reginaudo was informing me of this proceeding in the tone of one who personally holds a different view but feels that he should give an objective and respectful account of official opinion. His wife, however, with the habitual intolerance of women, was quite open about showing her aversion to the molasses system and interrupted her husband's remarks with little malicious laughs and ironic comments; this attitude of hers must have seemed to him out of place or too open, for he tried by his voice and manner to attenuate her defeatism, though not actually contradicting her entirely— perhaps because in private he said the same things, or worse —by making little compensating remarks such as: "Come now, you exaggerate, Claudia. . . . It's certainly not very effective, but it may help. . . . Then, they do it for nothing. One must wait a year or two before judging. . . ."

"A year or two? They've been putting that stuff down for twenty years, and every year the ants multiply."

Signor Reginaudo, rather than contradict her, preferred to turn the conversation to other services performed by the Corporation; and he told me about the boxes of manure which the ant man put in the gardens for the queens to go and lay their eggs in, and how they then came and took them away to burn.

I realized that Signor Reginaudo's tone was the best to use in explaining matters to my wife, who is suspicious and pessimistic by nature, and when I got back home I reported what our neighbor had said, taking care not to praise the system as in any way miraculous or speedy, but also avoiding Signora Claudia's ironic comments. My wife is one of those women who, when she goes by train, for example, thinks that the timetable, the make-up of the train, the requests of the ticket collectors, are all stupid and ill planned, without any possible justification, but to be accepted with submissive rancor; so though she considered this business of molasses to be absurd and ridiculous, she made ready for the visit of the ant man (who, I gathered, was called Signor Baudino), intending to make no protest or useless request for help.

The man entered our plot of land without asking permission, and we found ourselves face to face while we were still talking about him, which caused rather an unpleasant embarrassment. He was a little man of about fifty, in a worn, faded black suit, with rather a drunkard's face, and hair that was still dark, parted like a child's. Half-closed lids, a rather greasy little smile, reddish skin around his eyes and at the sides of his nose, prepared us for the intonations of a clucking, rather priestlike voice with a strong lilt of dialect. A nervous tic made the wrinkles pulsate at the corner of his mouth and nose.

If I describe Signor Baudino in such detail, it's to try to define the strange impression that he made on us; but was it strange, really? For it seemed to us that we'd have picked him out among thousands as the ant man. He had large, hairy hands; in one he held a sort of coffeepot and in the other a pile of little earthenware plates. He told us about the molasses he had to put down, and his voice betrayed a lazy indifference to the job; even the soft and dragging way he had of pronouncing the word "molasses" showed both disdain for the straits we were in and the complete lack of faith with which he carried out his task. I noticed that my wife was displaying exemplary calm as she showed him the main places where the ants passed. For myself, seeing him move so hesitantly, repeating again and again those few gestures of filling the dishes one after the other, nearly made me lose my patience. Watching him like that, I realized why he had made such a strange impression on me at first sight: he looked like an ant. It's difficult to tell exactly why, but he certainly did; perhaps it was because of the dull black of his clothes and hair, perhaps because of the proportions of that squat body of his, or the trembling at the corners of his mouth corresponding to the continuous quiver of antennae and claws. There was, however, one characteristic of the ant which he did not have, and that was their continuous busy movement. Signor Baudino moved slowly and awkwardly, as he now began daubing the house in an aimless way with a brush dipped in molasses.

As I followed the man's movements with increasing irritation I noticed that my wife was no longer with me; I looked around and saw her in a corner of the garden where the hedge of the Reginaudos' little house joined that of the Braunis'. Leaning over their respective hedges were Signora Claudia and Signora Aglaura, deep in talk, with my wife standing in the middle listening. Signor Baudino was now working on the yard at the back of the house, where he could mess around as much as he liked without having to be watched, so I went up to the women and heard Signora Brauni holding forth to the accompaniment of sharp angular gestures.

"He's come to give the ants a tonic, that man has; a tonic, not poison at all!"

Signora Reginaudo now chimed in, rather mellifluously: "What will the employees of the Corporation do when there are no more ants? So what can you expect of them, my dear Signora?"

"They just fatten the ants, that's what they do!" concluded Signora Aglaura angrily.

My wife stood listening quietly, as both the neighbors' remarks were addressed to her, but the way in which she was dilating her nostrils and curling her lips told me how furious she was at the deceit she was being forced to put up with. And I, too, I must say, found myself very near believing that this was more than women's gossip.

"And what about the boxes of manure for the eggs?" went on Signora Reginaudo. "They take them away, but do you think they'll burn them? Of course not!"

"Claudia, Claudia!" I heard her husband calling. Obviously these indiscreet remarks of his wife made him feel uneasy. Signora Reginaudo left us with an "Excuse me," in which vibrated a note of disdain for her husband's conventionality, while I thought I heard a kind of sardonic laugh echoing back from over the other hedge, where I caught sight of Captain Brauni walking up the graveled paths and correcting the slant of his traps. One of the earthenware dishes just filled by Signor Baudino lay overturned and smashed at his feet by a kick which might have been accidental or intended.

I don't know what my wife had brewing inside her against the ant man as we were returning toward the house; probably at that moment I should have done nothing to stop her, and might even have supported her. But on glancing around the outside and inside of the house, we realized that Signor Baudino had disappeared; and I remembered hearing our gate creaking and shutting as we came along. He must have gone that moment without saying good-by, leaving behind him those bowls of sticky, reddish molasses, which spread an unpleasant sweet smell, completely different from that of the ants, but somehow linked to it, I could not say how.

Since our son was sleeping, we thought that now was the moment to go up and see Signora Mauro. We had to go and visit her, not only as a duty call but to ask her for the key of a certain storeroom. The real reasons, though, why we were making this call so soon were to remonstrate with her for having rented us a place invaded with ants without warning us in any way, and chiefly to find out how our landlady defended herself against this scourge.

Signora Mauro's villa had a big garden running up the slope under tall palms with yellowed fanlike leaves. A winding path led to the house, which was all glass verandas and dormer windows, with a rusty weathercock turning creakily on its hinge on top of the roof, far less responsive to the wind than the palm leaves which waved and rustled at every gust.

My wife and I climbed the path and gazed down from the balustrade at the little house where we lived and which was still unfamiliar to us, at our patch of uncultivated land and the Reginaudos' garden looking like a warehouse yard, at the Braunis' garden looking as regular as a cemetery. And standing up there we could forget that all those places were black with ants; now we could see how they might have been without that menace which none of us could get away from even for an instant. At this distance it looked almost like a paradise, but the more we gazed down the more we pitied our life there, as if living in that wretched narrow valley we could never get away from our wretched narrow problems.

Signora Mauro was very old, thin, and tall. She received us in half darkness, sitting on a high-backed chair by a little table which opened to hold sewing things and writing materials. She was dressed in black, except for a white mannish collar; her thin face was lightly powdered, and her hair drawn severely back. She immediately handed us the key she had promised us the day before, but did not ask if we were all right, and this —it seemed to us—was a sign that she was already expecting our complaints.

"But the ants that there are down there, Signora . . ." said my wife in a tone which this time I wished had been less humble and resigned. Although she can be quite hard and often even aggressive, my wife is seized by shyness every now and then, and seeing her at these moments always makes me feel uncomfortable too.

I came to her support, and assuming a tone full of resentment, said: "You've rented us a house, Signora, which if I'd known about all those ants, I must tell you frankly . . ." and stopped there, thinking that I'd been clear enough.

The Signora did not even raise her eyes. "The house has been unoccupied for a long time," she said. "It's understandable that there are a few Argentine ants in it . . . they get wherever . . . wherever things aren't properly cleaned. You," she turned to me, "kept me waiting for four months before giving me a reply. If you'd taken the place immediately, there wouldn't be any ants by now."

We looked at the room, almost in darkness because of the half-closed blinds and curtains, at the high walls covered with antique tapestry, at the dark, inlaid furniture with the silver vases and teapots gleaming on top, and it seemed to us that this darkness and these heavy hangings served to hide the presence of streams of ants which must certainly be running through the old house from foundations to roof.

"And here . . ." said my wife, in an insinuating, almost ironic tone, "you haven't any ants?"

Signora Mauro drew in her lips. "No," she said curtly; and

then as if she felt she was not being believed, explained: "Here
we keep everything clean and shining as a mirror. As soon as
any ants enter the garden, we realize it and deal with them at
once."

"How?" my wife and I quickly asked in one voice, feeling
only hope and curiosity now.

"Oh," said the Signora, shrugging her shoulders, "we
chase them away, chase them away with brooms." At that
moment her expression of studied impassiveness was shaken as
if by a spasm of physical pain, and we saw that, as she sat, she
suddenly moved her weight to another side of the chair and
arched in her waist. Had it not contradicted her affirmations
I'd have said that an Argentine ant was passing under her
clothes and had just given her a bite; one or perhaps several
ants were surely crawling up her body and making her itch, for
in spite of her efforts not to move from the chair it was obvious
that she was unable to remain calm and composed as before
—she sat there tensely, while her face showed signs of sharper
and sharper suffering.

"But that bit of land in front of us is black with 'em," I
said hurriedly, "and however clean we keep the house, they
come from the garden in their thousands. . . ."

"Of course," said the Signora, her thin hand closing over
the arm of the chair, "of course it's rough uncultivated ground
that makes the ants increase so; I intended to put the land in
order four months ago. You made me wait, and now the damage is done; it's not only damaged you, but everyone else
around, because the ants breed . . ."

"Don't they breed up here too?" asked my wife, almost
smiling.

"No, not here!" said Signora Mauro, going pale, then, still
holding her right arm against the side of the chair, she began
making a little rotating movement of the shoulder and rubbing
her elbow against her ribs.

It occurred to me that the darkness, the ornaments, the size of the room, and her proud spirit were this woman's defenses against the ants, the reason why she was stronger than we were in face of them; but that everything we saw around us, beginning with her sitting there, was covered with ants even more pitiless than ours; some kind of African termite, perhaps, which destroyed everything and left only the husks, so that all that remained of this house were tapestries and curtains almost in powder, all on the point of crumbling into bits before her eyes.

"We really came to ask you if you could give us some advice on how to get rid of the pests," said my wife, who was now completely self-possessed.

"Keep the house clean and dig away at the ground. There's no other remedy. Work, just work," and she got to her feet, the sudden decision to say good-by to us coinciding with an instinctive start, as if she could keep still no longer. Then she composed herself and a shadow of relief passed over her pale face.

We went down through the garden, and my wife said: "Anyway, let's hope the baby hasn't waked up." I, too, was thinking of the baby. Even before we reached the house we heard him crying. We ran, took him in our arms, and tried to quiet him, but he went on crying shrilly. An ant had got into his ear; we could not understand at first why he cried so desperately without any apparent reason. My wife had said at once: "It must be an ant!" but I could not understand why he went on crying so, as we could find no ants on him or any signs of bites or irritation, and we'd undressed and carefully inspected him. We found some in the basket, however; I'd done my very best to isolate it properly, but we had overlooked the ant man's molasses—one of the clumsy streaks made by Signor Baudino seemed to have been put down on purpose to attract the insects up from the floor to the child's cot.

What with the baby's tears and my wife's cries, we had attracted all the neighboring women to the house: Signora Reginaudo, who was really very kind and sweet, Signora Brauni, who, I must say, did everything she could to help us, and other women I'd never seen before. They all gave ceaseless advice: to pour warm oil in his ear, make him hold his mouth open, blow his nose, and I don't know what else. They screamed and shouted and ended by giving us more trouble than help, although they'd been a certain comfort at first; and the more they fussed around our baby the more bitter we all felt against the ant man. My wife had blamed and cursed him to the four winds of heaven; and the neighbors all agreed with her that the man deserved all that was coming to him, and that he was doing all he could to help the ants increase so as not to lose his job, and that he was perfectly capable of having done this on purpose, because now he was always on the side of the ants and not on that of human beings. Exaggeration, of course, but in all this excitement, with the baby crying, I agreed too, and if I'd laid hands on Signor Baudino then I couldn't say what I'd have done to him either.

The warm oil got the ant out; the baby, half stunned with crying, took up a celluloid toy, waved it about, sucked it, and decided to forget us. I, too, felt the same need to be on my own and relax my nerves, but the women were still continuing their diatribe against Baudino, and they told my wife that he could probably be found in an enclosure nearby, where he had his warehouse. My wife exclaimed: "Ah, I'll go and see him, yes, go and see him and give him what he deserves!"

Then they formed a small procession, with my wife at the head and I, naturally, beside her, without giving any opinion on the usefulness of the undertaking, and other women who had incited my wife following and sometimes overtaking her to show her the way. Signora Claudia offered to hold the baby

and waved to us from the gate; I realized later that Signora
Aglaura was not with us either, although she had declared
herself to be one of Baudino's most violent enemies, and that
we were accompanied by a little group of women we had not
seen before. We went along a sort of alley, flanked by wooden
hovels, chicken coops, and vegetable gardens half full of rubbish. One or two of the women, in spite of all they'd said,
stopped when they got to their own homes, stood on the
threshold excitedly pointing out our direction, then retired
inside calling to the dirty children playing on the ground, or
disappeared to feed the chickens. Only a couple of women
followed us as far as Baudino's enclosure; but when the door
opened after heavy knocks by my wife we found that she and
I were the only ones to go in, though we felt ourselves followed
by the other women's eyes from windows or chicken coops;
they seemed to be continuing to incite us, but in very low
voices and without showing themselves at all.

The ant man was in the middle of his warehouse, a shack
three-quarters destroyed, to whose one surviving wooden wall
was tacked a yellow notice with letters a foot and a half long:
"Argentine Ant Control Corporation." Lying all around were
piles of those dishes for molasses and tins and bottles of every
description, all in a sort of rubbish heap full of bits of paper
with fish remains and other refuse, so that it immediately
occurred to one that this was the source of all the ants of the
area. Signor Baudino stood in front of us half smiling in an
irritating questioning way, showing the gaps in his teeth.

"You," my wife attacked him, recovering herself after a
moment of hesitation. "You should be ashamed of yourself!
Why d'you come to our house and dirty everything and let the
baby get an ant in his ear with your molasses?"

She had her fists under his face, and Signor Baudino,
without ceasing to give that decayed-looking smile of his, made

the movements of a wild animal trying to keep its escape open, at the same time shrugging his shoulders and glancing and winking around to me, since there was no one else in sight, as if to say: "She's bats." But his voice only uttered generalities and soft denials like: "No . . . No . . . Of course not."

"Why does everyone say that you give the ants a tonic instead of poisoning them?" shouted my wife, so he slipped out of the door into the road with my wife following him and screaming abuse. Now the shrugging and winking of Signor Baudino were addressed to the women of the surrounding hovels, and it seemed to me that they were playing some kind of double game, agreeing to be witnesses for him that my wife was insulting him; and yet when my wife looked at them they incited her, with sharp little jerks of the head and movements of the brooms, to attack the ant man. I did not intervene; what could I have done? I certainly did not want to lay hands on the little man, as my wife's fury with him was already roused enough; nor could I try to moderate it, as I did not want to defend Baudino. At last my wife in another burst of anger cried: "You've done my baby harm!" grasped him by his collar, and shook him hard.

I was just about to throw myself on them and separate them; but without touching her, he twisted around with movements that were becoming more and more antlike, until he managed to break away. Then he went off with a clumsy, running step, stopped, pulled himself together, and went on again, still shrugging his shoulders and muttering phrases like: "But what behavior . . . But who . . ." and making a gesture as if to say "She's crazy," to the people in the nearby hovels. From those people, the moment my wife threw herself on him, there rose an indistinct but confused mutter which stopped as soon as the man freed himself, then started up again in phrases not so much of protest and threat as of complaint and almost of supplication or sympathy, shouted out as if they were proud proclamations. "The ants are eating us alive. . . . Ants in the bed, ants in the dishes, ants every day, ants every night. We've little enough to eat anyway and have to feed them too. . . ."

I had taken my wife by the arm. She was still shaking her fist every now and again and shouting: "That's not the last of it! We know who is swindling whom! We know whom to thank!" and other threatening phrases which did not echo back, as the windows and doors of the hovels on our path closed again, and the inhabitants returned to their wretched lives with the ants.

So it was a sad return, as could have been foreseen. But what had particularly disappointed me was the way those women had behaved. I swore I'd never go around complaining about ants again in my life. I longed to shut myself up in silent tortured pride like Signora Mauro—but she was rich and we were poor. I had not yet found any solution to how we could go on living in these parts; and it seemed to me that none of the people here, who seemed so superior a short time ago, had found it, or were even on the way to finding it either.

We reached home; the baby was sucking his toy. My wife sat down on a chair. I looked at the ant-infested field and hedges, and beyond them at the cloud of insect powder rising from Signor Reginaudo's garden; and to the right there was the shady silence of the captain's garden, with that continuous dripping of his victims. This was my new home. I took my wife and child and said: "Let's go for a walk, let's go down to the sea."

It was evening. We went along alleys and streets of steps. The sun beat down on a sharp corner of the old town, on gray, porous stone, with lime-washed cornices to the windows and roofs green with moss. The town opened like a fan, undulating over slopes and hills, and the space between was full of limpid air, copper-colored at this hour. Our child was turning around in amazement at everything, and we had to pretend to take part in his marveling; it was a way of bringing us together, of reminding us of the mild flavor that life has at moments, and of reconciling us to the passing days.

We met old women balancing great baskets resting on head pads, walking rigidly with straight backs and lowered eyes; and in a nuns' garden a group of sewing girls ran along a railing to see a toad in a basin and said: "How awful!"; and behind an iron gate, under the wistaria, some young girls dressed in white were throwing a beach ball to and fro with a blind man; and a half-naked youth with a beard and hair down to his shoulders was gathering prickly pears from an old cactus with a forked stick; and sad and spectacled children were making soap bubbles at the window of a rich house; it was the hour when the bell sounded in the old folks' home and they began climbing up the steps, one behind the other with their sticks, their straw hats on their heads, each talking to himself; and then there were two telephone workers, and one was holding a ladder and saying to the other on the pole: "Come on down, time's up, we'll finish the job tomorrow."

And so we reached the port and the sea. There was also a line of palm trees and some stone benches. My wife and I sat down and the baby was quiet. My wife said: "There are no ants here." I replied: "And there's a fresh wind; it's pleasant."

The sea rose and fell against the rocks of the mole, making the fishing boats sway, and dark-skinned men were filling them with red nets and lobster pots for the evening's fishing. The water was calm, with just a slight continual change of color, blue and black, darker farthest away. I thought of the expanses of water like this, of the infinite grains of soft sand down there at the bottom of the sea where the currents leave white shells washed clean by the waves.

The Passage of Sono Nis

J. MICHAEL YATES

Once I left my familiar apartment building . . . no, like a prisoner sending his memory to regather trivia of time before his confinement—drinking a brandy, bagworms hard on the evergreens one year—let me say to myself again that small recollection: Once I left my familiar apartment building. That very last time.

I awoke that morning to the sound of colossal movement in the street outside. Perhaps a parade. But neither shouts nor music rose up to my second story. Another war? I listened, breathless. The sound was rather of running than marching feet. And there were no shots.

I started to rise, then, annoyed that my sleep had been disturbed long before time for my alarm, I turned toward the wall and pulled the quilt up about my ears. It would pass, and with no show of curiosity on my part.

Of course, it did not pass—rather whatever was passing continued to pass. For over an hour.

I went to the window.

The street seemed swollen with people running, but my observation was somewhat obscured by the heavy fog of dust sent into the air by thousands of feet.

Still a little annoyed, I dressed quickly and started down the stairs. The phenomenon had seized my interest.

What I encountered at the entrance below (responsible, too, I suppose, was the thick dust, the smell, and the heat of so many perspiring bodies) made me instantly faint; I grasped the rail with both hands. At the foot of my stairs lay five monstrously flattened corpses. Just beyond them and the opening of the doorway streamed the river of runners which had awakened me. In such close file they ran that noses seemed pressed painfully against backs of heads. Those at the edges of the current ran twisted sideways, like crabs, shoulders wrenched in away from the brutal promontories the doorways like my own threatened. The five unfortunates heaped in my doorway had been forced into the sharp stone archway with the thrust of running thousands, perhaps millions, behind them.

Even as I stood there, one fatigue-maddened runner attempted (with infinite will and impotent strength) to spring free of that flood into the safety of my entrance way. As I noticed his intent, in that fragment of a second, I was compelled to stumble forward over the corpses, my arms outstretched to aid him. He saw me and shot forth his hand, but the instant our finger-tips met, the force of the closing gap where he had been running for who knows how long, caused the stream to bow and he was driven with the energy of an avalanche against the granite corner of the archway—divided in two before my horrified eyes. As I stood there frozen in mid-gesture, those who, beyond their control, became his kill-ers, racked one against the other: some fell to their knees and rolled beneath a cataract of legs and feet around the corner to a fate I dared not visualize. Others were beaten and dismembered on the corner until the stream ceased to whip and heave.

"The murderers!" I felt my voice fly out of me toward them. But the titanic running absorbed every syllable, every distinction of sound, and every other distinction. Those who were forced into the dead man at my feet were themselves mutilated, some of them probably killed. Had I accused those stampeding animals of a deliberate act? The man's springing, itself, had been his own end and that of many others. I could as well name his act suicide, as theirs murder. The running was responsible. The running? That seemed to me grotesquely amusing: In the beginning was one verb: In the end. . . .

I stumbled hysterically back to my second-story and lay face down for a long time upon my bed.

My senses returned to me, gradually, and I began to consider my own position. I was, at least, safe in my apartment. That comforted me until I grew hungry and realized I had nothing to eat. Surely, I argued, the stream would pass by nightfall and I would be free to seek food before aiding the wounded and helping to dispose of the dead. But my feelings challenged that hypothesis again and again. Against all reason my soul began to fill with the suspicion there would never be an end to this running in the street.

And my mind had begun to trick me—try as I did, I couldn't conjure time before the running.

It struck me then that my doorway was already partially blocked by six dead. The hair at the base of my skull rose as I envisioned myself entombed alive there by the many others who would inevitably join the six if the running did not cease. The thought of slow starvation incarcerated in my own dwelling sent a wave of nausea through me.

I chose quickly and set about realization of my plan.

Precisely as I feared: there were now not six but ten deceased heaped askew on my lower stairs. Already the opening at the door had shrunk by nearly half.

As I, trembling, went about tugging and lifting torsos and limbs into position, still another alternative darted across the cold floor of my consideration. Had I not read of those ship-wrecked on remote isles who thus survived? In deep shame, I shut away that possibility and continued my work. Life was, no, not worth that.

Then it was clear there was yet insufficient volume for what I had in mind.

As I sat mid-way up my stairs, face in my hands, my mind fled in panic from the reality that there was I, waiting for more dead. My only hope for escape depended utterly on the certainty that more would die before me, driven in choice or against choice into the stone archway—men and women who might, like me, sit on a stairway fearing for their lives. But one must be alive to fear for his life. I clapped my head between my hands until the pain distracted me from further morbid deliberation. Soon my intentions turned again toward the work I had to find strength to do.

By and by a sufficient number accumulated. I laid them in rows up the stairs until there was a human runway from the top of the stairs to an opening at the doorway perhaps one-quarter its original height. The runway at the door was higher than the heads of the passing runners.

My plan was to dash from the top of my stairs full-tilt toward the doorway, stooping as I ran, then dive—literally—through the opening and as far out over the heads of the runners toward the center of the stream as my strength would carry me. The greatest jeopardy, clearly, lay at the edges of the hurtling mass. Once I cleared the edge, the next terror was the chance I might not succeed in wedging myself in among the runners. To fall horizontally between them, or head-first, would mean decisive destruction.

And if my feet found the pavement, then . . . that would have to attend to itself.

That suspended instant between the fate that might have befallen me in my home and that which awaited me as I fell upon the panic-stricken runners; what wouldn't I have given to perpetuate that flight through the air over the heads of the runners—or better: to drift up between the buildings and away. Anywhere away.

The terror of those next minutes as the hands and heads of the runners received my weight. They meant me no personal harm—simply, they feared for their lives. Feared I might upset their uncertain balance and send one or several of them down beneath the feet. They thrust me away as if to catapult me back into the air whence I dropped upon them. I rolled, spun, drifted, and tossed on a sea of frenzied hands, heads, and shoulders. I shot now dangerously near one bank of sharp stone facades, then toward the other. Over and over I rolled, fingers and fists at my eyes, driving me away and away as down the human rapids of the street the endless wave of us continued. I struggled compassionately when I could, mercilessly when necessary—seized hands, arms, clothes, ears with my finger-tips. When I veered suddenly toward a wall with its stone blades, my insides seemed to come loose and entangle and I kicked and lashed for my life. At last, just two runners from the deadly wall, my fingers found the long wiry curls of a flaming red head. Both my hands dove for the roots at the center of that isle of hair. With that head for an axis, around and around the hands sent me like a wheel of one spoke, the head turning as it could to relieve the torture of the twisted hair in my fists. After several of these terrible orbits around the carrot-colored head, I let go at the moment that my body seemed moving toward the center of the river. When I seemed almost exactly mid-stream, I stopped my drift upon the current of hands with an anchor-hand-hold in another head of hair. I then jammed one foot furiously between two runners, pushed against the back of the head of the one forward with the heel of my other foot, then wedged myself down between the two.

I was running.

How many lost their footing irrevocably and vanished during my struggle, I cannot bear to consider—how many went against the walls. . . . I was running. My feet found the blessed pavement and fell into erratic cadence. Where? Why? I knew only: I was running.

Those on either side seemed to throw me indignant glances as our shoulders jostled, but for a few blocks only. Then they gazed again glassily toward the heads before them.

One has better wind than he might suspect—when his life depends upon it. After an hour or so of painful stitches in my sides and chest, I felt fresher and began to be interested in my surroundings.

I asked the runner to my left, cheerily as I could under the circumstances: "Where are we going?" But the roar of feet from untold miles before and behind gave my voice nothing audible even to me. I ran along for a time before it occurred to me that he might read my lips. I nudged him—gently, really —in the side. Instantly his knees buckled, his white eyes rolled toward the sky in his dust-blackened face, and he was gone.

If thirst, by that time, hadn't claimed even that moisture, I wept.

How could I have known how long, how far the man had run? And I began to sense how tenuously we balanced there, for all of our thunderous running.

As I ran on wearily behind the shifting mirage of heads,

I felt more alone than I had ever been, notwithstanding that I was in closer contact with my own species than ever I had been.

Once again, I don't know how much later, I attempted to communicate with a fellow runner: when I nudged him, he struck me back so sharply with his elbow that I stumbled and would have fallen, surely, had I not grasped the shirt of the runner ahead of me. The rhythm was broken: the three of us and many around us only narrowly escaped going under.

The street widened and narrowed, I was swept closer to the buildings then away; there seemed, often, as much oblique movement among us as forward.

I learned soon, when those ahead of me bobbed a little, to prepare my balance for a small leap over some object in the street I dared not glance down to identify.

At eye-level before and to either side of me—an infinite landscape of wavering profiles and backs of heads. Overhead, above the shops, an endless passage of signs. The stone gazes of a thousand lonely gargoyles fell upon us from the ledges and roofcorners of tenements and office-buildings.

The dust claimed the color of my clothes and my skin.

I discovered—vaguely to my chagrin—I was as tireless a runner as the rest.

As I became less and less conscious of one weary foot following the other, of the occasional little leaps, of watching my distance between the walls, my perspicacity sharpened.

It occurred to me that nowhere in my cross-currents of miles, hours, and bodies, had I noticed a single child younger than, perhaps, sixteen or seventeen. Nor an adult older than, I should say, forty. Rarely did I see a woman, and when I did, she was as strong and masculine as the rest of us.

One of these was thrown next to me not long after I had awakened to how few women there were. She was, at first, repulsive to me, but loneliness overwhelmed me soon and it was of signal importance that she notice me. I nudged and gestured as well as I could for perhaps a mile. No response. I was bitterly hurt and began then—backhand—to commit every indignity I could think of with her person. I stopped only when it seemed likely that my own physical excitement at this activity was sapping strength I needed for running. I was furious, however, and even considered striking her down beneath the runners. Fear for my own balance prevented me.

Then she was shifted away and there were no more women.

I thought, occasionally, I glimpsed faces back a little from the light in upper-story windows. I was sure, once, I saw a man, shirtless, leaning out his window on his elbows, gnawing a joint of meat, perhaps the length of an arm between elbow and shoulder; but I attribute it now to my failing senses. Through the dust-mist over us, one could be certain of very little.

Some time thereafter, I noticed a commotion several heads ahead and to my right. As well as I could see, it seemed a runner had leapt upon the back of the one ahead of him and driven his teeth into the soft muscle where the neck joins the torso. His victim fought as valiantly as he could without turning. Pain, apparently, drove him at last to turn and down he, his assailant, and many around them went. That violence passed through us like rings from a stone tossed into a pool. We rocked with and against one another giddily until the shock subsided.

Time to time, the better thing seemed to be to drop as I had seen so many drop. When I faced the inevitability that without women and children, the race had no hope for perpetuity, no hope. . . . Often a deep wave of that feeling swept me. I had simply to relax my tortured body to end all running.

I didn't. There seemed no more justification for that than

for endless running. It was perhaps vanity: I might have been proud of my capacity to endure, unwilling to allow that my elaborate plan to escape my apartment had come to nothing —in any case, so much of my consciousness, my will, seemed invested. If running is insufficient, it is, at least, something.

My decision originally to dive headlong into the street— what possibility spurred me? It seemed likely, as I recall, that even if the running in the street continued, one could hope to eventuate in some countryside full of green clover where the river of runners could flood out harmlessly into soft grass and there rest and offer up thanks. Cities are not infinite. What of vacant lots, and what of intersections, one every block, why hadn't I, how many hundred intersections of alleys and streets had I passed? In the center where I ran there had been no break to either side in the on-surge of the running.

I allowed myself to drift—cautiously—toward the periphery as a large space between office buildings told me a crossing approached.

There, like the wheels and whirlpools of water at the confluence of two strong rivers, swirls of runners revolved against and crushed one another. It was one thing to die against a cold facework of stone—.

Some escaped, of course, from the stream my stream bisected into the midst of mine. I was momentarily happy to flow with the stronger current.

Soon my stream encountered one of greater force and I was carried to my left down another street, running warily in the center. I went on then for miles in that direction, running night and day, until a stronger stream turned me once again.

I began to look forward to these changes: there as the two forces met and interchanged, the pace slackened somewhat for a few moments, if precariously so.

By the time I was quite sure the same sequence of signs

appeared again and again overhead, I was beyond anything like horror or despair.

And I was not surprised to feel we were no longer running on the pavement.

More and more heads dropped from sight—from hunger, from fatigue, from the increasing difficulty to find footing. Yet, although more disappeared, concentration of the current never diminished. Perhaps more and more, like me, contrived ways to fling themselves into the stream (notwithstanding that, from my vantage at the middle of the flow, never did I notice one).

And then?

And then there was running.

To preoccupy myself, I shout this into the sound of our feet between us to you who hear nothing and know as much and as little as I.

•

A Very Old Man with Enormous Wings

GABRIEL GARCÍA MÁRQUEZ

Translated by Gregory Rabassa

A TALE FOR CHILDREN

On the third day of rain they had killed so many crabs inside the house that Pelayo had to cross his drenched courtyard and throw them into the sea, because the newborn child had a temperature all night and they thought it was due to the stench. The world had been sad since Tuesday. Sea and sky were a single ash-gray thing and the sands of the beach, which on March nights glimmered like powdered light, had become a stew of mud and rotten shellfish. The light was so weak at noon that when Pelayo was coming back to the house after throwing away the crabs, it was hard for him to see what it was that was moving and groaning in the rear of the courtyard. He had to go very close to see that it was an old man, a very old man, lying face down in the mud, who, in spite of his tremendous efforts, couldn't get up, impeded by his enormous wings.

Frightened by that nightmare, Pelayo ran to get Elisenda,

his wife, who was putting compresses on the sick child, and he
took her to the rear of the courtyard. They both looked at the
fallen body with mute stupor. He was dressed like a ragpicker.
There were only a few faded hairs left on his bald skull and very
few teeth in his mouth, and his pitiful condition of a drenched
great-grandfather had taken away any sense of grandeur he
might have had. His huge buzzard wings, dirty and half-
plucked, were forever entangled in the mud. They looked at
him so long and so closely that Pelayo and Elisenda very soon
overcame their surprise and in the end found him familiar.
Then they dared speak to him, and he answered in an incomprehensible dialect with a strong sailor's voice. That was how
they skipped over the inconvenience of the wings and quite
intelligently concluded that he was a lonely castaway from
some foreign ship wrecked by the storm. And yet, they called
in a neighbor woman who knew everything about life and
death to see him, and all she needed was one look to show them
their mistake.

"He's an angel," she told them. "He must have been
coming for the child, but the poor fellow is so old that the rain
knocked him down."

On the following day everyone knew that a flesh-and-
blood angel was held captive in Pelayo's house. Against the
judgment of the wise neighbor woman, for whom angels in
those times were the fugitive survivors of a celestial conspiracy,
they did not have the heart to club him to death. Pelayo
watched over him all afternoon from the kitchen, armed with
his bailiff's club, and before going to bed he dragged him out
of the mud and locked him up with the hens in the wire
chicken coop. In the middle of the night, when the rain
stopped, Pelayo and Elisenda were still killing crabs. A short
time afterward the child woke up without a fever and with a
desire to eat. Then they felt magnanimous and decided to put

the angel on a raft with fresh water and provisions for three days and leave him to his fate on the high seas. But when they went out into the courtyard with the first light of dawn, they found the whole neighborhood in front of the chicken coop having fun with the angel, without the slightest reverence, tossing him things to eat through the openings in the wire as if he weren't a supernatural creature but a circus animal.

Father Gonzaga arrived before seven o'clock, alarmed at the strange news. By that time onlookers less frivolous than those at dawn had already arrived and they were making all kinds of conjectures concerning the captive's future. The simplest among them thought that he should be named mayor of the world. Others of sterner mind felt that he should be promoted to the rank of five-star general in order to win all wars. Some visionaries hoped that he could be put to stud in order to implant on earth a race of winged wise men who could take charge of the universe. But Father Gonzaga, before becoming a priest, had been a robust woodcutter. Standing by the wire, he reviewed his catechism in an instant and asked them to open the door so that he could take a close look at that pitiful man who looked more like a huge decrepit hen among the fascinated chickens. He was lying in a corner drying his open wings in the sunlight among the fruit peels and breakfast leftovers that the early risers had thrown him. Alien to the impertinences of the world, he only lifted his antiquarian eyes and murmured something in his dialect when Father Gonzaga went into the chicken coop and said good morning to him in Latin. The parish priest had his first suspicion of an imposter when he saw that he did not understand the language of God or know how to greet His ministers. Then he noticed that seen close up he was much too human: he had an unbearable smell of the outdoors, the back side of his wings was strewn with parasites and his main feathers had been mistreated by terres-

trial winds, and nothing about him measured up to the proud
dignity of angels. Then he came out of the chicken coop and
in a brief sermon warned the curious against the risks of being
ingenuous. He reminded them that the devil had the bad habit
of making use of carnival tricks in order to confuse the unwary.
He argued that if wings were not the essential element in
determining the difference between a hawk and an airplane,
they were even less so in the recognition of angels. Nevertheless, he promised to write a letter to his bishop so that the latter
would write to his primate so that the latter would write to the
Supreme Pontiff in order to get the final verdict from the
highest courts.

His prudence fell on sterile hearts. The news of the captive angel spread with such rapidity that after a few hours the
courtyard had the bustle of a marketplace and they had to call
in troops with fixed bayonets to disperse the mob that was
about to knock the house down. Elisenda, her spine all twisted
from sweeping up so much marketplace trash, then got the idea
of fencing in the yard and charging five cents admission to see
the angel.

The curious came from far away. A traveling carnival
arrived with a flying acrobat who buzzed over the crowd several
times, but no one paid any attention to him because his wings
were not those of an angel but, rather, those of a sidereal bat.
The most unfortunate invalids on earth came in search of
health: a poor woman who since childhood had been counting
her heartbeats and had run out of numbers; a Portuguese man
who couldn't sleep because the noise of the stars disturbed him;
a sleepwalker who got up at night to undo the things he had
done while awake; and many others with less serious ailments.
In the midst of that shipwreck disorder that made the earth
tremble, Pelayo and Elisenda were happy with fatigue, for in
less than a week they had crammed their rooms with money

and the line of pilgrims waiting their turn to enter still reached beyond the horizon.

The angel was the only one who took no part in his own act. He spent his time trying to get comfortable in his borrowed nest, befuddled by the hellish heat of the oil lamps and sacramental candles that had been placed along the wire. At first they tried to make him eat some mothballs, which, according to the wisdom of the wise neighbor woman, were the food prescribed for angels. But he turned them down, just as he turned down the papal lunches that the penitents brought him, and they never found out whether it was because he was an angel or because he was an old man that in the end he ate nothing but eggplant mush. His only supernatural virtue seemed to be patience. Especially during the first days, when the hens pecked at him, searching for the stellar parasites that proliferated in his wings, and the cripples pulled out feathers to touch their defective parts with, and even the most merciful threw stones at him, trying to get him to rise so they could see him standing. The only time they succeeded in arousing him was when they burned his side with an iron for branding steers, for he had been motionless for so many hours that they thought he was dead. He awoke with a start, ranting in his hermetic language and with tears in his eyes, and he flapped his wings a couple of times, which brought on a whirlwind of chicken dung and lunar dust and a gale of panic that did not seem to be of this world. Although many thought that his reaction had been one not of rage but of pain, from then on they were careful not to annoy him, because the majority understood that his passivity was not that of a hero taking his ease but that of a cataclysm in repose.

Father Gonzaga held back the crowd's frivolity with formulas of maidservant inspiration while awaiting the arrival of a final judgment on the nature of the captive. But the mail from Rome showed no sense of urgency. They spent their time finding out if the prisoner had a navel, if his dialect had any connection with Aramaic, how many times he could fit on the head of a pin, or whether he wasn't just a Norwegian with wings. Those meager letters might have come and gone until the end of time if a providential event had not put an end to the priest's tribulations.

It so happened that during those days, among so many other carnival attractions, there arrived in town the traveling show of the woman who had been changed into a spider for having disobeyed her parents. The admission to see her was not only less than the admission to see the angel, but people were permitted to ask her all manner of questions about her absurd state and to examine her up and down so that no one would ever doubt the truth of her horror. She was a frightful tarantula the size of a ram and with the head of a sad maiden. What was most heart-rending, however, was not her outlandish shape but the sincere affliction with which she recounted the details of her misfortune. While still practically a child she had sneaked out of her parents' house to go to a dance, and while she was coming back through the woods after having danced all night without permission, a fearful thunderclap rent the sky in two and through the crack came the lightning bolt of brimstone that changed her into a spider. Her only nourishment came from the meatballs that charitable souls chose to toss into her mouth. A spectacle like that, full of so much human truth and with such a fearful lesson, was bound to defeat without even trying that of a haughty angel who scarcely deigned to look at mortals. Besides, the few miracles attributed to the angel showed a certain mental disorder, like the blind man who didn't recover his sight but grew three new teeth, or the paralytic who didn't get to walk but almost won the lottery, and the leper whose sores sprouted sunflowers. Those consolation miracles, which were more like mocking fun, had already ruined the angel's reputation when the woman who had been changed into a spider finally crushed him completely. That was how Father Gonzaga was cured forever of his insomnia and Pelayo's courtyard went back to being as empty as during the time it had rained for three days and crabs walked through the bedrooms.

The owners of the house had no reason to lament. With the money they saved they built a two-story mansion with balconies and gardens and high netting so that crabs wouldn't get in during the winter, and with iron bars on the windows so that angels wouldn't get in. Pelayo also set up a rabbit warren close to town and gave up his job as bailiff for good, and Elisenda bought some satin pumps with high heels and many dresses of iridescent silk, the kind worn on Sunday by the most desirable women in those times. The chicken coop was the only thing that didn't receive any attention. If they washed it down with creolin and burned tears of myrrh inside it every so often, it was not in homage to the angel but to drive away the dungheap stench that still hung everywhere like a ghost and was turning the new house into an old one. At first, when the child learned to walk, they were careful that he not get too close to the chicken coop. But then they began to lose their fears and got used to the smell, and before the child got his second teeth he'd gone inside the chicken coop to play, where the wires were falling apart. The angel was no less standoffish with him than with other mortals, but he tolerated the most ingenious infamies with the patience of a dog who had no illusions. They both came down with chicken pox at the same time. The doctor who took care of the child couldn't resist the temptation to listen to the angel's heart, and he found so much whistling in the heart and so many sounds in his kidneys that it seemed impossible for him to be alive. What surprised him most, however, was the logic of his wings. They seemed so natural on that completely human organism that he couldn't understand why other men didn't have them too.

When the child began school it had been some time since the sun and rain had caused the collapse of the chicken coop. The angel went dragging himself about here and there like a stray dying man. They would drive him out of the bedroom with a broom and a moment later find him in the kitchen. He seemed to be in so many places at the same time that they grew to think that he'd been duplicated, that he was reproducing himself all through the house, and the exasperated and unhinged Elisenda shouted that it was awful living in that hell full of angels. He could scarcely eat and his antiquarian eyes had also become so foggy that he went about bumping into posts. All he had left were the bare cannulae of his last feathers. Pelayo threw a blanket over him and extended him the charity of letting him sleep in the shed, and only then did they notice that he had a temperature at night, and was delirious with the tongue twisters of an old Norwegian. That was one of the few times they became alarmed, for they thought he was going to die and not even the wise neighbor woman had been able to tell them what to do with dead angels.

And yet he not only survived his worst winter, but seemed improved with the first sunny days. He remained motionless for several days in the farthest corner of the courtyard, where no one would see him, and at the beginning of December some large, stiff feathers began to grow on his wings, the feathers of a scarecrow, which looked more like another misfortune of decrepitude. But he must have known the reason for those changes, for he was quite careful that no one should notice them, that no one should hear the sea chanteys that he sometimes sang under the stars. One morning Elisenda was cutting some bunches of onions for lunch when a wind that seemed to come from the high seas blew into the kitchen. Then she went to the window and caught the angel in his first attempts at flight. They were so clumsy that his fingernails opened a furrow in the vegetable patch and he was on the point of knocking the shed down with the ungainly flapping that slipped on the light and couldn't get a grip on the air. But he did manage to gain altitude. Elisenda let out a sigh of relief, for herself and for him, when she saw him pass over the last houses, holding himself up in some way with the risky flapping of a senile vulture. She kept watching him even when she was through cutting the onions and she kept on watching until it was no longer possible for her to see him, because then he was no longer an annoyance in her life but an imaginary dot on the horizon of the sea.

The Southern Thruway

JULIO CORTÁZAR

Translated by Suzanne Jill Levine

> Sweltering motorists do not seem to
> have a history . . . As a reality a
> traffic jam is impressive, but it doesn't
> say much.
> —*Arrigo Benedetti,* L'Espresso,
> *Rome, 6.21.64*

At first the girl in the Dauphine had insisted on keeping track of the time, but the engineer in the Peugeot 404 didn't care any more. Anyone could look at his watch, but it was as if that time strapped to your right wrist or the beep beep on the radio were measuring something else—the time of those who haven't made the blunder of trying to return to Paris on the southern thruway on a Sunday afternoon and, just past Fontainebleau, have had to slow down to a crawl, stop, six rows of cars on either side (everyone knows that on Sundays both sides of the thruway are reserved for those returning to the capital), start the engine, move three yards, stop, talk with the two nuns in the 2CV on the right, look in the rear-view mirror at the

---

The translator wishes to thank Roberto González Echevarria for his collaboration in the translation of this story.

pale man driving the Caravelle, ironically envy the birdlike contentment of the couple in the Peugeot 203 (behind the girl's Dauphine) playing with their little girl, joking, and eating cheese, or suffer the exasperated outbursts of the two boys in the Simca, in front of the Peugeot 404, and even get out at the stops to explore, not wandering off too far (no one knows when the cars up front will start moving again, and you have to run back so that those behind you won't begin their battle of horn blasts and curses), and thus move up along a Taunus in front of the girl's Dauphine—she is still watching the time—and exchange a few discouraged or mocking words with the two men traveling with the little blond boy, whose great joy at this particular moment is running his toy car over the seats and the rear ledge of the Taunus, or to dare and move up just a bit, since it doesn't seem the cars up ahead will budge very soon, and observe with some pity the elderly couple in the ID Citroën that looks like a big purple bathtub with the little old man and woman swimming around inside, he resting his arms on the wheel with an air of resigned fatigue, she nibbling on an apple, fastidious rather than hungry.

By the fourth time he had seen all that, done all that, the engineer decided not to leave his car again and to just wait for the police to somehow dissolve the bottleneck. The August heat mingled with the tire-level temperature and made immobility increasingly irritating. All was gasoline fumes, screechy screams from the boys in the Simca, the sun's glare bouncing off glass and chrome frames, and to top it off, the contradictory sensation of being trapped in a jungle of cars made to run. The engineer's 404 occupied the second lane on the right, counting from the median, which meant that he had four cars on his right and seven on his left, although, in fact, he could see distinctly only the eight cars surrounding him and their occupants, whom he was already tired of observing. He had chatted with them all, except for the boys in the Simca, whom he disliked. Between stops the situation had been discussed down to the smallest detail, and the general impression was that, up to Corbeil-Essonnes, they would move more or less slowly, but that between Corbeil and Juvisy things would pick up once the helicopters and motorcycle police managed to break up the worst of the bottleneck. No one doubted that a serious accident had taken place in the area, which could be the only explanation for such an incredible delay. And with that, the government, taxes, road conditions, one topic after another, three yards, another commonplace, five yards, a sententious phrase or a restrained curse.

The two little nuns in the 2CV wanted so much to get to Milly-la-Forêt before eight because they were bringing a basket of greens for the cook. The couple in the Peugeot 203 were particularly interested in not missing the games on television at nine-thirty; the girl in the Dauphine had told the engineer that she didn't care if she got to Paris a little late, she was complaining only as a matter of principle because she thought it was a crime to subject thousands of people to the discomforts of a camel caravan. In the last few hours (it must have been around five, but the heat was unbearable) they had moved about fifty yards according to the engineer's calculations, but one of the men from the Taunus who had come to talk, bringing his little boy with him, pointed ironically to the top of a solitary plane tree, and the girl in the Dauphine remembered that this plane (if it wasn't a chestnut) had been in line with her car for such a long time that she would no longer bother looking at her watch, since all calculations were useless.

Night would never come; the sun's vibrations on the highway and cars pushed vertigo to the edge of nausea. Dark glasses, handkerchiefs moistened with cologne pressed against fore-

heads, the measures improvised to protect oneself from screaming reflections or from the foul breath expelled by exhaust pipes
at every start, were being organized, perfected, and were the
object of reflection and commentary. The engineer got out
again to stretch his legs, exchanged a few words with the couple
(who looked like farmers) traveling in the Ariane in front of the
nuns' 2CV. Behind the 2CV was a Volkswagen with a soldier
and a girl who looked like newlyweds. The third line toward the
edge of the road no longer interested him because he would
have had to go dangerously far from the 404; he could distinguish colors, shapes, Mercedes Benz, ID, Lancia, Skoda, Mor-
ris Minor, the whole catalog. To the left, on the opposite side
of the road, an unreachable jungle of Renaults, Anglias, Peu-
geots, Porsches, Volvos. It was so monotonous that finally, after
chatting with the two men in the Taunus and unsuccessfully
trying to exchange views with the solitary driver of the Caravelle, there was nothing better to do than to go back to the 404
and pick up the same conversation about the time, distances,
and the movies with the girl in the Dauphine.

Sometimes a stranger would appear, someone coming
from the opposite side of the road or from the outside lanes on
the right, who would slip between cars to bring some news,
probably false, relayed from car to car along the hot miles. The
stranger would savor the impact of his news, the slamming of
doors as passengers rushed back to comment on the events; but
after a while a horn, or an engine starting up, would drive the
stranger away, zigzagging through the cars, rushing to get into
his and away from the justified anger of the others. And so, all
afternoon, they heard about the crash of a Floride and a 2CV
near Corbeil—three dead and one child wounded; the double
collision of a Fiat 1500 and a Renault station wagon, which in
turn smashed into an Austin full of English tourists; the over-
turning of an Orly airport bus, teeming with passengers from

the Copenhagen flight. The engineer was sure that almost everything was false, although something awful must have happened near Corbeil or even near Paris itself to have paralyzed traffic to such an extent. The farmers in the Ariane, who had a farm near Montereau and knew the region well, told them about another Sunday when traffic had been at a standstill for five hours, but even that much time seemed ludicrous now that the sun, going down on the left side of the road, poured a last avalanche of orange jelly into each car, making metals boil and clouding vision, the treetops behind them never completely disappearing, the shadow barely seen in the distance up ahead never getting near enough so that you could feel the line of cars was moving, even if only a little, even if you had to start and then slam on the brakes and never leave first gear; the dejection of again going from first to neutral, brake, hand brake, stop, and the same thing time and time again.

At one point, tired of inactivity, the engineer decided to take advantage of a particularly endless stop to make a tour of the lanes on the left and, leaving the Dauphine behind he found a DKW, another 2CV, a Fiat 600, and he stopped by a De Soto to chat with an astonished tourist from Washington, D.C., who barely understood French, but had to be at the Place de l'Opéra at eight sharp, you understand, my wife will be awfully anxious, damn it, and they were talking about things in general when a traveling salesman type emerged from the DKW to tell them that someone had come by before saying that a Piper Cub had crashed in the middle of the highway, several dead. The American couldn't give a damn about the Piper Cub, likewise the engineer who, hearing a chorus of horns, rushed back to the 404, passing on the news as he went to the men in the Taunus and the couple in the 203. He saved a more detailed account for the girl in the Dauphine as the cars moved a few slow yards. (Now the Dauphine was slightly behind in relation to the 404, later it would be the opposite; actually, the twelve rows moved as a block, as if an invisible traffic cop at the end of the highway were ordering them to advance in unison, not letting anyone get ahead.) A Piper Cub, Miss, is a small touring plane. Oh. Some nerve crashing right on the thruway on a Sunday afternoon! Really. If only it weren't so hot in these damn cars, if those trees to the right were finally behind us, if the last number in the odometer were finally to fall into its little black hole instead of hanging by its tail, endlessly.

At one point (night was softly falling, the horizon of car tops was turning purple), a big white butterfly landed on the Dauphine's windshield, and the girl and the engineer admired its wings, spread in brief and perfect suspension while it rested; then with acute nostalgia, they watched it fly away over the Taunus and the old çouple's ID, head toward the Simca, where a hunter's hand tried vainly to catch it, wing amiably over the Ariane, where the two farmers seemed to be eating something, and finally disappear to the right. At dusk, the line of cars made a first big move of about forty yards; when the engineer looked absently at the odometer, one half of the six had vanished, and the seven was beginning to move down. Almost everybody listened to the radio, and the boys in the Simca had theirs at full blast, singing along with a twist, rocking the car with their gyrations; the nuns were saying their rosaries; the little boy in the Taunus had fallen asleep with his face against the window, the toy car still in his hand. At one point (it was nighttime now), some strangers came with more news, as contradictory as the news already forgotten. It wasn't a Piper, but a glider flown by a general's daughter. It was true that a Renault van had smashed into an Austin, not in Juvisy though, but practically at the gates of Paris. One of the strangers explained to the couple in the 203 that the pavement had caved in around Igny, and five cars had overturned when their front wheels got caught in the cracks. The idea of a natural catastrophe spread all the way to the engineer, who shrugged without a comment. Later, thinking of those first few hours of darkness when they had begun to breathe more easily, he remembered that, at one point, he had stuck his arm out of his window to tap on the Dauphine and wake up the girl; she had fallen asleep, oblivious to a new advance. It was perhaps already midnight when one of the nuns timidly offered him a ham sandwich, assuming that he was hungry. The engineer accepted it (although, in fact, he felt nauseous) and asked if he could share it with the girl in the Dauphine, who accepted and voraciously ate the sandwich and a chocolate bar she got from the traveling salesman in the DKW, her neighbor to the left. A lot of people had stepped out of the stuffy cars, because again it had been hours since the last advance; thirst was prevalent, the bottles of lemonade and even the wine on board were already exhausted. The first to complain was the little girl in the 203, and the soldier and the engineer left their cars to go with her father to get water. In front of the Simca, where the radio seemed to provide ample nourishment, the engineer found a Beaulieu occupied by an older woman with nervous eyes. No, she didn't have any water, but she could give him some candy for the little girl. The couple in the ID consulted each other briefly before the old woman pulled a small can of fruit juice out of her bag. The engineer expressed his gratitude and asked if they were hungry, or if he could be of any service; the old man shook his head, but the old lady seemed to accept his offer silently. Later, the girl from the Dauphine and the engineer explored the rows on the left, without going too far; they came back with a few pastries and gave them to the old lady in the ID, just in time to run back to their own cars under a shower of horn blasts.

Aside from those quick jaunts, there was so little to do

that the hours began to blend together, becoming one in the memory; at one point, the engineer thought of striking that day from his appointments book and had to keep from laughing out loud, but later, when the nuns, the men in the Taunus, and the girl in the Dauphine began to make contradictory calculations, he realized it would have been better to keep track of time. The local radio stations stopped transmitting for the day, and only the traveling salesman had a short-wave radio, which insisted on reporting exclusively on the stock market. Around three, it seemed as if a tacit agreement had been reached, and the line didn't move until dawn. The boys in the Simca pulled out inflatable beds and laid down by their car; the engineer lowered the back of the front seat of the 404 and offered the cushions to the nuns, who refused them; before lying down for a while, the engineer thought of the girl in the Dauphine, who was still at the wheel, and, pretending it didn't make any difference to him, offered to switch cars with her until dawn, but she refused, claiming that she could sleep fine in any position. For a while, you could hear the boy in the Taunus cry; he was lying on the back seat and probably suffering from the heat. The nuns were still praying when the engineer laid down on the seat and began falling asleep, but his sleep was too close to wakefulness, and he finally awoke sweaty and nervous, not realizing at first where he was. Sitting up straight, he began to perceive confused movements outside, a gliding of shadows between the cars, and then he saw a black bulk disappear toward the edge of the highway; he guessed why, and later he, too, left his car to relieve himself at the edge of the road; there were no hedges or trees, only the starless black fields, something that looked like an abstract wall fencing off the white strip of asphalt with its motionless river of cars. He almost bumped into the farmer from the Ariane, who mumbled something unintelligible; the smell of gasoline over the road now mingled with the more acid presence of man, and the engineer hurried back to his car as soon as he could. The girl in the Dauphine slept leaning on the steering wheel, a lock of hair in her eyes. Before climbing into the 404, the engineer amused himself by watching her shadow, divining the curve of her slightly puckered lips. On the other side, smoking silently, the man in the DKW was also watching the girl sleep.

In the morning they moved a little, enough to give them hope that by afternoon the route to Paris would open up. At nine, a stranger brought good news: The cracks on the road had been filled, and traffic would soon be back to normal. The boys in the Simca turned on the radio, and one of them climbed on top of the car singing and shouting. The engineer told himself that the news was as false as last night's and that the stranger had taken advantage of the group's happiness to ask for and get an orange from the couple in the Ariane. Later another stranger came and tried the same trick, but got nothing. The heat was beginning to rise, and the people preferred to stay in their cars and wait for the good news to come true. At noon, the little girl in the 203 began crying again, and the girl in the Dauphine went to play with her and made friends with her parents. The 203's had no luck: On the right they had the silent man in the Caravelle, oblivious to everything happening around him, and from their left they had to endure the verbose indignation of the driver of the Floride, for whom the bottleneck was a personal affront. When the little girl complained of thirst again, the engineer decided to talk to the couple in the Ariane, convinced that there were many provisions in that car. To his surprise, the farmers were very friendly; they realized that in a situation like this it was necessary to help one another, and they thought that if someone took charge of the group (the woman made a circular gesture with her hand, encompassing the dozen cars surrounding them), they would have enough to get them to Paris. The idea of appointing himself organizer bothered him, and he chose to call the men from the Taunus for a meeting with the couple in the Ariane. A while later, the rest of the group was consulted one by one. The young soldier in the Volkswagen agreed immediately, and the couple in the 203 offered the few provisions they had left. (The girl in the Dauphine had gotten a glass of pomegranate juice for the little girl, who was now laughing and playing.) One of the Taunus men who went to consult with the boys in the Simca received only mocking consent; the pale man in the Caravelle said it made no difference to him, they could do whatever they wanted. The old couple in the ID and the lady in the Beaulieu reacted with visible joy, as if they felt more protected now. The drivers of the Floride and DKW made no comment, and the American looked at them astonished, saying something about God's will. The engineer found it easy to nominate one of the Taunus men, in whom he had instinctive confidence, as coordinator of all activities. No one would have to go hungry for the time being, but they needed water; the leader, whom the boys in the Simca called Taunus for fun, asked the engineer, the soldier, and one of the boys to explore the zone of highway around them, offering food in exchange for beverages. Taunus, who evidently knew how to command, figured that they should obtain supplies for a maximum of a day and a half, taking the most pessimistic view. In the nuns' 2CV and the farmer's Ariane there were enough supplies for such a period of time and, if the explorers returned with water, all problems would be solved. But only the soldier returned with a full flask, and its owner had demanded food for two people in exchange. The engineer failed to find anyone who could give him water, but his trip allowed him to observe that beyond his group other cells were being organized and were facing similar problems; at a given moment, the driver of an Alfa Romeo refused to speak to him, referring him to the leader of his group five cars behind. Later, the boy from the Simca came back without any water, but Taunus figured they already had enough water for the two children, the old lady in the ID, and the rest of the women. The engineer was telling the girl in the Dauphine about his trip around the periphery (it was one in the afternoon, and the sun kept them in their cars), when she interrupted him with a gesture and pointed to the Simca. In two leaps the engineer reached the car and grabbed the elbow of the boy sprawled in the seat and drinking in great gulps from a flask he had brought back hidden in his jacket. To the boy's angry gesture the engineer responded by increasing the pressure on his arm; the other boy got out of the car and jumped on the engineer, who took two steps back and waited for him, almost with pity. The soldier was already running toward them, and the nuns' shrieks alerted Taunus and his companion. Taunus listened to what had happened, approached the boy with the flask, and slapped him twice. Sobbing, the boy screamed and protested, while the other grumbled without daring to intervene. The engineer took the flask away and gave it to Taunus. Horns began to blare, and everyone returned to his car, but to no avail, since the line moved barely five yards.

At siesta time, under a sun that was even stronger than the day before, one of the nuns took off her coif, and her companion doused her temples with cologne. The women improvised their Samaritan activities little by little, moving from one car to the next, taking care of the children to allow the men more freedom. No one complained, but the jokes were strained, always based on the same word plays, in snobbish skepticism. The greatest humiliation for the girl in the Dauphine and the engineer was to feel sweaty and dirty; the farmers' absolute indifference to the odor that emanated from their armpits moved them to pity. Toward dusk, the engineer looked casually into the rear-view mirror and found, as always, the pale face and tense features of the driver of the Caravelle who, like the fat driver of the Floride, had remained aloof from all the activities. He thought that his features had become sharper and wondered if he were sick. But later on, when he went to talk with the soldier and his wife, he had a chance to look at him more closely and told himself that the man was not sick, that it was something else, a separation, to give it a name. The soldier in the Volkswagen later told him that his wife was afraid of that silent man who never left the wheel and seemed to sleep awake. Conjectures arose; a folklore was created to fight against inactivity. The children in the Taunus and the 203 had become friends, quarreled, and later made up; their parents visited each other, and once in a while the girl in the Dauphine went to see how the old lady in the ID and the woman in the Beaulieu were doing. At dusk, when some gusts of wind swept through, and the sun went behind the clouds in the west, the people were happy, thinking it would get cooler. A few drops fell, coinciding with an extraordinary advance of almost 100 yards; far away, lightning glowed, and it got even hotter. There was so much electricity in the atmosphere that Taunus, with an instinct the engineer silently admired, left the group alone until night, as if he sensed the possible consequences of the heat and fatigue. At eight, the women took charge of distributing the food; it had been decided that the farmer's Ariane should be the general warehouse and the nuns' 2CV a supplementary depot. Taunus had gone in person to confer with the leaders of the four or five neighboring groups; later, with the help of the soldier and the man in the 203, he took an amount of food to the other groups and returned with more water and some wine. It was decided that the boys in the Simca would yield their inflatable beds to the old lady in the ID and the woman in the Beaulieu; the girl in the Dauphine also brought them two plaid blankets, and the engineer offered his car, which he mockingly called the "sleeping car," to whomever might need it. To his surprise, the girl in the Dauphine accepted the offer and that night shared the 404 cushions with one of the nuns; the other nun went to sleep in the 203 with the little girl and her mother, while the husband spent the night on the pavement wrapped in a blanket. The engineer was not sleepy and played dice with Taunus and his mate; at one point, the farmer in the Ariane joined them, and they talked about politics and drank a few shots of brandy that the farmer had turned over to Taunus that morning. The night wasn't bad; it had cooled down, and a few stars shone between the clouds.

Toward morning, they were overcome by sleep, that need to feel covered which came with the half-light of dawn. While Taunus slept beside the boy in the back seat, his friend and the engineer rested up front. Between two images of a dream, the engineer thought he heard screams in the distance and saw a vague glow; the leader of another group came to tell them that thirty cars ahead there had been the beginnings of a fire in an Estafette—someone had tried to boil vegetables on the sly. Taunus joked about the incident as he went from car to car to find out how they had spent the night, but everyone got his message. That morning, the line began to move very early, and there was an excited rush to pick up mattresses and blankets, but, since the same was probably happening all over, almost no one was impatient or blew his horn. Toward noon, they had moved more than fifty yards, and the shadow of a forest could be seen to the right of the highway. They envied those lucky people who at that moment could go to the shoulder of the road and enjoy the shade; maybe there was a brook or a faucet with running water. The girl in the Dauphine closed her eyes and thought of a shower falling down her neck and back, running down her legs; the engineer, observing her out of the corner of his eye, saw two tears streaming down her cheeks.

Taunus, who had moved up to the ID, came back to get the younger women to tend the old lady, who wasn't feeling well. The leader of the third group to the rear had a doctor among his men, and the soldier rushed to get him. The engineer, who had followed with ironical benevolence the efforts the boys in the Simca had been making to be forgiven, thought it was time to give them their chance. With the pieces of a tent the boys covered the windows of the 404, and the "sleeping car" became an ambulance where the old lady could sleep in relative darkness. Her husband lay down beside her, and everyone left them alone with the doctor. Later, the nuns attended to the old lady, who felt much better, and the engineer spent the afternoon as best he could, visiting other cars and resting in Taunus' when the sun bore down too hard; he had to run only three times to his car, where the old couple seemed to sleep, to move it up with the line to the next stop. Night came without their having made it to the forest.

Toward two in the morning, the temperature dropped, and those who had blankets were glad to bundle up. Since the line couldn't move until morning (it was something you felt in the air, that came from the horizon of motionless cars in the night), the engineer sat down to smoke with Taunus and to chat with the farmer in the Ariane and the soldier. Taunus' calculations no longer corresponded to reality, and he said so frankly; something would have to be done in the morning to get more provisions and water. The soldier went to get the leaders of the neighboring groups, who were not sleeping either, and they discussed the problem quietly so as not to wake up the women. The leaders had spoken with the leaders of faraway groups, in a radius of about eighty or 100 cars, and they were sure that the situation was analogous everywhere. The

farmer knew the region well and proposed that two or three
men from each group go out at dawn to buy provisions from
the neighboring farms, while Taunus appointed drivers for the
cars left unattended during the expedition. The idea was good,
and it was not difficult to collect money from those present; it
was decided that the farmer, the soldier, and Taunus' friend
would go together, taking all the paper bags, string bags, and
flasks available. The other leaders went back to their groups to
organize similar expeditions and, at dawn, the situation was
explained to the women, and the necessary preparations were
made, so that the line could keep moving. The girl in the
Dauphine told the engineer that the old lady felt better already
and insisted on going back to her ID; at eight, the doctor came
and saw no reason why the couple shouldn't return to their car.
In any case, Taunus decided that the 404 would be the official
ambulance; for fun the boys made a banner with a red cross
and put it on the antenna. For a while now, people preferred
to leave their cars as little as possible; the temperature continued to drop, and at noon, showers began to fall with lightning in the distance. The farmer's wife rushed to gather water
with a funnel and a plastic pitcher, to the special amusement
of the boys in the Simca. Watching all this, leaning on his
wheel with a book in front of him that he wasn't too interested
in, the engineer wondered why the expeditionaries were taking
so long; later, Taunus discreetly called him over to his car and,
when they got in, told him they had failed. Taunus' friend gave
details: The farms were either abandoned or the people refused
to sell to them, alleging regulations forbidding the sale to
private individuals and suspecting that they were inspectors
taking advantage of the circumstances to test them. In spite of
everything, they had been able to bring back a small amount
of water and some provisions, perhaps stolen by the soldier,
who was grinning and not going into details. Of course, the

bottleneck couldn't last much longer, but the food they had wasn't the best for the children or the old lady. The doctor, who came around four-thirty to see the sick woman, made a gesture of weariness and exasperation and told Taunus that the same thing was happening in all the neighboring groups. The radio had spoken about emergency measures being taken to clear up the thruway, but aside from a helicopter that appeared briefly at dusk, there was no action to be seen. At any rate, the heat was gradually tapering off, and people seemed to be waiting for night to cover up in their blankets and erase a few more hours of waiting in their sleep. From his car the engineer listened to the conversation between the girl in the Dauphine and the traveling salesman in the DKW, who was telling her jokes that made her laugh halfheartedly. He was surprised to see the lady from the Beaulieu, who never left her car, and got out to see if she needed something, but she only wanted the latest news and went over to talk with the nuns. A nameless tedium weighed upon them at nightfall; people expected more from sleep than from the always contradictory or unfounded news. Taunus' friend discreetly went to get the engineer, the soldier, and the man in the 203. Taunus informed them that the man in the Floride had just deserted; one of the boys in the Simca had seen the car empty and after a while started looking for the man just to kill time. No one knew the fat man in the Floride well. He had complained a lot the first day, but had turned out to be as silent as the driver of the Caravelle. When at five in the morning there was no longer any doubt that Floride, as the boys in the Simca got a kick out of calling him, had deserted, taking a handbag with him and leaving behind another filled with shirts and underwear, Taunus decided that one of the boys would take charge of the abandoned car so as not to immobilize the lane. They were all vaguely annoyed by this desertion in the dark and wondered how far

Floride could have gotten in his flight through the fields. Aside from this, it seemed to be the night for big decisions; lying on the seat cushion of his 404, the engineer seemed to hear a moan, but he figured it was coming from the soldier and his wife, which, after all, was understandable in the middle of the night and under such circumstances. But then he thought better and lifted the canvas that covered the rear window; by the light of one of the few stars shining, he saw the ever-present windshield of the Caravelle a yard and a half away, and behind it, as if glued to the glass and slightly slanted, the man's convulsed face. Quietly, he got out the left side so as not to wake up the nuns and approached the Caravelle. Then he looked for Taunus, and the soldier went to get the doctor. Obviously, the man had committed suicide by taking some kind of poison; a few lines scrawled in pencil in his appointments book were enough, plus the letter addressed to one Yvette, someone who had left him in Vierzon. Fortunately, the habit of sleeping in the cars was well established (the nights were so cold now that no one would have thought of staying outside), and few were bothered by others slipping between the cars toward the edges of the thruway to relieve themselves. Taunus called a war council, and the doctor agreed with his proposal. To leave the body on the edge of the road would mean to subject those coming behind to an at least painful surprise; to carry him further out into the fields could provoke a violent reaction from the villagers who, the night before, had threatened and beaten up a boy from another group, out looking for food. The farmer in the Ariane and the traveling salesman had what was needed to hermetically seal the Caravelle's trunk. The girl in the Dauphine joined them just as they were beginning their task, and hung on to the engineer's arm. He quietly explained what had happened and returned her, a little calmer, to her car. Taunus and his men had put the body in the trunk, and the traveling salesman worked with tubes of glue and Scotch tape by the light of the soldier's lantern. Since the woman in the 203 could drive, Taunus decided that her husband would take over the Caravelle, which was on the 203's right; so, in the morning, the little girl in the 203 discovered that her daddy had another car and played for hours at switching cars and putting some of her toys in the Caravelle.

For the first time, it felt cold during the day, and no one thought of taking off his coat. The girl in the Dauphine and the nuns made an inventory of coats available in the group. There were a few sweaters that turned up unexpectedly in the cars, or in some suitcase, a few blankets, a light overcoat or two. A list of priorities was drawn up, and the coats were distributed. Water was again scarce, and Taunus sent three of his men, including the engineer, to try to establish contact with the villagers. While impossible to say why, outside resistance was total. It was enough to step out of the thruway's boundaries for stones to come raining in from somewhere. In the middle of the night, someone threw a sickle that hit the top of the DKW and fell beside the Dauphine. The traveling salesman turned very pale and didn't move from his car, but the American in the De Soto (who was not in Taunus' group, but was appreciated by everyone for his guffaws and good humor) came running, twirled the sickle around and hurled it back with everything he had, shouting curse words. But Taunus did not think it wise to increase the hostility; perhaps it was still possible to make a trip for water.

Nobody kept track any more of how much they had moved in that day or days; the girl in the Dauphine thought that it was between eighty and two hundred yards; the engineer was not as optimistic, but amused himself by prolonging and confusing his neighbor's calculations, interested in stealing her away from the traveling salesman, who was courting her in his

professional manner. That same afternoon, the boy in charge
of the Floride came to tell Taunus that a Ford Mercury was
offering water at a good price. Taunus refused, but at nightfall
one of the nuns asked the engineer for a drink of water for the
old lady in the ID, who was suffering in silence, still holding
her husband's hand, and being tended alternately by the nuns
and the girl in the Dauphine. There was half a bottle of water
left, and the women assigned it to the old lady and the woman
in the Beaulieu. That same night Taunus paid out of his own
pocket for two bottles of water; the Ford Mercury promised to
get more the next day, at double the price.

It was difficult to get together and talk, because it was so
cold that no one would leave his car except for very pressing
reasons. The batteries were beginning to run down, and they
couldn't keep the heaters running all the time, so Taunus
decided to reserve the two best equipped cars for the sick,
should the situation arise. Wrapped in blankets (the boys in the
Simca had ripped off the inside covers of their car to make
coats and hats for themselves, and others started to imitate
them), everyone tried his best to open doors as little as possible
to preserve the heat. On one of those freezing nights the
engineer heard the girl in the Dauphine sobbing softly. Quietly
he opened her door and groped for her in the dark until he felt
a wet cheek. Almost without resistance, she let herself be
drawn to the 404; the engineer helped her lie down on the back
seat, covered her with his only blanket, and then with his
overcoat. Darkness was thicker in the ambulance car, its windows covered with the tent's canvas. At one point, the engineer
pulled down the two sun visors and hung his shirt and a sweater
from them to shut the car off completely. Toward dawn, she
whispered in his ear that before starting to cry she thought she
saw in the distance, on the right, the lights of a city.

Maybe it was a city, but in the morning mist you couldn't

see more than twenty yards away. Curiously, the line moved a lot more that day, perhaps two or three hundred yards. This coincided with new radio flashes. (Hardly anyone listened any more, with the exception of Taunus, who felt it was his duty to keep up.) The announcers talked emphatically about exceptional measures that would clear the thruway and referred to the weary toil of highway patrolmen and police forces. Suddenly, one of the nuns became delirious. As her companion looked on terrified, and the girl in the Dauphine dabbed her temples with what was left of the cologne, the nun spoke of Armageddon, the Ninth Day, the chain of cinnabar. The doctor came much later, making his way through the snow that had been falling since noon and that was gradually walling the cars in. He regretted the lack of sedatives and advised them to put the nun in a car with good heating. Taunus put her in his own car, and the little boy moved to the Caravelle with his little girl friend from the 203; they played with their toy cars and had a lot of fun, because they were the only ones who didn't go hungry. That day and the following days, it snowed almost continuously, and when the line moved up a few yards, the snow that had accumulated between cars had to be removed by improvised means.

No one would have conceived of being surprised at the way they were getting provisions and water. The only thing Taunus could do was administer the common fund and get as much as possible out of trades. The Ford Mercury and a Porsche came every night to traffic with food; Taunus and the engineer were in charge of distributing it according to the physical state of each one. Incredibly, the old lady in the ID was surviving, although sunken in a stupor that the women diligently fought off. The lady in the Beaulieu, who had been fainting and feeling nauseous a few days before, had recovered with the cold weather and was now one of the most active in

helping the nun take care of her companion, still weak and a
bit lost. The soldier's wife and 203's were in charge of the two
children; the traveling salesman in the DKW, perhaps to console himself for losing Dauphine to the engineer, spent hours
telling stories to the children. At night, the groups entered
another life, secret and private; doors would open or close to
let a frozen figure in or out; no one looked at the others; eyes
were as blind as darkness itself. Some kind of happiness endured here and there under dirty blankets, in hands with overgrown fingernails, in bodies smelling of unchanged clothes and
of days cramped inside. The girl in the Dauphine had not been
mistaken—a city sparkled in the distance, and they were approaching it slowly. In the afternoons, one of the boys in the
Simca would climb to the top of the car, relentless lookout
wrapped in pieces of seat covers and green burlap. Tired of
exploring the futile horizon, he'd look for the thousandth time
at the cars surrounding him; somewhat enviously he'd discover
Dauphine in 404's car, a hand caressing a neck, the end of a
kiss. To play a joke on them, now that he had regained 404's
friendship, he'd yell that the line was about to move. Dauphine
would have to leave 404 and go to her car, but after a while
she'd come back looking for warmth, and the boy in the Simca
would have liked so much to bring a girl from another group
to his car, but it was unthinkable with this cold and hunger,
not to mention that the group up front was openly hostile to
Taunus' because of some story about a can of condensed milk,
and except for official transactions with Ford Mercury and
Porsche, there was no possible contact with other groups. Then
the boy in the Simca would sigh unhappily and continue his
lookout until the snow and the cold forced him trembling back
into his car.

But the cold began to give way and, after a period of rains
and winds that enervated a few spirits and increased food

supply difficulties, came some cool sunny days when it was again possible to leave your car, pay visits, restore relations with neighboring groups. The leaders had discussed the situation, and peace was finally made with the group ahead. Ford Mercury's sudden disappearance was much talked about, although no one knew what could have happened to him. But Porsche kept coming and controlling the black market. Water and some preserves were never completely lacking, but the group's funds were diminishing, and Taunus and the engineer asked themselves what would happen the day when there was no more money to give Porsche. The possibility of an ambush was brought up, of taking him prisoner and forcing him to reveal the source of his supplies; but the line had advanced a good stretch, and the leaders preferred to wait some more and avoid the risk of ruining it all by a hasty decision. The engineer, who had given in to an almost pleasant indifference, was momentarily stunned by the timid news from the girl in the Dauphine, but later he understood that nothing could be done to avoid it, and the idea of having a child by her seemed as natural as the nightly distribution of supplies or the secret trips to the edge of the thruway. Nor could the death of the old lady in the ID surprise anyone. Again it was necessary to work at night, to console her husband, who just couldn't understand, and to keep him company. A fight broke out between the two groups up ahead, and Taunus had to act as mediator and tentatively solve the disagreement. Anything would happen at any moment, without prearranged schedules; the most important thing began when nobody expected it any more, and the least responsible was the first to find out. Standing on the roof of the Simca, the elated lookout had the impression that the horizon had changed (it was dusk; the meager, level light of a yellowish sun was slipping away) and that something unbelievable was happening five hundred, three hundred, two hundred and fifty yards away. He shouted it to 404, and 404 said something to Dauphine, and she dashed to her car, when Taunus, the soldier, and the farmer were already running, and from the roof of the Simca the boy was pointing ahead and endlessly repeating the news as if to convince himself that what he was seeing was true. Then they heard the rumble, as if a heavy but uncontrollable migratory wave were awakening from a long slumber and testing its strength. Taunus yelled at them to get back to their cars; the Beaulieu, the ID, the Fiat 600, and the De Soto started moving at once. Now the 2CV, the Taunus, the Simca, and the Ariane were beginning to move, and the boy in the Simca, proud of what was to him something of a personal triumph, turned to the 404 and waved his arm, while the 404, the Dauphine, the 2CV, and the DKW in turn started moving. But it all hinged on how long this was going to last, 404 thought almost routinely, as he kept pace with Dauphine and smiled encouragement to her. Behind them, the Volkswagen, the Caravelle, the 203, and the Floride started moving slowly, a stretch in first gear, then second, forever second, but already without having to clutch, as so many times before, with the foot firmly on the accelerator, waiting to move on to third. 404, reaching out to touch Dauphine's hand, barely grazed her fingertips, saw on her face a smile of incredulous hope, and thought that they would make it to Paris and take a bath, go somewhere together, to her house or his to take a bath, eat, bathe endlessly and eat and drink, and that later there would be furniture, a bedroom with furniture and a bathroom with shaving cream to really shave, and toilets, food and toilets and sheets, Paris was a toilet and two sheets and hot water running down his chest and legs, and a nail clipper, and white wine, they would drink white wine before kissing and smell each other's lavender water and cologne before really making love with the lights on, between clean sheets, and bathing again just for fun, to make love and bathe and drink and go to the barber shop, go into the bathroom, caress the sheets and caress each other between the sheets and make love among the suds and lavender water and toothbrushes, before beginning to think about what they were going to do, about the child and all the problems and the future, and all that as long as they didn't stop, just as long as the rows kept on moving, even though you couldn't go to third yet, just moving like that, in second, but moving. With his bumper touching the Simca, 404 leaned back, felt the speed picking up, felt that it was possible to accelerate without bumping into the Simca and that the Simca could accelerate without fear of crashing into Beaulieu, and that behind came the Caravelle and that they all accelerated more and more, and that it was O.K. to move on to third without forcing the engine, and the pace became even, and they all accelerated even more, and 404 looked around with surprise and tenderness, searching for Dauphine's eyes. But, naturally, speeding up like that the lanes could no longer stay parallel. Dauphine had moved almost a yard ahead of 404, and he saw her neck and barely her profile just as she was turning to look at him with surprise, noticing that the 404 was falling further behind. 404 calmed her down with a smile and accelerated abruptly, but he had to brake almost immediately, because he was about to bump the Simca; he blew the horn, and the boy looked at him in the rear-view mirror and made a gesture of helplessness, pointing to the Beaulieu, which was up against him. The Dauphine was three yards ahead, level with the Simca, and the little girl in the 203, now alongside the 404, waved her arms and showed him her doll. A red blot on his right confused 404; instead of the nuns' 2CV or the soldier's Volkswagen, he saw an unknown Chevrolet, and almost immediately the Chevrolet moved ahead followed by a Lancia and a Renault 8. To his left, an ID was gaining on him yard by yard, but before its place was taken by a 403, 404 was still able to make out up ahead the 203 that was already blocking Dauphine. The group was falling apart; it didn't exist any more. Taunus had to be at least twenty yards away, followed by Dauphine; at the same time, the third row on the left was falling behind since, instead of the traveling salesman's DKW, 404 could see only the rear end of an old black van, perhaps a Citroën or a Peugeot. The cars were in third, gaining or losing ground according to the pace of their lane, and on the side of the thruway trees and some houses in the thick mist and dusk sped by. Later, it was the red lights they all turned on, following the example of those ahead, the night that suddenly closed in on them. From time to time, horns blew, speedometer needles climbed more and more, some lanes were going at forty-five miles an hour, others at forty, some at thirty-five. 404 still hoped that with the gaining and losing of ground he would again catch up with Dauphine, but each minute that slipped by convinced him that it was useless, that the group had dissolved irrevocably, that the everyday meetings would never take place again, the few rituals, the war councils in Taunus' car, Dauphine's caresses in the quiet of night, the children's laughter as they played with their little cars, the nun's face as she said her rosary. When the Simca's brake lights came on, 404 slowed down with an absurd feeling of hope, and as soon as he put on the handbrake he bolted out and ran ahead. Outside of the Simca and the Beaulieu (the Caravelle would be behind him, but he didn't care), he didn't recognize any cars; through strange windows faces he'd never seen before stared at him in surprise and perhaps even outrage. Horns began to blare, and 404 had to go back to his car; the boy in the Simca made a friendly gesture, pointing with encouragement toward Paris. The line got moving again, slowly for a few minutes, and later as if the thruway were completely free. On

404's left was a Taunus, and for a second 404 had the impression that the group was coming together again, that everything was returning to order, that it would be possible to move ahead without destroying anything. But it was a green Taunus, and there was a woman with dark glasses at the wheel who looked straight ahead. There was nothing to do but give in to the pace, adapt mechanically to the speed of the cars around, and not think. His leather jacket must still be in the soldier's Volkswagen. Taunus had the novel he had been reading the first few days. An almost empty bottle of lavender water was in the nuns' 2CV. And he had, there where he touched it at times with his right hand, the teddy bear Dauphine had given him as a pet. He clung absurdly to the idea that at nine-thirty the food would be distributed and the sick would have to be visited, the situation would have to be examined with Taunus and the farmer in the Ariane; then it would be night, Dauphine sneaking into his car, stars or clouds, life. Yes, it had to be like that. All that couldn't have ended forever. Maybe the soldier would get some water, which had been scarce the last few hours; at any rate, you could always count on Porsche, as long as you paid his price. And on the car's antenna the red-cross flag waved madly, and you moved at fifty-five miles an hour toward the lights that kept growing, not knowing why all this hurry, why this mad race in the night among unknown cars, where no one knew anything about the others, where everyone looked straight ahead, only ahead.

The Bound Man

ILSE AICHINGER

Translated by Eric Mosbacher

Sunlight on his face woke him, but made him shut his eyes
again; it streamed unhindered down the slope, collected itself
into rivulets, attracted swarms of flies, which flew low over his
forehead, circled, sought to land, and were overtaken by fresh
swarms. When he tried to whisk them away, he discovered that
he was bound. A thick rope cut into his arms. He dropped
them, opened his eyes again, and looked down at himself. His
legs were tied all the way up to his thighs; a single length of
rope was tied round his ankles, criss-crossed up his legs, and
encircled his hips, his chest and his arms. He could not see
where it was knotted. He showed no sign of fear or hurry,
though he thought he was unable to move, until he discovered
that the rope allowed his legs some free play and that round
his body it was almost loose. His arms were tied to each other
but not to his body, and had some free play too. This made him

smile, and it occurred to him that perhaps children had been playing a practical joke on him.

He tried to feel for his knife, but again the rope cut softly into his flesh. He tried again, more cautiously this time, but his pocket was empty. Not only his knife, but the little money that he had on him, as well as his coat, were missing. His shoes had been pulled from his feet and taken too. When he moistened his lips he tasted blood, which had flowed from his temples down his cheeks, his chin, his neck, and under his shirt. His eyes were painful; if he kept them open for long he saw reddish stripes in the sky.

He decided to stand up. He drew his knees up as far as he could, rested his hands on the fresh grass and jerked himself to his feet. An elder branch stroked his cheek, the pain dazzled him, and the rope cut into his flesh. He collapsed to the ground again, half out of his mind with pain, and then tried again. He went on trying until the blood started flowing from his hidden weals. Then he lay still again for a long while and let the sun and the flies do what they liked.

When he awoke for the second time the elder bush had cast its shadow over him, and the coolness stored in it was pouring from between its branches. He must have been hit on the head. Then they must have laid him down carefully, just as a mother lays her baby behind a bush when she goes to work in the fields.

His chances all lay in the amount of free play allowed him by the rope. He dug his elbows into the ground and tested it. As soon as the rope tautened he stopped, and tried again more cautiously. If he had been able to reach the branch over his head he could have used it to drag himself to his feet, but he could not reach it. He laid his head back on the grass, rolled over, and struggled to his knees. He tested the ground with his toes, and then managed to stand up almost without effort.

A few paces away lay the path across the plateau, and in the grass were wild pinks and thistles in bloom. He tried to lift his foot to avoid trampling on them, but the rope round his ankles prevented him. He looked down at himself.

The rope was knotted at his ankles, and ran round his legs in a kind of playful pattern. He carefully bent and tried to loosen it, but, loose though it seemed to be, he could not make it any looser. To avoid treading on the thistles with his bare feet he hopped over them like a bird.

The cracking of a twig made him stop. People in this district were very prone to laughter. He was alarmed by the thought that he was in no position to defend himself. He hopped on until he reached the path. Bright fields stretched far below. He could see no sign of the nearest village, and if he could move no faster than this, night would fall before he reached it.

He tried walking and discovered that he could put one foot before another if he lifted each foot a definite distance from the ground and then put it down again before the rope tautened. In the same way he could actually swing his arms a little.

After the first step he fell. He fell right across the path, and made the dust fly. He expected this to be a sign for the long-suppressed laughter to break out, but all remained quiet. He was alone. As soon as the dust had settled he got up and went on. He looked down and watched the rope slacken, grow taut, and then slacken again.

When the first glow-worms appeared he managed to look up. He felt in control of himself again, and his impatience to reach the nearest village faded.

Hunger made him light-headed, and he seemed to be going so fast that not even a motorcycle could have overtaken him; alternatively he felt as if he were standing still and that the earth was rushing past him, like a river flowing past a man swimming against the stream. The stream carried branches which had been bent southward by the north wind, stunted young trees, and patches of grass with bright, long-stalked flowers. It ended by submerging the bushes and the young trees, leaving only the sky and the man above water level. The moon had risen, and illuminated the bare, curved summit of the plateau, the path, which was overgrown with young grass, the bound man making his way along it with quick, measured steps, and two hares, which ran across the hill just in front of him and vanished down the slope. Though the nights were still cool at this time of the year, before midnight the bound man lay down at the edge of the escarpment and went to sleep.

In the light of morning the animal-tamer who was camping with his circus in the field outside the village saw the bound man coming down the path, gazing thoughtfully at the ground. The bound man stopped and bent down. He held out one arm to help keep his balance and with the other picked up an empty wine bottle. Then he straightened himself and stood erect again. He moved slowly, to avoid being cut by the rope, but to the circus proprietor what he did suggested the voluntary limitation of an enormous swiftness of movement. He was enchanted by its extraordinary gracefulness, and while the bound man looked about for a stone on which to break the bottle, so that he could use the splintered neck to cut the rope, the animal-tamer walked across the field and approached him. The first leaps of a young panther had never filled him with such delight.

"Ladies and gentlemen, the bound man!" His very first movements let loose a storm of applause, which out of sheer excitement caused the blood to rush to the cheeks of the animal-

tamer standing at the edge of the arena. The bound man rose
to his feet. His surprise whenever he did this was like that of
a four-footed animal which has managed to stand on its hind
legs. He knelt, stood up, jumped, and turned cartwheels. The
spectators found it as astonishing as if they had seen a bird
which voluntarily remained earthbound, and confined itself to
hopping.

The bound man became an enormous draw. His absurd
steps and little jumps, his elementary exercises in movement,
made the rope dancer superfluous. His fame grew from village
to village, but the motions he went through were few and
always the same; they were really quite ordinary motions,
which he had continually to practice in the daytime in the
half-dark tent in order to retain his shackled freedom. In that
he remained entirely within the limits set by his rope he was
free of it, it did not confine him, but gave him wings and
endowed his leaps and jumps with purpose; just as the flights
of birds of passage have purpose when they take wing in the
warmth of summer and hesitantly make small circles in the sky.

All the children of the neighborhood started playing the
game of "bound man." They formed rival gangs, and one day
the circus people found a little girl lying bound in a ditch, with
a cord tied round her neck so that she could hardly breathe.
They released her, and at the end of the performance that
night the bound man made a speech. He announced briefly
that there was no sense in being tied up in such a way that you
could not jump. After that he was regarded as a comedian.

Grass and sunlight, tent pegs driven into the ground and
then pulled up again, and on to the next village. "Ladies and
gentlemen, the bound man!" The summer mounted toward its
climax. It bent its face deeper over the fish ponds in the
hollows, taking delight in its dark reflection, skimmed the
surface of the rivers, and made the plain into what it was.
Everyone who could walk went to see the bound man.

Many wanted a close-up view of how he was bound. So the circus proprietor announced after each performance that anyone who wanted to satisfy himself that the knots were real and the rope not made of rubber was at liberty to do so. The bound man generally waited for the crowd in the area outside the tent. He laughed or remained serious, and held out his arms for inspection. Many took the opportunity to look him in the face, others gravely tested the rope, tried the knots on his ankles, and wanted to know exactly how the lengths compared with the length of his limbs. They asked him how he had come to be tied up like that, and he answered patiently, always saying the same thing. Yes, he had been tied up, he said, and when he awoke he found that he had been robbed as well. Those who had done it must have been pressed for time, because they had tied him up somewhat too loosely for someone who was not supposed to be able to move and somewhat too tightly for someone who was expected to be able to move. But he did move, people pointed out. Yes, he replied, what else could he do?

Before he went to bed he always sat for a time in front of the fire. When the circus proprietor asked him why he didn't make up a better story he always answered that he hadn't made up that one, and blushed. He preferred staying in the shade.

The difference between him and the other performers was that when the show was over he did not take off his rope. The result was that every movement that he made was worth seeing, and the villagers used to hang about the camp for hours, just for the sake of seeing him get up from in front of the fire and roll himself in his blanket. Sometimes the sky was beginning to lighten when he saw their shadows disappear.

The circus proprietor often remarked that there was no reason why he should not be untied after the evening performance and tied up again next day. He pointed out that the rope dancers, for instance, did not stay on their rope overnight. But no one took the idea of untying him seriously.

For the bound man's fame rested on the fact that he was always bound, that whenever he washed himself he had to wash his clothes too and vice versa, and that his only way of doing so was to jump in the river just as he was every morning when the sun came out, and that he had to be careful not to go too far out for fear of being carried away by the stream.

The proprietor was well aware that what in the last resort protected the bound man from the jealousy of the other performers was his helplessness; he deliberately left them the pleasure of watching him groping painfully from stone to stone on the river bank every morning with his wet clothes clinging to him. When the proprietor's wife pointed out that even the best clothes would not stand up indefinitely to such treatment (and the bound man's clothes were by no means of the best), he replied curtly that it was not going to last forever. That was his answer to all objections—it was for the summer season only. But when he said this he was not being serious; he was talking like a gambler who has no intention of giving up his vice. In reality he would have been prepared cheerfully to sacrifice his lions and his rope dancers for the bound man.

He proved this on the night when the rope dancers jumped over the fire. Afterward he was convinced that they did it, not because it was midsummer's day, but because of the bound man, who as usual was lying and watching them with that peculiar smile that might have been real or might have been only the effect of the glow on his face. In any case no one knew anything about him because he never talked about anything that had happened to him before he emerged from the wood that day.

But that evening two of the performers suddenly picked him up by the arms and legs, carried him to the edge of the fire and started playfully swinging him to and fro, while two others held out their arms to catch him on the other side. In the end they threw him, but too short. The two men on the other side drew back—they explained afterward that they did so the better to take the shock. The result was that the bound man landed at the very edge of the flames and would have been burned if the circus proprietor had not seized his arms and quickly dragged him away to save the rope which was starting to get singed. He was certain that the object had been to burn the rope. He sacked the four men on the spot.

A few nights later the proprietor's wife was awakened by the sound of footsteps on the grass, and went outside just in time to prevent the clown from playing his last practical joke. He was carrying a pair of scissors. When he was asked for an explanation he insisted that he had had no intention of taking the bound man's life, but only wanted to cut his rope because he felt sorry for him. He was sacked too.

These antics amused the bound man because he could have freed himself if he had wanted to whenever he liked, but perhaps he wanted to learn a few new jumps first. The children's rhyme: "We travel with the circus, we travel with the circus" sometimes occurred to him while he lay awake at night. He could hear the voices of spectators on the opposite bank who had been driven too far downstream on the way home. He could see the river gleaming in the moonlight, and the young shoots growing out of the thick tops of the willow trees, and did not think about autumn yet.

The circus proprietor dreaded the danger that sleep involved for the bound man. Attempts were continually made to release him while he slept. The chief culprits were sacked rope dancers, or children who were bribed for the purpose. But measures could be taken to safeguard against these. A much bigger danger was that which he represented to himself. In his dreams he forgot his rope, and was surprised by it when he woke in the darkness of morning. He would angrily try to get up, but lose his balance and fall back again. The previous evening's applause was forgotten, sleep was still too near, his head and neck too free. He was just the opposite of a hanged man—his neck was the only part of him that was free. You had to make sure that at such moments no knife was within his reach. In the early hours of the morning the circus proprietor sometimes sent his wife to see whether the bound man was all right. If he was asleep she would bend over him and feel the rope. It had grown hard from dirt and damp. She would test the amount of free play it allowed him, and touch his tender wrists and ankles.

The most varied rumors circulated about the bound man. Some said he had tied himself up and invented the story of having been robbed, and toward the end of the summer that was the general opinion. Others maintained that he had been tied up at his own request, perhaps in league with the circus proprietor. The hesitant way in which he told his story, his habit of breaking off when the talk got round to the attack on him, contributed greatly to these rumors. Those who still believed in the robbery-with-violence story were laughed at. Nobody knew what difficulties the circus proprietor had in keeping the bound man, and how often he said he had had enough and wanted to clear off, for too much of the summer had passed.

Later, however, he stopped talking about clearing off. When the proprietor's wife brought him his food by the river and asked him how long he proposed to remain with them, he did not answer. She thought he had got used, not to being tied up, but to remembering every moment that he was tied up— the only thing that anyone in his position could get used to. She asked him whether he did not think it ridiculous to be tied up all the time, but he answered that he did not. Such a variety

of people—clowns, freaks, and comics, to say nothing of ele-
phants and tigers—traveled with circuses that he did not see
why a bound man should not travel with a circus too. He told
her about the movements he was practicing, the new ones he
had discovered, and about a new trick that had occurred to him
while he was whisking flies from the animals' eyes. He described to her how he always anticipated the effect of the rope
and always restrained his movements in such a way as to prevent it from ever tautening; and she knew that there were days
when he was hardly aware of the rope, when he jumped down
from the wagon and slapped the flanks of the horses in the
morning as if he were moving in a dream. She watched him
vault over the bars almost without touching them, and saw the
sun on his face, and he told her that sometimes he felt as if
he were not tied up at all. She answered that if he were
prepared to be untied, there would never be any need for him
to feel tied up. He agreed that he could be untied whenever
he felt like it.

The woman ended by not knowing whether she was more
concerned with the man or with the rope that tied him. She
told him that he could go on traveling with the circus without
his rope, but she did not believe it. For what would be the point
of his antics without his rope, and what would he amount to
without it? Without his rope he would leave them, and the
happy days would be over. She would no longer be able to sit
beside him on the stones by the river without arousing suspicion, and she knew that his continued presence, and her conversations with him, of which the rope was the only subject,
depended on it. Whenever she agreed that the rope had its
advantages, he would start talking about how troublesome it
was, and whenever he started talking about its advantages, she
would urge him to get rid of it. All this seemed as endless as
the summer itself.

At other times she was worried at the thought that she was herself hastening the end by her talk. Sometimes she would get up in the middle of the night and run across the grass to where he slept. She wanted to shake him, wake him up and ask him to keep the rope. But then she would see him lying there; he had thrown off his blanket, and there he lay like a corpse, with his legs outstretched and his arms close together, with the rope tied round them. His clothes had suffered from the heat and the water, but the rope had grown no thinner. She felt that he would go on traveling with the circus until the flesh fell from him and exposed the joints. Next morning she would plead with him more ardently than ever to get rid of his rope.

The increasing coolness of the weather gave her hope. Autumn was coming, and he would not be able to go on jumping into the river with his clothes on much longer. But the thought of losing his rope, about which he had felt indifferent earlier in the season, now depressed him.

The songs of the harvesters filled him with foreboding. "Summer has gone, summer has gone." But he realized that soon he would have to change his clothes, and he was certain that when he had been untied it would be impossible to tie him up again in exactly the same way. About this time the proprietor started talking about traveling south that year.

The heat changed without transition into quiet, dry cold, and the fire was kept going all day long. When the bound man jumped down from the wagon he felt the coldness of the grass under his feet. The stalks were bent with ripeness. The horses dreamed on their feet and the wild animals, crouching to leap even in their sleep, seemed to be collecting gloom under their skins which would break out later.

On one of these days a young wolf escaped. The circus proprietor kept quiet about it, to avoid spreading alarm, but the wolf soon started raiding cattle in the neighborhood. People at first believed that the wolf had been driven to these parts by the prospect of a severe winter, but the circus soon became suspect. The proprietor could not conceal the loss of the animal from his own employees, so the truth was bound to come out before long. The circus people offered the burgomasters of the neighboring villages their aid in tracking down the beast, but all their efforts were in vain. Eventually the circus was openly blamed for the damage and the danger, and spectators stayed away.

The bound man went on performing before half-empty seats without losing anything of his amazing freedom of movement. During the day he wandered among the surrounding hills under the thin-beaten silver of the autumn sky, and, whenever he could, lay down where the sun shone longest. Soon he found a place which the twilight reached last of all, and when at last it reached him he got up most unwillingly from the withered grass. In coming down the hill he had to pass through a little wood on its southern slope, and one evening he saw the gleam of two little green lights. He knew that they came from no church window, and was not for a moment under any illusion about what they were.

He stopped. The animal came toward him through the thinning foliage. He could make out its shape, the slant of its neck, its tail which swept the ground, and its receding head. If he had not been bound, perhaps he would have tried to run away, but as it was he did not even feel fear. He stood calmly with dangling arms and looked down at the wolf's bristling coat under which the muscles played like his own underneath the rope. He thought the evening wind was still between him and the wolf when the beast sprang. The man took care to obey his rope.

Moving with the deliberate care that he had so often put to the test, he seized the wolf by the throat. Tenderness for a fellow creature arose in him, tenderness for the upright being concealed in the four-footed. In a movement that resembled the drive of a great bird (he felt a sudden awareness that flying would be possible only if one were tied up in a special way) he flung himself at the animal and brought it to the ground. He felt a slight elation at having lost the fatal advantage of free limbs which causes men to be worsted.

The freedom he enjoyed in this struggle was having to adapt every movement of his limbs to the rope that tied him —the freedom of panthers, wolves, and the wild flowers that sway in the evening breeze. He ended up lying obliquely down the slope, clasping the animal's hind legs between his own bare feet and its head between his hands. He felt the gentleness of the faded foliage stroking the backs of his hands, and he felt his own grip almost effortlessly reaching its maximum, and he felt too how he was in no way hampered by the rope.

As he left the wood light rain began to fall and obscured the setting sun. He stopped for a while under the trees at the edge of the wood. Beyond the camp and the river he saw the fields where the cattle grazed, and the places where they crossed. Perhaps he would travel south with the circus after all. He laughed softly. It was against all reason. Even if he continued to put up with the sores that covered his joints and opened and bled when he made certain movements, his clothes would not stand up much longer to the friction of the rope.

The circus proprietor's wife tried to persuade her husband to announce the death of the wolf without mentioning that it had been killed by the bound man. She said that even at the time of his greatest popularity people would have refused to believe him capable of it, and in their present angry mood, with the nights getting cooler, they would be more incredulous than ever. The wolf had attacked a group of children at play that day, and nobody would believe that it had really been killed; for the circus proprietor had many wolves, and it was easy enough for him to hang a skin on the rail and allow free entry. But he was not to be dissuaded. He thought that the announcement of the bound man's act would revive the triumphs of the summer.

That evening the bound man's movements were uncertain. He stumbled in one of his jumps, and fell. Before he managed to get up he heard some low whistles and catcalls, rather like birds calling at dawn. He tried to get up too quickly, as he had done once or twice during the summer, with the result that he tautened the rope and fell back again. He lay still to regain his calm, and listened to the boos and catcalls growing into an uproar. "Well, bound man, and how did you kill the wolf?" they shouted, and: "Are you the man who killed the wolf?" If he had been one of them, he would not have believed it himself. He thought they had a perfect right to be angry: a circus at this time of year, a bound man, an escaped wolf, and all ending up with this. Some groups of spectators started arguing with others, but the greater part of the audience thought the whole thing a bad joke. By the time he had got to his feet there was such a hubbub that he was barely able to make out individual words.

He saw people surging up all round him, like faded leaves raised by a whirlwind in a circular valley at the center of which all was yet still. He thought of the golden sunsets of the last few days; and the sepulchral light which lay over the blight of all that he had built up during so many nights, the gold frame which the pious hang round dark, old pictures, this sudden collapse of everything, filled him with anger.

They wanted him to repeat his battle with the wolf. He said that such a thing had no place in a circus performance, and the proprietor declared that he did not keep animals to have them slaughtered in front of an audience. But the mob stormed the ring and forced them toward the cages. The proprietor's wife made her way between the seats to the exit and managed to get round to the cages from the other side. She pushed aside the attendant whom the crowd had forced to open a cage door, but the spectators dragged her back and prevented the door from being shut.

"Aren't you the woman who used to lie with him by the river in the summer?" they called out. "How does he hold you in his arms?" She shouted back at them that they needn't believe in the bound man if they didn't want to, they had never deserved him. Painted clowns were good enough for them.

The bound man felt as if the bursts of laughter were what he had been expecting ever since early May. What had smelt so sweet all through the summer now stank. But, if they insisted, he was ready to take on all the animals in the circus. He had never felt so much at one with his rope.

Gently he pushed the woman aside. Perhaps he would travel south with them after all. He stood in the open doorway of the cage, and he saw the wolf, a strong young animal, rise to its feet, and he heard the proprietor grumbling again about the loss of his exhibits. He clapped his hands to attract the animal's attention, and when it was near enough he turned to slam the cage door. He looked the woman in the face. Suddenly he remembered the proprietor's warning to suspect of murderous intentions anyone near him who had a sharp instrument in his hand. At the same moment he felt the blade on his wrists, as cool as the water of the river in autumn, which during the last few weeks he had been barely able to stand. The rope curled up in a tangle beside him while he struggled free. He pushed the woman back, but there was no point in anything he did now. Had he been insufficiently on his guard against those who wanted to release him, against the sympathy in which they wanted to lull him? Had he lain too long on the river bank? If she had cut the cord at any other moment it would have been better than this.

He stood in the middle of the cage, and rid himself of the rope like a snake discarding its skin. It amused him to see the spectators shrinking back. Did they realize that he had no choice now? Or that fighting the wolf now would prove nothing whatever? At the same time he felt all his blood rush to his feet. He felt suddenly weak.

The rope, which fell at its feet like a snare, angered the wolf more than the entry of a stranger into its cage. It crouched to spring. The man reeled, and grabbed the pistol that hung ready at the side of the cage. Then, before anyone could stop him, he shot the wolf between the eyes. The animal reared, and touched him in falling.

On the way to the river he heard the footsteps of his pursuers—spectators, the rope dancers, the circus proprietor, and the proprietor's wife, who persisted in the chase longer than anyone else. He hid in a clump of bushes and listened to them hurrying past, and later on streaming in the opposite direction back to the camp. The moon shone on the meadow; in that light its color was both of growth and of death.

When he came to the river his anger died away. At dawn it seemed to him as if lumps of ice were floating in the water, and as if snow had fallen, obliterating memory.

Nobody Will Laugh

MILAN KUNDERA

Translated by Suzanne Rappaport

1

"Pour me some more slivovits," said Klara, and I wasn't against it. It was by no means unusual for us to open a bottle and this time there was a genuine excuse for it. That day I had received a considerable sum for the last part of a study, which was being published in installments by a professional visual arts magazine.

Publishing the study hadn't been so easy—what I'd written was polemical and controversial. That's why my studies had previously been rejected by *Visual Arts Journal*, where the editors were old and cautious, and had then been published only in a minor rival periodical, where the editors were younger and not so conservative.

The mailman brought the payment to the university along with another letter; an unimportant letter; in the morning in the first flush of beatitude I had hardly read the letter. But now at home, when it was approaching midnight and the wine was nearly gone, I took it off the table to amuse us.

"Esteemed comrade and if you will permit the expression —my colleague!" I read aloud to Klara. "Please excuse me, a man whom you have never met, for writing to you. I am turning to you with a request that you should read the enclosed article. True, I do not know you, but I respect you as a man whose judgments, reflections, and conclusions astonish me by their agreement with the results of my own research; I am completely amazed by it. Thus, for example, even though I bow before your conclusions and your excellent comparative analysis, I wish to call attention emphatically to the thought that Czech art has always been close to the people. I voiced this opinion before reading your treatise. I could prove this quite easily, for among other things, I even have witnesses. However, this is only marginal, for your treatise . . ." There followed further praise of my excellence and then a request. Would I kindly write a review of his article, that is, a specialist's evaluation for *Visual Arts Journal,* where they had been underestimating and rejecting his article for more than six months. They had told him that my opinion would be decisive, so now I had become the writer's only hope, a single light in an otherwise total darkness.

We made fun of Mr. Zaturetsky, whose aristocratic name fascinated us. But it was just fun; fun that meant no harm, for the praise which he had lavished on me, along with the excellent slivovits, softened me. It softened me so that in those unforgettable moments I loved the whole world. However, out of the whole world, especially Klara, because she was sitting opposite me, while the rest of the world was hidden from me by the walls of my Vrshovits attic. And because at that moment I didn't have anything to reward the world with, I rewarded Klara; at least with promises.

Klara was a twenty-year-old girl from a good family. What am I saying, from a good family? From an excellent family! Her father had been a bank manager, and some time in the fifties, as a representative of the upper bourgeoisie, had been exiled to the village of Chelakovits, which was some distance from Prague. As a result, his daughter had a bad party record and worked as a seamstress in a large Prague dress factory. I can't bear prejudice. I don't believe that the extent of a father's property can leave its mark on his child's genes. I ask you, who today is really a plebeian and who is a patrician? Everything has been mixed up and has changed places so completely, that it's sometimes difficult to understand anything in terms of sociological concepts. I was far from feeling that I was sitting opposite a class enemy; on the contrary, I was sitting opposite a beautiful seamstress and trying to make her like me more by telling her lightheartedly about the advantages of a job I'd promised to get her through connections. I assured her that it was absurd for such a pretty girl to lose her beauty over a sewing machine, and I decided that she should become a model.

Klara didn't offer any resistance and we spent the night in happy understanding.

2

Man passes through the present with his eyes blindfolded. He is permitted merely to sense and guess at what he is actually experiencing. Only later when the cloth is untied can he glance at the past and find out *what* he has experienced and what meaning it has had.

That evening I thought I was drinking to my successes and didn't in the least suspect that it was the prelude to my undoing.

And because I didn't suspect anything I woke up the next

day in a good mood, and while Klara was still breathing contentedly by my side, I took the article, which was attached to the letter, and skimmed through it with amused indifference.

It was called "Mikolash Alesh, Master of Czech Drawing," and it really wasn't worth even the half hour of inattention that I devoted to it. It was a collection of platitudes heaped together with no sense of continuity and without the least intention of advancing through them some original thought.

Quite clearly it was pure nonsense. The very same day Dr. Kalousek, the editor of *Visual Arts Journal* (in other respects an unusually hostile man), confirmed my opinion over the telephone; he called me at the university: "Say, did you get that treatise from the Zaturetsky guy? . . . Then take care of it. Five lecturers have already cut him to pieces, but he keeps on bugging us; he's got it into his head that you're the only genuine authority. Tell him in two sentences that it's crap, you know how to do that, you know how to be really venomous; and then we'll all have some peace."

But something inside me protested: why should *I* have to be Mr. Zaturetsky's executioner? Was *I* the one receiving an editor's salary for this? Besides, I remembered very well that they had refused my article at *Visual Arts Journal* out of overcautiousness; what's more, Mr. Zaturetsky's name was firmly connected in my mind with Klara, slivovits, and a beautiful evening. And finally, I shan't deny it, it's human—I could have counted on one finger the people who think me "a genuine authority": why should I lose this only one?

I closed the conversation with some clever vaguery, which Kalousek considered a promise and I, an excuse. I put down the receiver firmly convinced that I would never write the review for Mr. Zaturetsky.

Instead I took some writing paper out of the drawer and wrote a letter to Mr. Zaturetsky, in which I avoided any kind of judgment of his work, excusing myself by saying that my opinions on nineteenth century art were commonly considered devious and eccentric, and therefore my intercession—especially with the editors of *Visual Arts Journal*—would harm rather than benefit his cause. At the same time, I overwhelmed Mr. Zaturetsky with friendly loquacity, from which it was impossible not to detect approval on my part.

As soon as I had put the letter in the mailbox I forgot Mr. Zaturetsky. But Mr. Zaturetsky did not forget me.

3

One day when I was about to end my lecture—I lecture at college on the history of art—there was a knock at the door; it was our secretary, Mary, a kind elderly lady, who occasionally prepares coffee for me, and says that I'm out when there are undesirable female voices on the telephone. She put her head in the doorway and said that some gentleman was looking for me.

I'm not afraid of gentlemen and so I took leave of the students and went good-humoredly out into the corridor. A smallish man in a shabby black suit and a white shirt bowed to me. He very respectfully informed me that he was Zaturetsky.

I invited the visitor into an empty room, offered him an armchair, and began pleasantly discussing everything possible with him, for instance what a bad summer it was and what exhibitions were on in Prague. Mr. Zaturetsky politely agreed with all of my chatter, but he soon tried to apply every remark of mine to his article, which lay invisibly between us like an irresistible magnet.

"Nothing would make me happier than to write a review

of your work," I said finally, "but as I explained to you in the letter, I am not considered an expert on the Czech nineteenth century, and, in addition, I'm on bad terms with the editors of *Visual Arts Journal,* who take me for a hardened modernist, so that a positive review from me could only harm you."

"Oh, you're too modest," said Mr. Zaturetsky, "how can you, who are such an expert, judge your own standing so blackly! In the editors' office they told me that everything depends on your review. If you support my article they'll publish it. You are my only recourse. It's the work of three years of study and three years of toil. Everything is now in your hands."

How carelessly and from what bad masonry does a man build his excuses! I didn't know how to reply to Mr. Zaturetsky. I involuntarily looked at his face and noticed there not only small, ancient, and innocent spectacles staring at me, but also a powerful, deep vertical wrinkle on his forehead. In a brief moment of clairvoyance a shiver shot down my spine. This wrinkle, concentrated and stubborn, betrayed not only the intellectual torment which its owner had gone through over Mikolash Alesh's drawings, but also unusually strong willpower. I lost my presence of mind and failed to find any clever excuse. I knew that I wouldn't write the review, but I also knew that I didn't have the strength to say so to this pathetic little man's face.

And then I began to smile and promise something vague. Mr. Zaturetsky thanked me and said that he would come again soon. We parted smiling.

In a couple of days he did come. I cleverly avoided him, but the next day I was told that he was searching for me again at the university. I realized that bad times were on the way; I went quickly to Mary so as to take appropriate steps.

"Mary dear, I beg you, if that man should come looking

for me again, say that I've gone to do some research in Germany and I'll be back in a month. And you should know about this: I have, as you know, all my lectures on Tuesday and Wednesday. I'll shift them secretly to Thursday and Friday. Only the students will know about this, don't tell anyone, and leave the schedule uncorrected. I'll have to disobey the rules."

4

Indeed Mr. Zaturetsky did soon come back to look me up and was miserable when the secretary informed him that I'd suddenly gone off to Germany. "But this is not possible. Mr. Klima has to write a review about me. How could he go away like this?" "I don't know," said Mary. "However, he'll be back in a month." "Another month . . .," moaned Mr. Zaturetsky: "And you don't know his address in Germany?" "I don't," said Mary.

And then I had a month of peace, but the month passed more quickly than I expected and Mr. Zaturetsky stood once again in the office. "No, he still hasn't returned," said Mary, and when she met me later about something she asked me imploringly: "Your little man was here again, what in heaven's name should I tell him?" "Tell him, Mary, that I got jaundice and am in the hospital in Jena." "In the hospital!" cried Mr. Zaturetsky, when Mary told him the story a few days later. "It's not possible! Don't you know that Mr. Klima has to write a review about me!" "Mr. Zaturetsky," said the secretary reproachfully, "Mr. Klima is lying in a hospital somewhere abroad seriously ill, and you think only about your review." Mr. Zaturetsky backed down and went away, but two weeks later was once again in the office: "I sent a registered letter to Mr. Klima in Jena. It is a small town, there can only be one hospital there, and the letter came back to me!" "Your little man is driving me crazy," said Mary to me the next day. "You mustn't get angry with me, what could I say to him? I told him that you've come back. You must deal with him by yourself now."

I didn't get angry with Mary. She had done what she could. Besides, I was far from considering myself beaten. I knew that I was not to be caught. I lived under cover all the time. I lectured secretly on Thursday and Friday; and every Tuesday and Wednesday, crouching in the doorway of a house opposite the school, I would rejoice at the sight of Mr. Zaturetsky, who kept watch in front of the school waiting for me to come out. I longed to put on a bowler hat and stick on a beard. I felt like Sherlock Holmes or the Invisible Man, who strides stealthily; I felt like a little boy.

One day, however, Mr. Zaturetsky finally got tired of keeping watch and jumped on Mary. "Where exactly does Comrade Klima lecture?" "There's the schedule," said Mary, pointing to the wall, where the times of all the lectures were laid out in exemplary fashion on a large, checkered board.

"I see that," said Mr. Zaturetsky, refusing to be put off. "Only Comrade Klima never lectures here on either Tuesday or Wednesday. Is he reported sick?"

"No," said Mary hesitantly. And then the little man turned again on Mary. He reproached her for the confusion in the schedule. He inquired ironically how it was that she didn't know where every teacher was at a given time. He told her that he was going to complain about her. He shouted. He said that he was also going to complain about Comrade Assistant Klima, who wasn't lecturing, although he was supposed to be. He asked if the dean was in.

Unfortunately, the dean was in. Mr. Zaturetsky knocked on his door and went in. Ten minutes later he returned to Mary's office and demanded the address of my apartment.

"Twenty Skalnik Street in Litomyshl," said Mary. "In Prague, Mr. Klima only has a temporary address and he doesn't want it disclosed . . ." "I'm asking you to give me the address of Assistant Klima's Prague apartment," cried the little man in a trembling voice.

Somehow Mary lost her presence of mind. She gave him the address of my attic, my poor little refuge, my sweet den, in which I would be caught.

5

Yes, my permanent address is in Litomyshl; there I have my mother, my friends, and memories of my father; I flee from Prague, as often as I can, and write at home in my mother's small apartment. So it happened that I kept my mother's apartment as my permanent residence and in Prague I didn't manage to get myself a proper bachelor's apartment, as you're supposed to do, but lived in Vrshovits in lodgings, in a small, completely private attic, whose existence I concealed as much as possible. I didn't register anywhere so as to prevent unnecessary meetings between undesirable guests and my various transient female roommates or visitors, whose comings and goings, I confess, were sometimes most disorganized. For precisely these reasons I didn't enjoy the best reputation in the house. Also, during my stays in Litomyshl I had several times lent my cozy little room to friends, who amused themselves only too well there, and didn't allow anyone in the house to get a wink of sleep. All this scandalized some of the occupants, who conducted a quiet war against me. Sometimes they had the local committee express unfavorable opinions of me and they even handed in a complaint to the apartment office.

At that time it was inconvenient for Klara to get to work

from such a distance as Chelakovits, and so she began to stay overnight at my place. At first she stayed timidly and as an exception, then she left one dress, then several dresses, and within a short time my two suits were stuffed into a corner of the wardrobe, and my little room was transformed into a woman's boudoir.

I really liked Klara; she was beautiful; it pleased me that people turned their heads when we went out together; she was at least thirteen years younger than me, which increased the students' respect for me; I had a thousand reasons for taking good care of her. But I didn't want it to be known that she was living with me. I was afraid of rumors and gossip about us in the house; I was afraid that someone would start attacking my good old landlord, who lived for the greater part of the year outside Prague, was discreet, and didn't concern himself about me; I was afraid that one day he would come to me, unhappy and with a heavy heart, and ask me to send the young lady away for the sake of his good name.

Klara had been strictly ordered not to open the door to anyone.

One day she was alone in the house. It was a sunny day and rather stuffy in the attic. She was lounging almost naked on my couch, occupying herself with an examination of the ceiling, when suddenly there was a pounding on the door.

There was nothing alarming in this. I didn't have a bell, so anyone who came had to knock. So Klara wasn't going to let herself be disturbed by the noise and didn't stop examining the ceiling. But the pounding didn't cease; on the contrary, it went on with imperturbable persistence. Klara was getting nervous. She began to imagine a man standing behind the door, a man who slowly and significantly turns up the lapels of his jacket, and who will later pounce on her demanding why she hadn't opened the door, what she was concealing, and whether she was registered. A feeling of guilt seized her; she lowered her eyes from the ceiling and tried to think where she had left her dress lying. But the pounding continued so stubbornly, that in the confusion she found nothing but my raincoat hanging in the hall. She put it on and opened the door.

Instead of an evil, querying face, she only saw a little man, who bowed: "Is Mr. Klima at home?" "No, he isn't." "That's a pity," said the little man and apologized for having disturbed her. "The thing is that Mr. Klima has to write a review about me. He promised me and it's very urgent. If you would permit it, I could at least leave him a message."

Klara gave him paper and pencil, and in the evening I read that the fate of the article about Mikolash Alesh was in my hands alone, and that Mr. Zaturetsky was waiting most respectfully for my review and would try to look me up again at the university.

6

The next day, Mary told me how Mr. Zaturetsky had threatened her, and how he had gone to complain about her; her voice trembled and she was on the verge of tears; I flew into a rage. I realized that the secretary, who until now had been laughing at my game of hide-and-seek (though I would bet anything that she did what she did out of kindness toward me, rather than simply from a sense of fun), was now feeling hurt and conceivably saw me as the cause of her troubles. When I also included the exposure of my attic, the ten-minute pounding on the door, and Klara's fright—my anger grew to a frenzy.

As I was walking back and forth in Mary's office, biting my lips, boiling with rage and thinking about revenge, the door opened and Mr. Zaturetsky appeared.

When he saw me a glimmer of happiness flashed over his face. He bowed and greeted me. He had come a little prematurely, he had come before I had managed to consider my revenge.

He asked if I had received his message yesterday.

I was silent. He repeated his question. "I received it," I replied.

"And will you, please, write the review?"

I saw him in front of me: sickly, obstinate, beseeching; I saw the vertical wrinkle—etched on his forehead, the line of a single passion—I examined this line and grasped that it was a straight line determined by two points, my review and his article; that beyond the vice of this maniacal straight line nothing existed in his life but saintly asceticism; and then a spiteful trick occurred to me.

"I hope that you understand that after yesterday I can't speak to you," I said.

"I don't understand you."

"Don't pretend. She told me everything. It's unnecessary for you to deny it."

"I don't understand you," repeated the little man once again; but this time more decidedly.

I assumed a genial, almost friendly tone. "Look here, Mr. Zaturetsky, I don't blame you. I chase women as well and I understand you. In your position I would have tried to seduce a beautiful girl like that, if I'd found myself alone in an apartment with her and she'd been naked beneath a man's raincoat."

"This is an outrage!" The little man turned pale.

"No, it's the truth, Mr. Zaturetsky."

"Did the lady tell you this?"

"She has no secrets from me."

"Comrade Assistant, this is an outrage! I'm a married

man. I have a wife! I have children!" The little man took a step forward, so that I had to step back.

"So much the worse for you, Mr. Zaturetsky."

"What do you mean, so much the worse?"

"I think being married must be a drawback to chasing women."

"Take it back!" said Mr. Zaturetsky menacingly.

"Well, all right," I conceded, "the matrimonial state need not always be an obstacle. Sometimes it can, on the contrary, excuse all sorts of things. But it makes no difference. I've already told you that I'm not angry with you and I understand you quite well. There's only one thing I don't understand. How can you still want a review from a man whose woman you've been trying to make?"

"Comrade Assistant! Dr. Kalousek, the editor of the magazine of the Academy of Sciences, *Visual Arts Journal*, is asking you for this review. And you must write the review!"

"The review or the woman. You can't ask for both."

"What kind of behavior is this, comrade!" screamed Mr. Zaturetsky in desperate anger.

The odd thing is that I suddenly felt that Mr. Zaturetsky had really wanted to seduce Klara. Seething with rage, I shouted, "You have the audacity to tell me off? You who should humbly apologize to me in front of my secretary?"

I turned my back on Mr. Zaturetsky, and, confused, he staggered out.

"Well then," I sighed with relief like a general after the victorious conclusion of a hard campaign, and I said to Mary, "Perhaps he won't want a review by me any more."

Mary smiled and after a moment timidly asked, "Just why is it you don't want to write this review?"

"Because, Mary my dear, what he's written is the most awful crap."

"Then why don't you write in your review that it's crap?"

"Why should I write it? Why do I have to antagonize people?"—but hardly had I said this when I realized that Mr. Zaturetsky was my enemy all the same and that my struggle not to write the review was an aimless and absurd struggle—unfortunately, there was nothing I could do either to stop it or to back down.

Mary was looking at me with an indulgent smile, as women look upon the foolishness of children; then the door opened and there stood Mr. Zaturetsky with his arm raised. "It's not me! It's you who will have to apologize," he shouted in a trembling voice and disappeared again.

7

I don't remember exactly when, perhaps that same day or perhaps a few days later, we found an envelope in my mailbox without an address.

Inside there was a letter in a clumsy, almost primitive handwriting:

> *Dear Madame:*
> *Present yourself at my house on Sunday regarding the insult to my husband. I shall be at home all day. If you don't present yourself, I shall be forced to take measures. Anna Zaturetsky, 14 Dalimilova Street, Prague 3.*

Klara was scared and began saying something about my guilt. I waved my hand, declaring that the purpose of life is to give amusement, and if life is too lazy for this, there is nothing left but to help it along a little. Man must constantly saddle events, those swift mares without which he would be dragging his feet in the dust like a weary foot-slogger. When Klara said that she didn't want to saddle any events, I assured her that she would never meet Mr. or Mrs. Zaturetsky, and that the event into whose saddle I had jumped, I'd take care of with one hand tied behind my back.

In the morning when we were leaving the house, the porter stopped us. The porter wasn't an enemy. Prudently, I had once bribed him with a fifty-crown bill, and I had lived until this time in the agreeable conviction that he'd learned not to know anything about me, and didn't add fuel to the fire, which my enemies in the house kept alight.

"Some couple was here looking for you yesterday," he said.

"What sort of couple?"

"A little guy with a woman."

"What did the woman look like?"

"Two heads taller. Terribly energetic. A stern woman. She was asking about all sorts of things." He turned to Klara. "Chiefly about you. Who you are and what your name is."

"Good heavens, what did you say to her?" exclaimed Klara.

"What could I say? How do I know who comes to see Mr. Klima? I told her that a different person comes every evening."

"Great!" I laughed and drew ten crowns from my pocket. "Just go on talking like that."

"Don't be afraid," I then said to Klara, "you won't go anywhere on Sunday and nobody will find you."

And Sunday came, and after Sunday, Monday, Tuesday, Wednesday; nothing happened. "You see," I said to Klara. But then came Thursday. I was lecturing to my students at the customary secret lecture about how feverishly and in what an atmosphere of unselfish camaraderie the young Fauvists had liberated color from its former impressionistic character, when Mary opened the door and whispered to me, "The wife of that

Zaturetsky is here." "But I'm not here," I said, "just show her the schedule!" But Mary shook her head. "I showed her, but she peeped into your office and saw your raincoat on the stand. Just then Assistant Professor Zeleny came by and assured her that it was yours. So now she's sitting in the corridor waiting."

Had fate been able to pursue me more systematically, it is quite possible that I would have been a success. A blind alley is the place for my best inspirations. I said to my favorite student:

"Be so kind as to do me a small favor. Run to my office, put on my raincoat, and go out of the building in it. Some woman will try to prove that you are me, and your task will be not to admit it at any price."

The student went off and returned in about a quarter of an hour. He told me that the mission had been completed, the coast was clear, and the woman was out of the building.

This time then I had won. But then came Friday, and in the afternoon Klara returned from work trembling almost like a leaf.

The polite gentleman who received customers in the tidy office of the dress factory had suddenly opened the door leading to the workroom, where my Klara and fifteen other seamstresses were sitting over their sewing machines, and cried:

"Does any one of you live at 5 Pushkin Street?"

Klara knew that it concerned her, because 5 Pushkin Street was my address. However, well-advised caution kept her quiet, for she knew that her living with me was a secret and that nobody knew anything about it.

"You see, that's what I've been telling her," said the polished gentleman when none of the seamstresses spoke up, and he went out again. Klara learned later that a strict female voice on the telephone had made him search through the directory of employees, and had talked for a quarter of an hour trying to convince him there must be a woman employee from 5 Pushkin Street in the factory.

The shadow of Mrs. Zaturetsky was cast over our idyllic room.

"But how could she have found out where you work? After all, here in the house nobody knows about you!" I yelled.

Yes, I was really convinced that nobody knew about us. I lived like an eccentric who thinks that he lives unobserved behind a high wall, while all the time one detail escapes him: the wall is made of transparent glass.

I had bribed the porter not to reveal that Klara lived with me, I had forced Klara into the most troublesome inconspicuousness and concealment and, meanwhile, the whole house knew about her. It was enough that once she had entered into an ill-advised conversation with a woman on the second floor —and they got to know where Klara was working.

Without suspecting it we had been living exposed for quite some time. What remained concealed from our persecutors was merely Klara's name and then one small detail: that she lived with me unregistered. These two were the final and only secrets behind which, for the time being, we eluded Mrs. Zaturetsky, who launched her attack so consistently and methodically that I was horror-struck.

I understood that it was going to be tough. The horse of my story was damnably saddled.

8

This was on Friday. And when Klara came back from work on Saturday, she was trembling again. Here is what had happened:

Mrs. Zaturetsky had set out with her husband for the factory. She had called beforehand and asked the manager to allow her and her husband to visit the workshop, to examine the faces of the seamstresses. It's true that this request astonished the comrade manager, but Mrs. Zaturetsky put on such an air that it was impossible to refuse. She said something vague about an insult, about a ruined existence, and about court. Mr. Zaturetsky stood beside her, frowned, and was silent.

They were shown into the workroom. The seamstresses raised their heads indifferently, and Klara recognized the little man; she turned pale and with conspicuous inconspicuousness quickly went on with her needlework.

"Here you are," exclaimed the manager with ironic politeness to the stiff-looking pair. Mrs. Zaturetsky realized that she must take the initiative and she urged her husband: "Well look!" Mr. Zaturetsky assumed a scowl and looked around. "Is it one of them?" whispered Mrs. Zaturetsky.

Even with his glasses Mr. Zaturetsky couldn't see clearly enough to examine the large room, which in any case wasn't easy to survey, full as it was of piled-up junk and dresses hanging from long horizontal bars, with fidgety seamstresses, who didn't sit neatly with their faces toward the door, but in various positions; they were turning round, getting up and down, and involuntarily averting their faces. Therefore, Mr. Zaturetsky had to step forward and try not to skip anyone.

When the women understood that they were being examined by someone, and in addition by someone so unsightly and unattractive, they felt vaguely insulted, and sneers and grumbling began to be heard. One of them, a robust young girl, impertinently burst out:

"He's searching all over Prague for the shrew who made him pregnant!"

The noisy, ribald mockery of the women overwhelmed the couple; they stood downcast, and then became resolute with a peculiar sort of dignity.

"Ma'am," the impertinent girl yelled again at Mrs. Zaturetsky, "you look after your little son badly! I would never have let such a nice little boy out of the house."

"Look some more," she whispered to her husband, and sullenly and timidly he went forward step by step as if he were running the gauntlet, but firmly all the same—and he didn't miss a face.

All the time the manager was smiling noncommittally; he knew his women and he knew that you couldn't do anything with them; and so he pretended not to hear their clamor, and he asked Mr. Zaturetsky, "Now please tell me, what is this woman supposed to look like?"

Mr. Zaturetsky turned to the manager and spoke slowly and seriously: "She was beautiful . . . She was very beautiful . . ."

Meanwhile Klara crouched in a corner, setting herself off from all the playful women by her agitation, her bent head, and her dogged activity. Oh, how badly she feigned her inconspicuousness and insignificance! And Mr. Zaturetsky was only a little way away from her; in the next minute he must look into her face.

"That isn't much, when you only remember that she was beautiful," said the polite comrade manager to Mr. Zaturetsky. "There are many beautiful women. Was she short or tall?"

"Tall," said Mr. Zaturetsky.

"Was she brunette or blonde?" Mr. Zaturetsky thought a moment and said, "She was blonde."

This part of the story could serve as a parable on the power of beauty. When Mr. Zaturetsky had seen Klara for the first time at my place, he was so dazzled that he actually hadn't seen her. Beauty created before her some opaque screen. A screen of light, behind which she was hidden as if beneath a veil.

For Klara is neither tall nor blonde. Only the inner greatness of beauty lent her in Mr. Zaturetsky's eyes a semblance of great physical size. And the glow, which emanates from beauty, lent her hair the appearance of gold.

And so when the little man finally approached the corner where Klara, in a brown work smock, was huddled over a shirt, he didn't recognize her, because he had never seen her.

9

When Klara had finished an incoherent and barely intelligible account of this event I said, "You see, we're lucky."

But amid sobs Klara said to me, "What kind of luck? If they didn't find me today, they'll find me tomorrow."

"I should like to know how."

"They'll come here for me, to your place."

"I won't let anyone in."

"And what when they send the police?"

"Come now, I'll make a joke of it. After all, it was just a joke and fun."

"Today there's no time for jokes, today everything gets serious. They'll say that I wanted to blacken his reputation. When they take a look at him, how could they ever believe that he was capable of trying to seduce a woman?"

"You're right, Klara," I said, "they'll probably lock you up. But look, Karel Havlichek Borovsky was also in jail and think how far he got; you must have learned about him in school."

"Stop chattering," said Klara. "You know it looks bad for me. I'll have to go before the disciplinary committee and I'll have it on my record, and I'll never get out of the workshop. Anyway, I'd like to know what's happening about the modeling job you promised me. I can't sleep at your place any longer. I'll always be afraid that they're coming for me. Today I'm going back to Chelakovits." This was one conversation.

And that afternoon after a departmental meeting I had a second.

The chairman of the department, a gray-haired art historian and a wise man, invited me into his office.

"I hope you know that you haven't helped yourself with that study that has just come out," he said to me.

"Yes, I know," I replied.

"Many of our professors think that it applies to them and the dean thinks that it was an attack on his views."

"What can be done about it?" I said.

"Nothing," replied the professor, "but your three-year period as a lecturer has expired and candidates will compete to fill the position. It is customary for the committee to give the position to someone who has already taught in the school, but are you so sure that this custom will be upheld in your case? But this is not what I wanted to speak about. So far it has spoken in your favor that you lectured regularly, that you were popular with the students, and that you taught them something. But now you can't even rely on this. The dean has informed me that for the last three months you haven't lectured at all. And quite without excuse. Well, this in itself would be enough for immediate dismissal."

I explained to the professor that I hadn't missed a single lecture, that it had all been a joke, and I told him the whole story about Mr. Zaturetsky and Klara.

"Fine, I believe you," said the professor, "but what does it matter if I believe you? Today the whole school says that you don't lecture and don't do anything. It has already been discussed at the union meeting and yesterday they took the matter to the board of regents."

"But why didn't they speak to me about it first?"

"What should they speak to you about? Everything is

clear to them. Now they are only looking back over your whole performance trying to find connections between your past and your present."

"What can they find bad in my past? You know yourself how much I like my work! I've never shirked! My conscience is clear."

"Every human life has many aspects," said the professor. "The past of each one of us can be just as easily arranged into the biography of a beloved statesman as into that of a criminal. Only look thoroughly at yourself. Nobody is denying that you like your work. But what if it served you above all as an opportunity for escape? You weren't often seen at meetings and when you did come, for the most part, you were silent. Nobody really knew what you thought. I myself remember that several times when a serious matter was being discussed you suddenly made a joke, which caused embarrassment. This embarrassment was of course immediately forgotten, but today, when it is retrieved from the past, it acquires a particular significance. Or remember how various women came looking for you at the university and how you refused to see them. Or else your last article, about which anyone who wishes can allege that it was written from suspicious premises. All these, of course, are isolated facts; but just look at them in the light of today's offense, and they suddenly unite into a totality of significant testimony about your character and attitude."

"But what sort of offense! Everything can be explained so easily! The facts are quite simple and clear!"

"Facts mean little compared to attitudes. To contradict rumor or sentiment is as futile as arguing against a believer's faith in the Immaculate Conception. You have simply become a victim of faith, Comrade Assistant."

"There's a lot of truth in what you say," I said, "but if a sentiment has arisen against me like an act of faith, I shall fight faith with reason. I shall explain before everyone the things that took place. If people are human they will have to laugh at it."

"As you like. But you'll learn either that people aren't human or that you don't know what humans are like. They will not laugh. If you place before them everything as it happened, it will then appear that not only did you fail to fulfill your obligations as they were indicated on the schedule—that you did not do what you should have done—but on top of this, you lectured secretly, that is, you did what you shouldn't have done. It will appear that you insulted a man who was asking for your help. It will appear that your private life is not in order, that you have some unregistered girl living with you, which will make a very unfavorable impression on the female chairman of the union. The issue will become confused and God knows what further rumors will arise. Whatever they are they will certainly be useful to those who have been provoked by your views, but were ashamed to be against you on account of them."

I knew that the professor wasn't trying to alarm or deceive me. In this matter, however, I considered him a crank and didn't want to give myself up to his skepticism. The scandal with Mr. Zaturetsky made me go cold all over, but it hadn't tired me out yet. For I had saddled this horse myself, so I couldn't let it tear the reins from my hands and carry me off wherever it wished. I was prepared to engage in a contest with it. And the horse did not avoid the contest. When I reached home, there in the mailbox was a summons to a meeting of the local committee, and I had no doubt as to what it was about.

10

I was not mistaken. The local committee, which was in session in what had been a store, was seated around a long table. The members assumed a gloomy expression when I came in. A grizzled man with glasses and a receding chin pointed to a chair. I said thank you, sat down, and this man took the floor. He informed me that the local committee had been watching me for some time, that it knew very well that I led an irregular private life; that this did not produce a good impression in my neighborhood; that the tenants from my apartment house had already complained about me once, when they couldn't sleep because of the uproar in my apartment; that all this was enough for the local committee to have formed a proper conception of me. And now, on top of all this, Comrade Madame Zaturetsky, the wife of a scientific worker, had turned to them for help. Six months ago I should have written a review about her husband's scientific work, and I hadn't done so, even though I well knew that the fate of the said work depended on my review.

"What the devil d'you mean by scientific work!" I interrupted the man with the little chin: "It's a patchwork of plagiarized thoughts."

"That is interesting, comrade." A fashionably dressed blonde of about thirty now joined in the discussion; on her face was permanently glued a beaming smile. "Permit me a question; what is your field?"

"I am an art theoretician."

"And Comrade Zaturetsky?"

"I don't know. Perhaps he's trying at something similar."

"You see," the blonde turned enthusiastically to the remaining members, "Comrade Klima sees a worker in the same field as a competitor and not as a comrade. This is the way that almost all our intellectuals think today."

"I shall continue," said the man with the receding chin. "Comrade Madame Zaturetsky told us that her husband visited your apartment and met some woman there. It is said that this woman accused Mr. Zaturetsky of wanting to molest her sexually. Comrade Madame Zaturetsky has in her hand documents which prove that her husband is not capable of such a thing. She wants to know the name of this woman who accused her husband, and to transfer the matter to the disciplinary section of the people's committee, because she claims this false accusation has damaged her husband's good name."

I tried again to cut this ridiculous affair short. "Look here, comrades," I said, "it isn't worth all the trouble. It's not a question of damaged reputation. The work is so weak that no one else could recommend it either. And if some misunderstanding occurred between this woman and Mr. Zaturetsky, it shouldn't really be necessary to summon a meeting."

"Fortunately, it is not you who will decide about our meetings, comrade," replied the man with the receding chin. "And when you now assert that Comrade Zaturetsky's work is bad, then we must look upon this as revenge. Comrade Madame Zaturetsky gave us a letter to read, which you wrote, after reading her husband's work."

"Yes. Only in that letter I didn't say a word about what the work was like."

"That is true. But you did write that you would be glad to help him; in this letter it is clearly implied that you respect Comrade Zaturetsky's work. And now you declare that it's a patchwork. Why didn't you say it to his face?"

"Comrade Klima has two faces," said the blonde.

At this moment an elderly woman with a permanent wave joined the discussion (she had an expression of self-sacrificing goodwill in examining the lives of others); she passed at once to the heart of the matter. "We would need to know, comrade, who this woman was whom Mr. Zaturetsky met at your home."

I understood unmistakably that it wasn't within my power to remove the senseless gravity from the whole affair, and that I could dispose of it in only one way: to confuse the traces, to lure them away from Klara, to lead them away from her as the partridge leads the hound away from its nest, offering its own body for the sake of its young.

"It's a bad business, I don't remember her name," I said.

"How is it that you don't remember the name of the woman you live with?" questioned the woman with the permanent wave.

"At one time, I used to write all this down, but then it occurred to me that it was stupid and I dropped it. It's hard for a man to rely on his memory."

"Perhaps, Comrade Klima, you have an exemplary relationship with women," said the blonde.

"Perhaps I could remember, but I should have to think about it. Do you know when it was that Mr. Zaturetsky visited me?"

"That was . . . wait a moment," the man with the receding chin looked at his papers, "the fourteenth, on Wednesday afternoon."

"On Wednesday . . . the fourteenth . . . wait . . ." I held my head in my hand and did some thinking. "Oh I remember That was Helena." I saw that they were all hanging expectantly on my words.

"Helena what?"

"What? I'm sorry, I don't know. I didn't want to ask her that. As a matter of fact, speaking frankly, I'm not even sure that her name was Helena. I only called her that because her husband seemed to me to be like red-haired Menelaus. But anyway she very much liked being called that. On Tuesday evening I met her in a wineshop and managed to talk to her for a while, when her Menelaus went to the bar to drink a cognac. The next day she came to my place and was there the whole afternoon. Only I had to leave her in the evening for a couple of hours, I had a meeting at the university. When I returned she was disgusted because some little man had molested her and she thought that I had put him up to it; she took offense and didn't want to know me any more. And so, you see, I didn't even manage to learn her correct name."

"Comrade Klima, whether you are telling the truth or not," went on the blonde, "it seems to me to be absolutely incomprehensible that you can educate our youth. Does our life really inspire in you nothing but the desire to carouse and abuse women? Be assured, we shall give our opinion about this in the proper places."

"The porter didn't speak about any Helena," broke in the elderly lady with the permanent wave, "but he did inform us that some unregistered girl from the dress factory has been living with you for a month. Don't forget, comrade, that you are in lodgings. How can you imagine that someone can live with you like this? Do you think that your house is a brothel?"

There flashed before my eyes the ten crowns which I'd given to the porter a couple of days ago, and I understood that the encirclement was complete. And the woman from the local committee continued: "If you don't want to tell us her name, the police will find it out."

11

The ground was slipping away beneath my feet. At the university I began to sense the malicious atmosphere which the professor had told me about. For the time being, I wasn't summoned to any interviews, but here and there I caught an allusion, and now and then Mary let something out, for the teachers drank coffee in her office and didn't watch their tongues. In a couple of days the selection committee, which was collecting evidence on all sides, was to meet. I imagined that its members had read the report of the local committee, a report about which I knew only that it was secret and that I couldn't refer to it.

There are moments in life when a man retreats defensively, when he must give ground, when he must surrender less important positions in order to protect the more important ones. But should it come to the very last, the most important one, at this point a man must halt and stand firm if he doesn't want to begin life all over again with idle hands and a feeling of being shipwrecked.

It seemed to me that this single, most important position was my love. Yes, in those troubled days I suddenly began to realize that I loved my fragile and unfortunate seamstress, who had been both beaten and pampered by life, and that I clung to her.

That day I met Klara at the museum. No, not at home. Do you think that home was still home? Is home a room with glass walls? A room observed through binoculars? A room where you must keep your beloved more carefully hidden than contraband?

Home was not home. There we felt like housebreakers who might be caught at any minute. Footsteps in the corridor made us nervous; we kept expecting someone to start pounding on the door. Klara was commuting from Chelakovits and we didn't feel like meeting in our alienated home for even a short while. So I had asked an artist friend to lend me his studio at night. That day I had got the key for the first time.

And so we found ourselves beneath a high roof in Vinohrady, in an enormous room with one small couch and a huge, slanting window, from which we could see all the lights of Prague. Amid the many paintings propped against the walls, the untidiness, and the carefree artist's squalor, a blessed feeling of freedom returned to me. I sprawled on the couch, pushed in the corkscrew and opened a bottle of wine. I chattered gaily and freely, and was looking forward to a beautiful evening and night.

However, the pressure, which I no longer felt, had fallen with its full weight on Klara.

I have already mentioned how Klara without any scruples and with the greatest naturalness had lived at one time in my attic. But now, when we found ourselves for a short time in someone else's studio, she felt put out. More than put out: "It's humiliating," she said.

"What's humiliating?" I asked her.

"That we have to borrow an apartment."

"Why is it humiliating that we have to borrow an apartment?"

"Because there's something humiliating about it," she replied.

"But we couldn't do anything else."

"I guess," she replied, "but in a borrowed apartment I feel like a whore."

"Good God, why should you feel like a whore in a *borrowed* apartment. Whores mostly operate in their own apartments, not in borrowed ones—"

It was futile to attack with reason the stout wall of irrational feeling that, as is known, is the stuff of which the female mind is made. From the beginning our conversation was ill-omened.

I told Klara what the professor had said, I told her what had happened at the local committee, and I was trying to convince her that in the end we would win if we loved each other and were together.

Klara was silent for a while and then said that I myself was guilty.

"Will you at least help me to get away from those seamstresses?"

I told her that this would have to be, at least temporarily, a time of forbearance.

"You see," said Klara, "you promised and in the end you do nothing. I won't be able to get out, even if somebody else wanted to help me, because I shall have my reputation ruined on your account."

I gave Klara my word that the incident with Mr. Zaturetsky couldn't harm her.

"I also don't understand," said Klara, "why you won't write the review. If you'd write it, then there'd be peace at once."

"It's too late, Klara," I said. "If I write this review they'll say that I'm condemning the work out of revenge and they'll be still more furious."

"And why must you condemn it? Write a favorable review!"

"I can't, Klara. This work is thoroughly absurd."

"So what? Why are you being truthful all of a sudden? Wasn't it a lie when you told the little man that they don't think much of you at *Visual Arts Journal?* And wasn't it a lie when you told the little man that he had tried to seduce me? And wasn't it a lie when you invented Helena? When you've told so many lies, what does it matter if you tell one more and praise him in the review? That's the only way you can smooth things out."

"You see, Klara," I said, "you think that a lie is a lie and it would seem that you're right. But you aren't. I can invent anything, make a fool of someone, carry out hoaxes and practical jokes—and I don't feel like a liar and I don't have a bad conscience. These lies, if you want to call them that, represent

myself as I really am. With such lies I'm not simulating anything, with such lies I am in fact speaking the truth. But there
are things which I can't lie about, things I've penetrated, whose
meaning I've grasped, which I love and take seriously. It's
impossible, don't ask me to do it, I can't."

We didn't understand each other.

But I really loved Klara and decided to do everything so
that she would have nothing to reproach me for. The following
day I wrote a letter to Mrs. Zaturetsky, saying that I would
expect her the day after tomorrow at two o'clock in my office.

12

True to her terrifying methodicalness, Mrs. Zaturetsky
knocked precisely at the appointed time. I opened the door and
asked her in.

Then I finally saw her. She was a tall woman, very tall with
a thin peasant's face and pale blue eyes. "Take off your things,"
I said, and with awkward movements she took off a long, dark
coat, narrow at the waist and oddly styled, a coat which God
knows why evoked the image of an ancient greatcoat.

I didn't want to attack at once; I wanted my adversary to
show me her cards first. After Mrs. Zaturetsky sat down, I got
her to speak by making a remark or two.

"Mr. Klima," she said in a serious voice, but without any
aggressiveness, "you know why I was looking for you. My
husband has always respected you very much as a specialist and
as a man of character. Everything depended on your review and
you didn't want to do it for him. It took my husband three
years to write this study. His life was harder than yours. He was
a teacher, he commuted daily twenty miles outside Prague.
Last year I forced him to stop that and devote himself to
research."

"Mr. Zaturetsky isn't employed?" I asked.

"No . . ."

"What does he live on?"

"For the time being I have to work hard myself. This research, Mr. Klima, is my husband's passion. If you knew how he studied everything. If you knew how many pages he rewrote. He always says that a real scholar must write three hundred pages so as to keep thirty. And on top of it, this woman. Believe me, Mr. Klima, I know him, I'm sure he didn't do it, so why did this woman accuse him? I don't believe it. Let her say it before me and before him. I know women, perhaps she likes you very much and you don't care for her. Perhaps she wanted to make you jealous. But you can believe me, Mr. Klima, my husband would never have dared!"

I was listening to Mrs. Zaturetsky, and all at once something strange happened to me: I ceased being aware that this was the woman for whose sake I should have to leave the university, and that this was the woman who caused the tension between myself and Klara, and for whose sake I'd wasted so many days in anger and unpleasantness. The connection between her and the incident, in which we'd both played a sad role, suddenly seemed vague, arbitrary, accidental, and not our fault. All at once I understood that it had only been my illusion that we ourselves saddle events and control their course. The truth is that they aren't *our* stories at all, that they are foisted upon us from somewhere *outside;* that in no way do they represent us; that we are not to blame for the queer path that they follow. They carry us away, since they are controlled by some *other* forces; no, I don't mean by supernatural forces, but by human forces, by the forces of those people who, when they unite, unfortunately still remain mutually *alien.*

When I looked at Mrs. Zaturetsky's eyes it seemed to me that these eyes couldn't see the consequences of my actions, that these eyes weren't seeing at all, that they were merely swimming in her face; that they were only stuck on.

"Perhaps you're right, Mrs. Zaturetsky," I said in a conciliatory tone: "Perhaps my girl didn't speak the truth, but you know how it is when a man's jealous . . . I believed her and was carried away. This can happen to anyone."

"Yes, certainly," said Mrs. Zaturetsky and it was evident that a weight had been lifted from her heart. "When you yourself see it, it's good. We were afraid that you believed her. This woman could have ruined my husband's whole life. I'm not speaking of the moral light it casts upon him. But my husband swears by your opinion. The editors assured him that it depended on you. My husband is convinced that if his article were published, he would finally be recognized as a scientific worker. I ask you, now that everything has been cleared up, will you write this review for him? And càn you do it quickly?"

Now came the moment to avenge myself on everything and appease my rage, only at this moment I didn't feel any rage, and when I spoke it was only because there was no escaping it: "Mrs. Zaturetsky, there is some difficulty regarding the review. I shall confess to you how it all happened. I don't like to say unpleasant things to people's faces. This is my weakness. I avoided Mr. Zaturetsky, and I thought that he would figure out why I was avoiding him. His paper is weak. It has no scientific value. Do you believe me?"

"I find it hard to believe. I can't believe you," said Mrs. Zaturetsky.

"Above all, this work is not original. Please understand, a scholar must always arrive at something new; a scholar can't copy what we already know, what others have written."

"My husband definitely didn't copy."

"Mrs. Zaturetsky, you've surely read this study . . ." I wanted to continue, but Mrs. Zaturetsky interrupted me: "No, I haven't." I was surprised. "You will read it then for yourself."

"I can't see," said Mrs. Zaturetsky. "I see only light and shadow, my eyes are bad. I haven't read a single line for five years, but I don't need to read to know if my husband's honest or not. This can be recognized in other ways. I know my husband, as a mother her children, I know everything about him. And I know that what he does is always honest."

I had to undergo worse. I read aloud to Mrs. Zaturetsky paragraphs from Mateychek, Pechirka, and Michek, whose thoughts and formulations Mr. Zaturetsky had taken over. It wasn't a question of willful plagiarism, but rather an unconscious submission to those authorities who inspired in Mr. Zaturetsky a feeling of sincere and inordinate respect. But anyone who had seen these passages compared must have understood that no serious scholarly magazine could publish Mr. Zaturetsky's work.

I don't know how much Mrs. Zaturetsky concentrated on my exposition, how much of it she followed and understood; she sat humbly in the armchair, humbly and obediently like a soldier, who knows that he may not leave his post. It took about half an hour for us to finish. Mrs. Zaturetsky got up from the armchair, fixed her transparent eyes upon me, and in a dull voice begged my pardon; but I knew that she hadn't lost faith in her husband and she didn't reproach anyone except herself for not knowing how to resist my arguments, which seemed obscure and unintelligible to her. She put on her military raincoat and I understood that this woman was a soldier in body and spirit, a sad and loyal soldier, a soldier tired from long marches, a soldier who doesn't understand the sense of an order and yet carries it out without objections, a soldier who goes away defeated but without dishonor.

After she'd gone, something remained in my office of her weariness, her loyalty, and her sadness. I suddenly forgot myself and my sorrows. The sorrow which seized me at that moment was purer, because it didn't issue from within me, but flowed from without, from afar.

13

"So now you don't have to be afraid of anything," I said to Klara, when later in the Dalmatian wineshop I repeated to her my conversation with Mrs. Zaturetsky.

"I didn't have anything to fear anyhow," replied Klara with a self-assurance that astonished me.

"How's that, you didn't? If it wasn't for you I wouldn't have met Mrs. Zaturetsky at all!"

"It's good that you did meet her, because what you did to them was cruel. Dr. Kalousek said that it's hard for an intelligent man to understand this."

"When did you meet Kalousek?"

"I've met him," said Klara.

"And did you tell him everything?"

"What? Is it a secret perhaps? Now I know exactly what you are."

"H'm."

"May I tell you what you are?"

"Please."

"A stereotyped cynic."

"You got that from Kalousek."

"Why from Kalousek? Do you think that I can't figure it out for myself? You actually think that I'm not capable of forming an opinion about you. You like to lead people by the nose. You promised Mr. Zaturetsky a review."

"I didn't promise him a review."

"That's one thing. And you promised me a job. You used me as an excuse to Mr. Zaturetsky, and you used Mr. Zaturetsky as an excuse to me. But you may be sure that I'll get that job."

"Through Kalousek?" I tried to be scornful.

"Not from you. You've gambled so much away and you don't even know yourself how much."

"And do you know?"

"Yes. Your contract won't be renewed and you'll be glad if they'll let you in some gallery as a clerk. But you must realize that all this was only your own mistake. If I can give you some advice: another time be honest and don't lie, because a man who lies can't be respected by any woman."

She got up, gave me (clearly for the last time) her hand, turned, and left.

Only after a while did it occur to me (in spite of the chilly silence which surrounded me) that my story was not of the tragic sort, but rather of the comic variety.

At any rate that afforded me some comfort.

I Am Writing to You from a Distant Country

HENRI MICHAUX

Translated by John Biguenet

1

We have here, she said, only one sun each month, and for only a short time. We rub our eyes days ahead. But in vain. Inexorable weather. The sun never arrives until its proper hour.

Then we have a world of things to do, while there is light, so that we hardly have time to look at one another.

The trouble, for us, comes during the night, when we must work, and we really must: dwarfs are born continually.

2

When you walk in the country, she further confided to him, you may happen to encounter considerable masses on the road. These are mountains, and sooner or later you must bend your knee to them. It is useless to resist; you could not go beyond, even by hurting yourself.

I do not say this in order to wound. I could say other things if I really wanted to wound.

3

The dawn is gray here, she continued. It was not always so. We do not know whom to accuse.

At night the cattle utter a great bellowing, long and flute-like at the end. One is compassionate, but what can be done?

The odor of eucalyptus surrounds us: a blessing, serenity, but it cannot protect us from everything, or else do you think that it actually can protect us from all things?

4

I add another word to you, a question rather.

Does the water flow in your country too? (I don't remember whether you have told me so) and it also gives chills, if it's the real thing.

Do I love it? I don't know. One feels so alone within when it is cold. It is altogether different when it is warm. So then? How to decide? How do you others decide, tell me, when you speak of it without disguise, with open heart?

5

I am writing to you from the end of the world. You must realize this. Often the trees tremble. We collect the leaves. They have a ridiculous number of veins. But why? There's nothing more between them and the tree, and we go away troubled.

Could not life on earth continue without the wind? Or is

it necessary that everything tremble, always, always?

There are also subterranean disturbances, and in the house, too, like angers which might come to find you, like stern creatures who would like to extract confessions.

One sees nothing, except what is of so little importance to see. Nothing, and yet we tremble. Why?

6

We here all live with tightened throats. You know that, although very young, in the past I was even younger, and my companions were too. What does that mean? There is surely something horrible in it.

And in the past when, as I have already told you, we were even younger, we were afraid. Anyone could have taken advantage of our confusion. Anyone could have told us: "You see, we are going to bury you. The moment has arrived." We, thinking: "It's true, we might as well be buried tonight, if it's definite that this is the moment."

And we did not dare run too much: breathless, at the end of a race, to arrive in front of a grave all prepared, and not the time to say a word, not the breath.

Tell me, what then is the secret in regard to this?

7

There are constantly, she further told him, lions in the village, who walk about without any restraints. On condition that we pay no attention to them, they pay no attention to us.

But if they see a young girl running before them, they don't care to excuse her excitement. No! they devour her at once.

That is why they constantly walk about the village where they have nothing to do, for quite obviously they could yawn just as well elsewhere.

8

For a long, long time, she confided to him, we have been at odds with the sea.

On the very rare occasions—blue, gentle—one might believe her to be contented. But that would not last. Her smell besides says it, a smell of rot (if it is not her bitterness).

Here I should explain the matter of the waves. It is ridiculously complicated, and the sea . . . I beg you, have confidence in me. Would I want to deceive you? She is not only a word. She is not only a fear. She exists, I swear it to you; one sees her constantly.

Who? Why we, we see her. She comes from very far away to quarrel and to terrify us.

When you come, you will see her yourself; you will be totally amazed. "Wow!" you'll say, for she is stupefying.

We will look at her together. I am sure that I will no longer be afraid. Tell me, will that never happen?

9

I cannot leave you with a doubt, she continued, with a lack of confidence. I would like to talk with you again of the sea. But the obstacle remains. The streams advance; but not she. Listen, don't be angry, I swear it to you, I wouldn't dream of deceiving you. She is like that. No matter how agitated she gets, she halts before a little sand. She is a great hesitater. She would certainly like to advance, but the fact is there.

Later on perhaps, one day she will advance.

10

"We are more than ever surrounded by ants," says her letter. Uneasily, stomach to earth they push the dust. They have no interest in us.

Not one raises its head.

This is the most tightly closed society which can exist, although outdoors they constantly spread out. No matter, their projects, their preoccupations . . . they are among themselves . . . everywhere.

And, up till the present, not one has raised its head toward us. It would rather be crushed.

11

She writes to him again:

"You can't imagine all that there is in the sky; you would have to see it to believe it. So, look, the . . . but I'm not going to tell you their name immediately."

Despite their airs of weighing so much and of occupying nearly all of the sky, they do not weigh, gigantic though they are, as much as a newborn baby.

We call them clouds.

It is true that water escapes from them, but not by compressing them, nor by grinding them. It would be useless, they have so little.

But, by reason of occupying lengths and lengths, widths

and widths, depths also and depths and of puffing themselves up, they manage in the long run to make fall a few droplets of water, yes, of water. And we are thoroughly wet. We run away furious to have been trapped; for nobody knows the moment when they are going to release their drops; sometimes they go for days without releasing them. And one would stay home in vain waiting for them.

12

The education regarding chills is not properly managed in this country. We are ignorant of the true rules and when the event occurs, we are taken by surprise.

It is Time, of course. (Is it the same with you?) One must arrive sooner than it does; you see what I mean, just a very little bit ahead. You know the story of the flea in the drawer? Yes, of course. And how true, isn't it! I don't know what more to say. When will we at last see each other?

The Word

MARGARITA KARAPANOU

Translated by N.C. Germanacos

One morning I went dumb. Still as a clock, waves turning back on themselves.

One morning I couldn't hear. I quarreled with sounds. I turned into a table. I turned transparent.

It rained from the sky, and the raindrops turned to tears on my cheeks. I chewed invisible tastes. Words turned to pebbles in my belly, so heavy I couldn't lift them. I changed shapes. (Dumb) words came out of my mouth, and the air around me tore them in pieces.

Letters turned to reptiles. The only thing I could hear was my heart: Bang—bang—bang—bang. I knew no other tune. I looked around me and listened to my heart: Bang—bang— bang—bang. I forgot everything else.

People spoke to me.

"Bang—bang—bang—bang," I answered.

At night, forgotten words tried to reach me. I listened

with my skin. Words tore my skin off, crept inside me and nestled down. I was a mass of wounds. I opened my mouth in front of the mirror: beasts lay asleep in my throat; they'd made it their home.

I was in a faraway land. Bang—bang—bang—bang. I'd forgotten everything else.

T—K—P—X: they were driving me crazy.

A—R: balsam.

Grandmother spoke: I bled.

Mother spoke: my thighs bled.

Peter: he knew. He lulled the beasts to sleep.

"My little cabbage, I'll take you away from here."

T—K—P—X: "Peter don't leave me."

"We'll go to the island."

Grandmother was cleaning Grandfather's pipe: "Would you like a cup of tea?"

On the island we closed the doors, shutters and curtains, and stuffed black paper in the cracks. Then we undressed and went to bed for years, months and weeks.

"Bang—bang—bang—bang."

"Gang—bang," he answered.

I suckled Peter between his legs, he turned into a woman. I suckled him to fall asleep. Yesterday a spider jumped out of my mouth. I was shrinking.

I suckled him every three hours, lizards died in my guts. Peter became a cave, and I lost my teeth too.

Peter's breasts grew. He opened out, and I shrank.

We drove sounds away. The ones left over we tamed and turned into dogs.

In the dark, in his arms, Peter took me for a stroll around the house.

"Bang—bang—bang—bang," something inside me began to respond.

A vein ran from Peter's heart into mine, and I was filled with tunes.

Naked we stood in front of the mirror.

"Open your mouth," Peter said.

"You," he said.

He licked me in the mirror.

"I," he said, pointing to himself.

He turned into a shelter and water.

One morning a word tottered on the brink.

"Come on, my little cabbage, it'll hurt. It'll hurt me too."

I crawled into his belly and grabbed hold. It was so peaceful I curled up and fell asleep.

Peter was pushing out, rhythmically.

"Bang—bang—bang—bang. Peter let me stay in here."

His whole body arched forward. I shot out.

The windows were open: air, and the sun warming my hair. I opened my eyes. Something fluttered in my mouth.

A word.

The Circular Ruins

JORGE LUIS BORGES

Translated by Anthony Bonner

And if he left off dreaming about you . . .
—*Through the Looking Glass, VI.*

No one saw him disembark in the unanimous night, no one saw the bamboo canoe sink into the sacred mud, but in a few days there was no one who did not know that the taciturn man came from the South and that his home had been one of those numberless villages upstream in the deeply cleft side of the mountain, where the Zend language has not been contaminated by Greek and where leprosy is infrequent. What is certain is that the gray man kissed the mud, climbed up the bank without pushing aside (probably, without feeling) the blades which were lacerating his flesh, and crawled, nauseated and bloodstained, up to the circular enclosure crowned with a stone tiger or horse, which sometimes was the color of flame and now was that of ashes. This circle was a temple which had been devoured by ancient fires, profaned by the miasmal jungle, and whose god no longer received the homage of men. The stranger stretched himself out beneath the pedestal. He was awakened by the sun high overhead. He was not astonished to find that his wounds had healed; he closed his pallid eyes and slept, not through weakness of flesh but through determination of will. He knew that this temple was the place required for his invincible intent; he knew that the incessant trees had not succeeded in strangling the ruins of another propitious temple downstream which had once belonged to gods now burned and dead; he knew that his immediate obligation was to dream. Toward midnight he was awakened by the inconsolable shriek of a bird. Tracks of bare feet, some figs and a jug warned him that the men of the region had been spying respectfully on his sleep, soliciting his protection or afraid of his magic. He felt a chill of fear, and sought out a sepulchral niche in the dilapidated wall where he concealed himself among unfamiliar leaves.

The purpose which guided him was not impossible, though supernatural. He wanted to dream a man; he wanted to dream him in minute entirety and impose him on reality. This magic project had exhausted the entire expanse of his mind; if someone had asked him his name or to relate some event of his former life, he would not have been able to give an answer. This uninhabited, ruined temple suited him, for it contained a minimum of visible world; the proximity of the workmen also suited him, for they took it upon themselves to provide for his frugal needs. The rice and fruit they brought him were nourishment enough for his body, which was consecrated to the sole task of sleeping and dreaming.

At first, his dreams were chaotic; then in a short while they became dialectic in nature. The stranger dreamed that he was in the center of a circular amphitheater which was more or less the burnt temple; clouds of taciturn students filled the tiers of seats; the faces of the farthest ones hung at a distance of many centuries and as high as the stars, but their features were completely precise. The man lectured his pupils on anatomy, cosmography, and magic: the faces listened anxiously and tried to answer understandingly, as if they guessed the importance of that examination which would redeem one of them from his condition of empty illusion and interpolate him into the real world. Asleep or awake, the man thought over the answers of his phantoms, did not allow himself to be deceived by impostors, and in certain perplexities he sensed a growing intelligence. He was seeking a soul worthy of participating in the universe.

After nine or ten nights he understood with a certain bitterness that he could expect nothing from those pupils who accepted his doctrine passively, but that he could expect something from those who occasionally dared to oppose him. The former group, although worthy of love and affection, could not ascend to the level of individuals; the latter pre-existed to a slightly greater degree. One afternoon (now afternoons were also given over to sleep, now he was only awake for a couple of hours at daybreak) he dismissed the vast illusory student body for good and kept only one pupil. He was a taciturn, sallow boy, at times intractable, and whose sharp features resembled those of his dreamer. The brusque elimination of his fellow students did not disconcert him for long; after a few private lessons, his progress was enough to astound the teacher. Nevertheless, a catastrophe took place. One day, the man emerged from his sleep as if from a viscous desert, looked at the useless afternoon light which he immediately confused with the dawn, and understood that he had not dreamed. All that night and all day long, the intolerable lucidity of insomnia fell upon him. He tried exploring the forest, to lose his strength; among the hemlock he barely succeeded in experiencing several short snatches of sleep, veined with fleeting, rudimentary visions that were useless. He tried to assemble the student body but scarcely had he articulated a few brief words of exhortation when it became deformed and was then erased. In his almost perpetual vigil, tears of anger burned his old eyes.

He understood that modeling the incoherent and vertiginous matter of which dreams are composed was the most difficult task that a man could undertake, even though he should penetrate all the enigmas of a superior and inferior order; much more difficult than weaving a rope out of sand or coining the faceless wind. He swore he would forget the enormous hallucination which had thrown him off at first, and he sought another method of work. Before putting it into execution, he spent a month recovering his strength, which had been squandered by his delirium. He abandoned all premeditation of dreaming and almost immediately succeeded in sleeping a reasonable part of each day. The few times that he had dreams during this period, he paid no attention to them. Before resuming his task, he waited until the moon's disk was perfect. Then, in the afternoon, he purified himself in the waters of the river, worshiped the planetary gods, pronounced the prescribed syllables of a mighty name, and went to sleep. He dreamed almost immediately, with his heart throbbing.

He dreamed that it was warm, secret, about the size of a clenched fist, and of a garnet color within the penumbra of a human body as yet without face or sex; during fourteen lucid nights he dreamt of it with meticulous love. Every night he perceived it more clearly. He did not touch it; he only permitted himself to witness it, to observe it, and occasionally to rectify it with a glance. He perceived it and lived it from all angles and distances. On the fourteenth night he lightly touched the pulmonary artery with his index finger, then the whole heart, outside and inside. He was satisfied with the examination. He deliberately did not dream for a night; he then took up the heart again, invoked the name of a planet, and undertook the vision of another of the principle organs. Within a year he had come to the skeleton and the eyelids. The innumerable hair was perhaps the most difficult task. He dreamed an entire man—a young man, but who did not sit up or talk, who was unable to open his eyes. Night after night, the man dreamt him asleep.

In the Gnostic cosmogonies, demiurges fashion a red Adam who cannot stand; as clumsy, crude and elemental as this Adam of dust was the Adam of dreams forged by the wizard's nights. One afternoon, the man almost destroyed his entire work, but then changed his mind. (It would have been better had he destroyed it.) When he had exhausted all supplications to the deities of the earth, he threw himself at the feet of the effigy which was perhaps a tiger or perhaps a colt and implored its unknown help. That evening, at twilight, he dreamt of the statue. He dreamt it was alive, tremulous: it was not an atrocious bastard of a tiger and a colt, but at the same time these two fiery creatures and also a bull, a rose, and a storm. This multiple god revealed to him that his earthly name was Fire, and that in this circular temple (and in others like it) people had once made sacrifices to him and worshiped him, and that he would magically animate the dreamed phantom, in such a way that all creatures, except Fire itself and the dreamer, would believe it to be a man of flesh and blood. He commanded that once this man had been instructed in all the rites, he should be sent to the other ruined temple whose pyramids were still standing downstream, so that some voice would glorify him in that deserted edifice. In the dream of the man that dreamed, the dreamed one awoke.

The wizard carried out the orders he had been given. He devoted a certain length of time (which finally proved to be two years) to instructing him in the mysteries of the universe and

the cult of fire. Secretly, he was pained at the idea of being
separated from him. On the pretext of pedagogical necessity,
each day he increased the number of hours dedicated to dreaming. He also remade the right shoulder, which was somewhat
defective. At times, he was disturbed by the impression that all
this had already happened. . . . In general, his days were happy;
when he closed his eyes, he thought: *Now I will be with my son.*
Or, more rarely: *The son I have engendered is waiting for me
and will not exist if I do not go to him.*

Gradually, he began accustoming him to reality. Once he
ordered him to place a flag on a faraway peak. The next day
the flag was fluttering on the peak. He tried other analogous
experiments, each time more audacious. With a certain bitterness, he understood that his son was ready to be born—and
perhaps impatient. That night he kissed him for the first time
and sent him off to the other temple whose remains were
turning white downstream, across many miles of inextricable
jungle and marshes. Before doing this (and so that his son
should never know that he was a phantom, so that he should
think himself a man like any other) he destroyed in him all
memory of his years of apprenticeship.

His victory and peace became blurred with boredom. In
the twilight times of dusk and dawn, he would prostrate himself before the stone figure, perhaps imagining his unreal son
carrying out identical rites in other circular ruins downstream;
at night he no longer dreamed, or dreamed as any man does.
His perceptions of the sounds and forms of the universe became somewhat pallid: his absent son was being nourished by
these diminutions of his soul. The purpose of his life had been
fulfilled; the man remained in a kind of ecstasy. After a certain
time, which some chroniclers prefer to compute in years and
others in decades, two oarsmen awoke him at midnight; he
could not see their faces, but they spoke to him of a charmed

man in a temple of the North, capable of walking on fire without burning himself. The wizard suddenly remembered the words of the god. He remembered that of all the creatures that people the earth, Fire was the only one who knew his son to be a phantom. This memory, which at first calmed him, ended by tormenting him. He feared lest his son should meditate on this abnormal privilege and by some means find out he was a mere simulacrum. Not to be a man, to be a projection of another man's dreams—what an incomparable humiliation, what madness! Any father is interested in the sons he has procreated (or permitted) out of the mere confusion of happiness; it was natural that the wizard should fear for the future of that son whom he had thought out entrail by entrail, feature by feature, in a thousand and one secret nights.

His misgivings ended abruptly, but not without certain forewarnings. First (after a long drought) a remote cloud, as light as a bird, appeared on a hill; then, toward the South, the sky took on the rose color of leopard's gums; then came clouds of smoke which rusted the metal of the nights; afterwards came the panic-stricken flight of wild animals. For what had happened many centuries before was repeating itself. The ruins of the sanctuary of the god of Fire was destroyed by fire. In a dawn without birds, the wizard saw the concentric fire licking the walls. For a moment, he thought of taking refuge in the water, but then he understood that death was coming to crown his old age and absolve him from his labors. He walked toward the sheets of flame. They did not bite his flesh, they caressed him and flooded him without heat or combustion. With relief, with humiliation, with terror, he understood that he also was an illusion, that someone else was dreaming him.

The Future Kings

ADOLFO BIOY CASARES

Translated by Ruth L.C. Simms

Perhaps this story should begin with the memory of a circus performance held in 1918. That was when my dazzled eyes first beheld—in antics that, although admittedly humble, seemed prodigious to me then—the animals that deserve our deepest respect: seals. As for the feeling of joy I unconsciously associate with those memories—now I attribute it (but let us not forget that in these unhappy times we are subject to obsessions) to the noble, blissful intoxication of victory; but when I try to relive my feelings of that time with greater exactitude I am aware that at the root of my happiness, like symbols of future mysteries, were the enormous flag-bedecked circus tent and three children—Helen, Mark, and I—hand in hand on an ominous threshold.

When the seals had finished their performance, Mark left our box. A chimpanzee was riding a bicycle around the red circumference of the ring. The animal was not looking at his narrow path; his eyes were riveted on Helen. Suddenly things began to happen. Helen cried; Mark came back and said that he had obtained permission for us to visit the seals and the other animals; Helen implored and threatened: she said that if I went she would never speak to me again; I followed Mark.

Even then Mark was the secret and indomitable agent who organized everything in our lives. He was very intelligent, very strong, very rich. Much of our childhood we spent together at his homes: the town house or the large country estate of Saint Remi.

Only Helen seemed to resist his influence. With a calm and spontaneous insistence that somehow had the power to thwart him, Helen continued to prefer me, to believe in me and not in him.

After we finished college I entered law school. I attended classes regularly for four years. When I heard about students who had graduated in one or two years, I was skeptical.

"What good can you possibly derive," I would ask, "from reading hundreds of pages in such a short time?"

Mark did not study. He read for his own enjoyment and directed our reading. Under his guidance I made a frivolous and profitable inquiry into the history of the quadrature of the circle, the progress made by Arab navigators, the possibilities of logistics, the nature and multiplication of chromosomes, the works of Resta on comparative cosmographies.

Later Mark became a student at the School of Natural Science. As a friend remarked, that seemed to confirm the fact that he did not take life seriously. Even so, the course is long and difficult. Mark graduated in a year.

"I have decided to devote my life to study," he told me one night. "I shall live in seclusion at Saint Remi. I need a companion, an intelligent girl, to live with me and be my assistant."

Inexplicably I felt alarmed. I realized that I was to find

that girl for him. Against my will, uncertainly, I began to search for her in a mental cataloguing of the women I knew. Very soon I abandoned the search.

Helen went with Mark. I withdrew from law practice and went to Australia. There were no good-byes. Helen and Mark were already ensconced at the villa; I did not have time to visit them, or even call.

In Australia I was the assistant administrator, then the administrator, of a ranch. Sometimes, in the afternoons, I would count the orange-colored flagstones of the patio, and each stone would represent one of the women in my life. Two memories stood out more poignantly than the rest: one, very sad, was of Helen; the other was of Louise, the grocer's daughter, who lived across from Saint Remi. We used to play with her each afternoon, and she was a pleasant, but no longer vivid, memory of that time. I wondered what had become of her. We had shared a part of our childhood, and then I had forgotten her. What vestige of her was left to me? Only the metal pencil I am writing with (she gave it to me once for a birthday present and I always carry it with me) and a desperate, tender reproach that seems to haunt me.

To dispel the boredom of my afternoons I wrote novels about espionage. Under the pseudonym of Speculator I published six or seven books in Melbourne. They ran to several editions, but the critics were not enthusiastic.

I spent nine years among the dunghills and the sheep-folds, until war was declared and I returned to my country. They said I was too old for the front and so, to my own surprise, I became a counterspy. Perhaps my novels made them think I was qualified for such work.

One afternoon I learned from conversation with a friend that the office had become suspicious of the people who lived at Saint Remi. I spoke to my chief about it. He suspected that enemy planes were being directed from the villa to bomb that section of the city. I convinced him that I was the man to head the investigation.

2

Early the next morning I left my quarters and crossed the noisy street. A pure sky was overhead as I descended into the cavernous recesses of the subway. I had to wait on the platform until the people who had taken shelter there during the night came out of the tunnels with their bags and mattresses. It was ten o'clock before the trains started running again. I rode to the end of the line and then emerged, by means of a labyrinthine iron stairway, into the quiet suburb darkened by trees. There, amid a conglomeration of indifferent materialized memories, were the garage adorned with medallions (it was formerly the stable), the picnic grounds, the tennis courts. I looked in vain for a taxi, or even a horse and carriage, to take me to the villa. I began to feel tired as I walked down an avenue of very tall and leafy trees with dark trunks, lustrous foliage, and orange-colored flowers, which did not coincide exactly with my memories. When I passed the trees I began to recognize the place. I had the impression that the area had been badly hit by the bombings (but the attack that is going on at this moment must be the worst one of all). I walked on, past undamaged houses, streets without perforations. Then I came to the wall that surrounds the estate of Saint Remi; it was in a ruinous condition. From the outside I could not determine whether the house had been hit by the bombings. I skirted the wall, feeling that I was in a dream of endless fatigue.

The neighborhood had changed, but the store that had belonged to Louise's parents was still standing directly opposite

the main gate of Saint Remi. I entered the store. As my feet
touched the smooth planks of oak that had once been a part
of the dining room at Saint Remi, I felt a sensation of love, the
first I had experienced in many years, pervade my soul. In the
dark room a man and woman I did not recognize stood waiting
to serve me. I took them for the new owners of the store, and
asked if I could buy something to eat.

"We don't have very much," said the grocer. He was a
disheveled man with a sallow complexion.

"Well, we have just as much as other places," said the
woman vaguely. She went to prepare lunch for me.

I spoke of the bombings, the food shortages, high prices,
the black market, man's descent from the monkey, our need
to be indulgent with the government, how the sacrifice of the
war had affected all of us, the winners of last Sunday's game,
and, finally, the country estate of Saint Remi.

"We've often wondered what goes on there," said the
man. "Especially lately!"

I heard the woman's voice from the back room, "People
are talking!"

"The people who live at Saint Remi never go out," explained the man. "And no one ever goes in."

"Why worry," said the woman. "I guess you'll find eccen-
trics in every neighborhood."

"We don't know what goes on behind that wall," said the
man darkly. After a pause he continued, "And we haven't
known for a long time!"

"What difference does it make?" supplied the woman.

She placed a voluminous plate of cabbage on the counter
and invited me to sit down. Then she brought a small glass of
sour wine and a piece of bread.

I summoned courage and asked, "Who knows about the
goings-on at the villa?"

"Not a soul," whispered the woman, squinting.

"The man who delivers the fish knows," said the man.

He was due to pass the store at one o'clock, or thereabouts, and was the only person who ever went near the villa.

"You mean he goes in the house every day?" I inquired.

"No, never," said the woman with a smile.

"He leaves the fish at the door," explained the man.

The fish peddler came along after one-thirty, in a horse-drawn cart.

"Do you deliver fish to Saint Remi?" I asked.

"Sure thing," he said. "Been doing it for years."

"Do you ever see the man who lives there?"

"Every day."

"Are you the only person who makes deliveries to the villa?"

"Naturally. Fish is all they eat. They eat more fish than an army. Because of them I was able to get my wagon, and now I have a horse too!"

I decided not to go to Saint Remi until evening. I asked the grocer if it would be possible to rest in one of the upstairs rooms. He took me up to the top floor, to a room that was long and narrow, with a door at each end.

I fell asleep, and then awoke with the sensation of having slept for a long time. I looked at my watch and saw that it was ten to five. I was afraid I had slept all day, all night, and that it was the morning of the next day. Bemused by sleep, I went to the door to call the man. I chose the wrong door; I opened it—Instead of the rickety stairway I expected to find, there was an orderly room with pictures, bookcases, lamps, draperies, rugs. A girl was seated at a desk. She raised her head and looked at me with kind and honest eyes. It was Louise. She pronounced my name.

"But—your parents?" I asked.

She told me that her parents had sold the store to some relatives and had gone to live in the country. She rented the room from them. I believe she was as touched and happy as I was.

Perhaps because it all seemed like a dream, I dared to tell her I had thought about her many times.

She interrupted me with a sudden anxious question, "Promise you won't go into the villa?"

We heard steps on the stairway.

"We mustn't be seen together. I don't want anyone to know who I am," I whispered. "I'll be back around eight-thirty."

I closed the door. The grocer was standing at the other door, asking if he might have a word with me.

"I know about your mission," he said. "I want to help you."

"My mission?"

"The bombings," he replied. "They have leveled the whole area, but this is an island."

"Have any bombs fallen here?"

"Lately, yes. A few. They were dropped by mistake or on purpose by some green planes flying at a very high altitude."

"All right," I replied. "And what can you tell me about the people who live at the villa?"

"You will hear that the owner of the villa has kidnapped the lady. Don't believe it!"

"Then the lady has not been kidnapped?"

"They have both been kidnapped."

As we went downstairs, I asked, "And who are the kidnappers?"

"I suspect no one knows. People give the most fantastic explanations."

"But do they all live in the villa?"

"Yes. They all live there."

He spoke some more without explaining anything. I conjectured that a sudden secret prefiguring of my ineptitude for this adventure or the ineffable or atrocious nature of his confidences had convinced him that it was useless to talk to me. I did not insist too much with my questions: it was not advisable to show eagerness. We said good-bye to each other, and I asked him not to tell anyone about our conversation.

I walked away from the store, trying to stay out of sight of a possible observer at the upstairs window. About ten minutes later I came to a place where the wall was almost totally disintegrated. I looked around to make certain that no one was watching; then I climbed over the crumbled remains of the wall and jumped down onto the grounds of the estate.

The degree to which that noble and beautiful garden had been neglected impressed me profoundly. I do not mean that the garden in that condition—with insects and plants allowed to develop freely, as if it were a jungle—seemed less noble or less beautiful. A partially destroyed summerhouse; a tree with ashen foliage, which disappeared in the summer sky beyond the brilliant leaves of the creeping vine that was choking it to death; a fallen statue of Diana; a dry fountain; a bush covered with fragrant yellow flowers, embedded in a monstrous ant hill; benches along the solitary pathways that seemed to be waiting for persons from another age; very tall trees with no leaves on their uppermost branches; precarious walls with windows edged in gray, green or blue—Now, in the light of what I have learned, I see in that combination of abundance and decrepitude, in that infinitely pathetic beauty, a symbol of the transitory reign of men.

I glanced at my watch. I had three hours of daylight left for my investigation, and then I would see Louise. I knew where to find her. There was—I thought—no reason for me to feel so impatient.

From my vantage point the house was not visible. I ad-

vanced cautiously, hiding behind the trees. Except for a continuous buzzing of bees and, now and then, a gust of wind that
shook the leaves, the silence was almost complete. Feeling that
I was being observed, I crouched down by a bust of Phaedrus.
I looked around. No one was there. I wanted to run, but I did
not have the necessary strength. I had the impression that I was
moving, hiding in the presence of invisible eyes; I was terrified,
but I thought I knew—and this will seem like an indication of
my unbalanced mental state—that there was no malevolence
in those secret eyes.

(I know that this story is confused. I am writing automati-
cally; in spite of my fatigue and my suffering, the habit of
literary composition is writing these lines. They say that we
remember our whole life at the moment of drowning. But it
is one thing to remember; another, to write.)

I fell to the ground. An attack was just beginning; it did
not seem far away. I remember thinking that I should take
advantage of the bombing to enter the house. Some green
planes flew overhead at an excessive altitude; then I peered out
through the foliage of a tree and saw the villa in all its vastness
at the end of the path. I don't know how long I stayed there.
I remember thinking that the building sprawling between the
trees reminded me of a huge antediluvian animal. Trying to
protect myself, dragging myself over the ground, running when
I lost control of my nerves, I reached the porch. I peered
through the window at what had been, in former days, the
children's dining room. Everything was exactly as I remembered it, but covered with a layer of dust and cobwebs. I pushed
the window open and climbed through. The pictures of wild
horses were still hanging on the wall; seeing them reassured me
somewhat. I walked down the hall; I went through the guest
wing; I tried to enter the game room. It was filled with small
mounds of earth that looked like wasp nests, and infinite num-

bers of black ants were crawling on the floor. On the walls and the furniture of the ballroom I saw some white caterpillars that looked like very large silkworms; they had white skin and almost-human faces, and their round, greenish eyes stared at me with attentive immobility. I fled up the stairs. Night had fallen and the moon's splendor was filtering through the cracks in the ceiling; through the cracks in the floor I saw the music room with its dark furniture covered with yellow damask. I saw that walls no longer separated the music room, the dining room, the ballroom, and the small red room. Where the red room should have been, I saw a kind of swamp or lake with rushes growing in it and some viscous forms swimming in the dark water; I saw, or thought I saw, a mermaid on the muddy bank.

I heard footsteps approaching. I went down the stairs, out to the winter garden, and hid behind a blue porcelain urn. Someone was walking heavily in the music room. If I crawled to the door, I would be able to see who it was. I heard splashing noises, the sound of churning water, and then a long silence intervened; then I heard the steps again. I peeked out cautiously. At first I saw nothing strange: my eyes, glancing over the yellow damask furniture, the imitation of Netscher's *Henrietta*, the tapestry with the two figures of Eridanus, the harmonium, the bronze statue of Mercury, finally came to the water. There I saw a seal (it was what I had taken for a mermaid a few moments before); and then I saw a group of seals, eagerly devouring fish. The footsteps were drawing near again. A ragged woman came in—Helen, in rags, looking old and dirty—carrying a net filled with fish.

She let the heavy load fall to the floor. We looked into each other's eyes. I said, "Let me take you away from all this."

I said it out of loyalty to my former feelings, the feelings that had become a habit through the years. But I thought with rancor, "She owes all this to Mark"—not "I owe all this to

Mark," as I used to think. "Mark has degraded her like this."

A door opened. Mark came in, in tatters, looking as old and dirty as Helen. Feeling genuinely sorry for him, I held out my hands in a gesture of friendship. His raucous gaiety and the look of relief and interest with which he greeted me denoted (I am sure of it now) a hidden meaning.

"What's going on here?" I asked.

"Nothing," said Mark.

"We were expecting you," said Helen. "We've always been expecting you."

"I've come to take you away," I said.

Mark turned to Helen. "Take the fish," he ordered.

"We must get away from here," I said.

As if he had not heard me, Mark placed the heavy burden on her back. Helen staggered away with it.

"Where is she going?" I asked.

"To take the fish to the seals."

"Why do you make her work like that?"

"I don't make her do anything," he replied vaguely.

I looked at my watch. I had the impression that it stopped at that instant.

"It is nine o'clock," I thought. "It's time for me to go. Louise is waiting."

I found myself thinking the prayer: "I must go because Louise is waiting" in algebraic terms. I was gratified to observe that I had mastered symbolic logic. I wanted to continue my mental gymnastics. And then I found myself in my habitual poverty, feeling (as I always feel after a dream) that by a vehement effort of my memory I would be able to recuperate the lost treasures. I was alone.

I experienced an intimate heaviness in my arms and legs. I groped my way in the dark, as if I could not see. My hands were trembling. I came to a hall covered with mosaic tile; there were skylights on the ceiling and paintings from the Flemish school on the walls. Mark stood at the end of the hall, in the moonlight. I called to him. I asked him where he was going.

"To bring in another load of fish," he replied.

"You and Helen have become the servants of the seals," I observed bitterly.

He gave me a long smile. Then he said, "We could ask for nothing better."

"Perhaps not—but at least think of Helen—" Then I added imploringly, "We must get away from this place!"

"No," he said slowly. "No. And now you are going to stay here too."

At that moment the sirens wailed three times, announcing the approach of enemy aircraft. Unaccountably I felt relieved.

"Are you going to force me to stay here?" I asked.

"You will want to stay of your own accord. We have accomplished some interesting things, and now the seals will carry on our work. I am sure you will want to be here to observe it. Do you recall how enthusiastic we were when I discovered Darwin? The infinite number of books on evolution that I read in a few days? The evolution wrought on a species by the blind action of nature takes thousands of years to accomplish. I wanted to achieve the same result in a shorter time by means of a definite plan. Man is a provisional result on one evolutionary path. But there are other ways: those of other mammals, birds, fish, the amphibians, the insects—I conquered the gregarious instinct of the ants: now they build individual anthills. But the seals are our masterpiece. We have tortured the young to find out what could be done with a vigilance that was ever alert; we have worked on cells and embryos; we have made a comparative study of the chromosomes of the frozen fossils from Siberia. But it was not enough to work on individual animals; we had to establish genetic patterns."

"And have you taught your seals how to talk?" I asked ironically.

"There is no need for them to talk. They communicate with their thoughts. They reproach me for not having changed their flippers into hands. But they are infinitely kind, and they bear no grudges. They are interested in man's evolutionary possibilities; they did not wish to force Helen and me to do anything, because that would have meant that one of us would have had to operate on the other, and they know how much we love each other. All these years they have kept repeating, 'Wait until someone from the outside world comes!' "

"And now I am here," I thought uneasily. Immediately I found myself thinking that the seals, assisted by Mark and Helen, had produced radical changes on the white caterpillars in the ballroom. The caterpillars were almost unreal creatures, bereft of the indispensable defenses required by an active life. Now they lived in a world like the one dreamed about by idealists, where reality consisted of the clear, precise ideas they had the ability to project.

The bombs began to fall; they seemed to be very close. Mark ran to the music room.

I heard an explosion. I felt a sharp pain in my back. I coughed, I choked. I was lying on the ground—I was sobbing. Some dust—perhaps from pieces of shattered plaster—was floating in the air.

Outside my line of vision, something that seemed to be animated with a life of its own was disintegrating.

Mark was standing beside me. "I'm going to give you an injection," he said.

I could not resist. My legs seemed to be paralyzed. The pain was intolerable. More bombs fell. I thought that the whole villa was about to collapse. There was a smell of mud, a smell of fish.

"The green planes are flying so high that the seals cannot drive them away," I thought.

I turned around. Mark was not at my side. Perhaps everyone in the house had been killed. I tried to remember Helen. I recaptured the image of Louise asking me if I planned to go into the villa, Louise telling me she rented that room, Louise smiling at me sadly when I left.

I felt the effect of the injection almost immediately. The pain stopped. I was afraid that I was bleeding to death. Struggling, I managed to look, to touch myself. There was no blood.

"I won't have time to see Louise tonight," I thought.

Then it occurred to me that I might not ever see her again, that I might be an invalid for the rest of my life.

I lay there feeling perplexed, trying very hard to control my breathing, resigning myself to the inevitable, fortifying my soul. I remembered that the pencil Louise had given me and my notebook were both in my pocket. I decided to write everything down before the effect of the anesthetic wore off.

I wrote with extraordinary rapidity, as if a superior will impelled me and helped me.

The bombing has just begun again. I am growing weaker —And now my solitude is all-encompassing.

The Great Theater

ANDRÉ PIEYRE DE MANDIARGUES

Translated by John Biguenet

All the actors (and actresses) finished the same day, on a decree of the khan that they be, after strangulation, mummified within their own wax effigies, painted and costumed, in order to preserve for future generations the image of drama and comedy as this century loved them. The great theater is no longer open except on the coldest mornings of the season, when the mercury is a Chinese fingernail below zero. The masters have maintained the hall, which is as it was before, except for the roof above the stage which was destroyed for no reason. When the curtain rises, frigid air enters and swirls. So one only goes in furs, with double-lined gloves of wool, trimmed in cat's fur, to the orchestra or to the balcony; the boxes are abandoned, because black tie and bare shoulders are still *de rigueur*. One no longer goes to the great theater except to see the snow fall into the emptiness there, against the backdrop of purple and gold, and to listen to the sound of the snow beating softly upon the velvet.

The Entry of Christ in Havana

SEVERO SARDUY

Translated by Suzanne Jill Levine

"The serpent, the emerald clarity, I saw it by my head, splatter-
ing vinegar; but not Mortal, not even his footsteps in the dust
I swallow searching for him, in the stones that cut my feet, in
the red bramble. Of what did he drink? Of the pasture of what
animals has he eaten? Did thirst kill him? Turn his bones to
ashes? Dry his throat and eyes? Are they the ones that look at
me, burnt, ashen, flanked with threads of blood? Is this the
promised orchard, this absence of trees, this gnashing of
teeth?"

Mercy could see herself finding him, draped in damasks,
carrying her bleeding breasts on a tray. She saw herself as an
infanta, flower of Aragon, open-winged plateresque bird, fixed
among apples and snakes from Flemish tapestries, on her head
the felt miter, the cardinal's hat of worsted tassels, the three-
cornered hat, the round and octagonal gold hat; tattooed in
Mudéjar borders, engraved in the heraldic purple of the

Courts, written in the sky of an engraving among masts and contorted angels, pointing toward the port of Cadiz. She dreamed her face was deformed by the churrigueresque style, by provincial woodworks, by a rock garden reflected in the volute of a mimbar. She imagined herself, the poor thing, leaving the Palace of Two Waters, bent under the weight of crackling jewels, the pace of her sorrel horse punctuated by a band of Moroccan tambourines, convoyed by Indians, yes, Indians with Brazilian parakeets, baskets of tobacco and sugar cane. She even sniffed the nearby scent of brown sugar, and of the black sweat she tasted with her fingertip, an expert sampler, and of aguardiente and rotten orchids.

That's what Mercy wanted to be, conqueror of Mortal and the world, a new Cid, bastion of Castille, inquisitor of the Mohammedans and the circumcised; she wanted to cross the Manchegan dust again, galloping over broken turrets with a drove of steeds, swaying baroque incensories over shit-stained Korans, founding monasteries, beheading Almoravide princes, then washing herself with holy water.

. . . "He would travel in the morning. The branches would sprinkle dewdrops upon his horse's mane, and would hide the sun from him as he proceeded, letting through only the necessary light. The growing clarity sowed pieces of gold in his clothing, elusive to his fingers. There were fruits so full and of such delicate skin, that they seemed like liqueurs waiting to be imbibed without the need of a glass, and there were running waters where pebbles crackled like jewels in the hands of beautiful women . . ."[1]

It didn't last long. Of little use were so many gold trinkets. Banners and rumpled rags, mitered and scabby heads: they all rot. Whose stench is it? Who tilts the scale of the vanities? On

[1] Adaptation of a poem by Mutanabbí (915–965) *wafir, nun,* number 175, translated by Emilio García Gómez.

one plate of the balance, the dried, bald heads of Help and
Mercy, crowning the diadems that once crowned them; on the
other their bibles and viscera. Who will save them? Who's the
highest bidder? Going through his Mansions, searching for
Mortal dead or alive, pregnant with him, so did the Faithful
fall on the Sierra of Ronda, so did the pistol shots surprise
them, the cracking of Toledan swords clearing the way, the
hoarse "hands up" of the bandits and hands pawing their hips,
the smell of men and wine.

They defended themselves with their nails. They waved
papal bulls and amulets in their faces. The blasphemers' thirst
was greater. Now they're rolling on the ground, two-bit whores,
courtesans for a glass of sangría, their cheeks bitten, their
shoulders tattooed with enemy coats of arms. Swinging their
hips they go, flamenco dancing in the farmhouses, dragging
their Saint Theresa sandals, yes, with those dried and porous
nougat faces, and wine-flushed eyes, bent over their nags like
harassed picadors, dragging, downtrodden Easter Virgins with
their false gold trinkets.

In spite of those spites they want to dance. They shout
"I have the blood of kings in the palm of my hand!" and they
tap their heels again and again. But they yawn. The guitars are
out of tune. They fall out of step. Remain nailed to the platform. Get rings under their eyes. Cramps. They sweat. Their
eyes go dry on them, and then they see by their heads a serpent,
an emerald clarity.

Threadbare Virgins? Never! They retrieve their money
(but their honor, oh no!—they say). Under those rags they
wear silks, that pregnancy has been girdled by wide sashes, and
they bear the signatures of Córdoban silversmiths on forged
bracelets, lockets of saints' bones, charms that Mortal once
wore, coffer to keep his locks in. Do you feel sorry for them,
wearing the common wide hats of ruffians and muleteers?

Well, underneath are turbans that are jugs of doubloons and, of the sandals, the double sole is a genealogical tree of repoussé leather. Yes, they wear their ancestry on their feet, the gaudy things; they step on the grapevines of more than one crown:

That wine made viceroyships of provinces, ennobled generations of dealers and slave drivers. They search for an impossible, it's true, but they travel equipped for anything. They peddle advertisements for gambling houses and bee-hives—the brothels of Malaga—; in those cells, Apocryphal beggars, fortune-tellers, procuresses bribe black princesses, houris of Magreb harems, badly castrated eunuchs who answer them with their contralto voices:

HELP and MERCY *(hands clasped, eyes turned toward the sky— and in them the cross reflected, of course):* Sad hermaphrodites, by the law of contrasts you must know of him, he slept in these beds, did you not wash his private parts in the ablutions of before and after the act, did you not kiss the rings on his feet, anoint his chest with holy oils and cinnamon, perfume the air, as he passed, with jasmine pomegranates?

And the chorus of smeared fat men answers moaning over the orange-studded crowns, rending their white cloaks.

THE CHORUS *(the languid sopranos in their cells, accompanied by cymbals):* Yes! We saw him twice, twice did he honor our beds. We tasted of his juice and today we felt his thirst more inextinguishable than the *ayma;*[2] he tempered us like guitars, filled our cups . . . he left for Córdoba, he left for Medina, he stayed, all at once, because he is everywhere!

---

[2] A thirst, which the ancient Arabs had, for she-camel milk.

THE WAIT IN MEDINA-AZ-ZAHARA[3]

Not capitals, but wooden caps perforated with Koranic letters; the tortoiseshell of the texts appears once and again around those heads like the small animals in a Zirí dynasty plate, forming praises and precepts, and from those star-shaped symmetries a jet-black foliage descends—the matted hair of the Moorish Mademoiselles—twisted around the marble columns of their bodies. At their feet, a still river, the blue dust that was once paved with ponds and fountains. In it, water within water, the Azahara had dissolved.

That murmur of cisterns now belongs to the growing bramble; that dampness, an orange glow, levitates over the ground: a garden which the sun duplicates and evaporates; those terraces, cellars, their celebrations, mournings.

Help and Mercy bend down to listen: nothing, not even the birds have remained. So do the Veiled and Vigilant spend day and night at the ruins, waiting.

"Waiting is to become nothing"—they hum from time to time, and over their quartered bodies they let serpents creep. They are salamanders, sweet vermin; they offer that stillness to Mortal.

They neither eat, nor drink, nor join their stiffened eyelids. They decipher the neighboring capitals and from that reading receive omens of The Arrival and patience. Then they smile with their floury cracks, move their pupils of white and pink radii, and think that the joyful day is near.

So passes a time that has neither direction nor measure, until a crew of excavators approaches the palace. Stucco ruins, someone points out, and they crumble. From that rubbish,

[3]Medina-Az-Zahara, near Córdoba, palace built in 936 by Adb Er Rahman Anasir III for his favorite Azahara.

dusting themselves, two lady wildcat and bible vendors step out. Again they arouse the peasants' surprise, standing there in the middle of the chorus, frozen in speech-making poses; in their baskets, felines battle among psalms.

"Not for these rough stones, oh peasants, nor for archeological treasure whatsoever did we come; but rather for signs of our lord. You look for empty palaces; we a king who deserves them. The stones are already ascending. Pray tell us if near them he has passed. His name is Mortal and 'he wears the celestial robe from the looms of Almería.'"[4]

The Sancho Panzas want to mount their horses and run from the almond-eyed divinities.

IN A DREAM

Questioning, the Majas jump up and down in front of the foreman. Carriers of banderillas, they wave them like double piccolos and extricate their little feet from the ground, crossing them, striking first one hip then the other with them, dancers of the Aragonese jota. Are they going to hurl a javelin? No, they run, jump, touch each other in air; the crack is that of two small mildewed plates, or of a tambourine full of water.

The foreman wants to catch them and runs below, his hands open, awkward sunflowers, following the route of the Skilled Ones.

The Dog Heads picture themselves: in levitation, disarrayed angels, made of striated cubes, heads on backward, false tresses—tiaras of stones and sticks—falling, gold in gold, in a goblet which they raise between their hands. An indigo cloth covers them and on it, concentric creases, elbows and knees are insinuated. These touch (and cross), because the Princesses are

[4]Verse from Ben Guzmán, twelfth century.

two mountebanks, and the ground the letters of the gospel.

The foreman, way below, bearded, following them with his eyes, throwing pieces of earthen jugs at them to make them trip and fall, yes, they see him with half-moon horns, lanceolated ears and a tail of black bristles wagging in the air (not to mention the other, that exposed and overflowing earthen vessel); he drools, he wants to lick their feet.

They, naked intertwined herons over a plate of grapes and laurels, nailed upon a wooden heraldry, in red on the white half, in Prussian blue on the feathered half.

Help and Mercy were sleeping on a pallet, among bull and satyr heads, knees, volutes of Corinthian capitals and pieces of Omeyan plates. So did day discover the rubble and aforementioned plate of grapes, and the foreman the other giver of fire, their bodies sweetly naked under the sheets. It is true that, as in the dream, he licked their feet. He drank of them. He left on their breasts a smell of olives. They awoke damp and startled. Help shouted: "rascals, scoundrels, satyrs." And Mercy: "heretics, fiends." They leapt from the cushions, and not to the dust but to a carpet which covered it. Where the foreman had left the trace of his calloused feet when, playing the innocent, he came to them.

"Here, oh chaste mothers, is this souvenir *(and he pointed to the carpet with a king-of-hearts gesture),* a sign of Mortal's stay here that he left before he moved on. Give it to them— he said to me—so that they will love it as they love me." (And he turned dancingly on his heel.) Let it not surprise us then that the Fat Heads, still naked, parade the carpet among the ruins. They caress it, yes, they offer it raisins, fresh cheese, and goat's milk, they stand in front of it so that the sun won't fade it, they call it "banner," or "godgiven," or "burnt water."

HELP *(yawning):* Mortal thought of our honor: a carpet to carpet us. Sold, it would make our fortune, pawned, our bed and board, traded to the looms of Almería, our heaviest jewel.

MERCY *(who perfumed it with incense):* Shut up, magpie, potbelly. Giving it to you is like throwing rare diamonds to swine. Fool, these threads of gold have meaning, Mortal's tongue is in them. A woven message; it cannot be taken for tatters.

Does Help wave hers? No. It's her laugh: little bones in a tumbler, sand dragged away by the river.

"You numbskull, you're stuffed with vulgar sayings. Nothing says nothing. Let's sell it quickly, or it will be coveted by bandits and rats. Dust comes to dust. Water rots the threads."

"Those threads of your fate are already stinking, Sancha, Pot of Meatballs. Go away! Here's your part. Finish it off in pork and beans."

The scissor grates, bites the plush along the middle, like it does the fate of the Pale Ones. It's when the carpet is already cut that they look at each other, look again and immediately embrace in a jeremiad, howling. The unhappy creatures blow out their snot, riprap their clothes, bend over as if with stomach cramps, twitched into grimaces that cannot possibly disfigure them more than they are now. They're a lament, a breast-beating, a flamenco cry that doesn't stop.

"Look what we have done" *(and they pat each other on the back).*

"It was my fault. I, the transcendental, the fool" (Mercy).

"No, mine: the sweet tooth, never full" (Help).

And they hug and kiss. But it's too late.

Note: In the carpet, FAITH, a naked young woman (she covers one breast and her sex with her hands), hurries to enter the dining room, but already in front of the door, blocking her way, is EXPERIENCE, a hook-nosed and bilious old woman. Who in turn is stopped by a lazy round-faced page covered with a hat

of feathers which open like lyres before the dried face of the
old woman. The women whisper and nudge each other, relishing the banquet.

The blond prince has tasted the soup and is smiling.
Under the table, between his legs, a frightened boy hides and
two greyhounds play. The main dish, hog or wild boar meat,
has been presented in a bowl in the shape of a ship, the sail
is speckled skin and the wooden mast ends in a capital shaped
like a pineapple. There are three lit tapers, goblets full of nuts,
and a plate of open pomegranates.

(Mercy inquired into the meaning of the cloth. She unstitched it from the lining to see if it hid a written message;
she only found the unraveled back of plates and heads: islands
of knots, black stitches. The scar of the stitches traced another
banquet in the canvas that was like a joke on the visible one,
dull and full of clods. The plate of pomegranates was a dark
green patch; the dinner guests cross-eyed puppets. Next to the
border a left hand pointed to a striated piece of material,
separated from the rest.

Tearful Mercy resewed the carpet, pricking her fingers.)

A dark young man, HICCUPS, turns down the splendid
food and gives orders to the band. Which consists of three
flutists with puffed cheeks, a mandolin, harp, and drum. The
harpist, almost a dwarf, seems to be conducting the group. To
his right the mandolin player bends his head under the weight
of an abundantly convoluted turban, and to his left, the sad
drummer tightens his muscles to hold up his instrument (a
barrel with two leather skins and a chain) and press a perforated
piccolo in his mouth.

Next to him another character (a musician) is showing
FAITH and EXPERIENCE something, but we can't see what it is,
because there's a darning patch in its place.

MERCY

would redden stones with burning ash, and wait over the coals
for dawn, like a thief in ambush. She would fast standing, in
the dampest part of the cloister, repeat short prayers and Salve
Reginas. She abandoned, for their leniency, her confessors and
taking her half of the carpet (which she had unstitched again,
interpreted according to numbers and stars, and made into the
object of prayers), she spread it before a calvary, so that the
faithful would step on it, and stain it with their scabs and tears.

She begged. She lived on bread and water. She suffered
the hair shirt. She scourged herself. She drank bile and vinegar.
She considered herself a strumpet and begged them to scorn
her.

Her eyes sank into the back of her head from keeping
watch at night, her feet were cracked from walking barefoot.
She was reduced to mere bones. She lost her hair.

Note: By the right edge of the cloth, on a strip that feet had
not profaned, remained an arm of the prince and the body of
HICCUPS. A very pious little nun believed she saw in him our
Lord. So she cut him off, framed him in a shroud, and hung
him behind a door.

HELP

What a smell of cinnamon! It's just that Help, along with
cowbells and cowskulls, had placed fragrant timber among her
tresses, certain that so much fragrance can only favor the sale.
Although stiff, one would say that a hundred goats are grazing
when she moves, such is the chiming of her tins. She comes
wrapped in the merchandise: the purchase is the temptation to
another more pleasureful one. In other words: she covers her

nakedness with her half of the carpet, and apart from that, she wears only the tuneful hairdo.

So to the Palace she went. And lost both cloths: the brocade, and the one I leave to your imagination. She came out dressed, and if she was clinking, it was less from tin cans than from gold trinkets.

The marquis, who was a veteran, did not with this act do injustice to his past victories. Surprise did not unnerve him, and he consummated the conquest with the ritual chimings. When he finally sheathed his saber, they celebrated copiously with aged wines.

Note: The carpet ended up in a winter dining room. Since the scissor snippings left the prince armless, the embroiderers decided to eliminate him and with him the floral border that framed three of the sides. They hung it among horns and rifles, on a wooden closet, sewn to a blue wreath with goats and *puttis.* They made bedspreads with the fringes; the body of the prince, the victim of two restorations, ended up in the garbage.

TO HELP

You came out laden with gold trinkets, but you quickly went downhill. You broke your incensory dancing the *pompompero,* your palms and heels grew calloused, you lost honor and hair. You dragged yourself, hide and bones, smeared white and carmine, down the roads of Fuengirolas like a beggarly holy-man without once listening to a muezzin, or seeing the white of domes, or hearing any voice to break your fast. Your last shreds were spent on *manzanilla* and *anis del Mono;* you shuffled around, getting drunk in the holds of Magreb ships; at night you anointed yourself with perfumes and went out to wait for the harvesters. They left you their sweat, semen, and a few nickels. You returned with rings under your eyes, yel-

lowed hair, bitten lips. You sang, you were an Arabian cantor
with a great pink bow, a timbrel player; you pierced your
graying pompom with an arrow of sparkles.

They called you Easy Francie, the Living-Dead. You
couldn't even drag your own bones around any more and you
cursed Mortal, the carpet, and the day you were born; you were
a hook-nosed and bilious old woman.

TO MERCY

You deprived yourself of bracelets and of the honey crullers you
so much liked; you gave up your veil for the stain and to the
poor, your garments. You called yourself Ruin, Servant, you
kissed the feet of the lepers and shared with them your water
with noodles. You mortified your hide to the point of swoon-
ing. You enjoyed raptures, ecstasy, the gift of tears; you even
got to hear voices, to see next to you a pillar of light that rose
to the sky; you made light with a fistful of grass (you covered
one breast and your sex with your hands); you forgot your
senses and saw the emerald clarity, the serpent that appears
before the chosen. The one you didn't see was Mortal, nor did
you know what happened to him, nor did you remove his face
from your chest, your only memory, sharper than thorns, looking at you, turning your guts inside out, buried in your heart
like an amber.

So one day Mercy, who—rosary in hand—was dragging her
feet over stones and bramble, thought she saw herself in the
distance, advancing toward herself.

"Another miracle!"—she thanked the Giver aloud. She
continued walking. Then she ran into Help.

"Let's sing!"—they exclaimed. *(And taking each other's
hand):*

There's neither scourge nor reward
faithful the infidel
The quick and the dead
Dance with the Minstrel.

And they cried in their joy.

"I don't know how to say it"—sobbed One; and the Other:—"I don't know how to say it."

And so on till they calmed down, and untied their tongues. They were just turning the place into a lachrymatory with their tears when a bunch of drunken peasants came by. They sang as they walked, with canteens and sickles flung over their shoulders and a pickled stag on a pole. They laughed in a grand manner, so outrageous and insane did they find the weepers. They wanted to dance with them. They made signs with their hands touching themselves you know where, and in fun; they poked at one another. The girls seemed in such great need, with such appetites, that they threw them rolls and raisins. Although starving they tossed them back like hot coals and shouted that "the hunger they suffered was another kind; only the news of a Spaniard with skin like tasseled corn, a chaste tongue, and javelin eyes would satisfy them."

The men, laughing heartily:

"To Cadiz he goes, and on wings."

Hearing this made them so smiley and content that they asked for the same rolls and raisins they had just refused, not to mention meat, wine, and spices. Swiftly, they left.

They spent a happy day. By the next morning they were already confined in black cloth, one of them in a hairnet of starched cambric, the other with her bald disgrace still exposed. They took with them a mare, and lame at that, a missal and a jug of ginger. Had they killed a nun? Pillaged a convent?

Where'd they get all those rags? I don't know.

Joy made them proliferate.

Already they play leapfrog and ring-around-the-rosy—"it is not weeping but the plucking of guitars that our Shepherd wants" —they lose the green ivy of their eyelids, they laugh, yes, just like the words say, they laugh and make haste, Mercy high on her saddle, under a fringed parasol which, opened, propels the animal when there's a good wind; Help in front, pulling the reins, parting the underbrush with her cane, crossing herself at every cliff.

MERCY: A day of merriment this is, since not of mourning. Let us not exhaust more hymnals since Mortal awaits us. He, before an absence split in two, is now a sole thirst drying us, a mute figure among stones.

HELP: Then we didn't know how to look for him. Ask for him. We felt his hunger and, crazy little feet, we ran all over the place.

MERCY: We were birds in air.

HELP: And now salamanders in fire!

Already the amazon unfolds parchments, wets her forefinger with saliva to feel the wind's direction, makes note of bird frequency, launches the filly to a gallop and hums: "east" or "northeast," with her little flute voice.

When blown from the stern their contentment is great; they think Mortal is promoting their union and pushing them toward him.

MERCY *(first voice):*

> Look at me, and you will have eyes
> and I yours, to refresh my own.

And HELP *(second voice):*

> You entered me. You anointed my tonsure
> and like burning coals left my senses.

The duo frightened birds and lizards; snakes and bucks glided behind the black bramble to spy on them. The creaking wicker of their hampers held rugs, wooden saints and carbines; in a pot, among small laurel leaves, cumin, capers, and red pepper, a deer tail and two ears clanked. A good bullfight they must have put on to deserve such distinguished trophies!

So they searched, ay, but didn't find. Wounded with love they walked, ran through the fields. They smelled only of sweet basil and rosemary; they ate only grass and flowers; painted birdies, they crossed forests and streams in one thrust, they shouted at the top of their lungs to see if he heard them; they inscribed on their rings—tin hoops that were still theirs—the word WOUNDER, and they trained homing pigeons to carry them in all directions.

They paused at every tree, to see if he had engraved his name; they distinguished the different greens in the grass, searching for the faded trace of his soles; they spent their nights in silence, watching: they heard the sap push out the buds, the gills of fish palpitate, and far away, on the other shore, the fire in the eyes of tigers, the sleep of men, the vigil of muezzins. A warm air enfolded them as if he had breathed it; then they dreamed intensely of him, to see if he'd appear, they repeated his name till they were breathless, to conjure it: they wanted to invent him with words, count all fish, birds, and fruit, all vermin and bugs, to see if those that nourished him, that he crushed with his step, were missing.

They searched, ay, but didn't find. They wanted to give up, be someone else.

Pigeons under the moon, in great strides they crossed bridges, nights, valleys of white ruins. Finally they saw beyond the hills a light as if from many bright lamps, bounded by a strip of palms. It was the sea: between lines of sand, a line of domes; between deltas of saltpeter, the blue dot of the fortified bay.

Comforted by the view of Cadiz, garland-clustered—guardian angels of the port—they praised and exalted as they laid a tablecloth down by a stream to thus recover their health and give thanks. They were relishing sunflowers with honey and gazing at ships cutting through terraces of foam, when they heard a sound like splitting rafts, and then some cries. Striped by the shadows of willows, fleeing mountain goats were approaching the bank. They jumped over the tablecloth. They turned over the pitcher of wine. After them came two naked, soaking shepherds. They stopped at the sight of wooden bowls, the toppled pitcher of red wine, the purple-stained grass, and frightened Help and Mercy, wounded partridges, open pomegranates in hand.

The Flamenco Girls stood up, and shyly turned their faces toward the stream. With one hand they covered their eyes—Help put a little mirror in front of hers to look at the shepherds without dishonoring herself—with the other, they pointed to the pitcher, accusingly.

The shepherds stammered "a good lunch to you," and with the wet underpants rumpled in their hands, they covered what they thought most urgent: the popular gesture of Modesty. Above the damp cloths their pubic hairs showed in minute spirals; other hairs, like down, shaded their chests. They were strong and golden and had identical beards and hair. The shepherds blushed at seeing them so covered: flowered cretonne fitted them snugly like shrouds from where their hands, desiccated herons, and shaven heads emerged; a white bow on their last lock crowned them like a weather vane. Under those consumptive butterflies the Deers smiled.

And offering the shepherds the bowl of pomegranates:

"Pray do not stop, your mountain goats are escaping."

"Yes, we were running after fleeing goats, and find our-selves before wounded fawns."

And that quaint music? It's hand organs. Look: turn the crank. Don't let the roll stop. That holey roll is the music. Time as a honeycombed parchment. Look at them. The Polliwogs enter Cadiz. The boys follow them in throngs, singing ballads and clapping. The organs of Cadiz slide their sounding boxes, painted with jumping turtles, silver flowers, and Indian birds, around Help and Mercy. And they escape, they don't want that music, they want Mortal's, which is silent music.[5]

They ask around for him. The saffron-haired players fol-low them, big puppets rolling cranks and heads. Hoods. And the girls cover their ears, hide in the doorways—are they cry-ing? They want to give up, be someone else.

They searched, yes, they asked, they bribed, they begged for advice from door to door. Nobody understood them. People would push them. Throw them old bread and pots of rotten soup. They caught their fingers in doors. Remained stuck there. Children threw stones at them. Cats came to sniff them.

FRAGMENTS FROM HELP AND MERCY'S
LOG BOOK

1

HELP: *(Isle and Islets of
the Queen.* [6]) Yes, I discern

[5] In this passage, and many others, may Saint John forgive me.
[6] An archipelago south of Camagüey.

this sea's roof is of fern,
and, its towers are lances.
Are they coral the lusters
on these insular clusters?
MERCY: No, they're holey countenances.
Don't you see that those red dots
are mushrooms and were eye slots
of turtles and drowned dancers?

FRAGMENTS FROM HELP AND MERCY'S LOG BOOK

2

Yesterday the sea was orange-hued and calm. We saw a school of sirens come near the ship, some of them caught on to the prow and kept us company during many leagues. The sailors threw them walnuts and hazelnuts, which they like so much. It was joyous to see them frolic in the water.

Afraid of running over tritons at night, we navigated cautiously; these besieged us in bands of as many as one hundred and did not leave us till dawn, remaining tangled in gulfweed. Many birds and angels, never further than a mile away from the coast, flew by; land must be near . . . "We saw a branch of fire fall into the sea."[7]

This morning, fish, green bands in the water—islands? Help danced for the sailors, clad only in sea shell necklaces . . . I said a Salve Regina.

A wind blows from the stern and sea horses stick on to the hull. Help caught some and fried them in oil. The sailors, it

[7]Columbus.

seems, found them delicious. A long siesta. We're running out
of drinking water.

SUBSEQUENT REPORTS identify Help and Mercy as two organists
in the cathedral of Santiago, Cuba. The Bacardí Museum holds
in its collection of engravings two scores that they composed
and, in all probability, in their own handwriting: one is a Stabat
Mater. If rather simple in instrumentation, the text is correct.
The other is a vernacular song about love and Cupid's artful
deceptions, followed by a quadrille for clavichord; both are
undated in the original. Which is the composer of each work,
and if a "Mourning Song" in two voices, for soprano and
contralto, also belongs to the composer of the first, and if "To
the pineapple and sun of Cuba," a song for mezzosoprano and
piano, clearly sweetened by the Italian operetta, belongs to the
composer of the second, are debatable matters, but after all,
secondary.

Other news less worthy of credit—handed down by dubi-
ous oral tradition—testifies that the famous women who, following the route of the liberating invasion, entertained the
island in sheds, or under white pilgrim and nomadic tents, are
none other than the Moorish Girls.

Engravings of the times, anonymous or signed by local
craftsmen, portray the *Ontos* Girls against a background of
banners and tapers.

But if these episodes are but rough drafts, written over
them have remained those that took place during the last days
of Cadiz and the first of Santiago. There's a log book in which
the Fixed Eyes bear witness to the exaltation which "the incan-
descence of the tropics" produced in them and they even
indulge in a dialogued ten-line stanza, silly and metrically precise, on the Isles and Islets of the Queen, an archipelago off the
southern coast of Camagüey.

It is after the landing that their common history branches

off, or duplicates itself in mocking inversion, as if the facts danced dizzily around themselves.

We shall follow the version that covers the days of choral glory in the Santiago cathedral, up until the disappearance of the organists in Havana, victims of a snowstorm.

DOMUS AUXILII

1: "Hey, by the way, what happened to Mortal? Don't they keep searching for him, have they forgotten him?"

"Why honey!"—Help answers, and cartwheels out of her hammock. "Have some, kid, it'll cool you off"—and she gives me a guanábana milk shake.

1 *(delicious!)* tips the glass: Through the bottom I see her within a milky circle, sugar-stained and concave.

"What can I do for you, sweetie?"—she continues *(How she's changed! I say to myself)*. "Reality is a simple matter of birth and death, so why worry ourselves sick? If you don't change, you get stuck, pal, so live and let live!"

I put the glass down to hear her better. She waves her hands, shuffles around, talks with her hands on her hips.

"Look, honey, we searched for him all right, but if he turns up, great, and if not *(she yawns, ooh, it looks like she's going to swallow me)* we'll get through the day with the help of siesta. Which of the two is blonder?" *(And she raises—what sunlight!—a bamboo curtain.)*

Pale sunflowers speckle her body: reflections from a stained-glass window. Shadows of arabesques break between her hands: iron grates, city blocks of pink glass. The light scratches her, a smell of molasses surrounds her, the purple of the roofs hardly differs from that of her eyes.

1: I've got to admit, Help, you're really at home here. The gold of these tropical fruits glows no brighter than the gold of your hair, angels of Caney county crown you with medlars, write your name on mameys.

HELP: Come on, sonny, don't be so Cuban. *(and calling)* Mercy, Mercy, listen to what this aborigine *(that's me)* is saying.

MERCY: In some mood for natives I am!—She comes in from the kitchen, half-naked, with a bunch of bananas hanging from her waist and singing:

> Mamá those singers so gay
> are they from ol' Havana bay?
> oh how I like their rhythm
> oh how I'd like to know them . . .

She flops in a wicker chair. And fans herself with a palm leaf, opening her legs in a way that to tell the truth leaves me perplexed. It's incredible how heat loosens folks up. But let's cut this short and move on to something else.

Let's climb to the lecterns of the Schola Cantorum. Before them the Passion Flowers have been decaying, extravagant vestry junk, holy water larvae. Poor things, they spend the night among these platforms, ringing the bells and oiling the organs. Their days go by in Te Deums, siestas, and bread with sardines. When they leave the cathedral, pious mustached women shout at them from behind curtains, envious of the clerical life they lead, organizing catechism and bingo parties (they nickname them The Bats). Sunday afternoons, services over, they slip away to dance at the Medlar, so they say. There they rub against mulattoes and slanty-eyed natives; they go drunk to the beer halls, to wait for morning—remembering Mortal?—in the bacchanal.

That winds them up for another week of climbing the tower. But, as they say, you can't ring the bell and march in the procession, and this gig of the Little Shopping Bags is in for a bad ending.

When did the Mulatto first come before them? How did his diplomaed tenor voice, his violin, fill that vociferous old age with enthusiasm? How did he gain access, not to chapels and vestry, but to tower platforms, and to the most secret beds? He made the organs resound and, long live the virgin!, the Cranachian bellies of their organists.

HELP: "He brought those yellowing texts back to life with his sweet breath!"

MERCY: "He scared away the moths with his nigger smell!"

These devout women were already moving from the Spanish ascesis to Creole mysticism; they were the martyrs and confessors of half of Santiago (virgins they were not), but they bore one dead weight: their scales. So, seeing them pedal in vain, and finger sixteenth notes instead of thirty-seconds, and scribbles instead of eighth notes, the Bishop of the diocese, that plump good-natured fellow with clammy hands, ordered that an "expert" assist them, since "it takes more than fervor to play the organ" and "my daughters, technique is everything in divine matters." Yes, the canon was a technocrat, so the next day, come what may, he unswervingly appeared in the deambulatory arm in arm with the violinist. The latter came in a Bachian jacket, with his kinky hair slicked down; when he took up the bow, his hands fluttered like two long-tailed doves. He was merry and frolicsome, and from the minute he saw Help and Mercy he knew that high music was in store for them.

"If in the towers"—said the sepia Paganini, taking from his sleeves a lace handkerchief—"there were spiral ramps for carriages, we could set up the clavichords and, chorus raised, sing a Salve Regina that would be heard out to sea!"—And he drew in the air with his handkerchief, the form of a pineapple.

"Oh!"—breathed Help, braking with the pedal.
"Let's sing!"—ordered Bruno. And he gave the key.

Oh the sadness, my friend, of those middays! Of cockroached
skies, yellow rain. Big birds would hover among the ropes of the
bell tower or fall shrieking, beheaded against the lightning rod.
But neither the little heads throbbing between the cracks of
the boarded floor, nor the blood-clotted feathers prevented
Help and Mercy from attacking the midday onion pie. They'd
eat it standing, among bunches of Easter ribbons, remains of
ransacked sepulchers, and moldings from the kneeling stool.

They would cry from two to four, rolled into balls among
the cushions of a confessional. They would cry and sneeze, and
it was neither snuff nor something similar that they smelled,
but rather the fine dust of the covers, sand that would saturate
the naves, suspending—golden asterisks—fleas and lice.

Figure it out: two hours daily of lachrymal secretion, with
the little they'd drink and the lot they'd urinate—thus the
prosperity of the east gardens: gargoyles emptied into them—
and you'll see why they were drying up, like pickled lizards.

Around four, that old devil siesta would start putting the
flea in their ear. To shake it out they'd ring bells and vespers
a few times, drink some cane liquor (which they'd send up in
a thermos bottle in the morning, along with other victuals) and
they'd give their all to the rigors of the ruled staff. On the bells,
fleeing the clappers, blind baby owls would bump their heads.

To judge by the concentric iridescent veins (so pretty!)
which daily tears left in the felt of the cushions, the weeping
season was long and full. You can see that they resisted—did
the memory of Mortal still sustain them?—the sudden attacks
of the honeyed heat; you can see that disorder frightened them.

Till one day: (1) They grew a little ovoid belly which
waddled before them as they'd climb the spiral staircase; (2)

they got bored with everything, they shat on scales and theory, they let their hairs split and dirt settle on the suspenders of their slips; (3) to everything they answered "whatever you say, pal" "no need to kill yourself." In short: siesta corroded their bones, turned them yellow, a malignant anemia; no big deal, it just gave them the Caribbean torpor (sweetly!) in its mildest form, which is the cabbage soup, and the daily *danzón,* and the mattress.

They'd remain stupified on the platforms for days on end, never descending to the maddening crowd, only opening tin cans and playing cards. So that at noon one day, the priest, accompanied by the plump theocrat, climbed the creaking steps on all fours and surprised them, at Te Deum hour, in full snore.

"Better tuned—exclaimed the servant of the servants of the lord—"are your fluty bronchial tubes, than those of this dilapidated harmonium!"

And in their drowsiness, talking through their noses, they flapped their hands in his face. "Come on pal, we're up to our necks in pedaling. We finger the keyboard all day long and not a single saint comes down. We entreat in vain. There's a great deafness up there. We've had it: our phalanx, second phalanx, and third phalanx hurt from fingering that keyboard so much!"

Now that you've heard them, darlings, you'll understand why when Bruno, jazzy violinist and steady drinker of Santiago *prú,* arrived, he found the way paved.

This will look redundant, but the classes began in perfect harmony. The virtuoso taught them Misereres, but also sarabands, so from the Salve Regina, alas, they soon went on to the chaconne. How did he introduce them to the daiquiri, the baroque crown of Oriente province drinks? How did they become so addicted to the Santiago *"chiringuito"*? Where did they learn the *"saoco"* recipe, that is: *agua-ardiente* with cocoanut milk, which they were already pronouncing like Cubans as *"agüecoco"*? Who taught them that bad habit: leaving tamales, pork pies, and deviled ham rolls among the organ strings, where they'd sometimes even rot?

Already the cover of the organ, shining more from varnish than from centenaries, was a washboard marked with whitish circles: the traces of small glasses of crushed ice, overflowing with Bacardí and maraschino cherries, which they left there, in the frantic dancing. And I say frantic dancing, because while One scribbled four or five *pasodobles* on the artefact, the Other danced off heat in the arms of the Maestro, when he wasn't in those of Rita Pla, the new pupil, an image seller and a soprano in her free time.

When they had celebrated the dancing gods, they'd go back to the lessons. How nice those trios were, with Bruno in the center of the organ and the Blond Cowlicks on either side, industriously following his hands with theirs, from C to C, from keyboard to knee, yes sir, they'd give him a finger and he'd take the rest! Do you remember Help, your hair messed by the blowing tubes, coiling your matted peroxide hair around them, golden serpents on golden pillars, musical taffy that you were, you naughty wench?

HELP *(a bit grief-stricken):* Yes, kid, of course I remember; how can I forget those times? Listen, get me a drink . . . What could have become of those waterfront bars, the Black and White, the Two Worlds, where we'd end up shipwrecked in the morning? What became of the Santiago by-the-hour hotels, those gardens open only for the few? Mercy would run naked among colonists and Haitian smugglers, dancing Lully's dances, as she would call those drum beatings . . .

(And we hear a Lully dance which becomes a vaudoux drumbeat. We go back to the times of the cathedral tower.)

AT THE SANTIAGO MUSEUM

neither detailed branches, earthly paradises, faces made of vegetables, nor patient gardens painted leaf by leaf were scarce.

Peeping out of the windows of their Noah's Arks, their manes in flames, varnished little blond giraffes passed by. Restorers had returned the eloquence of cockatoos and gold of roosters to the palms. On the same branches hummingbirds and mockingbirds perched. Among the stones, white and quartered like the giraffes, lizards slept; the one with little verticle ears, the rodent, would flit through the reeds—the raw red of its scalped hide denounced it—.

In the engravings Latin alternated with Old French in humpbacked letters.

"*Ara chloroptere! Boselphus Trago Canelus!*"—Mercy would exclaim pointing to the little spheres of fish scales bristled with thorns: miniatures of haddock and snappers.

And the hummingbird sewn to the wood, pinned flyer.

IN THE OTHER ROOM

"Place of Arms on The Night of the Military Parade" and a blurred "View of Havana," by Hill, were gathering dust. Sugary Indians displayed tobacco leaves and cassava pies. Then the collection, the Punishment of the Mace, Punishment of the Mask, and Punishment of the Stocks: Negros tainted in blood, kneeling among shackles and chains.

CHRIST SETS OUT FROM SANTIAGO

Along the naves, tapers in little cups of gilded edges were blinking; in the dark those signs were bat eyes nailed against the altars or swarms of glowworms coming out of a bottle. That light of drizzled sand over Help and Mercy would change them at times into water nymphs, and other times into little candy skulls, depending on how the shadows cut them.

The murmur of crackling wax would join the sound of a rusty clock and this the steps of their bare feet. The feet of the Devout Ones scarcely touched the floor, like a hanged man's feet. Beneath the gravestones they were stepping on, among mushrooms and withered relics, lay eight mitered generations: empty eyes would look at the same archivolts, the identical days would from the lantern yellow the circles of angels in the dome, as light as mist; bundles of bones held in place the gold of the tunics that were incrusted in them, and pressed together, dried cartilage, reliquaries and chalices.

Heads bowed, Help and Mercy advanced toward the vestry. They went reading the In Memoriam engraved in the marble. They touched dark green texts with the tip of their forefingers and crossed themselves. They heard a warbling: it was Rita Pla's vocal exercises. When they pushed open the doors, they found her before Bruno who was raising a baton, her mouth open like someone who's about to spell in the first reading book Acorn Air And.

There was a lukewarm air, of wax, among the closets, and a mustard light among the holy-water pots, incensories and purple puppets with their eyelids on backward. Light filtered through a yellow awning, stretched before the baroque iron work of the window; the wind stretched it—a drum—blowing it—a sail—. Birds were crossing lines on the cloth, and the trolleycars with their long sparking trolleys, in the background of the orange square, outlined by the iron bars, were gods of codices running with burning rattles.

Mercy opened the little platinum mesh pouch that she wore at her waist and out of it came a swollen key, with a double point. She carefully sank it into the lock. The click rang like a bell.

Sprawled in a corner of the display case, elbows folded against his chest and his arm in disks, the Redeemer, foot and headless, was resting. Hooks came out of his wrists and ankles, and from his neck, cut at the Adam's apple, a great screw. He had neither sex nor knee. A tortoise-shell varnish covered him and on his stomach, pale pink. He was worm-eaten. He smelled of incense and naphthalene. On the wounded side you could see a hinge.

On a slab of white wood, stained with ink from the sign HANDLE WITH CARE, his feet and a hand of ovaled nails were exhibited. The other, which gripped a golden flagstaff, and the head, were found in the back of a drawer among broken candelabrums, little Santa Lucía eyes and scapularies.

They put him together in the twinkling of an eye. Bruno screwed on his head until the two little threads of blood which ran down from his eyes continued into those of his neck. Rita combed his beard and with a beer-drenched curler twisted his wig of blond hemp into several snail shell curls which she fastened with a barbed-wire crown. Help perfumed him with her "Attractive and Winning." She took out her string of safety pins. They dressed him in a ruffled slip, crackling with starch and on top, a blanket of rubies and stones from El Cobre Mountain, and snail shells on a string. In his bullfighter's garb he balanced on his flat feet, in the middle of the vestry.

The Christ Fans stepped back to look at him. When they came forward again, they fell on their knees.

WITH GREEN BACKGROUND AND SHOUTING

"Praised be Jesus Christ our Lord who died on the cross to redeem us!"—Help shouted praises till she was hoarse, stretching the e's of "redeem" to the point of choking, catching the impulse in soprano and, poor wretch, ending in bass.

"Have pity on us, ay!" (That was Mercy, and she struck her chest as if she were seized with Saint Vitus's Dance.)

"Long live the King of the Jews and the Cubans!" (That was Rita and she sobbed with emotion.)

And He, before Bruno, looked at himself in the mirror.

"Look how handsome, look how handsome he is!"— shouted a little black girl hanging from the bars of the window.

On the street, cars with loudspeakers passed by; the nasal twang of amplifiers came in along with the crackling of broken glass and screeching of rails.

In the tarnished space of the mirror the small doors opened and the red square of the bonnet, the lace sleeve, the black shirt frills of lively golds appeared: it was the Bishop.

"Oh, my beloved!"—and he patted his stomach.

Through the crack between the shutters you could see a brightness in the naves: the dirty silver of the altars, reddish disks dancing clumsily—copper crosses—.

In the vestry's dampness the faithful were five hanged warriors, going around and around in the same place, dervishes, spinning tops, merry-go-rounds. The grass green, bottle green floor of rhombi met the orange walls at sharp angles, forming a cuneiform space where he reigned, duplicated in the river of quicksilver.

"Hurry up, girls, we'll be leaving in a minute!"—And the Lord Bishop shook a hand bell that was heard again, faraway, returning from the dome.

And he shook a hand bell that was heard again, another time, as if it had sounded in the Kingdom of Death.

"We're leaving!"—In the naves a band of cracked drums, water-filled guitars, and muted rattles broke out.

What a hissing of prayers! What a creaking of benches! Chest beatings. Ejaculations. The weepers sounded maracas—

they played maracas for this burial—and the hoodmasters their
mahogany clavichords. Little devils with palm-leaf skirts and
castles of yellow feathers on their heads crowded into the
baptistery.

He appeared in the door of the vestry, tottering under a
canopy of royal palms held up by Help and Mercy, within a
white white light, as from milk curds. Canticles and cheers.
Under his vault of greenery he advanced among purple strips
of stained-glass windows, shadows of banners, flags.

The sepulcher awaited Him.

You could hear a flapping of wings, like droves of geese:
it was the Black Oblates, they were dressed as angels.

These big Pious Babies were already lined up in the choir
aisle, rosy and smelling of Eau de Cologne, in white piqué
dresses and carrying large palm-leaf baskets, reciting a rosary of
river pebbles and sweating into initialed hankies.

Grumpy dwarfs were stamping their feet behind the altar,
wrapped in bunches of red felt ribbon.

The shrouds were replicas of his face, the standard-bear-
ers' ensigns the color of his blood, the cornets of the Municipal
Brass Band the silver of his tomb.

"Long live the King of Alto Songo!"—that was the hot-
headed misses of the diocese, who had been tippling as they
walked since morning. One of them rattled a maraca.

Electric tapers were lit. Crepe-paper flowers carpeted the
route to the sepulcher. Make way, people, here comes the Verb
of Santiago! The resurrected, sandpapered king was about to
begin the voyage on his aluminum throne. The blood barely
stained his nose and eyelids. Why, it looked like he was going
to laugh!

Now the leader shakes his baton (at his age, that's what he
shakes best). And the chorus sings the first Gloria—What a

triumph for Bruno! Mercy leaves the pulpy palm leaves on the pulpit staircase. She kisses him, sets him on the sepulcher.

Help shouts "Ready!" Someone breaks into tears.

The King totters, then takes off, balancing under a rainfall of jasmine. He advances toward the portico, between lamps of green glass. The flame flits over the chalk of his face, the shine of rotten fish. White and green, the rust of nails, flowers of tetanus, opens in his dried hands and pierced feet.

"Here comes the handsomest fellow of Caney county"— the children clap hands. And take out their bags of confetti.

Creole gentlemen follow him. You've got to admit, that humble vestry wine sure gives a man poise! They march in unison, foot to foot, their stomachs tucked in by In Excelsis Deo sashes.

The Minstrels march, the precious load on their shoulders: in front, Mercy sets the example in her Prussian blue rayon cloak with a cushion sewn on the left shoulder, and Rita Pla. a cushion on her right shoulder, struts in such a way that you'd think it's the lantern of The Bakers' Masked Ball that's being carried and not the Victor of Santiago on his tomb. The poor Redeemer up there, he must be eating himself up! At the rear, Help, in the best of her wigs, and Bruno hold the two back handles of the sepulcher. Look in wonder, brethren, at what four pillars carry the Blond of Blonds, at what caryatids fit for a mausoleum, in short, what four legs for a bench!

Already they're down the central nave. At his passing the faithful close their eyes, kneel; trembling, they kiss the carpet where he has passed. And make the sign of the cross. Others run. Push. Touch him. Tear white lilies from his funeral carriage.

Already they're near the portico. From the high altar you can see him from the back, outlined against the blue rectangle of night, shower of light; hands and handkerchiefs raised. The stones from El Cobre shrine, mortuary jewels, are already glittering on his cloak, stirred by the breeze in the square.

"Lower him!"—Mercy orders—"or his crown will short-circuit on the bulbs of the tympan!"

The bearers stoop. He's outside. The whole square lights up.

"Raise him again!"

And he ascends, standing erect over the sepulcher, proud as a pimp, hoisting a white flag. Behind, red stones, gold stains: the seal of his face on the Pantocrator of Italian mosaic. A silence. Rosary beads passing through fingers. Candles crackling.

The wind on the terraces, whistling through patio palm trees.

Then bells, the hymn. Gentlemen in drill suits and Panamas come out on their balconies, and little girls in straw hats empty baskets of petals. Cigar smoke sweetens the air in slow rings that will break among the fans. The square is full. The people of Santiago sing.

"Straight on, but *moderato*, gents, *per piacere!*"—orders Bruno. And the Blond descends the steps, following a gentle parabola as if on an escalator. The Bishop receives him.

No sooner did he set foot on the ground when beneath the portico appears the sorrowful, ash moon virgin. They've whitened her with rice powder, "so that she really looks pale," her mouth and cheeks, a heart. Her tears, and her seven daggers, are silver.

He crosses the square. Around him trumpets, the rim of the drums, crashing cymbals, shine. The Bishop makes way for him; covered in his hands, the chalice: over the red cloth of his sleeves, gilded lace. In front walk two acolytes swaying incensories. Sinuous ribbons of white smoke. The pale parson drops Latin mumbo jumbo as he goes, and makes crosses in the air with his right hand. Women in black mantillas and high shell combs, and stiff men with candles and branches of lilies, walk on either side.

"Come, people of Santiago, who's more stud than he, and who whiter?"—howl the Cornucopias of Craniums, beating their breasts.

HELP *(who has pinched a cloak with a black and white fiber hood.):* "You leave Santiago to enter Death!"

MERCY *(wielding a shroud in which you see Christ's face in an arrow-pierced heart with the inscription "C loves M."— Christ and Mercy):* "You enter Death to give us Life!"

The old people, bundled up, crowd together on the sidewalks, beneath the greenish halo of the street lamps. Joining hands they watch him go by in his Sunday best, and then withdraw in silence, to kneel on the cushions of the antechamber.

In cracked oil paintings the Virgin shines on her halfmoon, against a blackened sky of sugar mill chimneys, and in the yellowish cardboard of screens a mulatto Christ watches over Santiago: a labyrinth of small sugar plantations and boats.

> Look at them oh crack footed King,
> because you leave they cannot sing

It's Rita, when they stop in front of City Hall where gentlemen greet him from the gates, waving hats. Little devils jingle bells, dancing on one foot before the sepulcher. Against the white façades, the hood masters play their clavichords: black stitches around the holes of their eyes.

Then the procession moves on. Empty terraces, lighted lamps, wicker rocking chairs rocking are left behind, and in the shadows of interiors: burnished clocks, mirrors, opulent pineapple goblets, the ancestral portrait.

In the night's dampness they disappear into poplar groves, into the suburbs.

Now little by little, they are left alone. In the city the tapers' light has traced a white sign, a chalk omega, two inverted fish joined by a thread. Or perhaps a signature.

So they left the last lots behind, the whistle of the land breeze through the mangrove trees, the streaks of saltpeter on the eaves. When they started moving into the thick night, Bruno made him turn his head so that he'd see the rows of windows slowly disappear. Mercy tells that down his cheeks rolled two big tears, and also down his neck, as far as his shoulder blade.

When they straightened his head he saw before him other greens, the surprise of other birds in the calm, the Cuban peasants: little eyes behind windows, lighter than the royal palm leaves of the shutters, Chinese shadows—but in big Panama hats—in front of carbon lamps. They covered the cracks in their walls with newspapers, passed the latch, and between the planks of their whitewashed doors, they peeped out to see him go by. The huts were boxes of hemp, the cracks small yellow stained-glass windows with printed letters.

They followed the windings of a stream, the highway, they disappeared into the mist of a small forest, among the dark cones of the . . . (and here, the exhaustive enumeration of Cuban trees—horseflesh mahogany, guamá, jequi, oak, the anona tree, and so forth—with their botanical jargon)[8] . . . until Help and Mercy, Rita and Bruno, "dead tired," left the sepulcher on the grass.

In the early morning—or was it the turning of a rattlesnake among dry leaves, the flapping of an owl?—they heard Him cough. He woke up with stiff elbows and wrists; the joints of his ankles rigid. Well you see, it's just that accustomed as

[8]Phonetic delights never omitted in any Cuban tract, from the *Mirror of Patience*—1608—to the present day.

he was to vestry climate, tempered by the sighs and yawns of
so many fasters, the dampness had gotten into the sawdust of
his bones. His fingers stiffened, one foot hard in the air as if
on a step, he was petrified in a good-bye: poorly sewn puppet,
raffle picture card. His meeting with the Cuban countryside,
with insular space and its glowworms, had brought on arthritis.

They stretched His limbs as much as they could. They put
Him through calisthenics, recited an Ex Aegypto Israel. The
heat was—listen to Help—"thicker than pea soup." There was
something sweetish in the air, as if near a beehive or cane juice
stand.

The followers stretched—the few that were left: at the
sight of the jungle the rest had resigned themselves to urban
mysticism—shook the hay off their uniforms and cassocks and
ran into the woods to piss.

(Tarnished cornets, and on the drums, dew.)

He felt that something was jolting Him in the knees, that
his legs were giving way. A shiver ("Oh Father, have pity on
me, you who have gotten me into this mess"—he thought). His
whole body itched—Was it jigger fleas? He promised to
scourge himself. He wasn't going to wait much longer. Listen
to these morning prayers:

HELP (who was putting the pink back into her cheeks with
roucou): Now you carry Him for a while, why it's worse than
carrying a chimpanzee piggyback. He's got me crippled.

MERCY (who was bathing in a stream): You poke your own
hellfire, you lazybones, ramrod, thick clod. Etc., etc.

Stretching and bending they finally reached a town. What a
relief for their swollen feet: the square was paved in cobblestones and dark green water ran along the juncture of the
stones. It overflowed from the broken basin of the fountain.

What a smell of coffee, what nice smoke spiraling out the

doorways! Bowls of chipped china on shiny crimson table-cloths, the leaning tables, the stools, piled on top.

The women were doing the foot scratching dance, coming out in flowered slippers, the backs of them worn down: "oh boy, what a visitor." They opened their houses. Brought out lamps and hung them on the *guásima* trees in the patio, and gave away lumps of pan sugar from their cupboards. Why they combed their hair: to receive him!

THE NEXT DAY

An arcade stood facing the village, and another one almost parallel: the shadow of the first on the smooth, windowless façades. These successive arches supported unfinished walls, or ruins, a second portico, and the slope of roofs. On a stoop rested the handle of a coach, and over the shadow of its great wheels, on the adjacent wall, hung carbines, telescopes, pendulums, and perhaps pocket pistols and swords with tortoise-shell hilts. From there the early risers set forth in a throng, with great clamor and large red shawls around their necks. They brought accordions. Graters and maracas. What cute music they scratched! It would split anybody's sides! It was a thick-lipped mulatto with even, scorched kinky hair—Mercy's darling—who was shooting off like this, with his razor sharp voice:

> I have a little thing that you like
> that you like
> that you like

He wriggled like an eel, with a hand on his hip—what Dahoman rings!—pointing with the other to the object of such elliptic verse.

The aroma of honest-to-good coffee—accustomed as he was to that of incense—and that spicy odor emanating from the tables revived Him. He was delighted that they ran behind Him, that they wore down the wood of his feet with kisses, that they perfumed him with *agua-ardiente*. He wanted them to entreat Him, but with guitars and gourds; he wanted angels with royal palms. He thought himself a patriot, a Martilike orator frozen in the threads of an engraving; He pictured himself in a speech-making pose, raised to a tricolor tribune, or releasing a fighting cock with his calloused hands, its feathers crossing his dried, olive face. He would like you to see a blue sky behind him, and a sun of hard fog, a waning moon, several comets. He had the calling of a redeemer, blondie did, He liked flags.

Help immediately joined in on the fun, not to mention— which would be knocking your head against Redundance— Rita and Bruno, who didn't have to join it, since they had it in them since birth (according to Mercy).

It wasn't till they were in the store, with the "hurry up, we still have the fringes to put up," that they found out: the one they left slipping on the cobblestones outside in the square was not the object of this great fuss; the people were expecting a new candidate, who had promised "to give the town running water and to build a road that would connect them to their neighbors in nearby towns," to arrive at noon. For him the tournament, the cockfights, the "National" band, the tables of breadsticks and the taffy wrapped in colored papers.

Competition horses in checkered girths came from all over the county. And on foot, pulling their reins, smiling bow-legged riders already appeared in black and gold or blue and gold colors that reappeared on stirrups and blinders, bringing Guinea hens and Mandarin oranges and shopping bags of limes too.

"May you be struck down with lightning!"—Mercy exploded, she was cracking up, already wallowing in corners with some of the band players (according to Help), knocking machetes and spats off the walls.

"God, what am I doing here?"—and she ran toward the portico through the steam of boiled milk, the wake of clean pitchers and the marimbas.

She sensed that the party was leaving her. She saw Bruno call to her, between two open-mouthed guitarists, against a background of pots and swords.

In full force she crossed the square, fell on her knees before Christ and cried on His navel—that's as high as her disheveled head could reach.

"Forgive me Dear God, I didn't know what I was doing." *(and without any sense of dramatic transition)* Help adds: "Fungus! Pustules on his feet! He's rotting, eek!"

She took one step back, and another, without turning around. She opened her hands, drew them near her eyes, scrutinized the palms:

"And I've touched Him! I'm infected: alcohol!"

And He, to get a good look at her, squeezed his glass pupils, those opaque stones that have been dimmed by so much looking at the top of a locker. He was soaked with dew. Bagasse Christ. One foot was eczematous and green, and in the arch a milky flower, of mushrooms. His nose ran and so did the swollen edge of his eyelids.

"Alcohol, for God's sake!"—And she shot off to the store.

"And the best!"—answered Bruno who awaited her with open arms in the doorway. And he emptied on her head a glass of rum-on-the-rocks. From there he was dragged away. Help and Mercy, yoked together, pulled Him. He went on foot, tied to a beam, handcuffed. They had taken off his crown and put on a palm-leaf hat because it was drizzling, they had tossed lemon juice on his foot and cologne on his head. So that His sore couldn't be seen, they had surrounded Him with vases of wax flowers. So that the Rotten One emerged from an opaque garden whose leaves the cart's jolting could not shake off. They fell into gutters. Got stuck in bogs.

Mercy was getting eaten up by mosquitos; but stoically she sang:

> tonight it is raining
> tomorrow will be muddy,

When Help answered her the rain fell thicker:

> poor is the carter
> who pulls this cart

And the Foul One went through the drizzle, his feet among flowered urns, his legs among still flowers. Oh how it burns! Water surrounded him right up to his pustules.

"A bigamist I'll be, but not a fag"—he thought. And looked out the corner of his eye at Bruno, who was laughing, envious.

It was because the Two Women were rubbing Him with camphor balls, wrapping Him in blankets, inserting in each armpit "because you see, he had fever on only one side" a vulvous thermometer with filigrees and Roman numerals. They even pleaded with Saint Lazarus to rid Him of galloping leprosy.

They had to cross the rising Jobabo river, and hauled the cart by looping the rope through a ring that moved along a rope tied to a palm tree on each bank. And the last just men kept the balance.

Like a rolling barrel full of stones was the noise of the waters. Red turtles leapt to the beams, held on with their little nails, disappeared into slow eddies. Trout jumped up in rapid flight, flicked their tails, spattered water, and remained gasping between planks.

"They fish themselves, God's creatures! Let's pray He doesn't decide to multiply them now!" (Help)

Below, the current dragged away torn roots, and shrubs with nests.

"And the bluish hands of drowned men, saying goodbye!" (Adds Mercy, who scarcely breathes so as not to move, "not everybody walks on water.") They left the rest of the pilgrimage in Oriente province waving handkerchiefs and sneezing. Rita wanted to catch on to the rope and swim to the other side, but they finally convinced her to stay on land. Bruno left the violin cover and three candelabrums with her, to lighten the load. What a farewell! They could still see her from the other bank, behind the strip of mud, moving the three bronzes like a traffic cop. Then she became a blur with the others. At the landing a gust of wind carried away His hat. Bruno raised Him by the head and planted Him on the grass. Then they saw those plaques of pus which whitened his leg to the waist.

They stuck their ears to his stomach, the Magdalenas auscultated Him. Something was bubbling inside.

MERCY *(her eyes popping):* "The Evil Disease!"

The sweet felp of their earlobes and the pearls of their earrings rubbing His groin certainly seemed to make Him mighty happy. What a pity there wasn't a camera at hand: he was smiling!

ILLUSTRIOUS SHORES, but a feeble welcome did He receive from those of Santa María del Puerto del Príncipe.

Listen to those welcomes the Camagüeyan ladies forced on Him, sheltered behind the shutters and rails of their windows:

a. You will leave our towers mute, but the bronze of our many bells will sink your ships. *(They had taken Him for a pirate!)*

b. Ill wind from a leprosarium, angel of rebels, leader of escaped slaves.

c. Locust of cattle, salting of the water, etc.

He, who in so many Gobelins, on so many night tables: wounded pigeon, gentleman of painted plaster, with eyes of chemical blue like a Mexican doll, He, whose signs—parallel fish, crowns, crosses and nails—embellished the glass of every paperweight and, in cement, worn down by rains, the medallions of every façade,

He, who appeared in so many family portraits.

And yet they did not recognize Him.

He scratched what he thought most symbolic of the situation (he already had Cuban habits!) and gave Bruno the "forward march" signal.

The shadows of dates clouded his face, in the black gardens of las Mercedes, the chandelier of the choir loft's arches. He wanted to lose himself in the labyrinths of the angel makers, among the goldsmith stands and old book stalls. Along the banks of the Tínima River the display cases of Spanish flea markets, beneath the yellow halo of candles, were shining in the mist: Catalan panels with beheaded saints and all the arteries of their necks; paintings of balloons rising with sacks of sand and green ribbons: in the baskets, in smoking jackets, handlebar mustaches, and spectacles, brave Matías Perezes would observe the clouds.

BRUNO'S STATEMENT

It is here necessary to make note of a fact, so that written evidence shall remain which could serve the authoress in securing either total absolution or perpetual hellfire. Here it is: the Redeemer pointed to one of those balloons. It is well known that ascensions are His weak point.

I bear witness that, with the few pesos she had left, with no hope whatsoever of earning more, and much less in such chaste places, Help offered to get it for Him, perhaps because she had seen new stains on Him and knew that sooner or later she'd recover the gift. Whatever the case may be, she went out to buy it.

Every Venetian blind fell. Every salesman spat on her, threw the door in her face.

The lights went out. I hereby testify that that's how the Camagüeyan tour ended.

They saw black propellers among the palm trees: army helicopters were following them. Clean shaven young pilots descended to the villages He was going to pass through, to intimidate the people and buy Paloma de Castilla crackers. When the travelers arrived, little men in uniforms would point to them with large pencils and, terrified, take off. Through the plastic bellies of the crafts you could see them gesticulate and open maps.

To bother Him, the pilots powdered Him from above with bread crumbs.

Another rumble. They all stooped down—except Him, naturally, He would have hurt his pustules—but they didn't see anything. It was the subway.

There is no rule without the exception: the herbists of Ciego de Avila came out to receive him, and with a lot of noise. To entertain Him they brought out wooden serpents coiled around little mirrors, mortars, old pomander boxes with the names of leaves where letters were missing, the covers adorned with Florentine and French landscapes.

Mechanical gargoyles followed them, raising whirlwinds with their helices, five bakelite birds. Curtains of dust surrounded Him. If the three faithfuls would stop, the noise of the motors would decrease and the row of transparent machines would stand still in air, perpendicular to the highway. The whirlwinds would then spread and a spiral of straw would surround them.

If they'd flee to the grottos of reinforced concrete, or hide by the rivers, in the inns on abandoned piles, the patrol—and the dull buzzing—would escort them, forming a V whose vortex, a craft with two propellers, would plane over His head, like a Holy Spirit Dove.

HELP *(and the motors came on louder):* . . . . . . (she opened and closed her mouth—was she shouting?—; gusts of wind stiffened her face. A totally bald pate.)

MERCY: . . . . . . *(with calm gestures)*

Bruno touched them and pointed to the mouth of a subway. They went down the escalator, under the panel SUBWAY. With Him and the cart on their backs they passed through a lunch counter (ay, His toes were already spouting pus, falling off in pieces), the cabarets of River Side (pustules had begun on His other leg and, like a belt of rotting metals, they girded His stomach), corridors with amplifiers; on the radio the twelve o'clock noon gongs, the meowing sopranos on the Chinese programs and the Candado soap commercials.

They bathed Him in sulphur. They came up in the elevator content, out the other mouth of the subway. Motionless, like a band of scabby turkey buzzards, the helicopters were waiting for them at the exit.

The din of the choppers was breaking Help's eardrums; the corruption of the Corpus Christi, Mercy's heart.

The crafts were not following them at equal distances now, but rather, one by one, they dove down like kingfishers, almost flush with roofs and trees; then a hatch-door opened in the plexiglass shell, the copilot peered out a second "like the cuckoo of a clock" (Bruno), and took a flash photograph. The mosquito would then return to his place in the V. The next would come down.

Having reached the cherry orchards of Las Villas, He asked them to abandon him to His fate (he showed them the highway with a flabby hand, and with the other He grabbed on to a trunk), to let Him rot on the marabou.

At night they'd take off His blanket and leave Him in the open—so that the night dew would cool his sores—in the light of the V of blinking headlights. In the morning they'd find Him softened, tearful, pecked at by birds.

They hiked down the Villa Clara hills. In the distance, streaking the pink fields, you could see the black lines of the railroad disappearing under the roofs of the kirschwasser factories, branching off on the other side, crossing the pine groves and fishing villages, or else following the rivers which swept along rafts of white trunks, convoyed by signal flags and toads, until disappearing into the curve of inlets, under the red smoke cloud of the distilleries, among the tanks along the docks.

Near a curve in the road they heard call bells. When they turned the corner, they saw two yellow triangles with red edges light up and a barrier fall before them: blocking the way, an armored train had stopped at the crossing.

The bell stopped. What a silence! (They felt they were being watched.) Suddenly the cars opened, unglued boxes, and down the walls, now ramps, tanks rolled out. From their turrets came nets full of green sponges ("Giant pieces of mint!"— Help), portable radios, tape recorders whose tapes were running.

"Somehow we've got to appeal to the popular devotion!"— declared Help, and she stamped the first letter on one buttock.

Let me explain: she was dancing in front of a jukebox, and wildly, pardon me, and enthusiastically composing the Lord's texts on her naked body—which looked as if printed on brown paper—: with wooden blocks she engraved golden monograms.

No one had come to receive them in Santa Clara. She tore her clothes in anger, crossed herself, and bought a printing set: (to Him):

> I will make of my body Your book,
> they will read from me!

And Mercy *(to the frightened Villa Clara folk behind cracks—families squeezed into bunches—hidden under their mothers' skirts):*

> Come, children of God:
> Here is the flesh made word!

And Help went wild over burning tambourines and cornets from John Coltrane's band.

They came running, and *en masse.* At the beat of the drums, Help wriggled from head to toe, and from her navel, which projected an O, to the full stop of her knee letters shined all over her.

He couldn't take His eyes off the oscillating band of texts, nor hold back His feet: He wanted to dance, He knew that dance is the new birth, that after death they'll confront us with the mambo band. What a pity! He couldn't even clap hands. He stretched His arms and felt like His armpits were breaking. He was finished now: His nipples were purple, His chest in welts, His throat burning, He was choking, the ganglia of His neck hurt. If the band came on louder—the needle in the striped grooves, for Him it was like bottles breaking against each other, cornets playing under water.

"What wiggly hips!"—(said the faithful). Bruno took some steps around her, looking at her hips as if reading.

"But, what about the helicopters?"

They were there. Watching the show from the boxes. The

pilots eating popcorn. Whose bags they threw away when the record was over.

Let's not even talk about Matanzas.

THE ENTRY OF CHRIST IN HAVANA

What a reception in Havana! They were all waiting for Him. His picture was everywhere, endlessly repeated, to the point of ridicule or simply boredom: pasted up, ripped off, pulled apart, nailed on every door, pasted around every pole, decorated with mustaches, with pricks dripping into His mouth, even in colors —oh so blond and beautiful, just like Greta Garbo—not to mention the stained-glass reproductions in the Galiano subway. Wherever you look, He looks back.

Bruno: I'm gonna walk no more: I'm sitting right down. I'm at my wit's end: They take more pictures of him than of the Coca Cola bottle! Let somebody else carry Him. Here's where I'm staying.

And there he stayed, in a fit of hiccups.

Pictures, taken from above, but at different distances: a black spot, a winding line of the highway, tilled fields; a blond head, toes on a platform, a background of pavement, white locks, and up front His profile; close-up: His eyes. His eyes; white locks, profile; dark spot, highway.

A little black girl came running full steam ahead, with a banner waving in the breeze, white knee socks were all you could see of her tiny legs; she came running full steam ahead, her legs —pistons—were all over the place, her knees chugachuga- chuga—a Hittite lion—holding up high a banner that said INRI. You've finally come, she said, we were waiting for You. Her eyes became moist, she was speechless ("She swooned, in a trance, as if she had seen Paul Anka!"—said Help), she thrashed about wildly, out of joy, took a few steps toward Him, and fell.

He didn't have time to pick her up. Two others fell upon Him, more and more kept coming. Weeping and embracing Him. They came down from the hills, beating barrels and drums with sticks rolled up in rags. The women threw open their doors; dazed, they clapped their hands over their mouths; a cry; they dropped to their knees, tried to touch Him, kissed the ground where He passed. The children carried around His image in good luck charms, in little straw dolls. His name was in all the shop windows. They ate Him in mint candies. They dressed up like Him, wearing little crowns of thorns (their faces white with rice powder) and small blood flowers. It was all so pretty!

They came from every direction, climbed trees to see Him, asked for His autograph.

He coughed and suddenly felt that He was moving forward, the people pushing Him, that He was moving backward, driftwood floating in the tide, that He was moving forward again. Sweating. He had chills. They stepped on His feet. They blew their hot breath, thick fumes of Gold Label rum, into His face; the trumpets of Luyanó in His ears. (The flutists were two jaundiced and baggy-eyed dwarfs, puffy cheeks under black berets.) He felt slimy hands caressing Him, and on His thighs wet mollusk lips. The banners covered His sky, the poles fenced Him in like a palisade of red lances. He was gasping for air. He thrashed His arms in acid fumes. He really wasn't made for the proletariat: the masses stifled Him.

"I'll never make it," He said to Himself. He tightened His eyes, clinched His fists, bit His lips. He wanted to stamp and kick. Spin around with his arms outstretched (and, God willing, with knives in both hands), open a path, escape. His dangling limbs did not obey Him. (Horns, rattles, bells) His hand shook as if it were throwing dice. He tried to stop it: one foot trembled, or was it the other or His head. His hand moved on its own. His feet. He jumped. His body quivered, a goaded frog. An electric shock ran through Him. He was dancing unwillingly to a rock beat. (Balloons popped out of a balcony, doves from another.)

He listened as if someone were whispering in His ear. At the same time Help and Mercy turned toward Him. Once more (but the racket of brass bands, clapping, hurrahs): stuttering, babbling words ("African angels are speaking to Me," He thought). Without turning His head, He looked in the direction of the voices. Attentive, He heard "red," and right after: "It hurts in the back of my eyes."

He saw Help and Mercy shake their heads, stand still, raise their open hands—restored to the fervor of the catacombs—turn from white to yellow and back again to white. Now two great tears rolled down their cheeks. Now they muttered, sobbing, "A miracle, a miracle."

Then He realized He was speaking.

He heard Himself say: "I am freezing inside."

They wrapped Him in the Madonna's cloak from the main altar in the Church of Carmen. The thick cloth, embroidered with gold leaves hung straight down from His shoulders. Black cords intertwined in the shape of clover leaves and rosettes of pearls ran along its edges.

Each step of the bearers shook His blond head, his waxy eyelids, those sick eyes sank deeper. (From a distance He was the Madonna of a Siennese casket.) They threw flowers, they cheered Him. Without turning His head, with the solemnity of a princess in her Mercedes, He greeted the multitudes on the balconies. Carnations stuck to the garlands and brooches of His cloak.

"Blessed be ye, women, wise if not virgins, who have followed Me through thick and thin." He moved His forearm

three times like a piggy-bank black boy who bows and doffs his
cap. He suddenly unwound: His hands. They hung limp, like
rags. He could not quite touch His eyelids:

"How cold they are, oh God, what a pain in the back of
My eyes!" And they took off their cloaks, folded them like
sashes, wrapped them around His waist. Or transported by
mystical delirium ("May Your fire joyously consume me!"—
said Help), they padded them, and with the same burlap filled
in the gaps of His joints. They covered His hinges. They would
have torn out the pupils of their eyes to give Him. They wept
with only one eye, so He would not see. They turned violet,
their nails black, as if the Plague were devouring them.

(Thickness of the sky: terraces of wax.

And there, over the streets, the sea: fixed foam, a strip
of sand.) He glided over the mob—carried on their shoulders—swift, blinded by the flash bulbs, followed by the
cameras—concave green crossed the lenses—. Majestic, He
was like a redwood statue unearthed from a river bed: His
eyes sockets full of crabs, His face rotted, His arms broken,
His feet black sponges. Branches and leaves of holy Palm
trees opened before Him, like seaweed before the hull of a
ship.

Posing in place, in order of generations, the families looked
down at Him from their balconies. In the foreground, right
behind the railing, little boys dressed in white suits and
black bow ties, were rocking back and forth on their
wooden horses, chocolate cigars between their fingers. Little
girls, in starched dresses, held yellow hoops next to their
perfectly conical skirts, beach pails, and shovels. Behind
them, austere, the fathers with mustaches and goatees, and
bouquets of flowers in their hands, the mothers in their
fancy curls and bonnets, wrapped in shawls. And in the

background, leaning against the doors, grinning at the photographer's birdie, the grandparents, gray-haired, almost dead.

The squares: theaters with identical boxes. A parade of toy horses, hoops, bouquets, toy horses.

Such repetition made him dizzy, and the choruses too. Mercy touched His forehead with the back of her hand: It was burning. She pressed the wood and it crumbled. A white halo remaining. He had already rotted right through.

"King of the Four Roads, spare our sugar harvest!," shouted a reeling peasant with a bottle of rum in his hand, and he hung from Him, crying. Help tried to protect Him. But it was too late. The peasant had torn off a hand. A wooden stump remained, a splinter, out of which ants came scurrying.

The people came from all directions. They pushed. They squeezed together. It was a jungle of slender legs, knotty bamboo shoots supporting puffy buttocks, round like purple *caimitos*. Their trunks bent, swayed back, rocked by gusts of wind. In their midst, jumping over their wide feet, frightened black boys—little frogs—zigzagged around, fanning themselves.

A grandstand had been set up—with bleachers and platforms—and a red damask canopy hung over it, supported by four gilded halberds. Banners waved. Helicopters hovered above the square. From the platforms His followers threw them black balls which opened in midair: flowers of Chinese silk. They floated: black gardens. They fell; on the petals His name was imprinted: incomplete, backward, broken.

The sky was a crumpled piece of paper. A thick tent. Slow waves rolled through it: the ebb tide of a salty marsh. Something in the air was going to break.

"Come closer"—He said to them—"look at Me."

I am He who gives the Face. The big daddy-o. Mine is

the page of the Codex. Mine is the ink and the painted image. Where are you taking Me?

But an icy gust ripped open His cloak, tore down the flags.

The people trembled. They warmed each other with their breath. Their eyes were wide open. They murmured: "This is the day terror after death change rot House of the Black." They began to weep. They lowered their heads in prayer. They beat their brows. He heard Himself say: "Dear God, have pity on Me."

The families went inside: They closed the shutters. They bolted the doors. They piled up the furniture, and the children on top, against the doors so the wind would not blow them open. They covered the mirrors with sheets.

The storm raged. (The little black boys dropped their fans, clung to people's legs, buried their heads between their knees.) It grew dark. It was when they turned on the lights that they saw, in the lights' flickering cones, the white specks scrawling in the air, then orderly, with the slowness of stars, whirlwinds of sculptured water: it was snowing.

They huddled up under His cloak. They tried to warm Him "But He was already fucked up"—Help said—; and on to another prayer. The snow burned Him on the face, another kind of fever. He looked like a prisoner, a drowned man. His eyes were sunken and watery, the lids jaundiced, His lips oozing with pus, His neck bloated. Branches of black veins climbed to His throat. Knots of puffy ganglia, spongy animals, rotting between His bones and hide. When He coughed he felt something was burning inside. When He spat, bloody water stained the handkerchief. He was scarcely breathing, sounding like an asthmatic sucking in air. Hunched over. Gasping. A fish on dry land.

"Come on, You're looking great. You look just like a Virgin of Charity!" (it's Mercy, to make Him happy)

Parallel furrows in the pavement. A carpet of ceiba flowers. White moss.

And He:

"Of all the spectacles I've seen, none . . ."

A fit of coughing broke His bronchial tubes. A downpour of snowflakes pelted Him ("Tiny bird feathers!"—said Help); the whirling propellers scattered them.

"If I should die upon the road, on my grave I want no flowers" (He said)—And He tried to smile, to reassure the last of the faithful. But when they beat the drums they sprayed needles of ice.

Smooth, a tin sky covered almost the whole landscape. Bell towers and the arms of windmills jutted out over the red roofs. Open bridges, beached ships run aground: the Almendares River multiplied them. Along the snowy banks, stained at intervals by scaffolds and cranes, dying fish were jumping. Sea gulls swooped down to peck at them.

He tightened His throat. He felt that something was bursting in His neck. A taste of copper, warm salt, came up. He spat blood.

He was now a gargoyle, a snow white rag. Help, in a fit of tears, passed her hand over His head, dried the sweat from His brow, murmured in His ear, "It will soon be over, have faith, it will soon be over." And Mercy, in a fit of tears, patted Him on the back, kissed His temples, murmured in His ear: "It will soon be over, have faith, it will soon be over."

The snow slanted down. At the eaves, broken spirals, veins of white ink that He saw erased, with each gust of wind, to reappear, each time wider.

In the depths of their sockets, His eyes grew glassy. He did not move them. Help and Mercy dragged Him a few steps; they looked at each other: they turned to shout. His body shook. He was weeping. And when He calmed down:

"Why all this moaning?"—He said—. "Kicking the bucket is great fun. Life only begins after death, the life."

He was choking.

Cutting through the snow, a coach sped by.

Like zinc, from afar, the Havana lakes. Small covered bridges crossed them. On the shore there were austere towers of fortresses, palaces of cedar, tall dove cotes amidst cherry orchards, the ruins of synagogues, cut off minarets: there Infanta Street, frozen, crosses San Lázaro.

"Let's go, every man for himself!"—He heard them shout. He tried to raise His head. Then He saw the grandstand crushed by an avalanche. "Oh God"—He moaned—"Why didn't You throw in the towel?" The faithful left the square in groups, under yellow raincoats held over themselves with raised arms. The leaders carried lanterns. Helicopters spotlighted them with their floodlights: dotted lines.

"Who has stayed behind?"—(poor thing!)

And They:

"Loyal Ones, Followers, Shadows."

On the façades of colonial palaces the snow covered capitals, moldings, cement flowers. Closed gates; the blue shadow of the latches extended over the iron. Only half-moons, contorted masks, remained of the medallions with the heads of viceroys. Squirrels fled across the cornices.

Sunken gardens. Silent fountains: the tritons driveled threads of ice.

"Curtains of bread crumbs" (said Help).

"Who up there is shaking His tablecloth?" (said Mercy). One of His hands came loose. Swollen, it fell to the ground; in its palm, a sore.

It stayed there, for a moment, on the white cloth; purple knuckles. Three red drops fell upon it, from the wrist, it was buried by the snow.

THE ENTRY OF CHRIST INTO DEATH

He saw quick reddish stains in the snow, copper shadows. The ground moved away from him. He was losing footing. He felt he was entering another space. Burning zone, he heard water through swollen leaves, the sleep of rattlesnakes and birds, the ambush. Behind vines, the frightened flight of mockingbirds. Cascades of moss, thick dark green mats, fell from the highest fronds, clouding the day. Light tigers carried bleeding ducks in their teeth. He heard His steps in the mud, on damp leaves. With the sound of water among rocks, the strokes of a guitar reached His ear. Then the drums, yes: it was the mambo band, the one that greets us on the other side.

His body became strange to Him: a pile of rotting sticks under the snow. Help and Mercy closed His eyes. He saw himself twisted, a broken gargoyle.

Meanwhile, He crossed reverberating forests, stockades of sugar cane that ended in golden leaves. He was getting close. Already among the sputtering sparks of flowers you could see the musicians. He knew that He was going to dance. That dancing means meeting the Dead.

That if you dance well, you get in.

He saw himself crumble. He fell into pieces, with a moan. Wood falling in water. His bald, leprous head split in two. The empty holes of the eyes, the white, perforated lips, the nose in its bone, the ears plugged with two black clots. And further on, the forehead, the cold globes of the eyes, the trunk, with an

arm that sank into the snow as if looking for something buried.
And further up, the curve of the back. The legs in pieces; the
snow buried them.

And the foot that stamped three times, the belch, the first beat.
He jumped. Two more steps, two steps. He clapped hands to
the rhythm. He did a turn. Holding a white handkerchief. He
danced on one foot. The band players shook their little bells
near his ear. "Who can beat me?"—He said to Himself. And
he wiggled His hips. The musicians gathered around him.
Twice they suddenly changed the batá beat of the tambourines
and twice he caught up to them with a caper. He was blond
and handsome. And had white feet. He whirled around. Then
the other way. Superimposed on himself. He was blond. He
was naked. Holding a white handkerchief. He shouted again.
"Sugar!"—they shouted to Him. He laughed. He wore gold
bracelets. Not as shiny as his eyes.

He didn't know that the snow had stopped. Rivulets of mud
cracked the white cloth, creased it at the sewers. It was sunny.
Grating rails and throwing off sparks, the trolleys, full, passed
by again. The river ran. The ships cast off.
   (In the parks the old men chatted.)

Then the Faithful, the Fates, crossed the square. They started
picking Him up, searching in the mire. Piece by piece, they
wrapped Him in a cloth with loving care. They hurried away.
   They were already reaching the portals when, from the
helicopters, bullets rained down.

Rhinoceros

EUGÈNE IONESCO

Translated by Jean Stewart

In memory of André Frédérique

We were sitting outside the café, my friend Jean and I, peacefully talking about one thing and another, when we caught sight of it on the opposite pavement, huge and powerful, panting noisily, charging straight ahead and brushing against market stalls—a rhinoceros. People in the street stepped hurriedly aside to let it pass. A housewife uttered a cry of terror, her basket dropped from her hands, the wine from a broken bottle spread over the pavement, and some pedestrians, one of them an elderly man, rushed into the shops. It was all over like a flash of lightning. People emerged from their hiding-places and gathered in groups which watched the rhinoceros disappear into the distance, made some comments on the incident and then dispersed.

My own reactions are slowish. I absent-mindedly took in the image of the rushing beast, without ascribing any very great

importance to it. That morning, moreover, I was feeling tired
and my mouth was sour, as a result of the previous night's
excesses; we had been celebrating a friend's birthday. Jean had
not been at the party; and when the first moment of surprise
was over, he exclaimed:

"A rhinoceros at large in town! doesn't that surprise you?
It ought not to be allowed."

"True," I said, "I hadn't thought of that. It's dangerous."

"We ought to protest to the Town Council."

"Perhaps it's escaped from the Zoo," I said.

"You're dreaming," he replied. "There hasn't been a Zoo
in our town since the animals were decimated by the plague
in the seventeenth century."

"Perhaps it belongs to the circus?"

"What circus? The Council has forbidden itinerant enter-
tainers to stop on municipal territory. None have come here
since we were children."

"Perhaps it has lived here ever since, hidden in the marshy
woods round about," I answered with a yawn.

"You're completely lost in a dense alcoholic haze. . . ."

"Which rises from the stomach. . . ."

"Yes. And has pervaded your brain. What marshy woods
can you think of round about here? Our province is so arid they
call it Little Castile."

"Perhaps it sheltered under a pebble? Perhaps it made its
nest on a dry branch?"

"How tiresome you are with your paradoxes. You're quite
incapable of talking seriously."

"Today, particularly."

"Today and every other day."

"Don't lose your temper, my dear Jean. We're not going
to quarrel about that creature. . . ."

We changed the subject of our conversation and began to
talk about the weather again, about the rain which fell so rarely

in our region, about the need to provide our sky with artificial clouds, and other banal and insoluble questions.

We parted. It was Sunday. I went to bed and slept all day: another wasted Sunday. On Monday morning I went to the office, making a solemn promise to myself never to get drunk again, and particularly not on Saturdays, so as not to spoil the following Sundays. For I had one single free day a week and three weeks' holiday in the summer. Instead of drinking and making myself ill, wouldn't it be better to keep fit and healthy, to spend my precious moments of freedom in a more intelligent fashion: visiting museums, reading literary magazines and listening to lectures? And instead of spending all my available money on drink, wouldn't it be preferable to buy tickets for interesting plays? I was still unfamiliar with the avant-garde theatre, of which I had heard so much talk, I had never seen a play by Ionesco. Now or never was the time to bring myself up to date.

The following Sunday I met Jean once again at the same café.

"I've kept my promise," I said, shaking hands with him.

"What promise have you kept?" he asked.

"My promise to myself. I've vowed to give up drinking. Instead of drinking I've decided to cultivate my mind. Today I am clear-headed. This afternoon I'm going to the Municipal Museum and this evening I've a ticket for the theatre. Won't you come with me?"

"Let's hope your good intentions will last," replied Jean. "But I can't go with you. I'm meeting some friends at the brasserie."

"Oh, my dear fellow, now it's you who are setting a bad example. You'll get drunk!"

"Once in a way doesn't imply a habit," replied Jean irritably. "Whereas you. . . ."

The discussion was about to take a disagreeable turn,

when we heard a mighty trumpeting, the hurried clatter of some perissodactyl's hoofs, cries, a cat's mewing; almost simultaneously we saw a rhinoceros appear, then disappear, on the opposite pavement, panting noisily and charging straight ahead.

Immediately afterwards a woman appeared holding in her arms a shapeless, bloodstained little object:

"It's run over my cat," she wailed, "it's run over my cat!"

The poor dishevelled woman, who seemed the very embodiment of grief, was soon surrounded by people offering sympathy.

Jean and I got up. We rushed across the street to the side of the unfortunate woman.

"All cats are mortal," I said stupidly, not knowing how to console her.

"It came past my shop last week!" the grocer recalled.

"It wasn't the same one," Jean declared. "It wasn't the same one: last week's had two horns on its nose, it was an Asian rhinoceros; this one had only one, it's an African rhinoceros."

"You're talking nonsense," I said irritably. "How could you distinguish its horns? The animal rushed past so fast that we could hardly see it; you hadn't time to count them. . . ."

"I don't live in a haze," Jean retorted sharply. "I'm clearheaded, I'm quick at figures."

"He was charging with his head down."

"That made it all the easier to see."

"You're a pretentious fellow, Jean. You're a pedant, who isn't even sure of his own knowledge. For in the first place it's the Asian rhinoceros that has one horn on its nose, and the African rhinoceros that has two!"

"You're quite wrong, it's the other way about."

"Would you like to bet on it?"

"I won't bet against you. You're the one who has two

horns," he cried, red with fury, "you Asiatic you!" (He stuck to his guns.)

"I haven't any horns. I shall never wear them. And I'm not an Asiatic either. In any case, Asiatics are just like other people."

"They're yellow!" he shouted, beside himself with rage.

Jean turned his back on me and strode off, cursing.

I felt a fool. I ought to have been more conciliatory, and not contradicted him: for I knew he could not bear it. The slightest objection made him foam at the mouth. This was his only fault, for he had a heart of gold and had done me countless good turns. The few people who were there and who had been listening to us had, as a result, quite forgotten about the poor woman's squashed cat. They crowded round me, arguing: some maintained that the Asian rhinoceros was indeed one-horned, and that I was right; others maintained that on the contrary the African rhinoceros was one-horned, and that therefore the previous speaker had been right.

"That is not the question," interposed a gentleman (straw boater, small moustache, eyeglass, a typical logician's head) who had hitherto stood silent. "The discussion turned on a problem from which you have wandered. You began by asking yourselves whether today's rhinoceros is the same as last Sunday's or whether it is a different one. That is what must be decided. You may have seen one and the same one-horned rhinoceros on two occasions, or you may have seen one and the same two-horned rhinoceros on two occasions. Or again, you may have seen first one one-horned rhinoceros and then a second one-horned rhinoceros. Or else, first one two-horned rhinoceros and then a second two-horned rhinoceros. If on the first occasion you had seen a two-horned rhinoceros, and on the second a one-horned rhinoceros, that would not be conclusive either. It might be that since last week the rhinoceros had lost one of his horns, and that the one you saw today was the same. Or it might be that two two-horned rhinoceroses had each lost one of their horns. If you could prove that on the first occasion you had seen a one-horned rhinoceros, whether it was Asian or African, and today a two-horned rhinoceros, whether it was African or Asian—that doesn't matter—then we might conclude that two different rhinoceroses were involved, for it is most unlikely that a second horn could grow in a few days, to any visible extent, on a rhinoceros's nose; this would mean that an Asian, or African, rhinoceros had become an African, or Asian, rhinoceros, which is logically impossible, since the same creature cannot be born in two places at once or even successively."

"That seems clear to me," I said. "But it doesn't settle the question."

"Of course," retorted the gentleman, smiling with a knowledgeable air, "only the problem has now been stated correctly."

"That's not the problem either," interrupted the grocer, who being no doubt of an emotional nature cared little about logic. "Can we allow our cats to be run over under our eyes by two-horned or one-horned rhinoceroses, be they Asian or African?"

"He's right, he's right," everybody exclaimed. "We can't allow our cats to be run over, by rhinoceroses or anything else!"

The grocer pointed with a theatrical gesture to the poor weeping woman, who still held and rocked in her arms the shapeless, bleeding remains of what had once been her cat.

Next day, in the paper, under the heading Road Casualties among Cats, there were two lines describing the death of the poor creature, "crushed underfoot by a pachyderm," it was said, without further details.

On Sunday afternoon I hadn't visited a museum; in the evening I hadn't gone to the theatre. I had moped at home by myself, overwhelmed by remorse at having quarrelled with Jean.

"He's so susceptible, I ought to have spared his feelings," I told myself. "It's absurd to lose one's temper about something like that . . . about the horns of a rhinoceros that one had never seen before . . . a native of Africa or of India, such faraway countries, what could it matter to me? Whereas Jean had always been my friend, a friend who . . . to whom I owed so much . . . and who. . . ."

In short, while promising myself to go and see Jean as soon as possible and to make it up with him, I had drunk an entire bottle of brandy without noticing. But I did indeed notice it the next day: a sore head, a foul mouth, an uneasy conscience; I was really most uncomfortable. But duty before everything: I got to the office on time, or almost. I was able to sign the register just before it was taken away.

"Well, so you've seen rhinoceroses too?" asked the chief clerk, who, to my great surprise, was already there.

"Sure I've seen him," I said, taking off my town jacket and putting on my old jacket with the frayed sleeves, good enough for work.

"Oh, now you see, I'm not crazy!" exclaimed the typist Daisy excitedly. (How pretty she was, with her pink cheeks and fair hair! I found her terribly attractive. If I could fall in love with anybody, it would be with her. . . .) "A one-horned rhinoceros!"

"Two-horned!" corrected my colleague Emile Dudard, Bachelor of Law, eminent jurist, who looked forward to a brilliant future with the firm and, possibly, in Daisy's affections.

"*I've* not seen it! And I don't believe in it!" declared

Botard, an ex-schoolmaster who acted as archivist. "And no-body's ever seen one in this part of the world, except in the illustrations to school text-books. These rhinoceroses have blossomed only in the imagination of ignorant women. The thing's a myth, like flying saucers."

I was about to point out to Botard that the expression "blossomed" applied to a rhinoceros, or to a number of them, seemed to me inappropriate, when the jurist exclaimed:

"All the same, a cat was crushed, and before witnesses!"

"Collective psychosis," retorted Botard, who was a free-thinker, "just like religion, the opium of the people!"

"I believe in flying saucers myself," remarked Daisy.

The chief clerk cut short our argument:

"That'll do! Enough chatter! Rhinoceros or no rhinoceros, flying saucers or no flying saucers, work's got to be done."

The typist started typing. I sat down at my desk and became engrossed in my documents. Emile Dudard began correcting the proofs of a commentary on the Law for the Repression of Alcoholism, while the chief clerk, slamming the door, retired into his study.

"It's a hoax!" Botard grumbled once more, aiming his remarks at Dudard. "It's your propaganda that spreads these rumours!"

"It's not propaganda," I interposed.

"I saw it myself . . ." Daisy confirmed simultaneously.

"You make me laugh," said Dudard to Botard. "Propaganda? For what?"

"You know that better than I do! Don't act the simple-ton!"

"In any case, *I'm* not paid by the Pontenegrins!"

"That's an insult!" cried Botard, thumping the table with his fist. The door of the chief clerk's room opened suddenly and his head appeared.

"Monsieur Boeuf hasn't come in today."

"Quite true, he's not here," I said.

"Just when I needed him. Did he tell anyone he was ill? If this goes on I shall give him the sack. . . ."

It was not the first time that the chief clerk had threatened our colleague in this way.

"Has one of you got the key to his desk?" he went on.

Just then Madame Boeuf made her appearance. She seemed terrified.

"I must ask you to excuse my husband. He went to spend the weekend with relations. He's had a slight attack of 'flu. Look, that's what he says in his telegram. He hopes to be back on Wednesday. Give me a glass of water . . . and a chair!" she gasped, collapsing on to the chair we offered her.

"It's very tiresome! But it's no reason to get so alarmed!" remarked the chief clerk.

"I was pursued by a rhinoceros all the way from home," she stammered.

"With one horn or two?" I asked.

"You make me laugh!" exclaimed Botard.

"Why don't you let her speak!" protested Dudard.

Madame Boeuf had to make a great effort to be explicit:

"It's downstairs, in the doorway. It seems to be trying to come upstairs."

At that very moment a tremendous noise was heard: the stairs were undoubtedly giving way under a considerable weight. We rushed out on to the landing. And there, in fact, amidst the debris, was a rhinoceros, its head lowered, trumpeting in an agonized and agonizing voice and turning vainly round and round. I was able to make out two horns.

"It's an African rhinoceros . . ." I said, "or rather an Asian one."

My mind was so confused that I was no longer sure

whether two horns were characteristic of the Asian or of the African rhinoceros, whether a single horn was characteristic of the African or of the Asian rhinoceros, or whether on the contrary two horns . . . In short, I was floundering mentally, while Botard glared furiously at Dudard.

"It's an infamous plot!" and, with an orator's gesture, he pointed at the jurist: "It's your fault!"

"It's yours!" the other retorted.

"Keep calm, this is no time to quarrel!" declared Daisy, trying in vain to pacify them.

"For years now I've been asking the Board to let us have concrete steps instead of that rickety old staircase," said the chief clerk. "Something like this was bound to happen. It was predictable. I was quite right!"

"As usual," Daisy added ironically. "But how shall we get down?"

"I'll carry you in my arms," the chief clerk joked flirtatiously, stroking the typist's cheek, "and we'll jump together!"

"Don't put your horny hand on my face, you pachydermous creature!"

The chief clerk had not time to react. Madame Boeuf, who had got up and come to join us, and who had for some minutes been staring attentively at the rhinoceros, which was turning round and round below us, suddenly uttered a terrible cry:

"It's my husband! Boeuf, my poor dear Boeuf, what has happened to you?"

The rhinoceros, or rather Boeuf, responded with a violent and yet tender trumpeting, while Madame Boeuf fainted into my arms and Botard, raising his to heaven, stormed: "It's sheer lunacy! What a society!"

When we had recovered from our initial astonishment, we telephoned to the Fire Brigade, who drove up with their ladders and fetched us down. Madame Boeuf, although we advised her against it, rode off on her spouse's back towards their home. She had ample grounds for divorce (but who was the guilty party?) yet she chose rather not to desert her husband in his present state.

At the little bistro where we all went for lunch (all except the Boeufs, of course) we learnt that several rhinoceroses had been seen in various parts of the town: some people said seven, others seventeen, others again said thirty-two. In face of this accumulated evidence Botard could no longer deny the rhinoceric facts. But he knew, he declared, what to think about it. He would explain it to us some day. He knew the "why" of things, the "under-side" of the story, the names of those responsible, the aim and significance of the outrage. Going back to the office that afternoon, business or no business, was out of the question. We had to wait for the staircase to be repaired.

I took advantage of this to pay a call on Jean, with the intention of making it up with him. He was in bed.

"I don't feel very well!" he said.

"You know, Jean, we were both right. There are two-horned rhinoceroses in the town as well as one-horned ones. It really doesn't matter where either sort comes from. The only significant thing, in my opinion, is the existence of the rhinoceros in itself."

"I don't feel very well," my friend kept on saying without listening to me, "I don't feel very well!"

"What's the matter with you? I'm so sorry!"

"I'm rather feverish, and my head aches."

More precisely, it was his forehead which was aching. He must have had a knock, he said. And in fact a lump was swelling up there, just above his nose. He had gone a greenish colour, and his voice was hoarse.

"Have you got a sore throat? It may be tonsillitis."

I took his pulse. It was beating quite regularly.

"It can't be very serious. A few days' rest and you'll be all right. Have you sent for the doctor?"

As I was about to let go of his wrist I noticed that his veins were swollen and bulging out. Looking closely I observed that not only were the veins enlarged but that the skin all round them was visibly changing colour and growing hard.

"It may be more serious than I imagined," I thought. "We must send for the doctor." I said aloud.

"I felt uncomfortable in my clothes, and now my pyjamas are too tight," he said in a hoarse voice.

"What's the matter with your skin? It's like leather. . . ." Then, staring at him: "Do you know what happened to Boeuf? He's turned into a rhinoceros."

"Well, what about it? That's not such a bad thing! After all, rhinoceroses are creatures like ourselves, with just as much right to live. . . ."

"Provided they don't imperil our own lives. Aren't you aware of the difference in mentality?"

"Do you think ours is preferable?"

"All the same, we have our own moral code, which I consider incompatible with that of these animals. We have our philosophy, our irreplaceable system of values. . . ."

"Humanism is out of date! You're a ridiculous old sentimentalist. You're talking nonsense."

"I'm surprised to hear you say that, my dear Jean! Have you taken leave of your senses?"

It really looked like it. Blind fury had disfigured his face, and altered his voice to such an extent that I could scarcely understand the words that issued from his lips.

"Such assertions, coming from you. . . ." I tried to resume.

He did not give me a chance to do so. He flung back his blankets, tore off his pyjamas, and stood up in bed, entirely naked (he who was usually the most modest of men!) green with rage from head to foot.

The lump on his forehead had grown longer; he was staring fixedly at me, apparently without seeing me. Or, rather, he must have seen me quite clearly, for he charged at me with his head lowered. I barely had time to leap to one side; if I hadn't he would have pinned me to the wall.

"You are a rhinoceros!" I cried.

"I'll trample on you! I'll trample on you!" I made out these words as I dashed towards the door.

I went downstairs four steps at a time, while the walls shook as he butted them with his horn, and I heard him utter fearful angry trumpetings.

"Call the police! Call the police! You've got a rhinoceros in the house!" I called out to the tenants who, in great surprise, looked out of their flats as I passed each landing.

On the ground floor I had great difficulty in dodging the rhinoceros which emerged from the concierge's lodge and tried to charge me. At last I found myself out in the street, sweating, my legs limp, at the end of my tether.

Fortunately there was a bench by the edge of the pavement, and I sat down on it. Scarcely had I more or less got back my breath when I saw a herd of rhinoceroses hurrying down the avenue and nearing, at full speed, the place where I was. If only they had been content to stay in the middle of the street! But they were so many that there was not room for them all there, and they overflowed on to the pavement. I leapt off my bench and flattened myself against the wall: snorting, trumpeting, with a smell of leather and of wild animals in heat, they brushed past me and covered me with a cloud of dust. When they had disappeared, I could not go back to sit on the bench; the animals had demolished it and it lay in fragments on the pavement.

I did not find it easy to recover from such emotions. I had to stay at home for several days. Daisy came to see me and kept me informed as to the changes that were taking place.

The chief clerk had been the first to turn into a rhinoceros, to the great disgust of Botard who, nevertheless, became one himself twenty-four hours later.

"One must keep up with one's times!" were his last words as a man.

The case of Botard did not surprise me, in spite of his apparent strength of mind. I found it less easy to understand the chief clerk's transformation. Of course it might have been involuntary, but one would have expected him to put up more resistance.

Daisy recalled that she had commented on the roughness of his palms the very day that Boeuf had appeared in rhinoceros shape. This must have made a deep impression on him; he had not shown it, but he had certainly been cut to the quick.

"If I hadn't been so outspoken, if I had pointed it out to him more tactfully, perhaps this would never have happened."

"I blame myself, too, for not having been gentler with Jean. I ought to have been friendlier, shown more understanding," I said in my turn.

Daisy informed me that Dudard, too, had been transformed, as had also a cousin of hers whom I did not know. And there were others, mutual friends, strangers.

"There are a great many of them," she said, "about a quarter of the inhabitants of our town."

"They're still in the minority, however."

"The way things are going, that won't last long!" she sighed.

"Alas! And they're so much more efficient."

Herds of rhinoceroses rushing at top speed through the streets became a sight that no longer surprised anybody. People would stand aside to let them pass and then resume their stroll, or attend to their business, as if nothing had happened.

"How can anybody be a rhinoceros! It's unthinkable!" I protested in vain.

More of them kept emerging from courtyards and houses, even from windows, and went to join the rest.

There came a point when the authorities proposed to enclose them in huge parks. For humanitarian reasons, the Society for the Protection of Animals opposed this. Besides, everyone had some close relative or friend among the rhinoceroses, which, for obvious reasons, made the project well-nigh impracticable. It was abandoned.

The situation grew worse, which was only to be expected. One day a whole regiment of rhinoceroses, having knocked down the walls of the barracks, came out with drums at their head and poured on to the boulevards.

At the Ministry of Statistics, statisticians produced their statistics: census of animals, approximate reckoning of their daily increase, percentage of those with one horn, percentage of those with two. . . . What an opportunity for learned controversies! Soon there were defections among the statisticians themselves. The few who remained were paid fantastic sums.

One day, from my balcony, I caught sight of a rhinoceros charging forward with loud trumpetings, presumably to join his fellows; he wore a straw boater impaled on his horn.

"The logician!" I cried. "He's one too? is it possible?"

Just at that moment Daisy opened the door.

"The logician is a rhinoceros!" I told her.

She knew. She had just seen him in the street. She was bringing me a basket of provisions.

"Shall we have lunch together?" she suggested. "You know, it was difficult to find anything to eat. The shops have been ransacked; they devour everything. A number of shops are closed 'on account of transformations,' the notices say."

"I love you, Daisy, please never leave me."

"Close the window, darling. They make too much noise. And the dust comes in."

"So long as we're together, I'm afraid of nothing, I don't

mind about anything." Then, when I had closed the window: "I thought I should never be able to fall in love with a woman again."

I clasped her tightly in my arms. She responded to my embrace.

"How I'd like to make you happy! Could you be happy with me?"

"Why not? You declare you're afraid of nothing and yet you're scared of everything! What can happen to us?" .

"My love, my joy!" I stammered, kissing her lips with a passion such as I had forgotten, intense and agonizing.

The ringing of the telephone interrupted us.

She broke from my arms, went to pick up the receiver, then uttered a cry: "Listen. . . ."

I put the receiver to my ear. I heard ferocious trumpetings.

"They're playing tricks on us now!"

"Whatever can be happening?" she inquired in alarm.

We turned on the radio to hear the news; we heard more trumpetings. She was shaking with fear.

"Keep calm," I said, "keep calm!"

She cried out in terror: "They've taken over the broadcasting station!"

"Keep calm, keep calm!" I repeated, increasingly agitated myself.

Next day in the street they were running about in all directions. You could watch for hours without catching sight of a single human being. Our house was shaking under the weight of our perissodactylic neighbours' hoofs.

"What must be must be," said Daisy. "What can we do about it?"

"They've all gone mad. The world is sick."

"It's not you and I who'll cure it."

"We shan't be able to communicate with anybody. Can you understand them?"

"We ought to try to interpret their psychology, to learn their language."

"They have no language."

"What do you know about it?"

"Listen to me, Daisy, we shall have children, and then they will have children, it'll take time, but between us we can regenerate humanity. With a little courage. . . ."

"I don't want to have children."

"How do you hope to save the world, then?"

"Perhaps after all it's we who need saving. Perhaps we are the abnormal ones. Do you see anyone else like us?"

"Daisy, I can't have you talking like that!"

I looked at her in despair.

"It's we who are in the right, Daisy, I assure you."

"What arrogance! There's no absolute right. It's the whole world that is right—not you or me."

"Yes, Daisy, I *am* right. The proof is that you understand me and that I love you as much as a man can love a woman."

"I'm rather ashamed of what you call love, that morbid thing. . . . It cannot be compared with the extraordinary energy displayed by all these beings we see around us."

"Energy? Here's energy for you!" I cried, my powers of argument exhausted, giving her a slap.

Then, as she burst into tears: "I won't give in, no, I won't give in."

She rose, weeping, and flung her sweet-smelling arms round my neck.

"I'll stand fast, with you, to the end."

She was unable to keep her word. She grew melancholy, and visibly pined away. One morning when I woke up I saw that her place in the bed was empty. She had gone away without leaving any message.

The situation became literally unbearable for me. It was my fault if Daisy had gone. Who knows what had become of her? Another burden on my conscience. There was nobody who could help me to find her again. I imagined the worst, and felt myself responsible.

And on every side there were trumpetings and frenzied chargings, and clouds of dust. In vain did I shut myself up in my own room, putting cotton wool in my ears: at night I saw them in my dreams.

"The only way out is to convince them." But of what? Were these mutations reversible? And in order to convince them one would have to talk to them. In order for them to re-learn my language (which moreover I was beginning to for-get) I should first have to learn theirs. I could not distinguish one trumpeting from another, one rhinoceros from another rhinoceros.

One day, looking at myself in the glass, I took a dislike to my long face: I needed a horn, or even two, to give dignity to my flabby features.

And what if, as Daisy had said, it was they who were in the right? I was out of date, I had missed the boat, that was clear.

I discovered that their trumpetings had after all a certain charm, if a somewhat harsh one. I should have noticed that while there was still time. I tried to trumpet: how feeble the sound was, how lacking in vigour! When I made greater efforts I only succeeded in howling. Howlings are not trumpetings.

It is obvious that one must not always drift blindly behind events and that it's a good thing to maintain one's individual-ity. However, one must also make allowances for things; assert-ing one's own difference, to be sure, but yet . . . remaining akin to one's fellows. I no longer bore any likeness to anyone or to anything, except to ancient, old-fashioned photographs which had no connection with living beings.

Each morning I looked at my hands hoping that the palms would have hardened during my sleep. The skin remained flabby. I gazed at my too-white body, my hairy legs: oh for a hard skin and that magnificent green colour, a decent, hairless nudity, like theirs!

My conscience was increasingly uneasy, unhappy. I felt I was a monster. Alas, I would never become a rhinoceros. I could never change.

I dared no longer look at myself. I was ashamed. And yet I couldn't, no, I couldn't.

Solid Geometry

IAN McEWAN

In Melton Mowbray in 1875 at an auction of articles of "curiosity and worth," my great-grandfather, in the company of M his friend, bid for the penis of Captain Nicholls who died in Horsemonger jail in 1873. It was bottled in a glass twelve inches long, and, noted my great-grandfather in his diary that night, "in a beautiful state of preservation." Also for auction was "the unnamed portion of the late Lady Barrymore. It went to Sam Israels for fifty guineas." My great-grandfather was keen on the idea of having the two items as a pair, and M dissuaded him. This illustrates perfectly their friendship. My great-grandfather the excitable theorist, M the man of action who knew when to bid at auctions. My great-grandfather lived for sixty-nine years. For forty-five of them, at the end of every day, he sat down before going to bed and wrote his thoughts in a diary. These diaries are on my table now, forty-five volumes bound in calf leather, and to the left sits Capt. Nicholls in the glass jar. My great-grandfather lived on the income derived from the patent of an invention of his father, a handy fastener used by corset-makers right up till the outbreak of the First World War. My great-grandfather liked gossip, numbers and theories. He also liked tobacco, good port, jugged hare and, very occasionally, opium. He liked to think of himself as a mathematician, though he never had a job, and never published a book. Nor did he ever travel or get his name in *The Times*, even when he died. In 1869 he married Alice, only daughter of the Rev. Toby Shadwell, co-author of a not highly regarded book on English wild flowers. I believe my great-grandfather to have been a very fine diarist, and when I have finished editing the diaries and they are published I am certain he will receive the recognition due to him. When my work is over I will take a long holiday, travel somewhere cold and clean and treeless, Iceland or the Russian Steppes. I used to think that at the end of it all I would try, if it was possible, to divorce my wife Maisie, but now there is no need at all.

Often Maisie would shout in her sleep and I would have to wake her.

"Put your arm around me," she would say. "It was a horrible dream. I had it once before. I was in a plane flying over a desert. But it wasn't really a desert. I took the plane lower and I could see there were thousands of babies heaped up, stretching away into the horizon, all of them naked and climbing over each other. I was running out of fuel and I had to land the plane. I tried to find a space, I flew on and on looking for a space . . ."

"Go to sleep now," I said through a yawn. "It was only a dream."

"No," she cried. "I mustn't go to sleep, not just yet."

"Well, *I* have to sleep now," I told her. "I have to be up early in the morning."

She shook my shoulder. "Please don't go to sleep yet, don't leave me here."

"I'm in the same bed," I said. "I won't leave you."

"It makes no difference, don't leave me awake . . ." But my eyes were already closing.

Lately I have taken up my great-grandfather's habit. Before going to bed I sit down for half an hour and think over the day. I have no mathematical whimsies or sexual theories to note down. Mostly I write out what Maisie has said to me and what I have said to Maisie. Sometimes, for complete privacy, I lock myself in the bathroom, sit on the toilet seat and balance the writing-pad on my knees. Apart from me there is occasionally a spider or two in the bathroom. They climb up the waste pipe and crouch perfectly still on the glaring white enamel. They must wonder where they have come to. After hours of crouching they turn back, puzzled, or perhaps disappointed they could not learn more. As far as I can tell, my great-grandfather made only one reference to spiders. On May 8th, 1906, he wrote, "Bismarck is a spider."

In the afternoons Maisie used to bring me tea and tell me her nightmares. Usually I was going through old newspapers, compiling indexes, cataloguing items, putting down this volume, picking up another. Maisie said she was in a bad way. Recently she had been sitting around the house all day glancing at books on psychology and the occult, and almost every night she had bad dreams. Since the time we exchanged physical blows, lying in wait to hit each other with the same shoe outside the bathroom, I had had little sympathy for her. Part of her problem was jealousy. She was very jealous . . . of my great-grandfather's forty-five-volume diary, and of my purpose and energy in editing it. She was doing nothing. I was putting down one volume and picking up another when Maisie came in with the tea.

"Can I tell you my dream?" she asked. "I was flying this plane over a kind of desert . . ."

"Tell me later, Maisie," I said. "I'm in the middle of something here." After she had gone I stared at the wall in front of my desk and thought about M, who came to talk and dine with my great-grandfather regularly over a period of fifteen years up until his sudden and unexplained departure one evening in 1898. M, whoever he might have been, was something of an academic, as well as a man of action. For example, on the evening of August 9th, 1870, the two of them are talking about positions for lovemaking and M tells my great-grandfather that copulation *a posteriori* is the most natural way owing to the position of the clitoris and because other anthropoids favour this method. My great-grandfather, who copulated about half-a-dozen times in his entire life, and that with Alice during the first year of their marriage, wondered out loud what the Church's view was and straightaway M is able to tell him that the seventh-century theologian Theodore considered copulation *a posteriori* a sin ranking with masturbation and therefore worthy of forty penances. Later in the same evening my great-grandfather produced mathematical evidence that the maximum number of positions cannot exceed the prime number seventeen. M scoffed at this and told him he had seen a collection of drawings by Romano, a pupil of Raphael's, in which twenty-four positions were shown. And, he said, he had heard of a Mr F. K. Forberg who had accounted for ninety. By the time I remembered the tea Maisie had left by my elbow it was cold.

An important stage in the deterioration of our marriage was reached as follows. I was sitting in the bathroom one evening writing out a conversation Maisie and I had had about the Tarot pack when suddenly she was outside, rapping on the door and rattling the door-handle.

"Open the door," she called out. "I want to come in."

I said to her, "You'll have to wait a few minutes more. I've almost finished."

"Let me in now," she shouted. "You're not using the toilet."

"Wait," I replied, and wrote another line or two. Now Maisie was kicking the door.

"My period has started and I need to get something." I ignored her yells and finished my piece, which I considered to be particularly important. If I left it till later certain details would be lost. There was no sound from Maisie now and I assumed she was in the bedroom. But when I opened the door she was standing right in my way with a shoe in her hand. She brought the heel of it sharply down on my head, and I only had time to move slightly to one side. The heel caught the top of my ear and cut it badly.

"There," said Maisie, stepping round me to get to the bathroom, "now we are both bleeding," and she banged the door shut. I picked up the shoe and stood quietly and patiently outside the bathroom holding a handkerchief to my bleeding ear. Maisie was in the bathroom about ten minutes and as she came out I caught her neatly and squarely on the top of her head. I did not give her time to move. She stood perfectly still for a moment looking straight into my eyes.

"You worm," she breathed, and went down to the kitchen to nurse her head out of my sight.

During supper yesterday Maisie claimed that a man locked in a cell with only the Tarot cards would have access to all knowledge. She had been doing a reading that afternoon and the cards were still spread about the floor.

"Could he work out the street plan of Valparaiso from the cards?" I asked.

"You're being stupid," she replied.

"Could it tell him the best way to start a laundry business, the best way to make an omelette or a kidney machine?"

"Your mind is so narrow," she complained. "You're so narrow, so predictable."

"Could he," I insisted, "tell me who M is, or why . . ."

"Those things don't matter," she cried. "They're not necessary."

"They are still knowledge. Could he find them out?"

She hesitated. "Yes, he could."

I smiled, and said nothing.

"What's so funny?" she said. I shrugged, and she began to get angry. She wanted to be disproved. "Why did you ask all those pointless questions?"

I shrugged again. "I just wanted to know if you really meant *everything.*"

Maisie banged the table and screamed, "Damn you! Why are you always trying me out? Why don't you say something real?" And with that we both recognized we had reached the point where all our discussions led and we became bitterly silent.

Work on the diaries cannot proceed until I have cleared up the mystery surrounding M. After coming to dinner on and off for fifteen years and supplying my great-grandfather with a mass of material for his theories, M simply disappears from the pages of the diary. On Tuesday, December 6th, my great-grandfather invited M to dine on the following Saturday, and although M came, my great-grandfather in the entry for that day simply writes, "M to dinner." On any other day the conversation at these meals is recorded at great length. M had been to dinner on Monday, December 5th, and the conversation had been about geometry, and the entries for the rest of that week are entirely given over to the same subject. There is absolutely no hint of antagonism. Besides, my great-grandfa-

ther *needed* M. M provided his material, M knew what was
going on, he was familiar with London and he had been on the
Continent a number of times. He knew all about socialism and
Darwin, he had an acquaintance in the free love movement,
a friend of James Hinton. M was *in* the world in a way which
my great-grandfather, who left Melton Mowbray only once in
his lifetime, to visit Nottingham, was not. Even as a young man
my great-grandfather preferred to theorize by the fireside; all
he needed were the materials M supplied. For example, one
evening in June 1884 M, who was just back from London, gave
my great-grandfather an account of how the streets of the town
were fouled and clogged by horse dung. Now in that same week
my great-grandfather had been reading the essay by Malthus
called "On the Principle of Population." That night he made
an excited entry in the diary about a pamphlet he wanted to
write and have published. It was to be called "De Stercore
Equorum." The pamphlet was never published and probably
never written, but there are detailed notes in the diary entries
for the two weeks following that evening. In "De Stercore
Equorum" ("Concerning Horseshit") he assumes geometric
growth in the horse population, and working from detailed
street plans he predicted that the metropolis would be impassable by 1935. By impassable he took to mean an average thickness of one foot (compressed) in every major street. He described involved experiments outside his own stables to
determine the compressibility of horse dung, which he
managed to express mathematically. It was all pure theory, of
course. His results rested on the assumption that no dung
would be shoveled aside in the fifty years to come. Very likely
it was M who talked my great-grandfather out of the project.

One morning, after a long dark night of Maisie's nightmares, we were lying side by side in bed and I said,

"What is it you really want? Why don't you go back to

your job? These long walks, all this analysis, sitting around the house, lying in bed all morning, the Tarot pack, the nightmares . . . what is it you want?"

And she said, "I want to get my head straight," which she had said many times before.

I said, "Your head, your mind, it's not like a hotel kitchen, you know, you can't throw stuff out like old tin cans. It's more like a river than a place, moving and changing all the time. You can't make rivers flow straight."

"Don't go through all that again," she said. "I'm not trying to make rivers flow straight, I'm trying to get my head straight."

"You've got to *do* something," I told her. "You can't do nothing. Why not go back to your job? You didn't have nightmares when you were working. You were never so unhappy when you were working."

"I've got to stand back from all that," she said. "I'm not sure what any of it means."

"Fashion," I said, "it's all fashion. Fashionable metaphors, fashionable reading, fashionable malaise. What do you care about Jung, for example? You've read twelve pages in a month."

"Don't go on," she pleaded, "you know it leads nowhere."

But I went on.

"You've never been anywhere," I told her, "you've never done anything. You're a nice girl without even the blessing of an unhappy childhood. Your sentimental Buddhism, this junk-shop mysticism, joss-stick therapy, magazine astrology . . . none of it is yours, you've worked none of it out for yourself. You fell into it, you fell into a swamp of respectable intuitions. You haven't the originality or passion to intuit anything yourself beyond your own unhappiness. Why are you filling your mind with other people's mystic banalities and giving yourself nightmares?" I got out of bed, opened the curtains and began to get dressed.

"You talk like this was a fiction seminar," Maisie said. "Why are you trying to make things worse for me?" Self-pity began to well up from inside her, but she fought it down. "When you are talking," she went on, "I can feel myself, you know, being screwed up like a piece of paper."

"Perhaps we *are* in a fiction seminar," I said grimly. Maisie sat up in bed staring at her lap. Suddenly her tone changed. She patted the pillow beside her and said softly,

"Come over here. Come and sit here. I want to touch you, I want you to touch me . . ." But I was sighing, and already on my way to the kitchen.

In the kitchen I made myself some coffee and took it through to my study. It had occurred to me in my night of broken sleep that a possible clue to the disappearance of M might be found in the pages of geometry. I had always skipped through them before because mathematics does not interest me. On the Monday, December 5th, 1898, M and my great-grandfather discussed the *vescia piscis*, which apparently is the subject of Euclid's first proposition and a profound influence on the ground plans of many ancient religious buildings. I read through the account of the conversation carefully, trying to understand as best I could the geometry of it. Then, turning the page, I found a lengthy anecdote which M told my great-grandfather that same evening when the coffee had been brought in and the cigars were lit. Just as I was beginning to read Maisie came in.

"And what about you," she said, as if there had not been an hour break in our exchange, "all you have is books. Crawling over the past like a fly on a turd."

I was angry, of course, but I smiled and said cheerfully, "Crawling? Well, at least I'm moving."

"You don't speak to me any more," she said, "you play me like a pinball machine, for points."

"Good morning, Hamlet," I replied, and sat in my chair waiting patiently for what she had to say next. But she did not speak, she left, closing the study door softly behind her.

"In September 1870," M began to tell my great-grandfather,

I came into the possession of certain documents which not only invalidate everything fundamental to our science of solid geometry but also undermine the whole canon of our physical laws and force one to redefine one's place in Nature's scheme. These papers outweigh in importance the combined work of Marx and Darwin. They were entrusted to me by a young American mathematician, and they are the work of David Hunter, a mathematician too and a Scotsman. The American's name was Goodman. I had corresponded with his father over a number of years in connection with his work on the cyclical theory of menstruation which, incredibly enough, is still widely discredited in this country. I met the young Goodman in Vienna where, along with Hunter and mathematicians from a dozen countries, he had been attending an international conference on mathematics. Goodman was pale and greatly disturbed when I met him, and planned to return to America the following day even though the conference was not yet half complete. He gave the papers into my care with instructions that I was to deliver them to David Hunter if I was ever to learn of his whereabouts. And then, only after much persuasion and insistence on my part, he told me what he had witnessed on the third day of the conference. The conference met every morning at nine thirty when a paper was read and a general discus-

sion ensued. At eleven o'clock refreshments were brought
in and many of the mathematicians would get up from the
long, highly polished table round which they were all
gathered and stroll about the large, elegant room and
engage in informal discussions with their colleagues. Now,
the conference lasted two weeks, and by a long-standing
arrangement the most eminent of the mathematicians
read their papers first, followed by the slightly less eminent, and and so on, in a descending hierarchy throughout
the two weeks, which caused, as it is wont to do among
highly intelligent men, occasional but intense jealousies.
Hunter, though a brilliant mathematician, was young and
virtually unknown outside his university, which was Edin-
burgh. He had applied to deliver what he described as a
very important paper on solid geometry, and since he was
of little account in this pantheon he was assigned to read
to the conference on the last day but one, by which time
many of the most important figures would have returned
to their respective countries. And so on the third morning,
as the servants were bringing in the refreshments, Hunter
stood up suddenly and addressed his colleagues just as they
were rising from their seats. He was a large, shaggy man
and, though young, he had about him a certain presence
which reduced the hum of conversation to a complete
silence.

"Gentlemen," said Hunter, "I must ask you to forgive this improper form of address, but I have something
to tell you of the utmost importance. I have discovered
the plane without a surface." Amid derisive smiles and
gentle bemused laughter, Hunter picked up from the
table a large white sheet of paper. With a pocket-knife he
made an incision along its surface about three inches long
and slightly to one side of its centre. Then he made some

rapid, complicated folds and, holding the paper aloft so all could see, he appeared to draw one corner of it through the incision, and as he did so it disappeared.

"Behold, gentlemen," said Hunter, holding out his empty hands towards the company, "the plane without a surface."

Maisie came into my room, washed now and smelling faintly of perfumed soap. She came and stood behind my chair and placed her hands on my shoulders.

"What are you reading?" she said.

"Just bits of the diary which I haven't looked at before." She began to massage me gently at the base of my neck. I would have found it soothing if it had still been the first year of our marriage. But it was the sixth year and it generated a kind of tension which communicated itself the length of my spine. Maisie wanted something. To restrain her I placed my right hand on her left, and, mistaking this for affection, she leaned forward and kissed under my ear. Her breath smelled of toothpaste and toast. She tugged at my shoulder.

"Let's go in the bedroom," she whispered. "We haven't made love for nearly two weeks now."

"I know," I replied. "You know how it is . . . with my work." I felt no desire for Maisie or any other woman. All I wanted to do was turn the next page of my great-grandfather's diary. Maisie took her hands off my shoulders and stood by my side. There was such a sudden ferocity in her silence that I found myself tensing like a sprinter on the starting line. She stretched forward and picked up the sealed jar containing Capt. Nicholls. As she lifted it his penis drifted dreamily from one end of the glass to the other.

"You're so COMPLACENT," Maisie shrieked, just before she hurled the glass bottle at the wall in front of my table.

Instinctively I covered my face with my hands to shield off the
shattering glass. As I opened my eyes I heard myself saying,
    "Why did you do that? That belonged to my great-grand-
father." Amid the broken glass and the rising stench of formaldehyde lay Capt. Nicholls, slouched across the leather covers of a volume of the diary, grey, limp and menacing,
transformed from a treasured curiosity into a horrible obscen-
ity.
    "That was a terrible thing to do. Why did you do that?"
I said again.
    "I'm going for a walk," Maisie replied, and slammed the
door this time as she left the room.
    I did not move from my chair for a long time. Maisie had
destroyed an object of great value to me. It had stood in his
study while he lived, and then it had stood in mine, linking my
life with his. I picked a few splinters of glass from my lap and
stared at the 160-year-old piece of another human on my table.
I looked at it and thought of all the homunculi which had
swarmed down its length. I thought of all the places it had
been, Cape Town, Boston, Jerusalem, travelling in the dark,
fetid inside of Capt. Nicholls's leather breeches, emerging occasionally into the dazzling sunlight to discharge urine in some
jostling public place. I thought also of all the things it had
touched, all the molecules, of Captain Nicholls's exploring
hands on lonely unrequited nights at sea, the sweating walls of
cunts of young girls and old whores, their molecules must still
exist today, a fine dust blowing from Cheapside to Leicester-
shire. Who knows how long it might have lasted in its glass jar.
I began to clear up the mess. I brought the rubbish bucket in
from the kitchen. I swept and picked up all the glass I could
find and swabbed up the formaldehyde. Then, holding him by
just one end, I tried to ease Capt. Nicholls on to a sheet of
newspaper. My stomach heaved as the foreskin began to come

away in my fingers. Finally, with my eyes closed, I succeeded, and wrapping him carefully in the newspaper, I carried him into the garden and buried him under the geraniums. All this time I tried to prevent my resentment towards Maisie filling my mind. I wanted to continue with M's story. Back in my chair I dabbed at a few spots of formaldehyde which had blotted the ink, and read on.

For as long as a minute the room was frozen, and with each successive second it appeared to freeze harder. The first to speak was Dr Stanley Rose of Cambridge University, who had much to lose by Hunter's plane without a surface. His reputation, which was very considerable indeed, rested upon his "Principles of Solid Geometry."

"How dare you, sir. How dare you insult the dignity of this assembly with a worthless conjuror's trick." And bolstered by the rising murmur of concurrence behind him, he added, "You should be ashamed, young man, thoroughly ashamed." With that, the room erupted like a volcano. With the exception of young Goodman, and of the servants who still stood by with the refreshments, the whole room turned on Hunter and directed at him a senseless babble of denunciation, invective and threat. Some thumped on the table in their fury, others waved their clenched fists. One very frail German gentlemen fell to the floor in an apoplexy and had to be helped to a chair. And there stood Hunter, firm and outwardly unmoved, his head inclined slightly to one side, his fingers resting lightly on the surface of the long polished table. That such an uproar should follow a worthless conjuror's trick clearly demonstrated the extent of the underlying unease, and Hunter surely appreciated this. Raising his hand, and the company falling suddenly silent once more, he said,

"Gentlemen, your concern is understandable and I will effect another proof, the ultimate proof." This said, he sat down and removed his shoes, stood up and removed his jacket, and then called for a volunteer to assist him, at which Goodman came forward. Hunter strode through the crowd to a couch which stood along one of the walls, and while he settled himself upon it he told the mystified Goodman that when he returned to England he should take with him Hunter's papers and keep them there until he came to collect them. When the mathematicians had gathered round the couch Hunter rolled on to his stomach and clasped his hands behind his back in a strange posture to fashion a hoop with his arms. He asked Goodman to hold his arms in that position for him, and rolled on his side where he began a number of strenuous jerking movements which enabled him to pass one of his feet through the hoop. He asked his assistant to turn him on his other side, where he performed the same movements again and succeeded in passing his other foot between his arms, and at the same time bent his trunk in such a way that his head was able to pass through the hoop in the opposite direction to his feet. With the help of his assistant he began to pass his legs and head past each other through the hoop made by his arms. It was then that the distinguished assembly vented, as one man, a single yelp of utter incredulity. Hunter was beginning to disappear, and now, as his legs and head passed through his arms with greater facility, seemed even to be drawn through by some invisible power, he was almost gone. And now . . . he was gone, quite gone, and nothing remained.

M's story put my great-grandfather in a frenzy of excitement. In his diary that night he recorded how he tried "to prevail upon my guest to send for the papers upon the instant" even though it was by now two o'clock in the morning. M, however, was more sceptical about the whole thing. "Americans," he told my great-grandfather, "often indulge in fantastic tales." But he agreed to bring along the papers the following day. As it turned out M did not dine with my great-grandfather that night because of another engagement, but he called round in the late afternoon with the papers. Before he left he told my great-grandfather he had been through them a number of times and "there was no sense to be had out of them." He did not realize then how much he was underestimating my great-grandfather as an amateur mathematician. Over a glass of sherry in front of the drawing-room fire the two men arranged to dine together again at the end of the week, on Saturday. For the next three days my great-grandfather hardly paused from his reading of Hunter's theorems to eat or sleep. The diary is full of nothing else. The pages are covered with scribbles, diagrams and symbols. It seems that Hunter had to devise a new set of symbols, virtually a whole new language, to express his ideas. By the end of the second day my great-grandfather had made his first breakthrough. At the bottom of a page of mathematical scribble he wrote, "Dimensionality is a function of consciousness." Turning to the entry for the next day I read the words, "It disappeared in my hands." He had reestablished the plane without a surface. And there, spread out in front of me, were step by step instructions on how to fold the piece of paper. Turning the next page I suddenly understood the mystery of M's disappearance. Undoubtedly encouraged by my great-grandfather, he had taken part that evening in a scientific experiment, probably in a spirit of great scepticism. For here my great-grandfather had drawn a series of small sketches illustrating what at first glance looked like yoga positions. Clearly they were the secret of Hunter's disappearing act.

My hands were trembling as I cleared a space on my desk. I selected a clean sheet of typing paper and laid it in front of me. I fetched a razor blade from the bathroom. I rummaged in a drawer and found an old pair of compasses, sharpened a pencil and fitted it in. I searched through the house till I found an accurate steel ruler I had once used for fitting window panes, and then I was ready. First I had to cut the paper to size. The piece that Hunter had so casually picked up from the table had obviously been carefully prepared beforehand. The length of the sides had to express a specific ratio. Using the compasses I found the centre of the paper and through this point I drew a line parallel to one of the sides and continued it right to the edge. Then I had to construct a rectangle whose measurements bore a particular relation to those of the sides of the paper. The center of this rectangle occurred on the line in such a way as to dissect it by the Golden Mean. From the top of this rectangle I drew intersecting arcs, again of specified proportionate radii. This operation was repeated at the lower end of the rectangle, and when the two points of intersection were joined I had the line of incision. Then I started work on the folding lines. Each line seemed to express, in its length, angle of incline and point of intersection with other lines, some mysterious inner harmony of numbers. As I intersected arcs, drew lines and made folds, I felt I was blindly operating a system of the highest, most terrifying form of knowledge, the mathematics of the Absolute. By the time I had made the final fold the piece of paper was the shape of a geometric flower with three concentric rings arranged round the incision at the centre. There was something so tranquil and perfect about this design, something so remote and compelling, that as I stared into it I felt myself going into a light trance and my mind becoming clear and inactive. I shook my head and glanced away. It was time now to turn the flower in on itself and pull it through the incision.

This was a delicate operation and now my hands were trembling again. Only by staring into the centre of the design could I calm myself. With my thumbs I began to push the sides of the paper flower towards the centre, and as I did so I felt a numbness settle over the back of my skull. I pushed a little further, the paper glowed whiter for an instant and then it *seemed* to disappear. I say "seemed" because at first I could not be sure whether I could feel it still in my hands and not see it, or see it but not feel it, or whether I could sense it had disappeared while its external properties remained. The numbness had spread right across my head and shoulders. My senses seemed inadequate to grasp what was happening. "Dimensionality is a function of consciousness," I thought. I brought my hands together and there was nothing between them, but even when I opened them again and saw nothing I could not be sure the paper flower had completely gone. An impression remained, an after-image not on the retina but on the mind itself. Just then the door opened behind me, and Maisie said,

"What are you doing?"

I returned as if from a dream to the room and to the faint smell of formaldehyde. It was a long, long time ago now, the destruction of Capt. Nicholls, but the smell revived my resentment, which spread through me like the numbness. Maisie slouched in the doorway, muffled in a thick coat and woolen scarf. She seemed a long way off, and as I looked at her my resentment merged into a familiar weariness of our marriage. I thought, why did she break the glass? Because she wanted to make love? Because she wanted a penis? Because she was jealous of my work, and wanted to smash the connection it had with my great-grandfather's life?

"Why did you do it?" I said out loud, involuntarily. Maisie snorted. She had opened the door and found me hunched over my table staring at my hands.

"Have you been sitting there all afternoon," she asked, "thinking about *that?*" She giggled. "What happened to it, anyway? Did you suck it off?"

"I buried it," I said, "under the geraniums."

She came into the room a little way and said in a serious tone, "I'm sorry about that, I really am. I just did it before I knew what was happening. Do you forgive me?" I hesitated, and then, because my weariness had blossomed into a sudden resolution, I said,

"Yes, of course I forgive you. It was only a prick in pickle," and we both laughed. Maisie came over to me and kissed me, and I returned the kiss, prising open her lips with my tongue.

"Are you hungry?" she said, when we were done with kissing. "Shall I make some supper?"

"Yes," I said. "I would love that." Maisie kissed me on the top of my head and left the room, while I turned back to my studies, resolving to be as kind as I possibly could to Maisie that evening.

Later we sat in the kitchen eating the meal Maisie had cooked and getting mildly drunk on a bottle of wine. We smoked a joint, the first one we had had together in a very long time. Maisie told me how she was going to get a job with the Forestry Commission planting trees in Scotland next summer. And I told Maisie about the conversation M and my great-grandfather had had about *a posteriori*, and about my great-grandfather's theory that there could not be more than the prime number seventeen positions for making love. We both laughed, and Maisie squeezed my hand, and lovemaking hung in the air between us, in the warm fug of the kitchen. Then we put our coats on and went for a walk. It was almost a full moon. We walked along the main road which runs outside our house and then turned down a narrow street of tightly packed houses with immaculate and minute front gardens. We did not talk much, but our arms were linked and Maisie told me how very stoned and happy she was. We came to a small park which was locked and we stood outside the gates looking up at the moon through the almost leafless branches. When we came home Maisie took a leisurely hot bath while I browsed in my study, checking on a few details. Our bedroom is a warm, comfortable room, luxurious in its way. The bed is seven foot by eight, and I made it myself in the first year of our marriage. Maisie made the sheets, dyed them a deep, rich blue and embroidered the pillow cases. The only light in the room shone through a rough old goatskin lampshade Maisie bought from a man who came to the door. It was a long time since I had taken an interest in the bedroom. We lay side by side in the tangle of sheets and rugs, Maisie voluptuous and drowsy after her bath and stretched full out, and I propped up on my elbow. Maisie said sleepily,

"I was walking along the river this afternoon. The trees are beautiful now, the oaks, the elms . . . there are two copper beeches about a mile past the footbridge, you should see them now . . . ahh, that feels good." I had eased her on to her belly and was caressing her back as she spoke. "There are blackberries, the biggest ones I've ever seen, growing all along the path, and elderberries, too. I'm going to make some wine this autumn . . ." I leaned over her and kissed the nape of her neck and brought her arms behind her back. She liked to be manipulated in this way and she submitted warmly. "And the river is really still," she was saying. "You know, reflecting the trees, and the leaves are dropping into the river. Before the winter comes we should go there together, by the river, in the leaves. I found this little place. No one goes there . . ." Holding Maisie's arms in position with one hand, I worked her legs towards the "hoop" with the other. ". . . I sat in this place for half an hour without moving, like a tree. I saw a water-rat

running along the opposite bank, and different kinds of ducks
landing on the river and taking off. I heard these plopping
noises in the river but I didn't know what they were and I saw
two orange butterflies, they almost came on my hand." When
I had her legs in place Maisie said, "Position number eighteen," and we both laughed softly. "Let's go there tomorrow,
to the river," said Maisie as I carefully eased her head towards
her arms. "Careful, careful, that hurts," she suddenly shouted,
and tried to struggle. But it was too late now, her head and legs
were in place in the hoop of her arms, and I was beginning to
push them through, past each other. "What's happening?"
cried Maisie. Now the positioning of her limbs expressed the
breathtaking beauty, the nobility of the human form, and, as
in the paper flower, there was a fascinating power in its symme-
try. I felt the trance coming on again and the numbness set-
tling over the back of my head. As I drew her arms and legs
through, Maisie appeared to turn in on herself like a sock. "Oh
God," she sighed, "what's happening?" and her voice sounded
very far away. Then she was gone . . . and not gone. Her voice
was quite tiny, "What's happening?" and all that remained was
the echo of her question above the deep-blue sheets.

●

The Smallest Woman in the World

CLARICE LISPECTOR

Translated by Giovanni Pontiero

In the depths of equatorial Africa the French explorer, Marcel Pretre, hunter and man of the world, came across a tribe of pygmies of surprising minuteness. He was even more surprised, however, to learn that an even smaller race existed far beyond the forests. So he traveled more deeply into the jungle.

In the Central Congo he discovered, in fact, the smallest pygmies in the world. And—like a box inside another box, inside yet another box—among the smallest pygmies in the world, he found the smallest of the smallest pygmies in the world, answering, perhaps, to the need that Nature sometimes feels to surpass herself.

Among the mosquitoes and the trees moist with humidity, among the luxuriant vegetation of the most indolent green, Marcel Pretre came face to face with a woman no more than forty-five centimeters tall, mature, black, and silent. "As black as a monkey," he would inform the newspapers, and she lived at the top of a tree with her little mate. In the warm humidity of the forest, which matured the fruits quickly and gave them an unbearably sweet taste, she was pregnant. Meanwhile there she stood, the smallest woman in the world. For a second, in the drone of the jungle heat, it was as if the Frenchman had unexpectedly arrived at the end of the line. Certainly, it was only because he was sane that he managed to keep his head and not lose control. Sensing a sudden need to restore order, and to give a name to what exists, he called her Little Flower. And, in order to be able to classify her among the identifiable realities, he immediately began to gather data about her.

Her race is slowly being exterminated. Few human examples remain of their species which, were it not for the subtle dangers of Africa, would be a widely scattered race.

Excluding disease, the polluted air of its rivers, deficiencies of food, and wild beasts on the prowl, the greatest hazard for the few remaining Likoualas are the savage Bantus, a threat which surrounds them in the silent air as on the morning of battle. The Bantus pursue them with nets as they pursue monkeys. And they eat them. Just like that: they pursue them with nets and eat them. So this race of tiny people went on retreating and retreating until it finally settled in the heart of Africa where the fortunate explorer was to discover them. As a strategic defense, they live in the highest trees. The women come down in order to cook maize, grind mandioca, and gather green vegetables; the men to hunt. When a child is born, he is given his freedom almost at once. Often, one must concede, the child does not enjoy his freedom for long among the wild beasts of the jungle, but, at least, he cannot complain that for such a short life the labor had been long. Even the language that the child learns is short and simple, consisting only of the essentials. The Likoualas use few names and they refer to things by gestures and animal noises. As a spiritual enhancement, he possesses his drum. While they dance to the sound of the drum, a tiny male keeps watch for the Bantus, who appear from heaven knows where.

This, then, was how the explorer discovered at his feet the smallest human creature that exists. His heart pounded, for surely no emerald is so rare. Not even the teachings of the Indian sages are so rare, and even the richest man in the world has not witnessed such strange charm. There, before his eyes, stood a woman such as the delights of the most exquisite dream had never equaled. It was then that the explorer timidly pronounced with a delicacy of feeling of which even his wife would never have believed him capable, "You are Little Flower."

At that moment, Little Flower scratched herself where one never scratches oneself. The explorer—as if he were receiving the highest prize of chastity to which man, always so full of ideals, dare aspire—the explorer who has so much experience of life, turned away his eyes.

The photograph of Little Flower was published in the color supplement of the Sunday newspapers, where she was reproduced life size. She appeared wrapped in a shawl, with her belly in an advanced stage. Her nose was flat, her face black, her eyes deep-set, and her feet splayed. She looked just like a dog.

That same Sunday, in an apartment, a woman, glancing at the picture of Little Flower in the open newspaper, did not care to look a second time, "because it distresses me."

In another apartment, a woman felt such a perverse tenderness for the daintiness of the African woman that—prevention being better than cure—Little Flower should never be left alone with the tenderness of that woman. Who knows to what darkness of love her affection might extend. The woman passed a troubled day, overcome, one might say, by desire. Besides, it was spring and there was a dangerous longing in the air.

In another house, a little five-year-old girl, upon seeing Little Flower's picture and listening to the comments of her parents, became frightened. In that house of adults, this little girl had been, until now, the smallest of human beings. And, if this was the source of the nicest endearments, it was also the source of that first fear of tyrannical love. The existence of Little Flower caused the little girl to feel—with a vagueness which only many years later, and, for quite different reasons, she was to experience as a concrete thought—caused her to feel with premature awareness, that "misfortune knows no limits."

In another house, in the consecration of spring, a young girl about to be married burst out compassionately, "Mother, look at her picture, poor little thing! Just look at her sad expression!"

"Yes," replied the girl's mother—hard, defeated, and proud—"but that is the sadness of an animal, not of a human."

"Oh Mother!" the girl protested in despair.

It was in another house that a bright child had a bright idea.

"Mummy, what if I were to put this tiny woman in little Paul's bed while he is sleeping? When he wakes up, what a fright he'll get, eh? What a din he'll make when he finds her sitting up in bed beside him! And then we could play with her! We could make her our toy, eh!"

His mother, at that moment, was rolling her hair in front of the bathroom mirror, and she remembered what the cook had told her about her time as an orphan. Not having any dolls to play with, and maternal feelings already stirring furiously in their hearts, some deceitful girls in the orphanage had concealed from the nun in charge the death of one of their companions. They kept her body in a cupboard until Sister went out, and then they played with the dead girl, bathing her and feeding her little tidbits, and they punished her only to be able to kiss and comfort her afterward.

The mother recalled this in the bathroom and she lowered her awkward hands, full of hairpins. And she considered the cruel necessity of loving. She considered the malignity of our desire to be happy. She considered the ferocity with which we want to play. And the number of times when we murder for love. She then looked at her mischievous son as if she were looking at a dangerous stranger. And she was horrified at her own soul, which, more than her body, had engendered that being so apt for life and happiness. And thus she looked at him, attentively and with uneasy pride, her child already without two front teeth, his evolution, his evolution under way, his teeth falling out to make room for those which bite best. "I must buy him a new suit," she decided, looking at him intently. She obstinately dressed up her toothless child in fancy clothes, and obstinately insisted upon keeping him clean and tidy, as if cleanliness might give emphasis to a tranquilizing superficiality, obstinately perfecting the polite aspect of beauty. Obstinately removing herself, and removing him from something which must be as "black as a monkey." Then, looking into the bathroom mirror, the mother smiled, intentionally refined and polished, placing between that face of hers of abstract lines and the raw face of Little Flower, the insuperable distance of millennia. But with years of experience she knew that this would be a Sunday on which she would have to conceal from herself her anxiety, her dream, and the lost millennia.

In another house, against a wall, they set about the exciting business of calculating with a measuring tape the forty-five centimeters of Little Flower. And as they enjoyed themselves they made a startling discovery: she was even smaller than the most penetrating imagination could ever have invented. In the heart of each member of the family there arose the gnawing desire to possess that minute and indomitable thing for himself, that thing which had been saved from being devoured, that enduring fount of charity. The eager soul of that family was roused to dedication. And, indeed, who has not wanted to possess a human being just for himself? A thing, it is true, which would not always be convenient, for there are moments when one would choose not to have sentiments.

"I'll bet you if she lived here we would finish up quarreling," said the father, seated in his armchair, firmly turning the pages of the newspaper. "In this house everything finishes up with a quarrel."

"You are always such a pessimist, José," said the mother.

"Mother, can you imagine how tiny her little child will be?" their oldest girl, thirteen, asked intensely.

The father fidgeted behind his newspaper.

"It must be the smallest black baby in the world," replied the mother, melting with pleasure. "Just imagine her waiting on table here in the house! And with her swollen little belly."

"That's enough of that rubbish!" muttered the father, annoyed.

"You must admit," said the mother, unexpectedly peeved, "that the thing is unique. You are the one who is insensitive."

And what about the unique thing itself?

Meanwhile, in Africa, the unique thing itself felt in its heart—perhaps also black, because one can no longer have confidence in a Nature that had already blundered once—meanwhile the unique thing itself felt in its heart something still more rare, rather like the secret of its own secret: a minute child. Methodically, the explorer examined with his gaze the belly of the smallest mature human being. It was at that moment that the explorer, for the first time since he had known her—instead of experiencing curiosity, enthusiasm, a sense of triumph, or the excitement of discovery—felt distinctly ill at ease.

The fact is that the smallest woman in the world was smiling. She was smiling and warm, warm. Little Flower was enjoying herself. The unique thing itself was enjoying the ineffable sensation of not having been devoured yet. Not to have been devoured was something which at other times gave her the sudden impulse to leap from branch to branch. But at this tranquil moment, among the dense undergrowth of the Central Congo, she was not applying that impulse to an action— and the impulse concentrated itself completely in the very smallness of the unique thing itself. And suddenly she was smiling. It was a smile that only someone who does not speak can smile. A smile that the uncomfortable explorer did not succeed in classifying. And she went on enjoying her own gentle smile, she who was not being devoured. Not to be devoured is the most perfect sentiment. Not to be devoured is the secret objective of a whole existence. While she was not being devoured, her animal smile was as delicate as happiness. The explorer felt disconcerted.

In the second place, if the unique thing itself was smiling it was because, inside her minute body, a great darkness had started to stir.

It is that the unique thing itself felt her breast warm with that which might be called love. She loved that yellow explorer. If she knew how to speak and should say that she loved him, he would swell with pride. Pride that would diminish when she should add that she also adored the explorer's ring and his boots. And when he became deflated with disappointment, Little Flower would fail to understand. Because, not even remotely, would her love for the

explorer—one can even say her "deep love," because without other resources she was reduced to depth—since not
even remotely would her deep love for the explorer lose its
value because she also loved his boots. There is an old misunderstanding about the word "love," and if many children
are born on account of that mistake, many others have lost
the unique instant of birth simply on account of a suscepti-
bility which exacts that it should be me, me that should be
loved and not my money. But in the humidity of the jungle, there do not exist these cruel refinements; love is not
to be devoured, love is to find boots pretty, love is to like
the strange color of a man who is not black, love is to smile
out of love at a ring that shines. Little Flower blinked with
love and smiled, warm, small, pregnant, and warm.

The explorer tried to smile back at her, without knowing
exactly to which charm his smile was replying, and then became disturbed as only a full-grown man becomes disturbed.
He tried to conceal his uneasiness, by adjusting his helmet on
his head, and he blushed with embarrassment. He turned a
pretty color, his own, greenish pink hue, like that of a lime in
the morning light. He must be sour.

It was probably upon adjusting his symbolic helmet that
the explorer called himself to order, returned severely to the
discipline of work, and resumed taking notes. He had learned
to understand some of the few words articulated by the tribe
and to interpret their signs. He was already able to ask questions.

Little Flower answered "yes." That it was very nice to
have a tree in which to live by herself, all by herself. Because
—and this she did not say, but her eyes became so dark that
they said it—because it is nice to possess, so nice to possess.
The explorer blinked several times.

Marcel Pretre experienced a few difficult moments trying

to control himself. But at least he was kept occupied in taking notes. Anyone not taking notes had to get along as best he could.

"Well, it just goes to show," an old woman suddenly exclaimed, folding her newspaper with determination, "it just goes to show. I'll say one thing though—God knows what He's about."

Scene

ALAIN ROBBE-GRILLET

Translated by Bruce Morrissette

As the curtain opens, the first thing seen from the orchestra pit—between the sections of red velvet drawing slowly apart—the first thing glimpsed is an actor, with back turned, sitting at a worktable in the center of the brightly lighted stage.

The personage sits motionless, elbows and forearms resting on the table top. The head is turned toward the right—at about forty-five degrees—not enough to allow the features of the face to be discerned, except for the beginnings of an invisible profile: the cheek, the temple, the edge of the jaw, the outline of the ear. . . .

Nor can the hands be seen, although the attitude allows their relative position to be inferred: the left spread out flat on scattered sheets of paper, the other grasping a pen, lifted above an interrupted text for a moment of reflection. On either side are piled up in disorder a number of large books, whose shape and size would indicate them to be dictionaries—of a foreign language, no doubt—an ancient language, probably.

The head, turned toward the right, is raised: the glance has moved up from the books and the interrupted sentence. It is directed toward the back of the room, to the spot where heavy, red velvet curtains conceal, from floor to ceiling, some large bay window. The folds of the curtains are vertical and very regular, at close intervals, creating, in between, deep hollows of darkness. . . .

A violent noise attracts attention to the other end of the room: blows struck against a wooden panel, so loudly and insistently as to imply that they are now being repeated, at least for the second time.

Yet the individual remains silent and motionless. Then, with no movement of the bust, the head turns, slowly, toward the left. The raised glance thus traverses the whole wall which forms the back of the large room, a wall bare—that is, without furniture—but covered with dark wood paneling, from the red curtains of the window to the panel of the closed door, which is of ordinary, or slightly less than ordinary, height. There the glance stops, while the blows at that point sound loudly again, blows so violent that the wooden panel seems to tremble.

The features of the face remain invisible, in spite of this change of posture. In fact, after a rotation of about ninety degrees, the head now occupies a position symmetrical to that of the beginning, with respect to a common central axis through the room, the table, and the chair. Thus, of an invisible profile, we can discern the other cheek, the other temple, the other ear. . . .

Once more there is a knock at the door, but more feeble, like a last entreaty—or as if in hopelessness, or in a state of calm after anguish, or of lack of assurance, or in any other mood. A few seconds later, heavy steps are heard gradually growing fainter down a long corridor.

The actor again faces toward the red curtains on the right.

We hear a whistle, from between the teeth: a few notes of what must be a musical phrase—some popular song or melody—but deformed, fragmentary, difficult to identify.

Then, after a minute of silent immobility, the individual looks down again at the work to be done.

The head drops. The back hunches over. The chair back is a rectangular framework, completed by two vertical bars which support, in the center, a solid square of wood. Again we hear, weaker, even more disjointed, a few measures of the melody, whistled between the teeth.

Suddenly the personage looks up toward the door and freezes, motionless, neck tense. The position is held for many seconds —as if eavesdropping. Yet, from the auditorium, not the slightest noise can be heard.

The actor rises cautiously, pushes aside the chair without allowing it to drag or strike against the floor, and begins to walk silently toward the velvet curtains. Gently drawing forward the outer edge, on the right side, the personage looks out the window in the direction of the door—to the left. The left profile would then be discernible, if it were not hidden by the edge of red curtain held against the cheek. On the other hand, the sheets of white paper may now be seen spread out on the table.

There are a number of them, lying partially one over the other. The lower sheets, whose corners protrude on all sides in very irregular fashion, are crosshatched by closely written lines, in a very careful hand. The top sheet, the only one fully visible, is as yet only half covered with writing. The words end in the middle of a line, in an interrupted sentence, with no sign of punctuation after the last word.

From below the right edge of this sheet extends the corner of the sheet beneath: an elongated triangle, whose base measures about an inch and whose sharp point is directed toward the back part of the table, where the dictionaries are.

Still farther to the right, beyond this little point, but turned toward the side of the table, the corner of another page extends a whole hand's breadth; it, too, has a triangular form, this time close to that of a half square, cut along a diagonal. Between the peak of this last triangle and the nearest dictionary there lies, on the waxed wood of the table, a whitish object the size of a fist: a piece of rock polished by handling, hollowed out into a sort of thick cup—the thickness much greater than the depth of the cup—with irregular, rounded contours. In the bottom of the cuplike depression, a cigarette butt lies crushed out in its ashes. At the unburned end, the paper shows obvious traces of lipstick.

The actor present upon the stage, however, was—apparently —a man: hair cut short, coat and trousers. Looking up, we observe that the figure is now standing before the door, looking at it, that is, still facing away from the auditorium. From this attitude we would deduce that the actor is trying to overhear something, something going on beyond the panel of the door.

But no noise reaches the auditorium. Without turning about, the actor walks backward downstage, continuing to watch the door. From a position near the table, the right hand is placed on one corner of it and . . .

"More slowly!" a voice, at that instant, calls out from the orchestra pit. It is someone speaking through a megaphone, no doubt, since the syllables ring out with abnormal volume.

The actor stops. The voice again says:

"More slowly! Do that movement more slowly! Take it again from the door: take one step backward first—just one step—and then don't move for fifteen or twenty seconds. Then start your backward walk to the table, but much more slowly."

So the actor is again standing opposite the door, facing it, that is, still facing away from the hall. From that posture we deduce that the personage is trying to overhear something going on beyond the door. No noise reaches the auditorium. Without looking around, the actor takes one step back and again stands motionless. After a pause the figure again walks backward toward the table, where the work lies waiting, very slowly, with tiny, regularly spaced steps, while continuing to stare at the door. The motion is linear, and at constant speed. Above the legs which scarcely seem to move, the bust remains perfectly rigid, as do the two arms, held slightly apart from the body, and arched.

Reaching the vicinity of the table, the actor puts one hand —the right—on one corner, and, in order to move along the left edge, changes direction to a slight degree. Using the wooden edge as a guide, the personage moves—now, perpendicularly to the footlights . . . then, turning the corner, parallel to them . . . and sits down again on the chair, hiding with a wide back the sheets of paper spread out on the table.

The actor looks at the sheets of paper, then at the red curtains over the window, then again at the door; and, head turned in that direction, utters four or five indistinct words.

"Louder!" calls out the megaphone in the auditorium.

"And now, in this place, my life, once more . . ." says a voice of normal pitch, the voice of the actor on the stage.

"Louder!" the megaphone calls.

"And now, in this place, my life, once more . . ." the actor repeats, in a louder tone.

Then the person on the stage is again immersed in the work to be done.

On a Journey

SLAWOMIR MROZEK

Translated by Konrad Syrop

Just after B—— the road took us among damp, flat meadows.
Only here and there the expanse of green was broken by a
stubble field. In spite of mud and potholes the chaise was
moving at a brisk pace. Far ahead, level with the ears of the
horses, a blue band of the forest was stretching across the
horizon. As one would expect at that time of the year, there
was not a soul in sight.

Only after we had traveled for a while did I see the first
human being. As we approached his features became clear; he
was a man with an ordinary face and he wore a Post Office
uniform. He was standing still at the side of the road, and as
we passed he threw us an indifferent glance. No sooner had we
left him behind than I noticed another one, in a similar uniform, also standing motionless on the verge. I looked at him
carefully, but my attention was immediately attracted by the

third and then the fourth still figure by the roadside. Their
apathetic eyes were all fixed in the same direction, their uniforms were faded.

Intrigued by this spectacle I rose in my seat so that I could
glance over the shoulders of the cabman; indeed, ahead of us
another figure was standing erect. When we passed two more
of them my curiosity became irresistible. There they were,
standing quite a distance from each other, yet near enough to
be able to see the next man, holding the same posture and
paying as much attention to us as road signs do to passing
travellers. And as soon as we passed one, another came into our
field of vision. I was about to open my mouth to ask the
coachman about the meaning of those men, when, without
turning his head, he volunteered: "On duty."

We were just passing another still figure, staring indifferently into the distance.

"How's that?" I asked.

"Well, just normal. They are standing on duty," and he
urged the horses on.

The coachman showed no inclination to offer any further
elucidation; perhaps he thought it was superfluous. Cracking
his whip from time to time and shouting at the horses, he was
driving on. Roadside brambles, shrines and solitary willow trees
came to meet us and receded again in the distance; between
them, at regular intervals, I could see the now familiar sil-
houettes.

"What sort of duty are they doing?" I enquired.

"State duty, of course. Telegraph line."

"How's that? Surely for a telegraph line you need poles
and wires!"

The coachman looked at me and shrugged his shoulders.

"I can see that you've come from far away," he said. "Yes,
we know that for a telegraph you need poles and wires. But this

is wireless telegraph. We were supposed to have one with wires but the poles got stolen and there's no wire."

"What do you mean, no wire?"

"There simply isn't any," he said, and shouted at the horses.

Surprise silenced me for the moment but I had no intention of abandoning my enquiries.

"And how does it work without wires?"

"That's easy. The first one shouts what's needed to the second, the second repeats it to the third, the third to the fourth and so on until the telegram gets to where it's supposed to. Just now they aren't transmitting or you'd hear them yourself."

"And it works, this telegraph?"

"Why shouldn't it work? It works all right. But often the message gets twisted. It's worst, when one of them has had a drink too many. Then his imagination gets to work and various words get added. But otherwise it's even better than the usual telegraph with poles and wires. After all live men are more intelligent, you know. And there's no storm damage to repair and great saving on timber, and timber is short. Only in the winter there are sometimes interruptions. Wolves. But that can't be helped."

"And those men, are they satisfied?" I asked.

"Why not? The work isn't very hard, only they've got to know foreign words. And it'll get better still; the postmaster has gone to Warsaw to ask for megaphones for them so that they don't have to shout so much."

"And should one of them be hard of hearing?"

"Ah, they don't take such-like. Nor do they take men with a lisp. Once they took on a chap that stammered. He got his job through influence but he didn't keep it long because he was blocking the line. I hear that by the twenty kilometres' stone

there's one who went to a drama school. He shouts most
clearly."

His arguments confused me for a while. Deep in thought,
I no longer paid attention to the men by the road verge. The
chaise was jumping over potholes, moving towards the forest,
which was now occupying most of the horizon.

"All right," I said carefully, "but wouldn't you prefer to
have a new telegraph with poles and wires?"

"Good heavens, no." The coachman was shocked. "For
the first time it's easy to get a job in our district in the telegraph, that is. And people don't have to rely only on their
wages either. If someone expects a cable and is particularly
anxious not to have it twisted, then he takes his chaise along
the line and slips something into the pocket of each one of
the telegraph boys. After all a wireless telegraph is something
different from one with wires. More modern."

Over the rattle of the wheels I could hear a distant sound,
neither a cry nor a shout, but a sort of sustained wailing.

"Aaaeeeaaauuueeeaaaeeeaayayay."

The coachman turned in his seat and put his hand to his
ear.

"They are transmitting," he said. "Let's stop so that we
can hear better."

When the monotonous noise of our wheels ceased, total
silence enveloped the fields. In that silence the wailing, which
resembled the cry of birds on a moor, came nearer to us. His
hand cupped to his ear, the telegraph man nearby made ready
to receive.

"It'll get here in a moment," whispered the coachman.

Indeed. When the last distant "ayayay" died away, from
behind a clump of trees came the prolonged shout:

"Fa . . . th . . . er dea . . . d fu . . . ner . . . al Wed
. . . nes . . . day."

"May he rest in peace," sighed the coachman and cracked
his whip. We were entering the forest.

False Limits

VLADY KOCIANCICH

*Translated by Norman Thomas Di Giovanni
in collaboration with the author*

He would write a letter because to see his best friend and tell
him face to face was impossible. He had often thought about
speaking to him but never quite could; he imagined Enrique's
face, the way his expression would change, his look of astonishment, his interruptions ("But it can't be—are you sure?"),
which would force him to explain or perhaps excuse himself or
at worst confess that it had only been a joke.

Up to now it had never occurred to him that friendship
and love are, in certain cases, proofs of a helpless solitude. He
could not face Enrique because Enrique would not understand.
Someone not so close to him would have been better. He
thought, if I had such a friend I'd tell him everything. But
Enrique was so loyal, so good, that it was impossible to utter
a word to him. Writing him might keep up the illusion of an
understanding between them and at the same time give Enrique a chance to think over his reply, to weigh carefully each

reason he would use to convince him he had been dreaming.

He didn't think the letter would be enough, but as an introduction it would at least spare him Enrique's looks of expectancy and bewilderment. He hesitated, and while hesitating—out of an impulse that ran contrary to his will—he was writing: "It's about my wife." He filled the letter with labored sentences, with excuses, with evasions, and with justifications. Suddenly he stopped and looked around. He was alone. He was peacefully surrounded by everyday things, as if nothing had really happened. He read: "It's about my wife. It's about Elisa. She's not ill, nor is there another man mixed up in this. . . ." Denying, he could go on forever. Enrique would never find out the truth. Still roundabout in his approach, he gave one last trite explanation before getting down to the facts: "It's very hard to make certain things clear to outsiders, because to a married couple that's what others are—outsiders. How idiotic to think love unites. How sentimental. Two people living together stand as if on different planes, most of which are secret. I won't try explaining anything to you because I don't know myself what's happened, but here are the facts. . . ."

He stopped again. He had heard a noise behind him, the shuffle of slippers on the rug. Quickly he covered the letter with the first thing he could lay his hands on—a map of greater Buenos Aires—and began studying it: Adrogué, Lomas de Zamora, familiar routes. . . . He pronounced these names to himself, trying to escape Elisa and the silence, which was so obvious it was almost like another person in the room. But also, though he did not lift his eyes from the map, he listened hard for the faint sound of Elisa's approaching steps. Then, unable to bear it any longer, he called without turning around, "Elisa?"

"Yes?" Her voice was neutral, with the sweetness of utter indifference.

"Nothing—except that I'm going out."

"Oh."

"Do you want anything from town?" he asked, obedient to his old habit of adding a word or two when he felt guilty.

"No."

He got up hurriedly, relieved by her answer, which excused him from having to come back right away. He gathered up his papers, the letter among them, put everything into a leather briefcase, and, feeling both stupid and afraid, left for his office.

Of course, he did not mail the letter. He kept it in a pocket for several days, transferring it from one suit to another, but he never mailed it. At last Enrique rang him up, wondering why they had not been getting together for drinks. Elisa had spoken to him; she was surprised too. She said he was too old to break his habit of meeting Enrique either on Wednesday nights or Thursdays before seven. Elisa always teased him about his way of organizing his habits with the same thoroughness he applied to his work at the office. This time her remark sounded to him like mockery. The atmosphere of the house, the forced secrecy of horror, shattered Elisa's innocent words.

Up to that moment he had fought against all sorts of troubles and out of these battles he had emerged victorious; this had led him to believe that one of his rock bottom virtues was strength. Yes, he considered himself strong, able to face anything, even the worst situations, but how could he understand this madness which surrounded him now—in spite of the sensibleness of all his past acts and the smooth way his days had run—without any apparent cause?

A man like him does not become disturbed overnight; he waits to see what will happen and then takes the plunge into analysis. This had been his first impulse. At the very moment Elisa changed, he had thought, I must see an analyst.

He would call Enrique to find out if he knew a good one

—not one of those clowns who organize LSD sessions, of course, but a sensible doctor, an understanding listener. As a listener, Enrique would have done well, but, preferring the impersonality of science, he never once spoke to him. He waited. And while postponing the moment of coming to grips with his problem, he tried to imagine a dialogue which might begin in this way:

"It's about my wife."

The analyst would not risk any conclusions, he would let him talk.

"I never noticed anything strange about her. She's a silent, quiet woman. But her character—Elisa herself—has nothing to do with what's happening to me. She's outside all this."

That was exactly why he could not talk to her. He stopped himself to ask if it had been always this way—Elisa distant from him, he trapped in his own silence, both of them avoiding the mention of anything unpleasant or dangerous. They'd had such a peaceful life.

"Elisa and I never had a quarrel—well, maybe once. Yes, now I remember, years ago we once had a fight, but I don't know what about. Yesterday, while we were having breakfast, I noticed that Elisa had no hands. Or maybe she did, maybe I just couldn't see them. No hands. She was sitting there as usual, but without hands."

He would stop to watch the doctor's reaction, but the doctor would display an impassive face so as not to lose his fee for subsequent visits. He would ask, very politely, "And what else?"

"I behaved as though nothing had happened. I tried to think—I still believe in this possibility—that it was only an hallucination, fatigue, overwork, my eyes."

That first day had been more uncomfortable than any-

thing else. He denied the change in her with all his strength
and with less courage than would have been required to take
it lightly, at the same time piling explanation on explanation
—his fatigue, his vision.

This visit to the doctor was so real that he decided not to
see him. He told himself that what he wanted was an answer,
not theories. Elisa without hands was a terrifying sight but still
bearable, since she had not lost them in an accident (there were
no traces of blood or of torn flesh). It was like the lingering
remnants of a nightmare, and one easily grows used to nightmares, so long as they don't make much sense. At some point
later on, weakened by fear and sorrow, he wondered why he
had not immediately run out of the house instead of trying to
grow gradually accustomed to the horror.

This attitude of well-mannered acceptance lasted till the
moment Elisa's eyes disappeared. She had lifted her empty face
to him for its morning kiss, and he stepped back instinctively
for the door. Moving clumsily in his fear, he got into his car,
the keys clinking together in his trembling hand, and started
the motor. Then a neighbor, a face he did not bother to
identify, was approaching him, wanting to be helped with his
car, which had gone dead or had sunk into a soft shoulder or
something of the kind. As at the outer limits of a nightmare,
he was held back by this series of efforts he was forced to make
against his will and by his neighbor's small talk, all the while
feeling Elisa's empty stare at the back of his head. But he did
not see a doctor, nor did he mail the letter to Enrique. He only
thought about escaping. It might have been a sensible decision
not to return home. But he could not leave. That would have
meant confronting Elisa and explaining why he was leaving
her. And where would he go? He put forward these and other
excuses so as not to have to admit the inexplicable feeling tying
him to his home and his wife. All he did was shut himself up

in his work. There was no detail into which he did not enter, no meeting he did not attend. His colleagues seemed not to mind, but were somewhat taken aback when he began meddling in the affairs of others. Now he was coming home very late; he would stay on at the office or at a bar, hoping on his return to find Elisa asleep.

Not wanting to wake her, he avoided turning on the lights. He would then grope for the bed and lie with his back to her, in one corner, like an angry child.

For a long time, for nearly a month, he let himself go on living in his nightmare, leaving home early each morning and coming back late at night. Not so late as to arouse Elisa's suspicions, however, but late enough to find her already asleep. With a glance at her side of the bed he could vaguely make out her head, a large spot of golden hair on the pillow. He would then be tempted to put his arms around her, not out of love but out of desperation, driven by a need to do something —anything. But he huddled in fear on his side of the bed and pulled the sheets over his head.

During the day, in a rush of endless tasks, he tried to forget his wife's gradual disappearance; but Elisa, handless, eyeless, like a broken doll, often broke into the conversation when he was lunching with other people, and made his blood run cold. He began to take little notice of his behavior. He was no longer able to cover up his fear before others and would stop a moment before any door and pray not to have Elisa open it for him.

He endured his nights stoically, sure there was no way of avoiding them, and, out of desperation, always managed to sleep. He had not had a single sleepless night, but in his dreams he found himself with Elisa. Once, he had cried out in his sleep and she stirred. He held his breath, rigid on his side of the bed. He heard her softly saying, "Are you all right? What is it?"

Close to tears in his fright, he begged her to go on sleeping, assuring her that he was perfectly all right. She turned her back to him without another word. They never talked again.

Now it was no more a matter of seeing an analyst or waiting for Enrique's advice. He had passed the limits of one nightmare and was entering into another, as if a last door had been closed on him. Motionless at the edge of the bed, knowing that if he stirred or got up she would come after him, he imagined the color of her hair in the dark. It was the only thing about her he still remembered.

He began to weep silently, while striking up an imaginary dialogue with his wife.

"Elisa, what's happening to us?"

He saw himself and Elisa in a trap, two figures drawn by the same hand, making up part of who knew what bewildering picture.

He began to regret the long-past time when they were both open and things were clear and they loved each other. With the certainty that nothing could now save him from his present horror, admitting for the first time that no tomorrow would come, all at once he understood everything. Violently, desperately frightened, he turned toward Elisa's incomplete body to take her in his arms, to try to hold together what little was left of her, feeling that this is what he should have done that first time. But there on the pillow lay nothing but a lock of golden hair, and in a matter of moments it too disappeared.

"These are the facts, Enrique," he wrote. "Elisa's gone. I can hear her. If I were to touch her, I could feel her skin; sometimes, when I brush against her, I can hear her breath. If she didn't exist, if she were really dead, I don't think it would matter to me. But living with her this way is unbearable and living without her is impossible. I have not gone back to work. I'm telling you all this without pain or fear because I have no other fate than to remain here. I care for nothing in this world but Elisa."

"Raúl."

It was his wife's voice calling him after such a long time. He got up from the desk, turned, and saw her. Elisa once again, Elisa tall, whole, beautiful, watching him with a grave look in her eyes, while he dared not speak for fear of breaking the spell of this new dream. He was trembling and had to support himself against the desk.

It took him an eternity to come back to life. It meant just that—to be living again in this small, simple world of manageable troubles, troubles shared with others. He would never be alone again.

When he came to his senses, to the almost unbearable happiness of being himself again, he heard Elisa explaining to him, perhaps for the fifth time, "I'm sorry, Raúl, but I'm leaving. I'm in love with another man."

Unexpected Guests

HEINRICH · BÖLL

Translated by Leila Vennewitz

I have nothing against animals; on the contrary, I like them, and I enjoy caressing our dog's coat in the evening while the cat sits on my lap. It gives me pleasure to watch the children feeding the tortoise in the corner of the living room. I have even grown fond of the baby hippopotamus we keep in our bathtub, and the rabbits running around loose in our apartment have long ceased to worry me. Besides, I am used to coming home in the evening and finding an unexpected visitor: a cheeping baby chick, or a stray dog my wife has taken in. For my wife is a good woman, she never turns anyone away from the door, neither man nor beast, and for many years now our children's evening prayers have wound up with the words: O Lord, please send us beggars and animals.

What is really worse is that my wife cannot say no to hawkers and peddlers, with the result that things accumulate in our home which I regard as superfluous: soap, razor blades, brushes and darning wool, and lying around in drawers are documents which cause me some concern: an assortment of insurance policies and purchase agreements. My sons are insured for their education, my daughters for their trousseaux, but we cannot feed them with either darning wool or soap until they get married or graduate, and it is only in exceptional cases that razor blades are beneficial to the human system.

It will be readily understood, therefore, that now and again I show signs of slight impatience, although generally speaking I am known to be a quiet man. I often catch myself looking enviously at the rabbits who have made themselves at home under the table, munching away peacefully at their carrots, and the stupid gaze of the hippopotamus, who is hastening the accumulation of silt in our bathtub, causes me at times to stick out my tongue at him. And the tortoise stoically eating its way through lettuce leaves has not the slightest notion of the anxieties that swell my breast: the longing for some fresh, fragrant coffee, for tobacco, bread and eggs, and the comforting warmth engendered by a schnapps in the throats of careworn men. My sole comfort at such times is Billy, our dog, who, like me, is yawning with hunger. If, on top of all this, unexpected guests arrive—men unshaven like myself, or mothers with babies who get fed warm milk and moistened zwieback —I have to get a grip on myself if I am to keep my temper. But I do keep it, because by this time it is practically the only thing I have left.

There are days when the mere sight of freshly boiled, snowy potatoes makes my mouth water; for—although I confess this reluctantly and with deep embarrassment—it is a long time since we have enjoyed "good home cooking." Our only meals are improvised ones of which we partake from time to time, standing up, surrounded by animals and human guests.

Fortunately it will be a while before my wife can buy useless articles again, for we have no more cash, my wages have been attached for an indefinite period, and I myself am reduced to spending the evenings going around the distant suburbs, in clothing that makes me unrecognizable, selling razor blades, soap and buttons far below cost; for our situation has become grave. Nevertheless, we own several hundredweight of soap, thousands of razor blades, and buttons of every description, and toward midnight I stagger into the house and go through my pockets for money: my children, my animals, my wife stand around me with shining eyes, for I have usually bought some things on the way home: bread, apples, lard, coffee and potatoes—the latter, by the way, in great demand among the children as well as the animals—and during the nocturnal hours we gather together for a cheerful meal: contented animals, contented children are all about me, my wife smiles at me, and we leave the living-room door open so the hippopotamus will not feel left out, his joyful grunts resounding from the bathroom. At that point my wife usually confesses to me that she has an extra guest hidden in the storeroom, who is only brought out when my nerves have been fortified by food: shy, unshaven men, rubbing their hands, take their place at table, women squeeze in between our children on the bench, milk is warmed up for crying babies. In this way I also make the acquaintance of animals that are new to me: seagulls, foxes and pigs, although once it was a small dromedary.

"Isn't it cute?" asked my wife, and I was obliged to say yes, it was, while I anxiously watched the tireless munching of this duffel-colored creature which looked at us out of slate-gray eyes. Fortunately the dromedary only stayed a week, and business was brisk: word had got round of the quality of my merchandise, my reduced prices, and now and again I was even able to sell shoelaces and brushes, articles otherwise not much in demand. As a result, we experienced a period of false prosperity, and my wife, completely blind to the economic facts, produced a remark which worried me: "Things are looking up!" But I saw our stocks of soap shrinking, the razor blades dwindling, and even the supply of brushes and darning wool was no longer substantial.

Just about this time, when I could have used some spiritual sustenance, our house was shaken one evening, while we were all sitting peacefully together, by a tremor resembling a fair-sized earthquake: the pictures rattled, the table rocked, and a ring of fried sausage rolled off my plate. I was about to jump up and see what the matter was when I noticed suppressed laughter on the faces of my children. "What's going on here?" I shouted, and for the first time in all my checkered experience I was really beside myself.

"Wilfred," said my wife quietly and put down her fork, "it's only Wally." She began to cry, and against her tears I have no defence, for she has borne me seven children.

"Who is Wally?" I asked wearily, and at that moment the house was rocked by another tremor. "Wally," said my youngest daughter, "is the elephant we've got in the basement."

I must admit I was at a loss, which is not really surprising. The largest animal we had housed so far had been the dromedary, and I considered an elephant too big for our apartment.

My wife and children, not in the least at a loss, supplied the facts: the animal had been brought to us for safekeeping by a bankrupt circus owner. Sliding down the chute which we otherwise use for our coal, it had had no trouble entering the basement. "He rolled himself up into a ball," said my oldest son, "really an intelligent animal." I did not doubt it, accepted the fact of Wally's presence, and was led down in triumph into the basement. The animal was not as large as all that; he waggled his ears and seemed quite at home with us, especially as he had a bale of hay at his disposal. "Isn't he cute?" asked my wife, but I refused to agree. Cute did not seem to be the right word. Anyway the family appeared disappointed at the limited extent of my enthusiasm, and my wife said, as we left the basement: "How cruel you are, do you want him to be put up for auction?"

"What d'you mean, auction," I said, "and why cruel? Besides, it's against the law to conceal bankruptcy assets."

"I don't care," said my wife, "nothing must happen to the animal."

In the middle of the night we were awakened by the circus owner, a diffident, dark-haired man, who asked us whether we had room for one more animal. "It's my sole possession, all I have left in the world. Only for a night. How is the elephant, by the way?"

"He's fine," said my wife, "only I'm a bit worried about his bowels."

"That'll soon settle down," said the circus owner. "It's just the new surroundings. Animals are so sensitive. How about it then: will you take the cat too—just for the night?" He looked at me, and my wife nudged me and said: "Don't be so unkind."

"Unkind," I said, "no, I certainly don't want to be that. If you like, you can put the cat in the kitchen."

"I've got it outside in the car," said the man.

I left my wife to look after the cat and crawled back into bed. My wife was a bit pale when she came to bed, and she seemed to be trembling. "Are you cold?" I asked.

"Yes," she said, "I've got such funny chills."

"You're just tired."

"Maybe," said my wife, but she gave me a queer look as she said it. We slept quietly, but in my dreams I still saw that queer look of my wife's, and a strange compulsion made me wake up earlier than usual. I decided to shave for once.

Lying under our kitchen table was a medium-sized lion; he was sleeping peacefully, only his tail moved gently and made a sound like someone playing with a very light ball.

I carefully lathered my face and tried not to make any noise, but when I turned my chin to the right to shave my left cheek I saw that the lion had his eyes open and was watching me. "They really do look like cats," I thought. What the lion was thinking I don't know; he went on watching me, and I shaved, without cutting myself, but I must admit it is a strange feeling to shave with a lion looking on. My experience of handling wild beasts was practically non-existent, and I confined myself to looking sternly at the lion, then I dried my face and went back to the bedroom. My wife was already awake, she was just about to say something, but I cut her short and exclaimed: "What's the use of talking about it!" My wife began to cry, and I put my hand on her head and said: "It's unusual, to say the least, you must admit that."

"What isn't unusual?" said my wife, and I had no answer.

Meanwhile the rabbits had awakened, the children were making a racket in the bathroom, the hippopotamus—his name was Gottlieb—was already trumpeting away, Billy was stretching and yawning, only the tortoise was still asleep, but it sleeps most of the time anyway.

I let the rabbits into the kitchen, where their feed box is kept under the cupboard; the rabbits sniffed at the lion, the lion at the rabbits, and my children—uninhibited and used to animals as they are—were already in the kitchen. I almost had the feeling the lion was smiling; my third-youngest son immediately found a name for him: Bombilus. And Bombilus he remained.

A few days later someone came to take away the elephant and the lion. I must confess I saw the last of the elephant without regret; he seemed silly to me, while the lion's quiet, friendly dignity had endeared him to me; I felt a pang at Bombilus' departure. I had grown so used to him; he was really the first animal to enjoy my wholehearted affection.

Tropism: V

NATHALIE SARRAUTE

Translated by Maria Jolas

On hot July days, the wall opposite cast a brilliant, harsh light into the damp little courtyard.

Underneath this heat there was a great void, silence, everything seemed in suspense: the only thing to be heard, aggressive, strident, was the creaking of a chair being dragged across the tiles, the slamming of a door. In this heat, in this silence, it was a sudden coldness, a rending.

And she remained motionless on the edge of her bed, occupying the least possible space, tense, as though waiting for something to burst, to crash down upon her in the threatening silence.

At times the shrill notes of locusts in a meadow petrified by the sun and as though dead, induce this sensation of cold, of solitude, of abandonment in a hostile universe in which something anguishing is impending.

In the silence, penetrating the length of the old blue-striped wallpaper in the hall, the length of the dingy paint, she heard the little click of the key in the front door. She heard the study door close.

She remained there hunched up, waiting, doing nothing. The slightest act, such as going to the bathroom to wash her hands, letting the water run from the tap, seemed like a provocation, a sudden leap into the void, an extremely daring action. In the suspended silence, the sudden sound of water would be like a signal, like an appeal directed towards them; it would be like some horrible contact, like touching a jellyfish with the end of a stick and then waiting with loathing for it suddenly to shudder, rise up and fall back down again.

She sensed them like that, spread out, motionless, on the other side of the walls, and ready to shudder, to stir.

She did not move. And about her the entire house, the street, seemed to encourage her, seemed to consider this motionlessness natural.

It appeared certain, when you opened the door and saw the stairway filled with relentless, impersonal, colorless calm, a stairway that did not seem to have retained the slightest trace of the persons who had walked on it, not the slightest memory of their presence, when you stood behind the dining room window and looked at the house fronts, the shops, the old women and little children walking along the street, it seemed certain that, for as long as possible, she would have to wait, remain motionless like that, do nothing, not move, that the highest degree of comprehension, real intelligence, was that, to undertake nothing, keep as still as possible, do nothing.

At the most, by being careful not to wake anybody, you could go down without looking at the dark, dead, stairway, and proceed unobtrusively along the pavements, along the walls, just to get a breath, to move about a bit, without knowing where you were going, without wanting to go anywhere, and then come back home, sit down on the edge of the bed and, once more, wait, curled up, motionless.

Journey through the Night

JAKOV LIND

Translated by Ralph Manheim

What do you see when you look back? Not a thing. And when you look ahead? Even less. That's right. That's how it is.

It was three o'clock in the morning and raining. The train didn't stop anywhere. There were lights somewhere in the countryside, but you couldn't be sure if they were windows or stars.

The tracks were tracks—but why shouldn't there be tracks in the clouds?

Paris was somewhere at the end of the trip. Which Paris? The earthly Paris—with cafés, green buses, fountains, and grimy whitewashed walls? Or the heavenly Paris? Carpeted bathrooms with a view of the Bois de Boulogne?

The fellow-passenger looked still paler in the bluish light. His nose was straight, his lips thin, his teeth uncommonly small. He had slick hair like a seal. A moustache, that's what he needs. He could do a balancing act on his nose. Under his clothes he is wet. Why doesn't he show his tusks?

After "that's how it is" he said nothing. That settled everything. Now he is smoking.

His skin is gray, that's obvious—it's taut, too. If he scratches himself it will tear. What else is there to look at? He has only one face and his suitcase. What has he got in the suitcase? Tools? Saw, hammer and chisel? Maybe a drill? What does he need a drill for? To bore holes in skulls? Some people drink beer that way. When empty, they can be painted. Will he paint my face? What colors? Water-color or oil? And what for? Children at Eastertime play with empty eggshells. His play with skulls.

Well, he said noncommittally, putting out his cigarette. He crushed it against the aluminum, making a scratching sound. Well, how about it?

I don't know, I said. I can't make up my mind. Doesn't the fellow understand a joke?

Maybe you need a little more spunk, he said. Now's the time to make up your mind; in half an hour you'll be asleep anyway, then I'll do what I want with you.

I won't sleep tonight, I said. You've given me fair warning.

Warning won't do you any good, he said. Between three and four everybody falls into a dead sleep. You're educated, you should know that.

Yes, I know. But I got self-control.

Between three and four, said the man, rubbing the moustache that was yet to grow, all of us get locked away in our little cubicles, don't hear nothing, don't see nothing. We die, every last one of us. Dying restores us, after four we wake up and life goes on. Without that people couldn't stick it out so long.

I don't believe a word of it. You can't saw me up.

I can't eat you as you are, he said. Sawing's the only way.
First the legs, then the arms, then the head. Everything in its
proper order.

What do you do with the eyes?

Suck 'em.

Can the ears be digested or have they got bones in them?

No bones, but they're tough. Anyway, I don't eat everything, do you think I'm a pig?

A seal is what I thought.

That's more like it. So he admitted it. A seal, I knew it.
How come he speaks German? Seals speak Danish and nobody
can understand them.

How is it you don't speak Danish?

I was born in Sankt Pölten, he said. We didn't speak
Danish in our family. He's being evasive. What would you
expect? But maybe he is from Sankt Pölten; I've heard there
are such people in the region.

And you live in France?

What's it to you? In half an hour you'll be gone. It's useful
to know things when you've a future ahead of you, but in your
situation . . .

Of course he's insane, but what can I do? He has locked
the compartment (where did he get the keys?), Paris will never
come. He's picked the right kind of weather. You can't see a
thing and it's raining; of course he can kill me. When you're
scared you've got to talk fast. Would you kindly describe it
again. Kindly will flatter his vanity. Murderers are sick. Sick
people are vain. The kindly is getting results.

Well, first comes the wooden mallet, he said, exactly like
a schoolteacher . . . you always have to explain everything twice
to stupid pupils; stupidity is a kind of fear, teachers give out
cuffs or marks.

. . . then after the mallet comes the razor, you've got to
let the blood out, most of it at least, even so you always mess

up your chin on the liver; well, and then, as we were saying, comes the saw.

Do you take off the leg at the hip or the knee?

Usually at the hip, sometimes the knee. At the knee when I have time.

And the arms?

The arms? Never at the elbow, always at the shoulder. Why?

Maybe it's just a habit, don't ask me. There isn't much meat on the forearm, in your case there's none at all, but when it's attached, it looks like something. How do you eat the leg of a roast chicken?

He was right.

If you want pointers about eating people, ask a cannibal. Do you use spices?

Only salt. Human flesh is sweet, you know that yourself. Who likes sweet meat?

He opened the suitcase. No, I screamed, I'm not asleep yet.

Don't be afraid, you scarecat, I just wanted to show you I wasn't kidding. He fished about among the tools. There were only five implements in the suitcase, but they were lying around loose. It was a small suitcase, rather like a doctor's bag. But a doctor's instruments are strapped to the velvet lid. Here they were lying around loose. Hammer, saw, drill, chisel and pliers. Ordinary carpenter's tools. There was also a rag. Wrapped in the rag was the salt-cellar. A common glass salt-cellar such as you find on the tables in cheap restaurants. He's stolen it somewhere, I said to myself. He's a thief.

He held the salt-cellar under my nose. There was salt in it. He shook some out on my hand. Taste it, he said, first-class salt. He saw the rage in my face, I was speechless. He laughed. Those little teeth revolted me.

Yes, he said and laughed again, I bet you'd rather be salted alive than eaten dead.

He shut the suitcase and lit another cigarette. It was half past three. The train was flying over the rails, but there won't be any Paris at the end. Neither earthly nor heavenly. I was in a trap. Death comes to every man. Does it really matter how you die? You can get run over, you can get shot by accident, at a certain age your heart is likely to give out, or you can die of lung cancer, which is very common nowadays. One way or another you kick the bucket. Why not be eaten by a madman in the Nice-Paris express?

All is vanity, what else. You've got to die, only you don't want to. You don't have to live, but you want to. Only necessary things are important. Big fish eat little ones, the lark eats the worm and yet how sweetly he sings, cats eat mice and no one ever killed a cat for it—every animal eats every other just to stay alive, men eat men, what's unnatural about that? Is it more natural to eat pigs or calves? Does it hurt more when you can say "it hurts"? Animals don't cry, human beings cry when a relative dies, but how can anybody cry over his own death? Am I so fond of myself? So it must be vanity. Nobody's heart breaks over his own death. That's the way it is.

A feeling of warmth and well-being came over me. Here is a madman, he wants to eat me. But at least he wants something. What do I want? Not to eat anybody. Is that so noble? What's left when you don't want to do what you certainly ought to do?

If you don't do that which disgusts you, what becomes of your disgust? It sticks in your throat. Nothing sticks in the throat of the man from Sankt Pölten. He swallows all.

A voice spoke very softly, it sounded almost affectionate: There, you see you're getting sleepy, that comes from thinking. What have you got to look forward to in Paris? Paris is only a city. Whom do you need anyway, and who needs you? You're going to Paris. Well, what of it? Sex and drinking won't make you any happier. And certainly working won't. Money won't do you a particle of good. What are you getting out of life? Just go to sleep. You won't wake up, I can promise you.

But I don't want to die, I whispered. Not yet. I want . . . to go for a walk in Paris.

Go for a walk in Paris? Big deal. It will only make you tired. There are enough people taking walks and looking at the shop windows. The restaurants are overcrowded. So are the whore-houses. Nobody needs you in Paris. Just do me a favor, go to sleep. The night won't go on forever; I'll have to gobble everything down so fast you'll give me a belly-ache.

I've got to eat you. In the first place I'm hungry, and in the second place I like you. I told you right off that I liked you and you thought, the guy is a queer. But now you know. I'm a simple cannibal. It's not a profession, it's a need. Good Lord, man, try to understand: now you've got an aim in life. Your life has purpose, thanks to me. You think it was by accident you came into my compartment? There's no such thing as an accident. I watched you all along the platform in Nice. And then you came into my compartment. Why mine and not someone else's? Because I'm so good-looking? Don't make me laugh. Is a seal good-looking? You came in here because you knew there'd be something doing.

Very slowly he opened the little suitcase. He took out the mallet and closed the suitcase. He held the mallet in his hand.

Well, how about it? he said.

Just a minute, I said. Just a minute. And suddenly I stood up. God only knows how I did it, but I stood up on my two feet and stretched out my hand. The little wire snapped, the lead seal fell, the train hissed and screeched. Screams came from next door. Then the train stopped. The man from Sankt

Pölten stowed the mallet quickly in his suitcase and took his coat; he was at the door in a flash. He opened the door and looked around: I pity you, he said. This bit of foolishness is going to cost you a ten-thousand-franc fine, you nitwit, now you'll have to take your walk in Paris.

People crowded into the compartment, a conductor and a policeman appeared. Two soldiers and a pregnant woman shook their fists at me.

Already the seal from Sankt Pölten was outside, right under my window. He shouted something. I opened the window: See, he shouted, you've made an ass of yourself for life. Look who wants to live. He spat and shrugged his shoulders. Carrying his suitcase in his right hand, he stepped cautiously down the embankment and vanished in the dark. Like a country doctor on his way to deliver a baby.

●

Undine Goes

INGEBORG BACHMANN

Translated by Michael Bullock

You humans! You monsters!

You monsters named Hans! Bearing this name that I can never forget.

Every time I walked through a clearing and the branches parted, when the twigs struck the water from my arms, the leaves licked the drops from my hair, I met a man called Hans.

Yes, I have learnt this piece of logic, that a man has to be called Hans, that you are all called Hans, one like the other, and yet only one. Always there is only one who bears this name that I can never forget, even if I forget you all, completely forget how I loved you utterly. And long after your kisses and your seed have been washed off and carried away

by the great waters—rains, rivers, sea—the name is still
there, propagating itself under water, because I cannot stop
crying it out, Hans, Hans . . .

You monsters with the firm and restless hands, with the
short pale fingernails, the grazed nails with black rims, the
white cuffs round the wrists, the ragged sweaters, the uniform
gray suits, the coarse leather jackets and the loose summer
shirts. But let me be exact, you monsters, and now make you
contemptible, for I shall not come back, shall never again
follow your beckoning, never again accept your invitation to a
glass of wine, to a journey, to a theater. I shall never come back,
never again say "Yes" and "You" and "Yes." All these words
will never again be spoken, and perhaps I shall tell you why.
For you know the questions, and they all begin with "Why?"
There are no questions in my life. I love the water, its dense
transparency, the green in the water and the dumb creatures
(I too shall soon be equally dumb), my hair among them, in it,
the just water, the indifferent mirror that forbids me to see you
differently. The wet frontier between me and me. . . .

I have no children by you because I knew no questions, no
demands, no caution, no intention, no future and did not know
how to occupy a place in another life. I needed no support, no
protestations and assurances, only air, night air, sea air, frontier
air, in order to be able again and again to draw breath for fresh
words, fresh kisses, for an unceasing confession: Yes. Yes.
When the confession had been made, I was condemned to
love; when one day I was released from love, I had to go back
into the water, into that element in which no one builds a nest,
raises a roof over rafters, covers himself with an awning. To be
nowhere, to stay nowhere. To dive, to rest, to move without
effort—and one day to stop and think, to rise to the surface
again, to walk through a clearing, to see *him* and say "Hans."
To begin at the beginning.

"Good evening."
"Good evening."
"How far is it to your place?"
"It's a long way, a long way."
"And it's a long way to my place."

Always to repeat a mistake, to make the mistake by which one is marked. And what use is it then to be washed by all the waters, by the waters of the Danube and the Rhine, by the waters of the Tiber and the Nile, the bright waters of the frozen oceans, the inky waters of the high seas and the magical pools? The violent human women sharpen their tongues and flash their eyes; the gentle human women quietly let fall a few tears; they also do their job. But the men say nothing to this. They faithfully stroke their wives' hair, their childrens' hair, open the newspaper, look through the bills or turn the radio up loud and yet hear above it the note of the shell, the fanfare of the wind, and then again, later, when it is dark in the house, they secretly get up, open the door, listen down the passage, into the garden, down the avenues, and now they hear it quite distinctly. The note of anguish, the cry from afar, the ghostly music. Come! Come! Come just once!

You monsters with your wives!

Didn't you say, "It's hell, and no one will be able to understand why I stay with her." Didn't you say, "My wife, yes, she's a wonderful person, yes, she needs me, she wouldn't know how to live without me." Didn't you say that? And didn't you laugh and say in high spirits, "Never take it seriously, never take anything like that seriously." Didn't you say, "It should always be like this, and the other shouldn't be, it doesn't count!" You monsters with your phrases, you who seek the phrases of women so that you have all you need, so that the world is round. You who make women your mistresses and wives, one-day wives, week-end wives, lifetime wives and let yourselves be made into their husbands. (Perhaps that is worth waking up for.) You with your jealousy of your women, with your arrogant forbearance and tyranny, your search for sanctuary with your women; you with your housekeeping money and your joint good-night conversations, those sources of new strength, of the conviction that you are right in your conflicts with the outside world, you with your helplessly skillful, helplessly absent-minded embraces. I was amazed to see that you give your wives money for the shopping and for clothes and for the summer holiday, then you invite them out (invite them, that means you pay, of course). You buy and let yourselves be bought. I can't help laughing and being amazed at you, Hans, Hans, at you little students and honest workmen, you who take wives who work with you, then you both work, each of you grows cleverer in a different field, each of you makes progress in a different factory, you work hard, save money and harness yourselves to the future. Yes, that is another reason why you take wives, so that the future is made solid for you, so that they shall bear children; you grow gentle when they go about fearful and happy with the children in their bellies. Or you forbid your wives to have children, you want to be undisturbed and you hurry into old age with your saved-up youth. O that would be worth a great awakening! You deceivers and you deceived. Don't try that with me. Not with me!

You with your muses and beasts of burden and your learned, understanding female companions whom you allow to speak. . . . My laughter has long stirred the waters, a gurgling laughter which you have often imitated with terror in the night. For you have always known that it is laughable and terrifying and that you are sufficient to yourselves and that you have never agreed. Therefore it is better not to get up in the night, not to go down the passage, not to listen in the yard, nor in the garden, because it would be nothing but a confession

that you are more easily seduced by a note of anguish, by its
sound, its enticement, than by anything else, and that you long
for the great betrayal. You have never been in agreement with
yourselves. Never in agreement with your houses, with all that
which fixed and laid down. You were secretly pleased about
every tile that blew away, every intimation of collapse. You
enjoyed playing with the thought of fiasco, of flight, of disgrace, of the loneliness that would have set you free from
everything at present existing. Too much, you enjoyed playing
with all this in thought. When I came, when a breath of wind
announced my arrival, you jumped up and knew that the hour
was near, disgrace, expulsion, ruin, incomprehensible events.
The call to the end. To the end. You monsters, that was why
I loved you, because you knew what the call meant, because
you allowed yourselves to be called, because you were never in
agreement with yourselves. And I, when was I ever in agreement? When you were alone, quite alone, and when your
thoughts were thinking nothing useful, nothing usable, when
the lamp looked after the room, the clearing came into being,
the room was damp and smoky when you stood there like that,
lost, forever lost, lost through insight, then it was time for me.
I could enter with the look that challenges: Think! Be! Speak
out!—I never understood you while you knew that you were
understood by any third party. I said, "I don't understand you,
don't understand, can't understand!" This was a splendid time
that lasted a long while, this time when you were not understood and yourselves did not understand, didn't understand
why this and why that, why frontiers and politics and newspapers and banks and stock exchanges and trade, all going on and
on.

Then I understood the refinements of politics, your ideas, your
convictions, opinions. I understood them very well and a bit
more besides. That was exactly why I didn't understand you.

I understood the conferences so completely, your threats, proofs, evasions, that they were no longer comprehensible. And that was what moved you, the incomprehensibility of all this. Because in this incomprehensibility lay your really great, concealed idea of the world, and I conjured up your great idea out of you, your unpractical idea in which time and death appeared and flamed, burning down everything, order wearing the cloak of crime, night misused for sleep. Your wives, sick with your present, your children, condemned to the future, they did not teach you death, they only showed you little bits of it at a time. But I taught you with one look, when everything was perfect, bright and raging—I said to you, "There is death in it." And "There is time in it." And at the same time, "Go death!" And "Stand still, time!" That's what I said to you. And you talked, my beloved, in a slow voice, completely true and saved, free of everything in between, you turned your sad spirit inside out, your sad, great spirit that is like the spirit of all men and of the kind that is not intended for any use. Because I am not intended for any use and you didn't know what use you were intended for, everything was good between us. We loved each other. We were of the same spirit.

I knew a man called Hans and he was different from all others. I knew another man who was also different from all others. Then one who was completely different from all others and he was called Hans; I loved him. I met him in the clearing and we walked on like that, without direction; it was in the Danube country, he went on the giant wheel with me; it was in the Black Forest; under plane trees on the great boulevards, he drank Pernod with me. I loved him. We stood on a station for the north, and the train left before midnight. I didn't wave; I made a sign with my hand meaning this is the end. The end that has no end. It never came to an end. One should have no hesitation in making the sign. It isn't a sad sign, it doesn't put a circle of black crape round stations and highways, less so than the deceptive wave with which so much comes to an end. Go, death, and stand still, time. Use no magic, no tears, no wringing of the hands, no vows, no entreaties. None of all that. The commandment is: leave one another, let eyes suffice for the eyes, let a green suffice, let the easiest thing suffice. Obey the law and not an emotion. Obey loneliness. Loneliness into which nobody will follow me.

Do you understand? I shall never share your loneliness, because mine is here, from a long time ago, for a long time to come. I am not made to share your worries. Not those worries. How could I ever recognize them without betraying my law? How could I ever believe in the importance of your entanglements? How can I believe you so long as I really believe you, believe completely that you are more than your weak, vain utterances, your shabby actions, your foolish casting of suspicion? I have always believed that you are more, a knight, an idol, not far from a soul that is worthy of the most royal of all names. When you could think of nothing more to do with your life, then you spoke entirely truthfully, but only then. Then all the waters overflowed their banks, the rivers rose, the water-lilies blossomed and drowned by hundreds, and the sea was a mighty sigh, it beat, beat and ran and rolled towards the earth, its lips dripping with white foam.

Traitors! When nothing else helped you, then abuse helped. Then you suddenly knew what was suspicious about me, water and veils and whatever cannot be firmly grasped. Then I was suddenly a danger that you recognized in time, and I was cursed and in a flash everything was repented. You repented on church benches, before your wives, your

children, your public. Before your great, great authorities
you were so courageous as to repent me and to make secure
all that which had become uncertain in you. You were in
safety. You quickly set up the altars and brought me to the
sacrifice. Did my blood taste good? Did it taste a little of
the blood of the hind and the blood of the white whale?
Of their dumbness?

So be it! You will be much loved, and much will be
forgiven you. But do not forget that you called me into the
world, that you dreamed of me, of the others, of the other, who
is of your spirit yet not of your shape, of the unknown woman
who raises the cry of lament at your weddings, who comes on
wet feet, and from whose kiss you fear to die as you wish to
die and now no longer die: in disorder, in ecstasy and yet most
rational.

Why should I not utter it, why should I not make you
contemptible, before I go?

I'm going now.

For I have seen you once again, have heard you speaking
in a language which you ought not to speak with me. My
memory is inhuman. I had to think of everything, of every
treachery and every baseness. I saw you again in the same
places; the places that had once been bright now seemed to me
places of shame. What have you done! I was silent, I spoke not
a word. You must tell yourselves. I have sprinkled a handful of
water over those places so that they shall turn green like graves.
So that finally they shall stay bright.

But I cannot go like this. Therefore let me say something good
about you again, so that we do not part like this. So that
nothing is parted.

In spite of everything your talk was good, your wonder-

ing, your zeal and your renunciation of the whole truth, so
that the half is spoken, so that light falls on the one half of
the world that you just had time to perceive in your zeal.
You were so brave and brave against the others—and cowardly too, of course, and often brave so as not to appear
cowardly. When you saw disaster coming from the fight
you nevertheless fought on and kept your word, although
you gained nothing by it. You fought against property and
for property, for non-violence and for weapons, for the old
and for the new, for rivers and for the regulation of rivers,
for the oath and against the swearing of oaths. And you
know that you are striving against your silence, and yet you
go on striving. That is perhaps to be praised.

In your clumsy bodies your gentleness is to be praised.
Something so particularly gentle appears when you do someone
a favour, do something kind. Your gentleness is much gentler
than the gentleness of all your women, when you give your
word or listen to someone and understand him. Your heavy
bodies sit there, but you are quite weightless, and your melancholy, your smile can be such that for a moment even the vast
suspicion of your friends goes unfed.

Your hands are to be praised, when you pick up fragile
things, protect them and know how to preserve them, and
when you carry burdens and clear away heavy things from a
path. And it is good when you treat the bodies of humans and
animals and very carefully rid the world of a pain. Your hands
produce much that is limited, but also much good that will
speak in your favour.

You are also to be admired when you bend over engines
and machines, when you make and understand and explain
them, till all your explanations turn them into a mystery again.
Didn't you say it was this principle and that energy? Wasn't
that well and beautifully said? Never again will anyone be able

to talk like that about currents and forces, magnets and mechanisms and about the core of all things.

Never again will anyone talk like that about the elements, the universe and all the planets.

Never has anyone spoken like that about the earth, about its shape, its ages. In your speech everything was so clear: the crystals, the volcanoes and ashes, the ice and the molten centre.

No one has ever spoken like that about men, about the conditions under which they live, about their servitude, goods, ideas, about the people on this earth, on an earlier and a future earth. It was right to speak like that and to reflect upon so much.

Never was there so much magic over things as when you spoke, and never were words so powerful. You could make speech flare up, become muddled or mighty. You did everything with words and sentences, came to an understanding with them or transmuted them, gave things a new name; and objects, which understand neither the straight nor the crooked words, almost took their being from your words.

Oh, nobody was ever able to play so well, you monsters! You invented all games, number games and word games, dream games and love games.

Never did anyone speak of himself like that. Almost truthfully. Almost murderously truthfully. Bent over the water, almost abandoned. The world is already dark and I cannot put on the necklace of shells. There will be no clearing. You different from all the others. I am under water. Am under water.

And now someone is walking up above and hates water and hates green and does not understand, will never understand. As I have never understood.

Almost mute,
almost still
hearing
the call.

Come. Just once.
Come.

The Third Bank of the River

JOÃO GUIMARÃES ROSA

Translated by Barbara Shelby

Father was a reliable, law-abiding, practical man, and had been
ever since he was a boy, as various people of good sense testified
when I asked them about him. I don't remember that he
seemed any crazier or even any moodier than anyone else we
knew. He just didn't talk much. It was our mother who gave
the orders and scolded us every day—my sister, my brother,
and me. Then one day my father ordered a canoe for himself.

He took the matter very seriously. He had the canoe made
to his specifications of fine *vinhático* wood; a small one, with
a narrow board in the stern as though to leave only enough
room for the oarsman. Every bit of it was hand-hewn of special
strong wood carefully shaped, fit to last in the water for twenty
or thirty years. Mother railed at the idea. How could a man
who had never fiddled away his time on such tricks propose to
go fishing and hunting now, at his time of life? Father said

nothing. Our house was closer to the river then than it is now, less than a quarter of a league away: there rolled the river, great, deep, and silent, always silent. It was so wide that you could hardly see the bank on the other side. I can never forget the day the canoe was ready.

Neither happy nor excited nor downcast, Father pulled his hat well down on his head and said one firm goodbye. He spoke not another word, took neither food nor other supplies, gave no parting advice. We thought Mother would have a fit, but she only blanched white, bit her lip, and said bitterly: "Go or stay; but if you go, don't you ever come back!" Father left his answer in suspense. He gave me a mild look and motioned me to go aside with him a few steps. I was afraid of Mother's anger, but I obeyed anyway, that time. The turn things had taken gave me the courage to ask: "Father, will you take me with you in that canoe?" But he just gave me a long look in return: gave me his blessing and motioned me to go back. I pretended to go, but instead turned off into a deep woodsy hollow to watch. Father stepped into the canoe, untied it, and began to paddle off. The canoe slipped away, a straight, even shadow like an alligator, slithery, long.

Our father never came back. He hadn't gone anywhere. He stuck to that stretch of the river, staying halfway across, always in the canoe, never to spring out of it, ever again. The strangeness of that truth was enough to dismay us all. What had never been before, was. Our relatives, the neighbors, and all our acquaintances met and took counsel together.

Mother, though, behaved very reasonably, with the result that everybody believed what no one wanted to put into words about our father: that he was mad. Only a few of them thought he might be keeping a vow, or—who could tell—maybe he was sick with some hideous disease like leprosy, and that was what had made him desert us to live out another life, close to his family and yet far enough away. The news spread by word of mouth, carried by people like travelers and those who lived along the banks of the river, who said of Father that he never landed at spit or cove, by day or by night, but always stuck to the river, lonely and outside human society. Finally, Mother and our relatives realized that the provisions he had hidden in the canoe must be getting low and thought that he would have to either land somewhere and go away from us for good—that seemed the most likely—or repent once and for all and come back home.

But they were wrong. I had made myself responsible for stealing a bit of food for him every day, an idea that had come to me the very first night, when the family had lighted bonfires on the riverbank and in their glare prayed and called out to Father. Every day from then on I went back to the river with a lump of hard brown sugar, some corn bread, or a bunch of bananas. Once, at the end of an hour of waiting that had dragged on and on, I caught sight of Father; he was way off, sitting in the bottom of the canoe as if suspended in the mirror smoothness of the river. He saw me, but he did not paddle over or make any sign. I held up the things to eat and then laid them in a hollowed-out rock in the river bluff, safe from any animals who might nose around and where they would be kept dry in rain or dew. Time after time, day after day, I did the same thing. Much later I had a surprise: Mother knew about my mission but, saying nothing and pretending she didn't, made it easier for me by putting out leftovers where I was sure to find them. Mother almost never showed what she was thinking.

Finally she sent for an uncle of ours, her brother, to help with the farm and with money matters, and she got a tutor for us children. She also arranged for the priest to come in his vestments to the river edge to exorcise Father and call upon him to desist from his sad obsession. Another time, she tried to scare Father by getting two soldiers to come. But none of it was any use. Father passed by at a distance, discernible only dimly through the river haze, going by in the canoe without ever letting anyone go close enough to touch him or even talk to him. The reporters who went out in a launch and tried to take his picture not long ago failed just like everybody else; Father crossed over to the other bank and steered the canoe into the thick swamp that goes on for miles, part reeds and part brush. Only he knew every hand's breadth of its blackness.

We just had to try to get used to it. But it was hard, and we never really managed. I'm judging by myself, of course. Whether I wanted to or not, my thoughts kept circling back and I found myself thinking of Father. The hard nub of it was that I couldn't begin to understand how he could hold out. Day and night, in bright sunshine or in rainstorms, in muggy heat or in the terrible cold spells in the middle of the year, without shelter or any protection but the old hat on his head, all through the weeks, and months, and years—he marked in no way the passing of his life. Father never landed, never put in at either shore or stopped at any of the river islands or sandbars; and he never again stepped onto grass or solid earth. It was true that in order to catch a little sleep he may have tied up the canoe at some concealed islet-spit. But he never lighted a fire on shore, had no lamp or candle, never struck a match again. He did no more than taste food; even the morsels he took from what we left for him along the roots of the fig tree or in the hollow stone at the foot of the cliff could not have been enough to keep him alive. Wasn't he ever sick? And what constant strength he must have had in his arms to maintain himself and the canoe ready for the piling up of the floodwaters where danger rolls on the great current, sweeping the bodies of dead animals and tree trunks downstream—frightening, threatening, crashing into him. And he never spoke another word to a

living soul. We never talked about him, either. We only
thought of him. Father could never be forgotten; and if, for
short periods of time, we pretended to ourselves that we had
forgotten, it was only to find ourselves roused suddenly by his
memory, startled by it again and again.

My sister married; but Mother would have no festivities.
He came into our minds whenever we ate something especially
tasty, and when we were wrapped up snugly at night we
thought of those bare unsheltered nights of cold, heavy rain,
and Father with only his hand and maybe a calabash to bail the
storm water out of the canoe. Every so often someone who
knew us would remark that I was getting to look more and more
like my father. But I knew that now he must be bushy-haired
and bearded, his nails long, his body cadaverous and gaunt,
burnt black by the sun, hairy as a beast and almost as naked,
even with the pieces of clothing we left for him at intervals.

He never felt the need to know anything about us; had
he no family affection? But out of love, love and respect,
whenever I was praised for something good I had done, I would
say: "It was Father who taught me how to do it that way." It
wasn't true, exactly, but it was a truthful kind of lie. If he didn't
remember us any more and didn't want to know how we were,
why didn't he go farther up the river or down it, away to
landing places where he would never be found? Only he knew.
When my sister had a baby boy, she got it into her head that
she must show Father his grandson. All of us went and stood
on the bluff. The day was fine and my sister was wearing the
white dress she had worn at her wedding. She lifted the baby
up in her arms and her husband held a parasol over the two of
them. We called and we waited. Our father didn't come. My
sister wept; we all cried and hugged one another as we stood
there.

After that my sister moved far away with her husband,

and my brother decided to go live in the city. Times changed, with the slow swiftness of time. Mother went away too in the end, to live with my sister because she was growing old. I stayed on here, the only one of the family who was left. I could never think of marriage. I stayed where I was, burdened down with all life's cumbrous baggage. I knew Father needed me, as he wandered up and down on the river in the wilderness, even though he never gave a reason for what he had done. When at last I made up my mind that I had to know and finally made a firm attempt to find out, people told me rumor had it that Father might have given some explanation to the man who made the canoe for him. But now the builder was dead; and no one really knew or could recollect any more except that there had been some silly talk in the beginning, when the river was first swollen by such endless torrents of rain that everyone was afraid the world was coming to an end; then they had said that Father might have received a warning, like Noah, and so prepared the canoe ahead of time. I could half-recall the story. I could not even blame my father. And a few first white hairs began to appear on my head.

I was a man whose words were all sorrowful. Why did I feel so guilty, so guilty? Was it because of my father, who made his absence felt always, and because of the river-river-river, the river—flowing forever? I was suffering the onset of old age— this life of mine only postponed the inevitable. I had bed spells, pains in the belly, dizziness, twinges of rheumatism. And he? Why, oh why must he do what he did? He must suffer terribly. Old as he was, was he not bound to weaken in vigor sooner or later and let the canoe overturn or, when the river rose, let it drift unguided for hours downstream, until it finally went over the brink of the loud rushing fall of the cataract, with its wild boiling and death? My heart shrank. He was out there, with none of my easy security. I was guilty of I knew not what, filled with boundless sorrow in the deepest part of me. If I only knew —if only things were otherwise. And then, little by little, the idea came to me.

I could not even wait until next day. Was I crazy? No. In our house, the word *crazy* was not spoken, had never been spoken again in all those years; no one was condemned as crazy. Either no one is crazy, or everyone is. I just went, taking along a sheet to wave with. I was very much in my right mind. I waited. After a long time he appeared; his indistinct bulk took form. He was there, sitting in the stern. He was there, a shout away. I called out several times. And I said the words which were making me say them, the sworn promise, the declaration. I had to force my voice to say: "Father, you're getting old, you've done your part. . . . You can come back now, you don't have to stay any longer. . . . You come back, and I'll do it, right now or whenever you want me to; it's what we both want. I'll take your place in the canoe!" And as I said it my heart beat to the rhythm of what was truest and best in me.

He heard me. He got to his feet. He dipped the paddle in the water, the bow pointed toward me; he had agreed. And suddenly I shuddered deeply, because he had lifted his arm and gestured a greeting—the first, after so many years. And I could not. . . . Panic-stricken, my hair standing on end, I ran, I fled, I left the place behind me in a mad headlong rush. For he seemed to be coming from the hereafter. And I am pleading, pleading, pleading for forgiveness.

I was struck by the solemn ice of fear, and I fell ill. I knew that no one ever heard of him again. Can I be a man, after having thus failed him? I am what never was—the unspeakable. I know it is too late for salvation now, but I am afraid to cut life short in the shallows of the world. At least, when death comes to the body, let them take me and put me in a wretched little canoe, and on the water that flows forever past its unending banks, let me go—down the river, away from the river, into the river—the river.

●

For to End Yet Again

SAMUEL BECKETT

Translated by the author

For to end yet again skull alone in a dark place pent bowed on
a board to begin. Long thus to begin till the place fades followed by the board long after. For to end yet again skull alone
in the dark the void no neck no face just the box last place of
all in the dark the void. Place of remains where once used to
gleam in the dark on and off used to glimmer a remain. Remains of the days of the light of day never light so faint as theirs
so pale. Thus then the skull makes to glimmer again in lieu of
going out. There in the end all at once or by degrees there
dawns and magic lingers a leaden dawn. By degrees less dark
till final gray or all at once as if switched on gray sand as far
as eye can see beneath gray cloudless sky same gray. Skull last
place of all black void within without till all at once or by
degrees at last this leaden dawn checked no sooner dawned.
Gray cloudless sky gray sand as far as eye can see long desert

to begin. Sand pale as dust ah but dust indeed deep to engulf the haughtiest monuments which too it once was here and there. There in the end same gray invisible to any other eye stark erect amidst his ruins the expelled. Same gray all that little body from head to feet sunk ankle deep were it not for the eyes last bright of all. The arms still cleave to the trunk and to each other the legs made for flight. Gray cloudless sky ocean of dust not a ripple mock confines verge upon verge hell air not a breath. Mingling with the dust slowly sinking some almost quite sunk the ruins of the refuge. First change of all in the end a fragment comes away and falls. With slow fall for so dense a body it lights like cork on water and scarce breaks the surface. Thus then the skull last place of all makes to glimmer again in lieu of going out. Gray cloudless sky verge upon verge gray timeless air of those nor for God nor for his enemies. There again in the end way amidst the verges a light in the gray two white dwarfs. Long at first mere whiteness from afar they toil step by step through the gray dust linked by a litter same white seen from above in the gray air. Slowly it sweeps the dust so bowed the backs and long the arms compared with the legs and deep sunk the feet. Bleached as one same wilderness they are so alike the eye cannot tell them apart. They carry face to face and relay each other often so that turn about they backward lead the way. His who follows who knows to shape the course much as the coxswain with light touch the skiff. Let him veer to the north or other cardinal point and promptly the other by as much to the antipode. Let one stop short and the other about this pivot slew the litter through a semi-circle and thereon the roles are reversed. Bone white of the sheet seen from above and the shafts fore and aft and the dwarfs to the crowns of their massy skulls. From time to time impelled as one they let fall the litter then again as one take it up again without having to stoop. It is the dung litter of laughable memory with

shafts twice as long as the couch. Swelling the sheet now fore
now aft as permutations list a pillow marks the place of the
head. At the end of the arms the four hands open as one and
the litter so close to the dust already settles without a sound.
Monstrous extremities including skulls stunted legs and trunks
monstrous arms stunted faces. In the end the feet as one lift
clear the left forward backward the right and the amble
resumes. Gray dust as far as eye can see beneath gray cloudless
sky and there all at once or by degrees this whiteness to decipher. Yet to imagine if he can see it the last expelled amidst
his ruins if he can ever see it and seeing believe his eyes.
Between him and it bird's-eye view the space grows no less but
has only even now appeared last desert to be crossed. Little
body last stage of all stark erect still amidst his ruins all silent
and marble still. First change of all a fragment comes away
from mother ruin and with slow fall scarce stirs the dust. Dust
having engulfed so much it can engulf no more and woe the
little on the surface still. Or mere digestive torpor as once the
boas which past with one last gulp clean sweep at last. Dwarfs
distant whiteness sprung from nowhere motionless afar in the
gray air where dust alone possible. Wilderness and carriage
immemorial as one they advance as one retreat hither thither
halt move on again. He facing forward will sometimes halt and
hoist as best he can his head as if to scan the void and who
knows alter course. Then on so soft the eye does not see them
go driftless with heads sunk and lidded eyes. Long lifted to the
horizontal faces closer and closer strain as it will the eye
achieves no more than two tiny oval blanks. Atop the cyclopean
dome rising sheer from jut of brow yearns white to the gray sky
the bump of habitativity or love of home. Last change of all
in the end the expelled falls headlong down and lies back to
sky full little stretch amidst his ruins. Feet centre body radius
falls unbending as a statue falls faster and faster the space of

a quadrant. Eagle the eye that shall discern him now mingled with the ruins mingling with the dust beneath a sky forsaken of its scavengers. Breath has not left him though soundless still and exhaling scarce ruffles the dust. Eyes in their orbits blue still unlike the doll's the fall has not shut nor yet the dust stopped up. No fear henceforth of his ever having not to believe them before that whiteness afar where sky and dust merge. Whiteness neither on earth nor above of the dwarfs as if at the end of their trials the litter left lying between them the white bodies marble still. Ruins all silent marble still little body prostrate at attention wash blue deep in gaping sockets. As in the days erect the arms still cleave to the trunk and to each other the legs made for flight. Fallen unbending all his little length as though pushed from behind by some helping hand or by the wind but not a breath. Or murmur from some dreg of life after the lifelong stand fall fall never fear no fear of your rising again. Sepulchral skull is this then its last state all set for always litter and dwarfs ruins and little body gray cloudless sky glutted dust verge upon verge hell air not a breath. And dream of a way in a space with neither here nor there where all the footsteps ever fell can never fare nearer to anywhere nor from anywhere further away. No for in the end for to end yet again by degrees or as though switched on dark falls there again that certain dark that alone certain ashes can. Through it who knows yet another end beneath a cloudless sky same dark it earth and sky of a last end if ever there had to be another absolutely had to be.

About the Authors

ILSE AICHINGER was born in Vienna in 1921. After the war she began medical studies, but later became a publisher's reader. Her first novel, *Die grössere Hoffnung (Herod's Children)*, was published in 1948. She has lived in Upper Bavaria since her marriage to Gunter Eich, the German poet, in 1953. Besides distinguished work in fiction and poetry, she has also written a highly regarded radio drama, *Knöpfe (Buttons)*.
Works Available In English: The Bound Man and Other Stories (1956), *Herod's Children* (1963), *Eliza, Eliza* (1965), *Selected Short Stories and Dialogues* (1966).

INGEBORG BACHMANN, an Austrian poet, short-story writer and radio dramatist, was born in Klagenfurt in 1926. She took her doctorate in philosophy in Vienna and remained there to work in broadcasting. *Die gestundete Zeit (Borrowed Time)*, her first collection of poems, was published in 1953. A second volume, *Anrufung des grossen Bären (Invocation of the Great Bears)*, won the Bremer Literature Prize in 1957. She has often lived abroad.
Works Available In English: The Thirtieth Year (1964).

SAMUEL BECKETT was born in 1906 in Foxrock, near Dublin, Ireland. He graduated from Trinity College and soon after went to Paris, where he became James Joyce's secretary. His first novel, *Murphy*, was published in 1938. Shortly after the war, he began to write directly in French. His play *En attendant Godot (Waiting for Godot)* brought him worldwide recognition. He was awarded the Nobel Prize for Literature in 1969.
Works Available In English: Waiting for Godot (1954), *Molloy* (1955), *Malone Dies* (1956), *Murphy* (1957), *Proust* (1957), *Endgame* (1958), *The Unnamable* (1958), *Watt* (1959), *Krapp's Last Tape & Other Dramatic Pieces* (1960), *Happy Days* (1961), *Poems in English* (1963), *How It Is* (1964), *Stories & Texts for Nothing* (1967), *Cascando & Other Short Dramatic Pieces* (1969), *Film, a Film Script* (1969), *More Pricks Than Kicks* (1970), *The Lost Ones* (1972), *First Love & Other Shorts* (1974), *The Collected Works of Samuel Beckett* (1975), *Mercier & Camier* (1975), *Ends & Odds* (1976), *Fizzles* (1976), *I Can't Go on: I'll Go on* (1976).

ADOLFO BIOY CASARES was born in Buenos Aires in 1914. He published his first book, a miscellany entitled *Prologo (Prologue),* in 1929. He has collaborated with Jorge Luis Borges, a friend of forty years, on a number of books under the joint pseudonym of "Honorio Bustos Domecq." He was awarded the 1st Premio Nacional de Literatura in 1969 for *El Gran serafín (The Great Seraph).*
Works Available In English: The Invention of Morel and Other Stories (1964), *A Plan for Escape* (1975), *The Chronicles of Bustos Domecq* [with Jorge Luis Borges] (1976).

HEINRICH BÖLL, born in 1917 in Cologne, has written novels, short stories and radio plays. He served in the infantry during World War II; following the war he held various jobs until becoming a free-lance writer in 1951. His first book, *Der Zug war pünktlich (The Train Was on Time),* was published in 1949. He was awarded the Nobel Prize for Literature in 1972.
Works Available In English: Acquainted with the Night (1955), *Adam, Where Art Thou?* (1955), *The Train Was on Time* (1956), *Traveler, If You Come to Spa* (1956), *The Bread of Those Early Years* (1957), *The Unguarded House* (1957), *Absent Without Leave* (1965), *The Clown* (1965), *Eighteen Stories* (1966), *Irish Journal* (1967), *End of a Mission* (1968), *Children Are Civilians, Too* (1970), *Billiards at Half-Past Nine* (1973), *Group Portrait with Lady* (1973), *The Lost Honor of Katharina Blum* (1975).

JORGE LUIS BORGES was born in 1899 in Buenos Aires but was educated in Geneva. After three years in Spain, he returned to Buenos Aires in 1921. Two years later he published *Fervor de Buenos Aires (Fervor of Buenos Aires),* a collection of poems. His first volume of stories, *Historia universal de la infamia (A Universal History of Infamy),* did not appear until 1935. Following the fall of the Perón regime in 1955, he became director of the National Library of Argentina. He received Argentina's National Prize of Literature in 1956 and shared the International Publishers' Prize with Samuel Beckett in 1961. He has written about his blindness in a number of poems and essays.
Works Available In English: Ficciones (1962), *Dreamtigers* (1964), *Other Inquisitions* (1964), *A Personal Anthology* (1967), *The Book of Imaginary Beings* (1969), *Labyrinths* (1969), *The Aleph & Other Stories* (1970), *An Introduction to American Literature* (1971), *Doctor Brodie's Report* (1972),

Selected Poems, 1923–1967 (1972), *A Universal History of Infamy* (1972), *Borges on Writing* (1973), *In Praise of Darkness* (1974), *An Introduction to English Literature* (1974), *The Chronicles of Bustos Domecq* [with Adolfo Bioy Casares] (1976).

ITALO CALVINO was born in 1923 in Santiago de Las Vegas, Cuba, but grew up in San Remo on the Italian Riviera. He was a member of the partisans during the German occupation, and fought in the Garibaldi Brigade. After the war he worked as a salesman for the publishing firm of Einaudi and in 1947 became an editor there. His first novel, *Il sentiero dei nidi di ragno (The Path to the Nest of Spiders)*, won the Premio Riccione in 1947. He was awarded the Premio Feltrinelli per la Narrativa in 1972.

Works Available In English: The Path to the Nest of Spiders (1956), *Adam, One Afternoon and Other Stories* (1957), *The Baron of the Trees* (1959), *Italian Fables* (1961), *The Nonexistent Knight & the Cloven Viscount* (1962), *Cosmicomics* (1968), *The Watcher & Other Stories* (1971), *Invisible Cities* (1974), *t zero* (1976), *Tarots: The Visconti Pack in Bergamo & New York* (1976), *The Castle of Crossed Destinies* (1977).

JULIO CORTÁZAR, an Argentinian novelist and short-story writer, was born in Brussels in 1914. Raised in Argentina, he moved to Paris in 1952 because of his opposition to the dictatorship of Juan Perón. He published *Los Reyes (The Kings)*, a play, in 1949 and *Bestiario (Bestiary)*, a collection of short stories, in 1951. He works in Paris for UNESCO as a translator of French and English into Spanish. Among his translations are the works of Edgar Allan Poe.

Works Available In English: The Winners (1965), *Hopscotch* (1966), *Blow Up & Other Stories* (1968), *Cronopios and Famas* (1969), *62: A Model Kit* (1972), *All Fires the Fire & Other Stories* (1973).

GABRIEL GARCÍA MÁRQUEZ was born in 1928 in Aracataca, Colombia. He studied law at the University of Bogotá and later worked as a reporter and film critic for the Colombian paper *El Espectador*. *La hojarasca (Leaf Storm)*, his first novel, appeared in 1955 and was widely acclaimed by critics. Since 1955, he has lived abroad in Venezuela, France, Mexico and Spain.

Works Available In English: No One Writes to the Colonel and Other Stories (1968), *One Hundred Years of Solitude* (1970), *Leaf Storm and Other Stories* (1972), *The Autumn of the Patriarch* (1976).

JOAO GUIMARAES ROSA was born in Cordisburgo, Brazil, in 1908. He studied medicine but served as a career diplomat for Brazil in Germany, France and a number of other nations during the 1930's. His first novel, *Grande Sertao: Veredas (The Devil to Pay in the Backlands)*, was published in 1956. He died in Rio de Janeiro in 1967.

Works Available in English: The Devil to Pay in the Backlands (1963), *Sagarana* (1966), *The Third Bank of the River and Other Stories* (1968).

EUGÈNE IONESCO, the French playwright, was born in Slatina, Rumania, in 1912. He was brought to Paris as an infant, but he and his family returned to Rumania when he was thirteen. In 1938 he left Rumania to live in France. His first play, *La Cantatrice chauve (The Bald Soprano)*, was not written until 1950. His plays have since been performed in Germany, Yugoslavia, Italy, Poland, Israel, the United States and numerous other countries around the world.

Works Available In English: Four Plays (1958), *Plays* [8 vols.] (1958–1974), *Three Plays* (1958), *The Killer & Other Plays* (1960), *Rhinoceros & Other Plays* (1960), *Notes & Counternotes* (1964), *Exit the King* (1967), *Fragments of a Journal* (1968), *A Stroll in the Air* (1968), *The Colonel's Photograph & Other Stories* (1969), *Hunger & Thirst & Other Plays* (1969), *Present Past, Past Present* (1971), *Macbett* (1973), *Story Number 4* (1973), *The Hermit* (1974), *The Killing Game* (1974), *A Hell of a Mess* (1975), *The Man with the Suitcases* (1976).

MARGARITA KARAPANOU was born in Athens in 1946. She studied philosophy and cinematography in Paris. She has taught kindergarten, written numerous film reviews and directed her own short film. She now lives in Athens.

Works Available In English: Kassandra and the Wolf (1976).

VLADY KOCIANCICH was born in Buenos Aires in 1942. She has studied at the University of Buenos Aires. Her first collection of short stories, *Coraje (Courage)*, was published in 1970.

Works Available In English: Her stories appear in the American literary magazine *Mundus Artium*.

MILAN KUNDERA was born in 1929 in Brno, Czechoslovakia. He studied at the Film Faculty of the Prague Drama Academy. His play *Majitelé klícu (The Keeper of the Keys)* was written in 1962 and has been performed in fourteen

countries. In 1973 he received the Médicis award in France. He has been debarred from publication and banned from public libraries in Czechoslovakia since 1971.
Works Available In English: Laughable Loves (1974), *Life Is Elsewhere* (1974).

JAKOV LIND was born in Vienna in 1927 to a Jewish family. He escaped to Holland in 1938, lived for two years (1943–45) in Germany with forged papers, and finally emigrated to Palestine. He later spent two years at the Max Reinhardt Academy of Dramatic Art in Vienna. *Eine Seele aus Holz (Soul of Wood)*, his first collection of stories, was published in 1962 and has been translated into eleven languages. He now lives in London.
Works Available In English: Soul of Wood and Other Stories (1964), *Landscape in Concrete* (1966), *Ergo* (1968), *Counting My Steps* (1969), *The Silver Foxes Are Dead & Other Plays* (1969).

CLARICE LISPECTOR, a Brazilian novelist and short-story writer, was born in Tchetchelnik, Ukraine, in 1925. She spent her childhood at Recife and moved to Rio de Janeiro when she was twelve. Her first novel, *Perto do Coração Selvagem (Close to the Savage Heart)*, was published in 1944—the year in which she graduated from the National Faculty of Law. She has traveled widely and has lived in the United States and Europe.
Works Available In English: Family Ties (1972).

ANDRÉ PIEYRE DE MANDIARGUES was born in Paris in 1909. He graduated from the Sorbonne and holds a number of degrees. His first collection of stories, *Le Musée Noir (The Black Museum)*, was published in 1946. *Soleil des Loups (Sun of the Wolves)*, another collection of stories, was awarded the Prix des Critiques in 1951. He lives in Paris.
Works Available In English: The Girl beneath the Lion (1959), *The Motorcycle* (1965), *Chagall* (1975).

IAN MC EWAN was born in 1948 in Aldershot, England. He began writing in 1970. In 1975 his play *Jack Flea's Birthday Celebration* was produced by the British Broadcasting Corporation. *Conversation with a Cupboardman*, a radio drama, was also produced by the B.B.C. in the same year. He lives in London.
Works Available In English: First Love, Last Rites (1975).

HENRI MICHAUX was born in Namur, Belgium, in 1899. A sailor as a young man, he published two travel journals that were well received. *Ecuador (Ecuador)*, in 1929, and *Un barbare en Asie (A Barbarian in Asia)*, in 1932, followed the publication of his first book of poems, *Qui je fus (Who I Was)*, in 1927. He has experimented with and written at length about hallucinogenic drugs. He was awarded (and refused) France's Grand Prix National des Lettres. He is also a painter and has exhibited widely.

Works Available In English: A Barbarian in Asia (1949), *Miserable Miracle* (1963), *Light Through Darkness* (1963), *Selected Writings* (1968), *Ecuador* (1970), *The Major Ordeals of the Mind & the Countless Minor Ones* (1974).

SLAWOMIR MROZEK was born in Borzecin, Poland, in 1930. He studied architecture and painting, and has worked as a journalist for various Polish publications. His first collection of stories, *Slon (The Elephant)*, was awarded the Polish State Cultural Review's annual literary prize in 1957. His plays have been translated into almost every European language and have been produced throughout the Western world.

Works Available In English: The Elephant (1963), *Six Plays* (1967), *Tango* (1969), *Vatzlav* (1970), *Three Plays* (1973).

ALAIN ROBBE-GRILLET was born in 1922 in Brest, France. Trained in Paris as an agronomist, he worked in the National Institute of Statistics. He later traveled to Africa and the Antilles, where he studied tropical fruits. *Les gommes (The Erasers)*, his first novel, appeared in 1953. In his fiction and his essays, he has argued for *"un nouveau roman." L'année dernière à Marienbad (Last Year at Marienbad)*, a film he scripted, has brought him international renown.

Works Available In English: Voyeur (1958), *Two Novels* (1960), *Last Year at Marienbad* (1962), *The Erasers* (1964), *For a New Novel* (1965), *La Maison de Rendez-vous* (1966), *Snapshots* (1968), *Project for a Revolution in New York* (1972).

SEVERO SARDUY was born in Camagüey, Cuba, in 1937. He has lived in Paris since 1962, the same year his first novel was published. Another of his novels, *Cobra (Cobra)*, received the Médicis award for the best foreign novel to appear in France. He works as an editor in a publishing house.

Works Available In English: From Cuba with a Song [in *Triple Cross*] (1972), *Cobra* (1975).

NATHALIE SARRAUTE was born in Russia in 1903. She studied law and literature, and practiced law in Paris until 1939. Her first collection of short fictions, *Tropismes (Tropisms),* appeared that year. She is considered a leading writer of the New Novel. She was awarded the Prix Formentor for *Les fruits d'or (The Golden Fruits)* in 1964.

Works Available In English: Portrait of a Man Unknown (1958), *Martereau* (1959), *Planetarium* (1960), *Age of Suspicion* (1964), *The Golden Fruits* (1964), *Tropisms* (1967), *Between Life and Death* (1969), *Do You Hear Them?* (1973), *Fools Say* (1976).

J. MICHAEL YATES, a Canadian poet, short fiction writer and dramatist, was born in Fulton, Missouri, in 1938. He has studied comparative literature and has done free-lance work in broadcasting and advertising. His radio dramas have been produced in Canada and throughout Europe. His first collection of poems, *Spiral of Mirrors,* was published in 1967. He has lived in Mexico, the United States and Germany, and he currently works as an editor for a Vancouver publishing firm.

Works Available In English: Spiral of Mirrors (1967), *Hunt in an Unmapped Interior* (1967), *Canticle for Electronic Music* (1968), *Man in the Glass Octopus* (1968), *The Great Bear Lake Meditations* (1970), *The Abstract Beast* (1971), *Parallax* (1971), *Nothing Speaks for the Blue Moraines* (1973), *Breath of the Snow Leopard* (1974), *The Qualicum Physics (1975), Quarks* (1975), *Fazes in Elsewhen* (1976), *Latrodectus Shoicetans* (1976).

About the Editor

JOHN BIGUENET was born in New Orleans in 1949. His poetry, translations, criticism and plays have appeared widely in this country and in Canada. He has received many awards, including a Harper's Magazine Writing Award for film criticism. He has been writer-in-residence at the University of Arkansas at Little Rock and is currently teaching at Loyola University in New Orleans.